T0038268

LADYHOPPERS

by Sarah Thérèse Pelletier
and Scott James Taylor

LADYHOPPERS
Copyright © 2023 Sarah Thérèse Pelletier and Scott James Taylor. All
rights reserved.

Published by Outland Entertainment LLC
3119 Gillham Road
Kansas City, MO 64109

Founder/Creative Director: Jeremy D. Mohler
Editor-in-Chief: Alana Joli Abbott
Senior Editor: Scott Colby
Project Director: Anton Kromoff

ISBN: 978-1-954255-95-1
Ebook ISBN: 978-1-954255-96-8
Worldwide Rights
Created in the United States of America

Editor: Alana Joli Abbott
Copy editor: Ariel Kromoff
Galley proofer: Em Palladino
Cover Illustration: Chris Yarbrough
Cover Design: Jeremy D. Mohler
Interior Layout: Mikael Brodu
Section Logo Design: Shannon Potratz

The characters and events portrayed in this book are fictitious or
fictitious recreations of actual historical persons. Any similarity to
real persons, living or dead, is coincidental and not intended by the
authors unless otherwise specified. This book or any portion thereof
may not be reproduced or used in any manner whatsoever without
the express written permission of the publisher except for the use of
brief quotations in a book review.

Printed and bound in the United States of America.

Visit **outlandentertainment.com** to see more, or follow us on our
Facebook Page **facebook.com/outlandentertainment/**

To TR.

Chapter One

— NO TEARS —

As she jumped into a hole in reality, Charlie's biggest worry was that it might not be her that came out on the other side.

Early on, there had been a theory from one of the many scientists working the problem at Veritech that the only way to survive the trip would be to replicate a person's entire molecular structure from scratch on the other side. Even as they'd moved beyond that—even as it had seemed that someone sufficiently protected by the right materials and the right biological modifications could survive—this theory had worried Charlie. The idea that what arrived on the other side might simply be a copy of her with all of her memories had kept her up at night. She might be simply torn apart and replaced. She had feared, most of all, discontinuity of experience, some point where she passed out, fainted, and reawakened on the other side with no way of knowing if she was still really her.

If nothing else, she was conscious of the whole trip, could trace moment to moment even if she was utterly unable to relate, even to her own self, even to store the experience to memory, what those moments contained. She was compressed to the smallest of points; she was ethereal and adrift. Every sensory nerve fired at once; she was numb and paralyzed, a brain in a jar. There were colors, or maybe they were sounds, or maybe they were her, an experience akin to synesthesia the way a static shock from walking on carpet would to being hit by lightning. She was a speck falling through a universe that she could see in its entirety; she was connected to everything, borderless and on the verge of transcendence.

She slammed into the ground on the other side and immediately threw up in her cowl.

The colors were wrong. If the trip alone—that incomprehensible sensory catastrophe that she couldn't be certain was anything other than a very vivid hallucination brought on by neurons firing wildly and randomly as her body underwent stresses unlike any it could have ever been prepared for—if that hadn't done it, the colors would have. She was, now that she'd crawled several feet from where she'd initially landed, staring at a patch of grass. It was green. The green was wrong. It was too vivid, for one; it seemed brighter than the world could be, as if someone had turned the saturation up. For another, it was wrong in some way she couldn't quite tell beyond the fact that it made her want to throw up. Again. It was just somehow *off*. She knew it was green because grass was green, but if she'd seen it on a wall, on a color swatch... she'd have still said green, because it was green. It was as if it was skewed, the wavelength wrong, but if you changed the wavelength of a color you just got another color, and this was green.

It was just that green was wrong.

She rolled over to look at the sky instead. It wasn't any better. It was blue. Blue was wrong, too. It was that old first-year philosophy saw: how do I know the blue I see is the blue you see? Only now her brain seemed to be having an argument with itself and actively coming to blows about varying interpretations of the fact of subjective experience.

At least she was alive. Feeling sick was feeling something. The HUD indicated the air was safe, and she retracted the cowl to pull in her first breath from another world. She'd need to clean the cowl. That was secondary to dragging her arm across her face to clear away some of the sick. She was alive, and she was breathing air, and there was a world to be alive and breathing air in. She had traveled through a hole in reality and there had, after all, been another reality on the other side, another world that fortunately seemed enough like her own for her to navigate. Even if she'd only seen some grass, some bushes as she'd hauled herself to a new spot, and now the sky. Even if those seemed somehow out of whack. That seemed to be settling, though. She thought she was in a park, and that was a relief, too, that there was something she could so easily categorize, that fell into the realm of things she had referents for. It was not wholly alien. They had grass, and bushes, and put these things in parks, and...

She sat up and confirmed that the park in which she lay was not surrounded by temporary fences, by any kind of barrier, that it lacked any kind of sense of alarm. She realized what else she hadn't seen, and she turned her head until she found it.

The tear was smaller on this side, it seemed, a more subdued distortion. But there it was: the hint of texture in intermediary space, a dimming of colors in the stone wall. If she hadn't known what she was looking for, she might have written it off as her eyes playing tricks on her. She had to wonder if that had even been here before she'd tumbled through, because there were none of the destructive results she'd have expected from a tear active as long as this one had been. The wall still looked mostly solid. The park was pristine. There was a bilingual NO LITTERING sign, and next to it, one of the probes the CMC had ordered them to send through earlier that week, but to Charlie anything that was solid and real and in full wrong-color was pristine. A bird was singing.

Charlie frowned at the bird. She couldn't remember the last time she'd seen one in person. Montreal wasn't exactly known for its wildlife, and since the tears had started up, it was an exciting day when she saw a squirrel. Birds were especially sensitive to tears, but this one—a fat blue jay perched high above her head—seemed oblivious. Charlie was determined to keep it that way.

"Time to get to work," she murmured, and she tested out her legs, slowly pulling herself upright. For a moment her vision grayed around the edges, and she thought she was going to revisit the too-green grass, but soon her vitals leveled out and she managed to straighten fully. Peering through the trees, she could make out a suspiciously familiar metal structure that she could swear was the old Biosphere, but there was no one else around, no gawkers to stare at this interloper from another reality, not another living soul save the blue jay. Charlie entertained the notion that this was some kind of weird world ruled by bird people—*Are they still bird people if they're just birds with people-level smarts?*—before remembering she had more important things to do.

Saving the world was at the top of the list.

Charlie reached behind her and slid the Coupler from her pack. Though Veritech had always been more interested in exploration than war, the device resembled nothing so much as a gun, albeit a very simplistic looking one. It was sleek and well-balanced, fitting comfortably in Charlie's hand. Instead of bullets or lasers, though, it fired a pulse that triggered the second part of the device, an Einstein-Rosen Coupling, which was the size of a small ball and not shot but thrown. She detached the Coupling nested in the grip and lobbed it toward the tear, where it hovered, tenuously, in place. The tear seemed confused, unsure whether to repel or devour the device. The Coupling vibrated, torn apart and sewn together in an endless loop, and Charlie took in a deep breath, then exhaled, slowly, as she fired in the split instant the Coupling was whole.

A deafening suction sound threatened to split Charlie's eardrums. She resisted the urge to cover her ears. The tear shuddered, and its surface went smooth and still, reflective like a calm lake on a summer morning. It was working—the tear was stabilizing, realities were bending to human ingenuity, and Charlie couldn't help the smile forming at the corners of her mouth.

"Ha!" she crowed. She pumped her fists into the air and did a victory dance so embarrassing even the blue jay had to avert its eyes. With a shrill squawk, the bird flew away, surely off to tell its bird friends of the strange girl from another world who successfully stabilized a hole in reality.

The jay's distress really should've been her first clue that something had gone wrong. Charlie was mid-dance when the tear began to ripple, tendrils of reality unspooling like a ball of yarn. A disconcerting pop reverberated in her chest. The tear was no more. Only unmarred matter remained.

She'd fixed the tear, but by the wrong metric. The tear had been meant to stabilize: no longer shredding the world around it but still there, a link between two universes for her to return home. But it was *gone*. Charlie stared into space, struck dumb by the weight of the realization she was stuck. Only one word came to mind.

"Fuck."

Stumbling forward and swiping at the spot where the tear had been was probably not the most well-thought-out of responses, probably wasn't precisely scientific. But in the immediate moment, she just wanted to put her hands on the fabric of the world and pull it back open so she could transport herself back to her family and friends and the proper color green.

But there was nothing. There was unbroken air. If she'd been standing on the other side, it would have been a delight, a triumph. If this had happened in any of their efforts at home, they would have broken out the champagne, and considering that the Champagne region was nearly entirely unraveled, that wasn't a small celebratory gesture.

Verity had had some standing by. It was probably still standing by, along with Verity, Josie, Nate, and, god, her parents. They were last on the list because she'd tried to divert her mind from the fact, but now it was here. Now she was just imagining them standing there, in a waiting room, waiting, until eventually, someone remembered to tell them, so, uh, your daughter's way home kind of erased itself, which is great for us but bad for you.

It wasn't even that great for her team. Fixing tears was great, was world-saving, but if every tear required leaving someone on the other side...

There were a lot of tears, back home.

Turning in a slow circle, she put her hands to her temples and tried to think about something other than her parents sitting endlessly. Maybe there was something in the fact that there were a lot of tears. Her team had never known what was on the other side, and maybe all the tears went here, in which case she just had to find another one.

That was easy enough. She had gear for that. She could scan for that. After giving the cowl a quick wipedown, she slid it back into place. Wincing a little as she took an experimental sniff to see if she'd gotten all the smell out, she fired up the HUD and set it to scan for tears.

It scanned. And scanned. And scanned. And returned nothing. It returned so resolutely nothing that she wondered if it was working properly. Maybe going through the tear had busted her equipment, or the different vibrational frequencies on this side were mucking with the signs it was designed to detect. Maybe tears just presented differently on this side. They might be unidirectional, one-way sluices dumping disaster onto her world from another that remained entirely unaffected.

Not enough information. Before she went wandering, she had to try and see if she could salvage a way home out of the tear she knew had been there. Maybe it was still extant, under the surface of the world. She scooped up the lost probe and hurried back to the backpack, popping open the side of the Coupler as she went. Crouching and rummaging through the tools, Charlie began plucking them out and jamming them into the device before heedlessly tossing them back in and grabbing another, switching wires, circuits, trying to reconfigure it into something that could widen a tear, pull it back into being.

When she had something workable, she turned and tossed the Einstein-Rosen Coupling back through the air where she estimated the tear had been. It sailed through the air and landed with a *thwack* against the wall. She ran over, grabbed it, and threw again, this time firing once she estimated its arc was taking it through the spot the tear had been.

Again, *thwack.*

She went and retrieved it, again, and then simply planted it in the appropriate spot, backed up, pointed the Coupler at it, and activated it.

Reality remained firmly undisturbed. From a tree farther into the park, birdsong started up again. Word of the idiot who got herself stuck here was spreading.

It's fine. It's okay. That was plan A. There's a whole alphabet left.

There was still her other idea. See if there were any other tears. Usually, that wouldn't have been hard. Follow the sounds of a crisis. It was just… there were none. Maybe she couldn't expect there to be vehicles with sirens rushing past to conveniently follow to her way home, but there should have been something rushing here.

She tossed her equipment and the cannibalized probe back into the backpack, ignoring the carefully devised custom pouches and simply stuffing things in as quickly as she could, then swung it on. She wasn't going to do any good sitting here staring.

Unless...

She took a moment to consider the possibility Verity and the others would be working the same problem. What were the chances they'd get it back open from their side? What were the chances they'd try? It wasn't that she expected them to just abandon her to her fate, but Charlie had just eliminated one very destructive force from the world. (Well, their world. Here it hadn't seemed to be a danger.) Rushing to get it back, to inflict more damage to a reality that had been wearing pretty thin...

If I get back, I am absolutely not looking up who argued for what, there. I don't want to know.

But before she could valiantly try not to think about who'd voted to abandon her, she'd have to actually get back. So. She had to find... well, frankly, anything that wasn't a park and some birds. Find out where she was, what kind of world it was, and whether they had any tears that she could hitch a ride home on.

Find a tear. Stabilize the tear. Go home.

Simple enough.

It took ten minutes of purposeful wandering for Charlie to definitively conclude she was not only still in a version of Montreal, but that birds were not, in fact, the dominant life form. A cyclist in eye-searing orange nearly clipped her as she crossed her first street, a narrow winding road that looped around what Charlie knew as Île Sainte-Hélène back home. After hurling a few colorful epithets at the cyclist's back, she decided following him was more useful. People seemed to come out of the woodwork the farther she walked: gaggles of schoolchildren in neon day camp shirts and their harried chaperones; tourists engrossed by oversized laminated maps; young families with shrieking toddlers; teenagers stretching the bounds of their independence; construction workers taking their first coffee break of the morning; the dull roar of lawnmowers firing up in the distance. Even familiar sights seemed foreign. A group of men wearing shirts emblazoned with STAGEHAND on the back was putting up chain link fences, not to cordon off a tear, but to set up for a concert. Posters advertising for CHUPACABRA: THE GOAT TOUR papered trees and the windshields of parked, boxy-looking cars that seemed decades behind the times.

Or, at least, to Charlie the cars were behind the times. She had no idea what the day was, let alone the year. It was a whole new universe. Did they even use the same calendar?

Charlie shook her head. Thinking about calendars would just open a Pandora's box of other questions, like what were the odds she'd even land in another universe that had invented cars? Or the odds she had a home to go back to? Math for math's sake had always been more Josie's thing, anyway.

A ferry docked in the distance, and Charlie watched as more boxy cars, directed by a tanned police officer wearing white gloves, rolled off the ramps and onto the road. There was a placard instructing pedestrians to follow the signs for boarding, and Charlie found three of them before realizing she would likely need to pay. Who the hell knew what passed for currency in the Land of Wrong Green?

But there were easier ways off the island. While the metro in her world had been shut down years ago, Charlie still knew all the stations by heart. The Yellow Line ran through Île Sainte-Hélène, and skipping a turnstile was less complicated than stowing away on a boat.

The metro was more or less how she remembered it, which was an unsettling feeling to have about a place you'd never been, in a universe you didn't know existed—like she imagined déjà vu on LSD. The walls of the station were stark white, and the ceilings were low. It was warmer underground, and stuffy despite the occasional gushes of wind catching passengers unaware on the platform. When the next train pulled in a few short minutes later, she waited for a gaggle of young families and workmen to exit before boarding. The fashions in the metro were no more garish than those outside, but somehow the flat fluorescent lighting made everything worse. Maybe it was just the sheer volume of it—Charlie couldn't even remember the last time she'd seen so many people in one place. The sights, the sounds, the smells... it was dizzying. The Velo, R&D's affectionate nickname for her jumpsuit, might've stuck out like a sore thumb if anyone paid attention to her, but as it was, Charlie was relieved to discover an interuniversal truth: no one makes eye contact on public transit.

Arms wrapped around her backpack like it was a favored plush toy, Charlie was studiously upholding her side of this social contract when an ad caught her attention: VERITECH: THE FUTURE IS NOW / L'AVENIR C'EST MAINTENANT.

"What." The word escaped Charlie's mouth, incredulity winning out over not looking like a crazy person. The ad itself was as shocking as how it was displayed: on matte paper protected behind scratched plexiglass. *This* was the future? She got to her feet before the metro came to a complete stop and steadied herself against one of the poles, her grip tight as she stared at the familiar blue and white logo in the ad. Her thoughts raced through implications and equations, stumbling over probabilities like Josie at the company Christmas party two years ago—the last time they'd had champagne—and what were the odds, what were the odds, what were the odds?

The doors opened at Station Berri, and the insistent press of bodies carried Charlie out onto the platform. She was greeted by a succession of posters plastered on the wall. All bore the same picture: a woman about Charlie's age staring directly into the camera, her lips curved in a daring smirk, her arms held loosely out to the sides, palms up, an inviting gesture. Her dark hair was cut short, and she wore a metallic blue suit with a black, deep-v shirt. The same slogan as before, VERITECH: THE FUTURE IS NOW / L'AVENIR C'EST MAINTENANT, was written in block letters across the bottom, obscuring a pair of frankly fabulous leather ankle boots.

"What."

Charlie swung her backpack over her shoulder and took a step closer. Underneath the slogan, in smaller font, was an address in the Old Port. Another universe with cars was one thing, but another Verity?

Charlie didn't need to find a tear. All she needed to find was Dr. Verity Baum.

Chapter Two

— JUST VERA —

Verity didn't prove hard to find. The fact that her address was plastered across half the city didn't hurt, but Charlie could've found the Veritech building in her sleep. Which was lucky, considering the constant stream of familiar things made strange jockeying for her attention. The first time a car went by after she came back up to street level, she'd startled and watched it, waiting for it to break down before she finally realized that noise was just how it sounded. Fossil fuels, inside designs that seemed bigger than they needed to be, big and boxy with rounded edges. To her eye, they seemed... profligate, the product of a society that either hadn't yet run down their resources or hadn't realized they were doing so. On paper, it was only a five-minute walk from Palais des congrès to this world's Veritech, but it took Charlie closer to thirty after all her stopping and staring.

Flags bearing the Veritech logo lined the road running alongside the Fleuve. Back home, Veritech had set up downtown partly to leverage the historic nature of the location; if you wanted to study a tear, setting up in the kind of location that tended to attract them was a fair bet. Here… here Veritech had apparently purchased land in the Old Port to throw up a brand-new expanse of glass and metal, all sweeping curves, an incongruity amid old stone. It was a building that seemed built to declare "look at me." Charlie looked at it and had to fight down another bout of that seasick-esque dislocation.

What would it be like to work somewhere with actual windows, though? It'd be nice. But then, having a world to look at that wasn't ravaged by tears in reality probably helped. She wanted a window that looked out on her world, not this oddly accoutered and generally unsettling mirror. Behind one of those windows was, hopefully, Verity Baum, who would be able to help her get back where she needed to be. Charlie just needed to figure out how on Earth—how on the wrong Earth—she was going to get in to talk to her. Things might be different here, but she very much doubted this world's Verity would just take meetings with walk-ins off the street.

Charlie sat down on a bench outside the remarkably intact Pointe-à-Callière Museum and stared across the street at the unfamiliar building, thinking about her options. Then, she abruptly stood and headed straight for the entrance, trying to even her steps into the fast but not hurried pace of someone who knew exactly where they were going and had every right to be going there. She reached the street, looked both ways, looked both ways again as it occurred to her that she had no idea what the rules of the road were and hadn't been paying attention to which side people had been driving on, and then crossed. She passed through the large glass entryway and into the atrium, a slight hitch in her step as she glanced around to work out where employees went. Maybe security wouldn't notice.

Spotting a set of turnstiles with sensors to swipe an employee ID, she strode toward them. When did people usually take out their employee ID? Was it right before, or halfway there? Some people did it right before, surely; there'd been plenty of times she'd been right behind someone hunting down their ID in their purse.

She didn't have a purse, of course. She had a high tech jumpsuit with pockets and a backpack, which was the biggest flaw in this plan. Well, the second biggest. The biggest was that it relied on something she had no way of knowing.

Reaching the turnstile, she patted her pockets. She ostentatiously patted her pockets, trying to look like she was looking for something, then turned to the security guard at the desk beside them. She didn't have to pretend at looking hopeful, but the guard just looked at her blankly.

"Forgot my ID," she said, trying a smile. People who'd forgotten their ID smiled approximately that awkwardly, right? "Could you..." She inclined her head at the turnstile.

The guard tapped at the computer, but not, it seemed, to open her a way through, which had probably been too much to hope for.

"What's your name?" the guard asked.

This was it, then. The experimental hypothesis on which this plan hinged: if Verity Baum existed in this dimension, who else did? Was everyone else somehow transposed over? Was there a Charlotte Chase?

It was a weird thing to think about. She was already wondering what the other her would be like. The security guard didn't know her, obviously, so she wasn't the kind of person who stopped to chat with people she saw every day. She was trying not to markdown Hypothetical Other Charlotte Chase based on no evidence. Maybe the guard had a bad memory for faces. Maybe he was new.

"Charlotte Chase," she said. He tapped. He tapped some more. He squinted at his screen. "Charlie?" she ventured.

"There's no one in here by that name," he said, now looking back at her, looking increasingly dubious. Suspicious, even.

"Huh," she said, trying to sound absolutely bewildered as to why that might be. "That's—that's weird, I don't—you know what," she said, words coming out a little fast, stumbling a little as they ran up against what had always been a limited talent for performance. "I'm new, and—and they probably haven't put me in the system yet. I'll just call my, um, my manager, I'll be right, I'll—"

And then she was crossing back over the floor, pace a little less the purposeful stride of someone who belonged and a little more... fleeing.

Charlotte Chase didn't work at Veritech, then. Different life, different career. Maybe without the tears around... well, it was pointless to think about it. There were more important things than trying to look herself up. Clearly, it wasn't going to be as easy as just walking in. She'd either have to find some way of convincing this Verity to see her, of getting a message to her that would convince her Charlie was someone she needed to talk to... or she was going to have to break in.

Operation Message seemed doomed from the outset. What, exactly, could she tell anyone that wouldn't come off as the delusional ramblings of someone trying to meet a— Well, the word for Verity's position in this universe really seemed to be a celebrity. It wasn't that the Verity back home wasn't known, but there weren't magazine covers. This Verity likely had cranks writing to her all the time, and so even if Charlie were to find a way to pay for some time in an internet café—if they had internet cafés—what email could she possibly send?

Hi, you don't know me, but I know a version of you in another universe...

Hi, I'm from another universe and could really use a hand getting back...

Greetings, inhabitant of an undesignated new universe, I am a traveler FROM ANOTHER WORLD!!!

Mark as spam, delete. If she got hold of a phone, same problem, and that was after the problem of getting a phone. She didn't exactly have Verity's direct line. Or, she did, but there was very little chance that it would be the same number here. They probably didn't even have the same phone number format.

In-person, though, she could explain, she could present her story in a non-insane-sounding light. She could show Verity the equipment she'd brought with her.

So, she was breaking into the building belonging to the woman one magazine described as "a genuine Leonarda da Vinci." State of the art security, then.

Charlie watched another car blare past smoking at the exhaust and wondered what state that might be, exactly.

Verity's office was surprisingly spartan and devoid of the building exterior's ostentation. Given the visual clutter of the world outside, Charlie's eyes welcomed the break. Satisfied she hadn't tripped any silent alarms, she shut the door behind her. It was after hours, and Charlie's infiltration of Veritech had gone more smoothly than expected. The security guard from earlier—Jean-François, memory supplied from just a flash of his nametag, but she had a knack for names—had gone home for the night, and Charlie had taken advantage of the shift change. Human error was always the easiest system to exploit.

The second easiest was this computer network when you applied a tablet from another world to it. It turned out Charlie's state of the art had a whole lot more state to it than they did here.

The problem with breaking in after hours, though, was that there was no telling when Verity would come back. The Verity Charlie knew was the kind of woman who never went home, but beyond owning the same company, Charlie couldn't be sure the two Veritys were particularly similar. This one was definitely younger, if the metro poster was an accurate representation. Charlie's brain hurt enough from accommodating the probability of another not-so-different universe without adding time-travel to the perpetually unbalanced equation.

Instead, she snooped. She considered the artwork on the walls and the books lined up neatly on a glass desk meant more for show than for use. She looked for secret doors hidden in the walls and in the floor. She put her backpack down and kicked up her feet to test the leather chairs for comfort. Judging by the Velo's built-in clock—still set to Right Earth Eastern Standard Time—she hadn't slept in close to twenty-four hours. A nap was overdue.

Charlie didn't have time for a nap. A door slid open, and she froze, still reclined with her booted feet pressed against the blunt edge of the desk. Dr. Verity Baum, dressed in a violet damask suit with black satin lapels and no blouse underneath, strode into the room with a runway model's purpose, her heels *clack-clacking* on the polished floor. She stopped five steps into the room, and the silence was deafening. For a long moment the two women simply met each other's eyes. Verity's expression was unreadable, which was a new brand of disorienting. Charlie and Verity had fielded accusations of developing telepathy over the years, they were so inside each other's heads, but the woman who bore her friend and mentor's face might as well have been wearing a blank mask. Who would speak first?

"Lights."

Verity, then.

A pair of lamps on opposite ends of the office switched on. Charlie belatedly remembered to take her feet off the desk, which was followed by the sudden urge to stand up and launch into an introduction.

"*Bonjour*-Hi, I'm—"

"In my office," Verity interrupted. She raised an intimidating eyebrow.

"Well, yes, but I'm also Charlotte Chase," Charlie continued, debating whether she should offer a hand, which resulted in an awkward gesture when she decided against it. Yes, Operation In Person was getting off to a swell start.

Verity smirked. Charlie recognized the expression from the posters, but not personal experience.

"Chuck Chaste, huh?" Verity's gaze traveled with predatory focus down the length of Charlie's body, and her smirk twisted, widened into a grin that revealed perfect teeth framed between full, red lips. The Velo was utilitarian, designed for the singular purpose of jumping through a tear in reality, and covered her from neck to toe. It was also, the thought slowly occurred to Charlie, very tight. A million more important things were vying for her attention. None of them stopped Charlie from blushing.

"Not in that outfit, sweetheart," Verity purred, taking a step closer, still wearing that same feline grin. "Whose idea were you anyhow? No one told me it was my birthday."

Oh god. "I'm not—" Charlie threw up her hands. "Not that there's anything wrong with— But I'm not, I'm— Charlie Chase, not Chaste," she clarified, nerves ramping her voice up an octave.

"As in 'thrill of the...'" Verity replied. The eyebrow went up again.

"Yes," Charlie said, which was immediately followed by a firm and decisive, "no. I mean—"

"I'm curious."

"Good!" Charlie said, clapping her hands together in anxious enthusiasm. "That's good! Curiosity, especially, say, scientific curiosity—"

Verity frowned. *Maybe she's getting it.* "My lab coat's downstairs if we're doing the Professor Baum thing..."

She's not getting it.

"No!" Charlie said, and then she took a breath, waving Verity off to keep her from interrupting again. "No. Just. Listen. Please."

Verity's eyes narrowed, the interior mechanics behind them seeming to work terrifyingly fast. To Charlie's immense relief, however, Verity stepped back rather than forward and took the long way around to the desk Charlie had abandoned. Leaning back against it, Verity lifted a hand. Whatever desperation had been in Charlie's voice must have piqued her interest.

"The floor's all yours, Miss Chaste."

Charlie winced. Or not.

"Charlotte Chase," she said.

"Miss Chase," Verity said, pushing off the desk and walking around it, raising a hand and making small circles with her fingers. "You have—you broke in? You broke in. You're not here to seduce me," she said, pausing to make a caricatured sad face, bottom lip pushed out before the expression instantly reverted to what it had been. "You're not here to kidnap or kill me. You're here to sell me something." She reached her seat and sat down, flopping both elegantly tailored legs onto the desk and holding both hands out in Charlie's direction.

Charlie thought this had so far been both a rather broad definition of ceding her the floor and also generally a bad start, but there was only one way to go.

"I'm— I am not here to sell you something. I am— I mean, I guess it's an opportunity, but it's—"

"Do you want me to go out and come back in?"

"No, I—"

"Good, because that seems like a lot of work. Please, either start or bring out the giant cake."

"I'm from another world."

Charlie hadn't thought Verity's smirk had anywhere to go without having to turn into a proper smile, but it turned out she had underestimated how finely tuned an instrument it was; Verity's lips ratcheted up an infinitesimal distance.

"You're an alien?"

"No. Well—yes, but not in a little green woman sense."

"Well, of course not. You're wearing blue." She squinted. "You're wearing my blue. I think we have a copyright on that."

"Actually, it's gray," Charlie mumbled, gaze flicking down to her own arms. Maybe that was what was wrong with the colors here: there was simply more room for variation. What was gray at home was light blue here. She shook her head. Not important.

"I'm from an adjacent universe, an alternate Earth. I mean, not adjacent, but—"

"Congruent," Verity said. It was impossible at this point to tell what she was thinking. Either way, Charlie just had to barrel on, now.

"So, about fifteen years ago, in, uh, my version of the world, we started to get... tears. No one knew what it was, at first, it wasn't like... it's not like people wearing weird clothes started popping out—"

"Breaking into people's offices, not even bringing giant cakes," murmured Verity.

"—it was just." Charlie took a breath. "They were small, at first, but even the small ones, buildings would collapse. Buildings would blow up. People thought it was some kind of new weapon, something that destabilized things at an atomic level, but once one had opened the effect just... lingered. Anything that got too close was affected, and 'too close' would get wider and wider...

"No one lives in New York anymore. It consumed the whole city. And then it started hitting other places, just, the whole world, and it definitely wasn't a weapon, and people studied what was going on and eventually figured out that they were holes, basically. Leaking foreign matter, and I mean foreign, on an absolute and fundamental level foreign, such that when it interacted with normal matter—"

She smacked her hands together and spread them wide.

"It was like... stains, I guess. Or... bleach. Harsh chemicals. Pour them onto fabric and they eat through or the colors run or fade, except substitute 'the fundamental basis of reality' for—"

"You know I'm smart, right?" Verity interrupted. "The magazine covers tell me so. You don't have to do the cute metaphor thing."

"Right," Charlie said. "Right. Well, it's—"

"Kidding, do the cute metaphors. The cute metaphors are more fun. The fabric of reality has bleach on it. Or acid? Your reality is having a really bad laundry day."

This was not exactly the serious take on it Charlie had been going for. It didn't capture the gravity of the situation, which was pretty damned grave.

"My reality is full of holes and would be in serious trouble, even if that was all that was going on," she said. "But—so, people didn't come out, nothing like that. But before too long we did start getting extra-dimensional entities. I guess—in my terrible undersell of an analogy, they're moths. They eat fabric. A tear opens up and everything around it is changed in unfathomable ways at a quantum level, and then parasites come along and eat everything that's changed, and then they keep eating and eventually, you have no planet, or maybe just an uninhabitable one, and no one's sure if it ends there, but it doesn't really matter if it does because no planet is kind of a big deal, okay?"

"So... holes in reality, nothing comes through, anything near them is changed, maybe explodes, maybe gets eaten, maybe just, I don't know, gets bad indigestion." Verity steepled her fingers. "How is it you're here? You came from somewhere. And I am certain we don't have any tears in reality. Someone would have asked me about it. I'd have been interviewed about it by a well-meaning news anchor who just wanted me to dumb the whole thing down into a convenient metaphor about clothes, and then I would have gone and poked at it in person because, well, that sounds exciting."

"You kind of did," Charlie said, wrinkling her brow.

"I—wait, wait, wait," Verity said, taking her feet off the desk and sitting up. "I exist? This alternate universe has a me. Okay, I don't buy it. Can't be. I'd be here talking to me, not..." She waved vaguely at Charlie. "I'd listen to me." She paused, considered this, and then said, "Well, it depends."

"You—not you, Verity. The other— My world's Verity," Charlie said. The other Verity seemed too disloyal. *This* was the other Verity, this aggravating, flighty dilettante who appeared incapable of taking anything seriously. "She was near a tear when one opened, in New York. She's had heart problems ever since, being too near to it.... So—she's been working on the problem for years. I came onto the project a few years ago, a little after she'd worked out a way to get closer to tears. She discovered how to lessen the effect of the foreign matter, reduce the amount the surrounding area decayed, deter the parasites, and once we could get close enough to study the tear, we figured out a way to stabilize them. Dampen down the effect. Except... well, it never held. Our best theory was that it was because the tear came from somewhere, or went somewhere. It connected to somewhere, anyway. There was another universe on the other side that was bleeding into ours. Stabilizing one side didn't do any good because it was still unstable on the other side, and it'd just reverberate back to our side and destabilize again. We had to stabilize it on both sides."

"Enter Chuck Chaste," Verity said. "How are you not exploded?"

"The suit," she said, looking down at herself, and then kind of wishing she hadn't. It seemed tantamount to asking Verity to do the same, and she was very much hoping to avoid that happening again. "We call it the Velo. The Velo and a lot of gene therapy to make me resistant to the effect of tears on people at a cellular level.

Um. There was nothing we could do about further down, atomic or quantum, but we sort of hoped—"

"If you survived long enough to actually make the transition, the vibrational shift would align you with the new universe, and you'd interact normally with the matter on this side."

"That," Charlie agreed. Talking to this Verity was like walking on a plane during turbulence. It was hard to figure out which way it was going to move.

"Okay. So you put on your spandex, you threw yourself through a tear in reality into a brave new world, and then... it didn't work?" She snapped her fingers. "It didn't work, and you need me to come and figure out how to make it work."

"It worked. It just... we thought it would resolve into a stable link. But when I stabilized it on this side, it closed. I'm stuck. If there were any other tears, I could just repeat the process and get home, except—"

"There aren't any," Verity said.

"You'd have noticed," Charlie said.

"Leading to you breaking into my office—how'd you do that, by the way? Actually, don't tell me, I'll work it out, it'll be a fun exercise—to beseech me to use my very big brain in the service of sending you home. Which would also be a fun exercise."

"Yes," Charlie said, breathing a sigh of relief. "That is—that's a tremendous relief. You'll help?"

"Nope," said Verity, putting her feet back up on the desk. "It would be a fun exercise if the whole story weren't so obviously the inventive but deranged fabulist ramblings of a nut. I called security the moment I realized you broke in. I'm actually a little concerned—" She pitched her voice to the opening door, to the security people hurrying in and eyeing Charlie to work out what kind of problem she would be. Whether it would be the kind that required the use of tasers or batons. "This is our response time?" Verity concluded. "We have got to do something about that. But first—could we maybe remove the intruder? Her name is Chuck, she'll tell you a wonderful story on what will presumably be a slow and rambling trip back downstairs. It's a couple of floors. I mean, honestly. She gave me her entire backstory. We were just about to start talking about her childhood, what her parents were like. I assume robots."

Charlie bristled. The slight against her parents, whom—judging by the turn of this meeting—she might never see again, hit hard. Her hands curled into fists, nails biting into the flesh of her palms, but Verity steamrolled over her retort.

"You are a very strange woman, but I just, I feel like there's only room for one eccentric, and my name's on the door, so. Bye, Chuck."

Chapter Three

— WATER LILIES —

Two days after Charlie was escorted—well, thrown—out of Veritech, she was growing increasingly grateful it wasn't winter. The summer days were long and humid, leaving her hair sticky against the nape of her neck, but she'd take the heat over the particular misery of Montreal in January. Living on the streets was far from ideal, but with no money to her name and a conspicuous lack of personal belongings, Charlie was making do. She was still kicking herself over leaving her bag in Verity's office. *A rookie mistake,* her mind supplied in an endless loop, though it wasn't like there were experts in the field of Dealing with an Alternate Reality Version of Your Boss.

Verity followed Charlie everywhere she went. Her face was plastered on billboards, street signs, posters in the metro and, most disconcertingly, in bathroom stalls. She was a different animal from the Verity Charlie knew, that much was for certain: younger, sensual, more rock star than scientist in bearing, though no less intimidating in her intelligence. It had been silly to think

Verity, any Verity, would believe her story. Charlie knew it was insane—the woman from another world. Of course Verity wouldn't believe her. But while Veritech wasn't quite as futuristic as its ads claimed, given it was at least two decades behind the tech an average consumer had in Charlie's world, she didn't have a surplus of other options to turn to for help.

Breaking and entering might have to become a normal part of her routine. She needed the equipment in that backpack if she had any hope of getting home again, regardless of whether Verity would believe her or not.

The electronics store she was in bore that out. She hadn't been casing it exactly, mostly because she wasn't a criminal. She didn't case. She did recon. She had been reconnoitering the store to identify potential materiel that she might need to uplift for emergency operational purposes. It didn't look hopeful, and not just because a security guard had started to follow her around. From a distance. Because she smelled. She was trying—and failing—to think of that as a weird fringe benefit.

She'd been trying to see if there were any electronics she could jack and kludge together into something resembling her kit. What she was seeing instead, again, was Verity, on the screen of the TVs on display. Tired as Charlie was, it took a moment for her to process what exactly was happening. Not another puff piece or interview, not Verity working a camera with a finely tuned eyebrow or smirk, but a file photo—which admittedly had both eyebrow and smirk— and footage of a stretcher.

Verity was in the hospital. That could be a coincidence. Right? Charlie was finding it harder to balance what could or could not be coincidence, because she was in another universe where an identical but different version of her mentor existed. They'd had different life experiences. It could be anything. There were a lot of things that landed a person in hospital, not just the most significant hospital trip that had happened to the Verity Charlie knew.

The trip right after...

Well, she had to know. Physical security around Veritech had been beefed up, mostly in the form of a picture of Charlie being handed around, but she could still get in digitally.

At least, once she found a tucked away spot, she could eventually get in. Verity had been at work there, too. Charlie had to brute force her way in with tech several decades ahead, which felt slightly embarrassing. She could have been cleaner, she just didn't have time.

She found the cameras, found one for Verity's lab. There had been some kind of disaster in there, because everything was strewn haphazardly about. Paper everywhere, piles of equipment, although whatever had happened hadn't touched the weird art installation that Verity had in the middle. Charlie's eye kept going back to it. She zoomed in, and realized why.

It was Charlie's tech. Or at least, it had been, before a bunch of other tech had been grafted on, in some places simply surrounding equipment she'd brought over, in some places actually inserted into it. At least one component was now in two parts, on opposite sides of the contraption Verity had Frankensteined out of her stuff. Atop a pair of antennae, the purpose of which Charlie couldn't ascertain at first glance, Verity had affixed a pair of googly eyes. Quite possibly the purpose of the antenna was to be stands for the googly eyes.

Charlie's initial this-can't-be-coincidence assumption had been that Verity had gotten too close to a tear, suffered the same fate as her Verity. Now she was leaning more toward coincidence. Maybe Verity had just done a lot of drugs, made whatever this monstrosity was in the footage, and then collapsed.

She rewound until there were people in the footage, then rewound even further until those people weren't paramedics. Verity and another woman were walking around the lab. Verity gestured about, expounding, extemporizing.

It took the context cue of a recording device in the woman's hand for Charlie to identify what she was looking at as an interview. About…what? About Charlie's tech? About whatever Verity had built out of her tech?

She stared at the image for a while, then dug up the paper that had first broken the story, and the reporter, then dug into the reporter's files until she found the relevant recordings. She lined it up with the video she had and played them both. It wasn't exact, probably, but it was enough to, hardy har, get the picture.

"—so, the security guys escort her out, and I'm there, in my office, with this big bag of stuff. It's crazy person stuff, obviously, so at first, I figure it's either the head of the last person she tried to sell this story to, or it's a bomb. But I'm, you know, smart. I do due diligence on it, and there's none of the right chemical signatures for 'go boom.' I open it up, and there's—this stuff, this tech. It's maybe a bit too retiring, a bit too afraid to make a scene. It's very understated—maybe that's why she didn't want to show it to me—but part of that is because it's small. More on a circuit than we can fit on a circuit, and I know precisely how much we can fit on a circuit and how much we're going to fit on a circuit five years from now. There is nowhere in the world that can do what her tech has done. And so I think—okay, but maybe it's just someone ahead of me. Unlikely, but I guess theoretically it is possible. And then I think, well, what's it for? So I work out what it's for."

The reporter leaned in, seeming to hang on Verity's every word. "And what's it for?"

"Wrong question! It is no longer for that. That's— You know what? That is the same question, I should have led into that differently. It had a purpose. I have given it a new purpose. I'm just going to show you, that's more fun. It's going to change the world."

I'm never getting home. Anger accompanied weary resignation as the thought took root. Verity hadn't just made abstract art out of her tech, she was using it as the basis of some new product she was showing off to a journalist—

Who was having a rather different, more subdued reaction.

"What is that?" the Verity on the screen said, bustling by and flapping a hand at the journalist's face, moving on before she could swipe it out of the way. "That is exactly the wrong reaction. I made this in two days, and it's a work of art."

Because it costs a fortune and doesn't do anything? Charlie pinched her fingers to zoom in on the avant-garde horror Verity had wrought. The individual components didn't seem to be damaged, so it was salvageable. Maybe in all the chaos of Verity's hospitalization, Charlie would be able to get back in to retrieve it. There had to be a way to use it to make a way home. Something like what Verity had done to the Einstein-Rosen Coupling wouldn't be a bad start, and then you'd have to...

She zoomed back out. She stared at it. She stared at the whole thing, including the antennae with their googly eyes. She was still pretty sure the eyes themselves were optional, but her rock-solid certainty she wasn't going home had fled, because the weird, sideways, abstract logic of what Verity had done was becoming clear. The work of art it resembled most strongly was a Monet. If you looked at all the little dots you didn't see the water lilies.

Except she was pretty sure Monet had never painted any water lilies with crocodiles under them, which was what they had here.

"I will tell you, it involves saving an actual-facts-alien from another world. You thought this was a puff piece, well, wait until you get a load—of—"

The Verity on the screen flicked a switch. For a moment, nothing happened. Then she raised an arm, looked at it in consternation, and collapsed.

When she'd first looked at the footage, Charlie had thought the faint distortion near the center was digital noise, an artifact of the recording.

Now she sort of thought it was the end of the world, again.

The emergency room looked much the same as it might have in Charlie's world before the tears closed down most traditional hospitals, though she couldn't speak from personal experience. She'd spent more time in Afghan field clinics and Veritech's private labs than anywhere like the CHUM, which had managed to avoid tears in her world because of its recent move to a new, considerably less historic building. She passed a seated woman with a bloody nose in the waiting area and fought down the disquieting sense of heightened reality: the blood was too red just as the grass had been too green. It was almost like stepping onto the set of some TV medical drama.

A nurse in kaleidoscope scrubs bustled past and jostled Charlie back to attention. She scanned the signs hanging from the ceiling and decided on a course that led her to the Visitor Information desk, which was housed in a quieter lobby. As far as signs went, it kind of summed up her time in this universe so far. She was a visitor; she needed information.

Then again, "emergency room" also applied. She kept thinking about that flicker on the screen, the visual distortion. Kept almost imagining it, almost willing herself to see that grayscale weft cutting across nothing, the texture in what should have been vacant space, as if she were trying to bring on a migraine. Thinking about what it would smell like in that lab, now. Tears had a different smell about them. Not a specific different, not simply like one known quantity when it should have been something else, not even a phantom smell like those experienced during neurological trauma, but different, the brain's olfactory interpretation simply coming up empty.

She'd wanted to go straight to Veritech, try and go directly at the problem before it grew, but she wouldn't be able to get in. So she was here, in a hospital, about to try and get the help of a reckless fool who might well be about to undergo heart surgery.

She had no idea how she was going to do that. Any lie that would get her in that room would probably involve not looking like she'd been sleeping rough for days.

She scanned the room, looking for any gap that she might be able to use to just sneak in. Her eyes alighted instead on…someone she knew. Someone else she knew. Sort of. Josephine Watson was talking rapidly in French on a cellphone. Like the Josie in Charlie's world, she stood half a head shorter than Charlie. Her eyes and skin were dark, and her short black hair was secured away from her face with a simple gray headband. Her expression was grave as she hung up and scanned the room with the idle despair of someone who could do nothing but wait.

Until she saw Charlie. For a moment, Charlie thought, *Oh, finally,* as Josephine's look halted on her. Not relief, but the bright swelling bubble that would pop to become relief. But—the bubble sagged—it wasn't recognition. It was a narrowing of the eyes, a this-is-out-of-place. Charlie recognized it as the look Josie got when she was solving a problem, trying to fit all the numbers together.

The two of them started walking toward each other at the same moment. Charlie braced herself to once again talk to someone who looked like one of her closest friends but did not know her in the slightest. That was clear. This Josephine didn't know her. But it looked like she knew of her.

"You're the…alien," she said, with the slight dry lilt that said, "this is a quote from Verity, which means that it's weird but also that's normal." Josephine's gaze was analytical, lacking in both the heat this world's Verity had when they'd met and all of the warmth Charlie had come to expect from *her* Josie. "She specified you weren't little and green, but I didn't expect precisely this tall. What did you give her, and what has it done to her?"

"Give—" Charlie began, and then cut herself off. At a volume more appropriate for a room where people waited to learn how badly their loved ones were hurt, she said, "I left that equipment behind when she threw me out. I didn't give her anything. She shouldn't have—"

"But she did," Josephine said, cutting across. "That is what she does, so now what? What did your alien—" The lilt, again, that this was what she had been told but might not be true, and a hint under that that if it wasn't someone was going to pay. That someone might, anyway. It was so, so familiar, and it had never been directed at Charlie this way. As if she were the outsider, the potential threat. "—technology do to her."

"Best guess? Gave her a heart attack. That's what happened in my world, to my Verity."

"Your Verity."

"She didn't mention that part, huh?" Charlie sucked air through her teeth and pressed the heel of her hand to her forehead. "Look, Josie—"

"What." A statement, not a question.

"Josie?" Charlie tried again. "I'm sorry, maybe that level of familiarity isn't appropri—"

"No, it's Watts. Everyone calls me Watts."

"...right," Charlie said, rolling with the new information like the rock of a boat. Slowly but surely, she'd get her sea legs. "Watts, look, this is a long story we don't have time for. I really need to talk to her. To Verity. The fate of this world depends on it."

"Of this world," Josie—Watts—said, testing the words, applying pressure and seeing if they'd break. "My friend is in hospital and in trouble. Her fate is in trouble, I know that for sure, so I will need some part of the story."

"She tore a hole in reality and it's going to destroy your whole business and also the world if I don't close it. Look, here—" Charlie pulled out the tablet and showed Watts the image she'd paused on, the scene in the lab once everyone had left. That small distortion, the weft in the air. She was keenly aware that in a digital image it could just look like a mistake. An error.

Which it was. When you saw it in person it still looked like that.

"And you need to talk to my friend, who is in hospital, to achieve this...why? I could get you back into the building and your equipment." This very much did not sound like an offer. It sounded like a criticism of Charlie's approach, a hole in her story.

For a moment, Charlie considered whether it was. Not a hole in her story, that was all true, but whether that was what she should be trying for instead. Skip dealing with Verity entirely. She was in hospital, and so much more frivolous, couldn't Charlie just do it herself?

Except she didn't know what Verity had done to her equipment—there had been googly eyes, for god's sake—and she couldn't predict or assume she'd be able to follow whatever line of thought this Verity had followed to get where she had, the way she would with her own. "I need her to tell me what she did so I can undo it. We don't have time for me to reverse engineer whatever she did. I don't know how her brain works."

The corner of Watts's mouth tugged upwards. Expression still grim, but with a modicum of recognition, perhaps. "I will give you ten minutes, and you are not going to get her worked up."

"With my news about the world ending."

"You will do your best. And—it's just Vera. Not Verity."

Vera-not-Verity was roomed on the third floor of Wing C, and Charlie was almost surprised by the lack of security outside the door.

The room itself was unremarkable save for the fact that it had double occupancy. Vera's roommate, whose bed was closest to the door, was watching a particularly sleep-inducing game show judging by the volume of her snores. Charlie tiptoed across the room to the other side of the privacy curtain. Vera was awake and without visitors. A game of solitaire—with real cards—was laid out on her lap, and she was scribbling something in a hospital-branded notepad. Her gaze snapped up the moment Charlie stepped over to her side.

"Oh, good, I was wondering how to track you down. And then I figured it out, but I was in hospital and they're being very unaccommodating. Honestly, it's bad enough I'm—I had a minor health incident. I have to be bored as well?"

"A minor— Do you have any idea what you've done?"

"The doctors are working on it, but frankly I have some doubts about—"

"To the world." Charlie stopped herself, pinched the bridge of her nose. Both things mattered, ultimately.

"Changed it fundamentally, yes. A brand-new era awaits, once I've solved some teething troubles and gotten you ho—"

"Teething troubles? Teething troubles. No, you know what? That is appropriate. Your troubles definitely have teeth. You made a tear."

Sloppy with drugs as her expressions were, Vera's nevertheless took on an edged gleam of inappropriate triumph. Didn't she realize what she'd done?

"It worked? Oh, I definitely have to be back working on that."

"I have to be working on that," Charlie corrected. "You have to be staying here. You just had a pacemaker put in. Right?" Charlie retrieved Vera's chart from the end of the bed.

Wrong, as it turned out. She hadn't had surgery but was likely to need it. Charlie wasn't entirely sure what "aortic regurgitation" was, but she could figure out "abnormal valve, congenital (??????)." At least, she thought that's what it said. It could have been "oprennol raku." Either handwriting styles in this universe were different, or doctors' handwriting was universal.

"I did not, and I'm not going to get one here, because they're saying I have a congenital heart defect. Which I don't, because if I was born with a heart defect, they would have noticed that when I was born."

"I think maybe you didn't have an 'oprennol raku'—congenital heart defect before, but you do now. You were too close to a tear. It...changes things. My Verity, her heart's electrical activity just went completely out of whack. As if it was syncing to somewhere else entirely. They had to put in a pacemaker. Apparently, you picked up a late-in-life heart defect that you were born with. Tears. They're really fucking weird."

"Oh, so it's something the doctors here have absolutely zero experience with and don't know how to handle? And we should leave immediately?" Vera pushed the cards together into a single deck. "Got it. Let's go."

"They're really fucking weird and *really fucking dangerous*, and you made one."

"I can work out where I went wrong. It needs to be stabilized, right? It's leaking everywhere. It and my heart, bosom buddies."

"*I* can—"

The volume of the television next bed over had changed. The dinky game show music and canned applause were replaced by the flourish of a breaking news report: "anomaly," "Old Port," "Veritech." The details were lost to Vera's continuing complaints and attempts to retrieve her phone and her clothes, or at least establish the location of these objects.

"Can you just shut up?" Charlie snapped. She tore the privacy curtain back, ripping half of it off the plastic hooks attaching it to the rail. A breathless field reporter was on the scene, but Charlie was more interested in the chyron occupying the bottom third of the screen: ATTACK ON VERITECH? That might mean...

"I gotta get in there," Charlie said, tucking Vera's chart back into its pocket. Vera, meanwhile, was getting out of bed.

"Great, we're on the same page."

"No," Charlie insisted, moving to ease Vera back onto the bed, "we are decidedly not on the same page, you're—"

"About to lose my life's work to a tear in reality," Vera replied with surprising clarity. Her eyes seemed to sharpen, her keen intellect fighting against the effects of the painkillers. Charlie imagined adrenaline was to thank for that. "Also, you can't get into my lab without me."

For a moment they shared a stare. Charlie cleared her throat. "Well, when you put it that way..."

Vera smirked. The expression didn't quite ooze the same confidence as it did on her posters, but Charlie had to give credit where credit was due: you'd never have known the woman had been unconscious from a heart that wasn't pumping blood properly and still wasn't. She shrugged out from under Charlie's hands and padded over to the closet on the opposite wall to retrieve her clothes.

Charlie averted her eyes. "I'm driving, though."

Chapter Four
— WITH CROCODILES —

T he biggest problem getting out of the hospital was somehow evading the press corps who'd set up camp around Veritech. Charlie pulled the car over far enough down the street that none of them yet registered the presence of the extremely Vera Baum sports car as something that might be Vera Baum arriving on the scene. Maybe they should have taken the metro.

Although then she'd have been stuck taking public transport with Vera, which wasn't exactly discreet. Also, she suspected it would have driven her more insane than Vera's comments on her driving.

"Ideas?" she said, drumming her fingers on the steering wheel.

"I thought you were driving," Vera said, slightly slumped in the seat. Charlie couldn't tell if it was the drugs, a sulk, or if that was just how Vera sat in a passenger seat.

"Yeah, okay, if you were driving, I guess you'd just drive over them, but maybe something a little less—"

"Vera?" Nathaniel Salt's voice came through the speakers. Vera's assistant here as well, then. She pictured him, automatically. Whip thin, hair that matched the name…except maybe he didn't look like that at all. She didn't know this version of him. Another friend that would respond blankly should she speak up. It was the least of their worries right now, but still. She did not speak up. "Vera, what's going on? I called the hospital, and they said you weren't there. There are very weird and very bad things happening here."

"I know. I'm here."

There was a pause. Charlie wondered if Salt had just looked around whatever room he was in, just in case. "…Where?"

"I'm outside. I need to be inside, to actually fix whatever it is that's happening, but the vulture corps are circling. I need you to talk to them."

"And tell them what? I don't know anything, just that—"

"Weird and bad, I got it. Just come out, say you don't know anything, investigations are ongoing, the situation will be resolved shortly. The truth! You love the truth."

"Should you even be out of the hospital?"

"I—"

"Hate hospitals," Salt interrupted. "Vera."

"I'm fine. Heart is murmuring but it's not shouting, so that's okay. I'm okay, I swear. It'll be fine."

"You're going right back to the hospital once—"

"The world is no longer falling apart. Sure. Done," said Vera, who clearly did not share Salt's love of the truth. Charlie could tell she didn't mean a word of that from where she was sitting. From Salt's sign-off, it kind of sounded like he could, too.

From there, it was fairly straightforward. The moment a genuine high-ranking Veritech employee showed up at the front door, the press descended en masse. All Charlie and Vera had to do was find a side door they weren't covering and they were in.

They took the elevator. It was a risk since without knowing how big the tear was, there was no way of knowing what it had done to the building. If Charlie had been on her own, she would have simply torn down the stairs. But all the valves in her heart were pumping blood in the right direction.

The elevator doors opened, as they had so often for Charlie in the last few years, on a Veritech lab with a tear in the middle.

Except this one wasn't a custom space designed to hold it, had absolutely no measures to lessen the impact, no Einstein-Rosen Couplings. All it had was the broken remains of equipment that had been set up to cause the damn thing. Charlie took a breath, ignored the flare of nasal blank space, and looked for what they had in their favor. It was still small. It was growing, and fast, twitching and swelling as space cracked about it, but it was small. And maybe the equipment had been set up to cause it, but it had originally been designed to stabilize it. She just had to put it all back the way it had been while a hole in reality ate the space she was working in.

"What is that?" Vera said. Charlie had been about to snap at her when she realized Vera had sniffed before she said it. She could have explained, but Vera was constantly talking about how smart she was. She could just figure it out, Charlie had more important things to—

"Oh," Vera said. "Brain doesn't know what it's smelling. Can't relate to anything so it freaks out. Weird."

That was annoying, and it lacked the proper gravity. It sounded, in fact, as if Vera wanted to go sniff the thing up close. Letting her would essentially be having a tear in reality eat off her nose to spite her face.

"Do not go near it. That is not going to react well to, you know, you, and I don't want to be stepping around your exploded heart to fix this thing. Leave it to me."

"Sure," said Vera.

Charlie really should have become more suspicious than she did at that point. She'd already reached her Frankensteined equipment, though, and her mind was occupied with working out how to restore it to working order in the quickest time possible.

The first thing to do was to figure out how Vera had distributed all her parts. "Synchronizer, synchronizer, why did you tear out the—"

"The what?" said Vera, and Charlie was halfway to barking a rebuke to step away from the hole in reality when she realized the intercom light was on.

"The synchronizer!" Charlie snapped before it occurred to her that the parts weren't labeled. On the other hand, how the hell else did you describe a synchronizer? Vera was supposed to have some idea of how this all functioned if she'd taken it apart and used it to, say, tear a fucking hole in the world just to see what would happen. "It...synchronizes! So all the things do their thing at the same time!"

Perhaps not her most technically proficient description, but if the words she was using weren't the words Vera was using, what was the goddamned point?

"Oh, the metronome," Vera said, though her voice seemed muffled somehow—interference from the tear affecting the intercom, perhaps. "I didn't need it, so I taped it behind a googly eye so I wouldn't lose it."

There was no time to go into this latest example of lunacy. Still stripping components out of the slightly battered part she'd thrown, Charlie crossed to the part still standing. There was, indeed, a chip taped behind one of the googly eyes. She tore it loose and set to reassembly, casting a glance over her shoulder. To the naked eye, the tear didn't look any bigger, but that only meant so much. Frowning, she refocused on the task at hand.

"All right, now where'd you put—" Another chip appeared in her line of vision. It was held by a curiously gloved hand, which was attached to what appeared to be some kind of bulky spacesuit.

The suit's visor snapped open, and Vera greeted her with a smile. "Less staring, more fixing. C'mon."

"What the hell are you wearing?"

"Ah, this old thing?" Vera had the audacity to twirl. The effect was lost on Charlie, whose eyes had rolled so hard she briefly caught a glimpse of her own gray matter. "Proof of concept I designed for the CSA."

So it really was a spacesuit. Charlie huffed a breath in annoyance. The Velo drew inspiration from NASA's latest designs, sure, but Vera's suit looked like a damn marshmallow.

"And you're wearing it...why?"

"It's cutting-edge hazard protection, and that is—there's a big hazard to fix. Now I can help and no exploding hearts."

"There's no cutting edge on that; it's a goddamn rolling pin. You just waddle over there, I'll be fine without your—"

The lights flickered. Okay, it could just be a regular power failure. Then they flickered and flared and one actually burned out, and when Charlie said, "Help," it wasn't as a continuation of the previous sentence. It was an actual plea for help, because as little as she trusted Vera, she did work fast, and hopefully still could with tin cans glued to her extremities. If they didn't fix this soon, they were both going to be dead. Even more dead than just from the tear alone.

"Sorry, you paused, was that—"

"Help me get this stable or we're going to die."

"—an actual request," Vera confirmed. "I am helping! This is what you were about to ask for."

"That is absolutely not what I was asking for. I need like three other things before I need that thing."

"Yeah, but if—"

"We are not redesigning it right now because we are going to die. Put it back in the—" She cut herself off before giving a technical name Vera wouldn't recognize. "The throw-y part. The part you throw. The part you're *meant* to throw," Charlie corrected. "Goes in the tear, centers the effects to provide stabilization?"

"Oh," Vera said, "the softball," before crossing the floor with surprising alacrity. Motorized support. Why Vera had thought a powered exoskeleton was the thing for work in a gravity-free vacuum, Charlie didn't know, but at least it sped up the process right now. Vera snapped the circuits back into place. Charlie seized some more leftover parts and snapped them back onto what she was working on, now beginning to resemble what it had been when originally constructed.

"Why the sudden hurry? You sound...suddenly extra terrified. You were concerned, but now we're quote-unquote—"

The parasite came through the wall. It was visible before it came through the wall, as if they were seeing it on a spectrum that shouldn't be available to the naked eye, the chitinous slither of it defying the eye's attempt to place it in perspective in the room, but then it was through the wall, and you could tell because the wall was no longer there.

"—going to die," said Vera, mouth clearly running on autopilot while the rest of her brain very clearly seized up. Charlie couldn't blame her. She'd seen these things up close before, and the only thing more appropriate than blind paralyzing terror was blind, fleeing terror. The parasite had too many tentacles. Not just a lot, but too many. A throng of chitin-coated protuberances, but if you counted the number of them leaving the main insectile body, and then the number of tips exploring the air, the numbers didn't match; if you tried to follow one back you simply couldn't do it. It was the optical illusion where the three poles became two at the other side of the drawing, except in three dimensions—well, probably more, that was the problem—and with horrifying tentacles. It didn't ambulate on them, or at least they weren't touching the ground. It just floated, twitching through the air. There were competing hypotheses for how they got around, but no one had ever managed to capture one because the people who were stupid enough to try ended up dead. The only thing they knew for certain was that the parasites were drawn to tears.

"Charlotte," Vera said, in a tone so completely devoid of her previous over-animation that in comparison it sounded like she was awkwardly reading off a cue card, "there's a non-Euclidean cockroach squid in my lab. Why is there a non-Euclidean cockroach squid in my lab?"

"It's a parasite. It's going to eat us," Charlie told her. "And your lab. And a lot of people."

"Oh," said Vera. Then she reached out, twisted part of the equipment back into place, mashed the button with a fist and said, "Yeah, no."

The stabilization kicked in; the tear pulsed into a steadier arrangement. A dozen tentacles snapped to point at Vera as if they were divining rods to water. Charlie opened her mouth to suggest she-didn't-know-what, just hoping something would occur to her when Vera took two steps left and threw herself into the tear.

Charlie stared in numb disbelief, swift and sudden grief robbing her urgency. There was no way Vera could have survived, no way that fucking *marshmallow* could've protected her from the worst of the tear. Her heart had stopped just *standing* near the damn thing, and—

The parasite followed Vera.

"Shit-*fuck*!" Charlie pressed her hands to her head, fingers curling in on themselves so her nails dug into her scalp. Then she grabbed her bag and deployed the cowl. There was only one way to close the tear, and it was on the other side with the rest of her tech, Vera—or what was left of her—and a parasite they had no known means of killing.

Charlie jumped.

Chapter Five

— THE WASTELAND —

Charlie hit the ground of a new world running. Where Vera's reality was oversaturated, this one was colorless, barren. A wasteland of tears crackled in the near and middle distance, swallowing matter with the carelessness of a hungry dog. The only hint of life was a deadened tree, whose petrified roots jutted out from the cracked, thirsty earth. A handful of skeletal buildings stood along the street in spite of reason, foundations riddled with smaller tears, though it was hard to tell where one tear ended and another began. Charlie's stomach lurched when she caught sight of a street sign dangling from a defunct traffic light: Sherbrooke. The storied street had been in rough shape when she'd left, its most famous landmarks devoured by parasites and tears, but this was devastation at an incomprehensible order of magnitude greater than she remembered. She looked around wildly, attempting to orient herself, and realized with a start that the solitary half-eaten pillar in front of her was all that remained of Roddick Gates, McGill University's main entrance. The familiar domed roof of the Arts Building was nowhere to be seen. The entire downtown campus was seemingly leveled. Mount Royal itself was gone, the once hilly terrain reduced to an eye-wateringly hazy horizon that defied any geographic descriptor.

Charlie swallowed down bile and tried to convince herself it was only because she'd just jumped through another goddamn hole in the universe.

She looked reality—realities—in the eye and refused it. This wasn't home, couldn't be home, and there was no time for sightseeing, no time for anything other than instinct. Her body thrummed with adrenaline, and with that adrenaline came clarity of purpose: close the tear, evade certain death—though possibly not in that order.

There was a wet cough to her right. It came from the marshmallowian form of Vera, who was, somewhat miraculously, not dead. Technicolor vomit streaked the inside of her visor and Charlie managed a sympathetic grimace through her own considerable surprise. But any sense of relief was short-lived. The parasite was circling.

While no one had ever managed to kill a parasite, they had devised ways of distracting them long enough to evacuate areas under siege. Charlie pressed on one of the segmented compartments of her belt, ejecting a palm-sized, malleable disc that contained materials contaminated by a tear, the kind parasites tended to eat first: a lure. She grabbed the Reality Jig from her belt, loaded it, and took aim in the opposite direction from Vera.

Charlie fired, and about half, or a third, or two-thirds—who could fucking tell?—*some measure* of the tentacles snapped about as if they were on puppet strings suddenly yanked tautly, an almost magnetic attraction. Tracking the lure. No one had any idea if parasites thought, as such, if there was a brain in there or what. But whatever decision-making process they had, whether pure instinct or something more complex, decided to follow the lure.

The rest of the parasite stuttered around, a swivel like a movie with several frames removed, and then darted after it, short shots through the air like a prowling fish.

Vera groaned, pushing herself up onto her knees. Charlie hauled her to her feet and pried the Frankensteined tear tech from Vera's exoskeleton-powered grasp. A million ways to call the woman an idiot sat at the tip of Charlie's tongue, but instead, she went through the motions to close the stabilized tear. Vera made her bed when she jumped. They couldn't risk damning her world to the threat of a parasite.

"You wanted to get back here?" Vera said as Charlie finished calibrating the Einstein-Rosen Coupling as best she could. Vera's head wasn't quite centered in her helmet, as though she was slumped inside of the Marshmallow. The only thing keeping her vertical was the suit.

"This is not my world," Charlie said, convincing herself.

She lobbed the Coupling into the heart of the tear, took aim and stabilized it, keeping half an eye there and the rest on the parasite. The tear winked out of existence. The lure wouldn't distract it long, but with the nearest tear gone, would the parasite lose interest in her and Vera? They'd never had a chance to test, having never been able to close tears before. Parasites weren't as interested in tears that were half-stable, or Charlie's Veritech would have been overrun long past, countermeasures or no countermeasures. She hoped the parasite would be distracted by one of the myriad other visible tears, leading who-knew-where. The chances of it being back to either of their worlds seemed slimmer, now that a simple dynamic between the two was out of the equation.

"Do you think this is where they live? I think this might be where they live," Vera said. Her voice had that nerveless monotone about it again. Charlie supposed the first trip to a new dimension would do that. Maybe she'd learn something out of the experience if they both didn't die in the next couple of minutes.

"There's only one, and it followed us here, so, no," she said.

"About that," Vera said, and there was only one place that phrase led, and so Charlie risked taking her eyes off the parasite to crane around to look where Vera was looking. At the throng. The swarm. Small, but getting larger, and there was that trouble with placing them in perspective. Experience meant she could hazard an estimate, though, and she was going to have to retract any thoughts of Vera having time to learn lessons, aside from the lesson of what it felt like to have a parasite consume you out of existence.

Parasites one way, parasite exploring a lure another way...at least a desolate wasteland provided a lot of compass points to pick an escape route from. But none of them offered anything to hide behind or distract the swarm. Then again, Roddick Gates wouldn't have given much coverage even if it had been intact.

"How much cockroach nip do you have?" Vera asked.

"Lures," corrected Charlie, who'd been mentally assessing their chances. "And not enough." She loaded one all the same. "Some of them will pile on, the rest will just keep on, and then the ones that piled on will finish up..." She sighed. "We get maybe a little more time. And I don't want the one behind us deciding it wants to go through us to look at the new lure, so...run first."

She turned, picked the direction that bisected the paths of the swarm and the lone follower parasite, and threw herself into motion, hearing, after a frantic shout of "Auto-pilot," the pneumatic whir of Vera's suit doing the same a moment later, the louder thud of it over the dry, ashen ground. The sound would have worried her, if parasites hunted by sound, but as far as anyone could tell their senses were stranger and finer than that. It didn't matter if you were quiet. It mattered that you existed.

After a few moments of desperate sprinting where they weren't yet dead, she twisted to point the Reality Jig behind her, angled up, and fired into the distance between them and the swarm. She turned back and willed some extra speed into her legs, already burning with flight-or-even-more-flight-god-let-it-be-enough-flight adrenaline. Tears crackled ahead. If they could make it to one, to any of them, then maybe.

But that look behind her had given her a glance at how much ground the swarm had made on them already. They were closer than the nearest tear. It was simple math. There was no way it came out to anything other than them caught and devoured before they got there, lure or no lure.

She could try, though, she could load another lure, turn, prepare to fire—

And see Vera twist and go sideways as she stumbled out of the way of a parasite that had just come up through a small cavity in the ground it shouldn't have fit through—hadn't fit through but had come out of anyway, a couple of stuttering twitch-darts forward to hover over her, its tentacles probing out.

Charlie aimed the Jig as best she could to fire right past the parasite's head, or what she thought of as the parasite's head—the end of the main body that it turned toward whatever it was going to eat. Toward, right then, Vera.

Before she could pull the trigger, it lunged.

Before the parasite could devour Vera, a blur of dark-metaled mass slammed into it head-on—an impression of teeth and slashing dark limbs that somehow met the parasite and was not unmade—driving it off Vera and some feet further on. Tentacles battered it, raising it in the air as the pair spun and snapped and squeezed. The rest of the swarm held its distance, exhibiting some hitherto unknown form of self-preservation.

Charlie stood transfixed. Who knew the parasites needed self-preservation skills? All reports—and she'd read through a lot of them—suggested they were nigh unstoppable predators of reality itself. What did they have to be afraid of?

The big bad wolf.

It was easier to make out than the parasite it was fighting, bound, as far as Charlie could tell, by the known laws of physics. It was roughly the size of a horse and behaved like normal matter, occupying some liminal space between machine and organic. It had an observable mass. It moved like, well, like a hound, all teeth and raw ferocity, and it consumed the parasite as though it were a harmless bunny rabbit instead of a destroyer of worlds.

Charlie didn't want to stick around in case it wanted dessert.

"Run." She grabbed Vera by the arm and pulled.

There was no argument. Together they ran all out, Charlie nimbler, though Vera's suit meant she could at least keep pace. There were too many tears to choose from, so Charlie made the executive decision to pick the closest one. This world was already dead; the priority was finding an exit.

Acutely aware of their dwindling supplies, Charlie let go of Vera's arm and pulled out the Einstein-Rosen Coupling. This had never been part of the plan. This was meant to be a simple recon mission. Charlie was either supposed to make it to the other side or die in the attempt, and they hadn't seen the need to weigh her down with an endless fucking supply of get out of jail free cards.

She lobbed the Coupling at the closest tear to stabilize it, caught Vera by the wrist, and swung her through the portal. Without so much as a backward glance, Charlie chased after, hoping she'd find her alive on the other side. The sensation of traveling between worlds would never become commonplace, but the mystery of it was gone. She knew to expect a hard landing, and she prepped herself for a roll, let her momentum carry her back onto her feet, where she pivoted, turned to face the tear, and closed it with a sharpshooter's precision.

Only then did she allow herself to breathe. Vera was once again on all-fours, visor open this time, the sound of her retches masked by the suction of reality knitting itself back together. Charlie averted her eyes to look at their new surroundings. The word that immediately sprang to mind was lush.

It was a step up from the Wasteland. They were in a glade, surrounded by ancient trees that stretched up toward a clear blue sky. Stone ruins littered the clearing behind the newly closed tear. There was a stillness to the air Charlie found welcoming, the scent of sweet wildflowers filling her nose and replacing the disorienting no-smell of the tear. She felt her pulse begin to slow, and she lowered the Coupler, though she wasn't yet lulled enough to put it away.

She wasn't home, that much was for certain. The colors still weren't quite right. This world was in soft focus, like she was looking out through a Vaseline-smeared lens. She resisted the urge to rub at her eyes, instead blinking hard and walking over to give Vera a hand up since she seemed to have stopped dry heaving for the moment.

Vera's face was pale, her bangs plastered to her clammy forehead. She had dark circles under her eyes and a stray line of vomit stretching from the corner of her mouth down her chin. Charlie frowned.

"You wanna sit?"

Vera shook her head—more of an abrupt twitch from side to side than a proper denial. "Do you work out?" she said, which didn't help the state of Charlie's frown. "Do shot put, maybe?" She stood with arms akimbo—a ridiculous pose to strike in her marshmallow suit—as though trying to regain some sense of normalcy, trying to reassert some authority after having survived an entirely powerless situation. Her expression shifted from curious to calculating. "This exoskeleton weighs 150 kilos without me in it, and I had a big lunch."

"I saw," Charlie said flatly, stepping away from Vera. Now hardly seemed time for exposition about all the enhancements she'd undergone for this mission: the surgeries, the drug therapies, the training. They were in another world—an *unknown* world—had just passed through some version of hell, and had no immediate means to return to either of their homeworlds. Charlie was pretty sure that took priority.

But she was spared the challenge of redirecting Vera's attention back to the real problem at hand when a large, suspiciously shaped shadow passed over their heads and disappeared above the forest.

"Was that...a dragon?"

Chapter Six

— CALISTHENICS —

Can't be," Vera said, in the very confident tone of someone who was used to being the smartest person in the room but nevertheless had no idea what they were talking about. She joined Charlie in peering up at the sky, though there was nothing left to see. "Whatever it is, it won't be a dragon. Aerodynamics, for one. You just couldn't get the musculature—and how would it even do the fire thing?"

"Look, Vera, I'm Team Science all the way, but if you're making bets on the nonexistence of dragons after we were just nearly eaten by a non-Euclidean cockroach squid, I will take that bet, and I will win."

"It wasn't a non-Euclidean lizard thing, though, was it? It had wings, and it was flapping them. It wasn't just floating around like—like—" Vera's brain had apparently stalled on trying to find a referent for the way parasites just superimposed themselves on the world however they damned liked, and if Charlie hadn't been so annoyed with her, if annoyed-at-Vera was not rapidly becoming the baseline emotion on which she operated, she might have been sympathetic.

"—like it swam out of the multiverse's equivalent of the deepest trenches of the ocean and didn't have the good manners to explode from the pressure differential."

Charlie had to admit that wasn't bad. A little arcane, probably too elaborate to be poetic, but not bad. But of course, there were going to be too many words, because it was Vera, who was still going. The adrenaline must've redirected from her body to her brain.

"Big, flappy wings. Couldn't possibly get the lift, but big, flappy wings. Maybe it's hollow. Lightweight frame, someone inside flying it around."

"You're more willing to believe in an elaborate fake dragon than the idea that we're in some world with dragons?"

"I'll believe it's a dragon when I see down its throat and see an actual throat spitting fire at me. Science."

"Well, if it comes back around, I'll feed you to it, okay? But until then, I'd still like to get home before it ends up like…"

This time it was Charlie's brain that stalled out as it shied away from superimposing the parasite-ravaged Wasteland upon her own world as she'd left it.

"Parasite Central," Vera said. "We could punch a hole. Well, we'd have to repurpose the tech, again, and then we wouldn't have anything to stabilize the hole, and we'd be eaten by non-Euclidean cockroach squid. Squids? What's the plural of non-Euclidean cockroach squid?"

"'Oh shit, we're gonna die,'" Charlie offered.

"We'd be eaten by an oh-shit-we're-gonna-die of non-Euclidean cockroach squid. I'm against it."

"You were the one who—" Charlie took a breath. "Right. No taking my gear apart to tear holes in a possibly perfectly innocent reality. We find out if there are any tears. I can do that without ripping my gear apart."

"Well, what are we standing around for? Time's wasting," Vera said as if she hadn't been standing around offering commentary on a brief glimpse of a scaled and winged and distinctly dragon-y flying object. She even started walking. Well, allowing herself to be moved by her exoskeleton. Charlie let her. Maybe it was petty, but there would be a certain satisfaction in seeing her realize she'd started off before Charlie had worked out the right direction and needed to turn back.

She turned on the HUD and found the direction. It was frustratingly more or less the direction Vera had chosen at random. Not exactly, but close enough to the same line that her dream of simply walking the other way and smugly letting Vera realize her mistake was dashed.

Charlie sighed and started walking.

Her dreams of leaving Vera behind turned out to be not so fruitless. After nearly an hour of walking, Vera had paused to rest and then simply hadn't started moving again, just stood where she was and let the suit hold her up. Two rapid jumps through reality itself were bound to have an effect.

Not that Charlie had any idea what those effects were. If things had gone to plan, she'd have been back at Veritech by now, having a full medical examination to find out. Instead, she was tromping over rolling green hills with a heart patient in a protective exoskeleton. It seemed like it had mostly inured Vera from the stresses of going through a tear, in that she was alive, but who knew what else had happened?

In any case, two trips through tears and the intermediary flight for their lives had clearly caught up with Vera, even if she wouldn't admit it, insisting that she was just taking a moment to take in the scenery—hadn't Charlie seen the scenery? It was lush and verdant and sort of hard to focus on, and so on.

It was starting to get dark, too, which at least forestalled that dumb argument. They made camp. There wasn't much camp to make, and an ax would've been particularly helpful, but they made camp. Given the only useful blades they had were Charlie's multi-tool and Jump Knife from her survival kit, the lean-to wasn't exactly the most sophisticated of shelters. They'd relied mostly on felled trees and built it over spongy moss to make it as comfortable as could be expected—they weren't kidding themselves that it was going to be a five-star stay. While Charlie'd slept through worse during her time outside the wire in Afghanistan, she was surprised by Vera's lack of complaint.

Then she realized Vera had fallen asleep standing up again.

"Hey," Charlie said, shaking Vera's shoulder. The suit wobbled a little, and Vera's head jerked up.

"I'm awake!"

"Good," Charlie replied, opting to play along rather than argue. "Then you can get started on the fire." She pointed to the small stash of branches, dead leaves, and dry grass she'd gathered in the past ten minutes. "Sensors say there's a stream about fifteen minutes north of here. I'll get us some water, and you try not to burn the forest down while I'm away, all right?"

Splitting up in an unknown environment with a potential dragon hanging around wasn't the best of tactics, but Vera would just slow her down and needed water more between the two of them anyhow. Better to give her something to focus on while Charlie was away, even if she was too sleepy to manage to succeed. It'd keep her awake and less vulnerable to attack.

"Don't let the spacesuit fool you," Vera quipped at Charlie's retreating back. "I can still hang with the cavemen." Charlie waved her off, dismissive, which only spurred Vera to add, "I'm hip!"

Getting water proved a milk run. The stream was as idyllic as the forest surrounding it, and Charlie filled both of her expandable canteens before slinging them over her shoulder. Each canteen carried about four liters, so they should be good for a while. The threat of dragons aside, the walk was peaceful, and her ears were grateful for the relative silence of being away from Vera. It was still strange how the same woman as her mentor could be so irritating in a younger iteration. Their similarities ran only skin deep, and it was almost easier to consider them as distinct individuals with the same taste in faces than as two sides of the same coin.

It was also easier to believe Vera would be all right. That there wouldn't be any lasting complications from the jumps. That her marshmallow suit would hold up if—when—they needed to jump again. Charlie might not necessarily like the woman, but they needed each other to get back. And, soldier or no, she didn't relish burying people. She joined the military to help—that the CAF covered her tuition was simply an added bonus.

"You're no knight!" shouted a man up ahead, surprising Charlie away from her thoughts. His voice carried high and loud, and his declaration was followed by an angry murmur of agreement. Charlie guessed there were about five people total, and the HUD confirmed her estimate. Through the trees, she could just spot Vera, still a marshmallow, holding court. She was surrounded.

The exoskeleton was impressive, but it wasn't armor. If any of the locals decided to take a swing, Vera was fucked. At least the outer shell of the Velo utilized multiple fabrics to optimize protection against projectiles; its cocktail of in-house Kevlar, resin, and thermoplastics doubtlessly made her sword-proof, but Charlie wasn't in a rush to test it. Not yet giving away her position, she pulled out her Browning and trained it on the angriest of the crowd.

They were a ragtag group, all dressed in shades of green. Charlie guessed they were thieves, but it was a whole new world—albeit another one that had followed a very similar linguistic path. The leader was within striking distance of Vera, but his followers were hanging back. All of them were gawking at Vera with dull, if curious, expressions.

The gun was maybe overkill, then. Charlie didn't lower it even as she made her approach, purposely stepping on a branch to signal her arrival. The thieves' heads turned in her direction, and Charlie fought to keep her mind from wandering to the way the parasite's tentacles stretched out, ramrod straight, toward the lure.

"Who's this then, eh?" asked Second Thief. He jutted his chin toward Charlie in a jittery manner that betrayed his nerves. He was young, maybe fifteen.

Never lowering the gun, Charlie took her place beside Vera, who was holding the end of a charred stick in one hand. They shot each other a sideways glance.

"My squire!" Vera announced.

Charlie bristled. Her what? And what the fuck was that accent she was putting on? But Vera ignored Charlie's incredulity and instead lifted one of the full canteens off Charlie's shoulder.

"Yes, see? She fetched me water from the stream," Vera carried on. "Good squire!"

Charlie braced herself to be patted on the head like a dog, but Vera had a survival instinct after all and kept her hands at her sides.

"What kind of knight doesn't have a mount?" asked one of them. He seemed to be addressing Charlie, as if being a squire also made her a spokesperson. Luckily, Vera answered, because Charlie was not about to become a part of this nonsense.

"I had a mount. Very sad story. Very long. Now temporarily mountless, but I still have my excellent armor, and it keeps me in good physical condition. You know. Calisthenics. We're big on calisthenics, knights."

"Knights are big on calisthenics," said Third Thief, nodding thoughtfully at Vera, which meant she missed the look of complete disbelief Charlie was throwing her way. "And that is expensive armor. You can tell because it's weird-looking. You only get weird-looking armor if you're real good."

"Or if you kill someone real good."

"Yeah, but, see, then she'd be even better, y'know?"

"They can do a flip in their armor. Can you do a flip in your armor?" said another.

"Yes," said Vera, with complete and utter confidence, (barely) standing where she was and not doing a flip in her armor. Charlie wondered if the exoskeleton had enough strength assist to back that up, but Vera did not appear to be about to find out. The thieves stood there for a moment, waiting, then there was some shuffling as they looked amongst each other to try and work out if it was rude to demand that Vera demonstrate on the spot.

"More importantly," said Third Thief, "can you kill a dragon?"

"Yes," said Vera. And then, "Wait, what?"

Chapter Seven

— DRAGONSLAYERS —

So now they were off to slay a dragon. Vera had signed them up to go slay a dragon. Vera hadn't even believed there was a real dragon but had signed them up to go kill it nonetheless, which she argued made more sense, not less.

"We'll find out what it really is and work from there. If it's fake, we unmask whoever's pretending to be a dragon for a land grab or whatever," she said the next morning when they finally had a moment they could talk without being overheard. Then it proved to only be a moment before one of their excited escorts was back within hearing distance, so Charlie hadn't been able to say what she was thinking, which was that an elaborate fake dragon wouldn't necessarily be any easier. It still flew around and spat fire.

Which was confirmed by their new entourage. The dragon spat fire and had been terrorizing the town. Carrying off livestock, burning buildings. "Your standard dragon havoc," Vera called it, cementing among her believers the impression that she'd handled her share of dragons before.

Charlie wanted to strangle her.

They'd barely seen the damn thing, but from their fleeting glimpse, she had to guess it was at least ten meters long, if not longer. Somehow Verity and Josie had never thought to put anti-dragon weapons into her pack, and unless Vera's spacesuit had hidden depths, Charlie was pretty sure they were fucked. She was growing increasingly familiar with that feeling. Oh, she had the Browning, sure, but its bullets weren't silver—*and wait, that's werewolves, isn't it?*

A piercing scream scattered Charlie's thoughts. Their party halted at different rates, resulting in Third Thief (a mother of three named, of all things, Robin, it turned out) walking straight into Charlie. The woman mumbled a clumsy apology that Charlie only half-heard. Her attention was focused up ahead. They'd been walking uphill for some time and had finally reached level ground. Thick, black smoke billowed from the valley below, the angry glow of fire accompanied by the disconcerting smell of barbecue. The village was burning.

The dragon was flying.

Charlie had never seen a bigger fuck-you to the whole notion of aerodynamics. It was an agile, serpentine beast about the size of a whale, covered in glittering black scales, and armed with twin rows of razor-sharp teeth. Its translucent violet wings thundered with every flap, and as it opened its mouth, the scream sounded again. Fire jetted out from between its teeth and engulfed a wooden house in flames.

"Pretty sure that's your cue, Sir Vera," Charlie said, nudging Vera.

"Sure is," said Vera, marching forward, which hadn't been Charlie's intent, exactly. She'd meant it more as a goad, and then when Vera realized the situation they were in, they'd come up with a plan. Instead, she was jogging forward, accelerating into a run. It wasn't quiet, but fortunately, neither was the dragon, which had landed and was busily engaged in peeling the roof off a house with one set of jaggedly protruding claws, like a tool-using raven—only scaled up, scaly, and also fire-breathing and a dragon and oh god, was Vera just going to punch it?

Vera closed in, wound back, and punched it fully in the leg; Charlie could hear the grind of the suit's machinery from here as it delivered all its assisted strength into the blow.

The dragon's leg might have moved, but not appreciably from Charlie's vantage point. The dragon's head, however, whipped right around on the end of that neck. It inhaled, the rest of its body shifting with a flap or two to reposition itself best to charbroil this new annoyance.

Charlie covered most of the ground between them in the time that extended breath took. Those scales were now confirmed to be solid, which meant a 9mm bullet wasn't going to do much, but maybe if she shot it in the eye—

She took the quickest route there...which was kicking off the half-collapsed wall of a building to land on the dragon's tail near where it joined the body. She'd expected it to try and buck her off.

She hadn't expected the tail to be so prehensile that the end could whip around and smack her off. She had a brief glimpse of Vera diving clear of a gout of flame that went wide before she slammed through a thatched roof into a still intact cottage.

At least the thatch had broken her fall, she supposed, and then broken it again when she'd gone straight through. On the other hand, the thatch was deeply flammable. She rolled to her feet and threw herself through the window before her body had a chance to start thinking about the fall, stumbled, and skidded between a pair of buildings, where she came to a halt, craning around to see if the dragon had tracked her movements.

A larger mass making a sound she couldn't identify came fast around the corner, and she was almost scrambling out of the way again before she realized it was Vera. The sound might have been cackling, but that couldn't possibly be right.

"So, it's definitely a dragon," Vera said, conversationally.

I should've let her get barbecued.

"It's really solid. I thought there'd at least be some concessions, low bone density, it'd have to be light, one good hit, y'know? But that thing is dense. Which has me thinking, bees."

"Bees?"

"Bees! You know, that thing people say, that the laws of aerodynamics say a bee can't fly—"

"That's a crock of—"

"That only people who don't know anything about science say, because obviously if you came up with a set of laws and did your equations and they said, 'this thing that's flying can't,' you wouldn't say, 'wow weird,' and carry on, you'd rethink your damn laws. Physics is different here! That's amazing! It's so exciting! What else is different? Maybe the whole ecosystem. I mean, when they said mounts, I assumed horses, but maybe they don't have horses! Maybe they have lizards! Or big bugs, the square-cube law might not—"

"Vera," Charlie said, a little too loudly. She prepared to run again, and Vera could do what she damned well liked, which was apparently sit where she was and mess with the wiring on one arm of her suit. "Dragon."

"Right. So I got a look down the, uh...gullet," she said, swallowing for a moment as if actually noting that she could have been a toasted marshmallow. "I think it has gas sacs that spit out a liquid that becomes flammable on contact with air. I was hoping for something I could ignite in situ, just blow it up, but I think no. I wanna try blinding it."

"What are you going to do?" Charlie said, seizing Vera by the arm she wasn't fiddling around with and yanking her around the corner, catching a brief glimpse of prowling snout before there were walls between them again. "Smile at it and hope for a really good reflection off your teeth?"

"Comms laser," Vera said, tapping her arm. "Spacesuit. Point laser at distant thing, switch on and off to talk, you know. I'm tweaking the wavelength and power to be more of a dragon deterrent."

"You're gonna have to shine it directly into its eyes, still," Charlie said. "Best we're gonna get is one eye, and I don't think it needs depth perception to set us on fire."

"Do you think they've invented mirrors? Our escorts make me kinda think nah, so we'll have to break mine—superstition, smuperstition—but a little refraction, a couple of mirrors..."

"A couple of mirrors that would have to be set up exactly right to hit a dragon standing in exactly the right place in the eyes. How're you going to..."

She stopped. Vera was looking at her.

"I am not the bait."

"I—I have the laser, I can't be the bait. I'm doing the shooting. Are you not—I'm slightly fireproof, are you not fireproof? You're unknowable-barrier-between-the-worlds-proof, but you're not fireproof?"

Charlie's shoulders drooped with something akin to defeat. She winced, and with great pain, she sighed. "Yeah, I'm fireproof."

Vera snapped her fingers, though the sound was muffled on account of her gloves. *If only they muffled the obnoxiousness of her pointing at me with that look on her face.*

"Bait!"

"Drop your hand," Charlie said, "or I will personally feed it to the dragon."

"Well, you'll be close enough to," Vera replied, but she dropped her hand to continue her tinkering. Charlie, meanwhile, redeployed her cowl. The plates slithered into place over her head and face, and she was greeted by the comforting hiss of the suit pressurizing. The HUD blinked to life, but then it just blinked, like there was some kind of interference. It was too distracting to keep on, so she shut it off.

"Care to do the honors?" Vera ripped off the business card-sized mirror from the sleeve of her suit and handed it to Charlie.

"Not like my luck can get any worse," Charlie replied. It was a stupid thing to say, maybe, a taunt sent out to the universe—the multiverse—to throw her another curveball, but she was a scientist, not a squire. The multiverse could already go fuck itself. She snapped the mirror in two and tried not to focus on how small the pieces were and *Jesus fucking Christ, I'm going along with the plan, aren't I?*

"It likes the wooden ones," Charlie noted. The only thing standing between them and the dragon was a stone wall, but the dragon was more interested in burning houses than exacting revenge on the two idiots who'd punched and ridden it, respectively. "I could get ahead of it. Place the mirrors around a tempting little bungalow while you get into position. Speaking of—" She looked Vera over. "—have you ever shot anything? In your life? 'Cause, uh, if the answer's no..."

Charlie hadn't been a sniper, but she was still a damn good shot. There wasn't time for an extended demo on how to hit a moving target, and even if there were, Vera was only, by her own admission, slightly fireproof.

"Please," Vera said. "I lived in the States for five years."

Well, that wasn't a no. Great.

"Great," Charlie said aloud because it bore repeating. "You ready?"

"Almost. I'll be ready when the mirrors are ready. We're running out of tempting death traps, go, get."

"This is a universe with weird rules and it's entirely possible ghosts are real and if you do not come through, I am going to haunt you," Charlie said, leaning out to cast her gaze around. And then, as the thought occurred to her, up. It could fly. She wasn't used to that. It was circling, now, and as she watched, the dragon let out another stream of fire and then followed the flames down, swatting at the burning building to scatter debris about.

"Dragons are gasholes," said Vera. Charlie ignored her, because injuring the dragon came first, and ducked out of their cover to dart toward a likely candidate building. Not close enough that it was likely to catch fire from an adjacent pyre, but close enough that the dragon might notice it.

Close enough that she felt like she was heading toward the dragon, and could certainly feel it getting warmer. She tried not to consider how fireproof the Velo was, and whether she might just cook alive inside her perfectly fireproof suit. All the dragon had to do was look around.

It looked around. Charlie threw herself into a low slide and fetched up low against her target building. Heard, fortunately, not the sound of the dragon inhaling or stomping closer, but the rush of air and the flare of warmth as it took to the sky again, each beat of its wings pushing debris and heat outwards with the downdraft.

Place two mirrors and then get a dragon to stand in the exact right place between them. Sure. Easy. A plan with zero downsides. Staying under the cover of the eaves, she very gingerly extended a foot to drag a stick over to herself, one of the non-flaming remnants of a destroyed building being strewn about. She took one half of the mirror, using duct tape from the survival kit to attach it to the stick.

"Simple geometry," she told herself, under her breath. Wedge the stick in here, requiring her to step out alarmingly into the open, shift it to an angle that would line up with the dragon if its head was in a particular spot—haha, why wouldn't it be, it would position its head right there because it was prepared to set some silly woman on fire. Then repeat on the other side. After Charlie took a cautious trip around the building, hugging the wall, and then back around a corner, the dragon's airborne circling brought it into view. She edged back out when the dragon carried on around...and landed, from the sounds of things, about three cottages down. She hurried out and set the mirror, took a breath, and got back into the shadow of the wall, peering out.

Trap primed.

"C'mon," she hissed, glancing about, spotting Vera positioning herself. Vera raised an arm. At this distance, Charlie couldn't tell if she was signaling ready or not ready, because of course, she wasn't using any recognizable hand signals.

There was another rush of air. Then, another burst of flame as another cottage—thankfully not the one she was crouching beside—went up. Then a second. Charlie was just thinking about whether the plan still worked if the building was on fire when the dragon landed. Began to inhale.

She stepped out to catch the attention of the large dragon preparing to set an entire building alight. Its eyes fixed on her. The position of its head shifted to track her. It kept inhaling. Charlie kept going sideways, the dragon's head swiveling as if it were a cat and she a red dot.

Well, today the red dot struck back. Charlie stopped. The inhalation stopped.

No lasers struck.

The dragon exhaled.

And, visible through the smoke and dust the dragon's passage had left, a flash of bright as the laser went on—

The dragon roared, head twisted, a jet of flame surging off target and then dying as the beast took two steps and slammed against a stone building, nearly caving it in, head whipping around in pain and distress—

Then stopping dead. Sideways to Charlie.

One good eye staring directly at her.

The exact right spot had always been a bit of an ask, she supposed.

The tail punched a hole right through the wall behind where she'd been standing, but she was running, and then in a dive. The tail brushed her back, then went up and stabbed at the spot she'd come to rest just as she rolled away. She came to her feet and went around the corner, ducking again as the tail slammed through the entire wall, debris raining on her back, knocking her to her knees, making her miss her grab for the mirror. She rummaged frantically, spotted the glint, and grabbed a full handful of dirt, closing her fist until she felt the solid mass of it.

She spun with the mirror extended and hoped Vera had the good sense to go for the follow-up shot. That she had juice for a follow-up shot.

The dragon landed on a roof, head still held side-on so its good eye could see her, its claw coming down. Charlie threw herself backward, raised the mirror again, and this time there was a flash off it. The dragon shrieked and careened backward with wild flaps of its wings that sent it into a hopping sideways stumble of destruction before finally, it took off, flapping erratically through the air.

Charlie watched it weave through the air, and thought that actually, the flight path did kind of look like a bee now that the dragon had no sense of direction or position, cracking trees until it gained enough height to fly directly into a mountain.

"Holy shit," she said, as Vera reached her, "we fought off a—"

"THE GREAT KNIGHT VERA HAS SLAIN THE DRAGON!" announced the most faithful of Vera's followers, a tiny thief by the name of Geoffrey who was more mustache than man. The least faithful, Pius Potter, declared he had been wrong to ever doubt her and led a failed effort to hoist her and the suit onto their shoulders for a victory parade through the (burning, debris-crowded) streets.

"It must be an honor, to be squire to such a great knight," said Second Thief, whose name was Jim.

"I cannot believe my luck, that's for sure," Charlie muttered. Had they even seen the fight? Probably not. They'd all been ducking for cover the moment Vera decided to charge in and just fucking punch the damned dragon, only popping back up once they saw it fly off and hit a mountain. As far as they were concerned, Vera might have just beaten the shit out of it with her fists.

"The things you must learn at her side! And, of course, you'll have prime position at her side during the feast..."

Charlie closed her mouth on the snide remark she'd been about to make. Because: "That's the best news I've had in days."

Well, aside from the part where she had to sit next to Vera, but she hadn't had a proper meal since she was in her proper universe. A feast sounded just like the thing.

And what a feast it was. Being made of stone, the local tavern was one of a handful of businesses still standing after the last of the fires had been put out. Priorities, Charlie supposed. The townsfolk were surprisingly cheerful given the day's events, and no effort was spared welcoming Vera and Charlie—mostly Vera, looking worse for wear, albeit in a stylish sort of way—into their company. In fact, it seemed most of the town was piled into the tavern. Long tables were set up so the majority could sit, but others huddled at the edges, waiting their turn for a morsel of this or that. Vera was, as promised, given a place of honor at the head table, and was seated between the town's Burgomaster and a very hungry Charlie.

Charlie didn't recognize most of the food beyond such broad classification as animal, vegetable, or mineral, but it smelled edible and was available in such embarrassingly large quantities that she wasn't going to question it too much. She ladled her third helping of what she'd mentally dubbed Fucking Good Stew onto her plate and sopped up the gravy with a hunk of bread the size of her fist. It didn't matter that her face was still covered in sweat and soot. If she managed a hot shower and a soft bed at the end of all this, it'd be a real banner day, dragon or no.

The tavern buzzed with conversation and clinking cutlery. There was the occasional shouted demand for a cheer in Vera's name, and Charlie couldn't even bring herself to feel annoyed for being left out. There was food and a place to sit and besides, she couldn't keep eyes on the mysterious cloaked figure seated at the bar if she kept rolling them.

The cloaked figure had neither eaten nor drunk since arriving at the tavern, though a tankard of what Charlie presumed was ale was placed within arm's reach. Like most of the feast's attendees, however, her—another presumption—attention was fixed on Vera, who was retelling an embellished version of their (first, though that fact was carefully ignored) foray into dragon-slaying.

"...obviously can't just punch a dragon. Although, funny story, the first time I fought a dragon, I actually tried that? Just ran up and punched it. I learned a lot about dodging dragons in a very short time, believe you me. Which came in handy here, of course, with yon vicious beastie lashing that tail and taking swipes at me, huge claws rending at the terrain. Which was on fire, because it was also spitting fire everywhere. You've seen what's left of the town. So, there I am, ducking and diving—we train to be especially agile in our armor, of course, knights—"

"They can do flips," said Geoffrey.

"—and doing flips, when I realize the dragon's attention is fixed somewhere else. Which is weird, right, because why wouldn't you be looking at me?" Vera winked at someone. Charlie followed where she was looking and hoped this was one of those socially forward fantasy universes, and not one of the ones where they felt "olden times" necessitated "specifically bigoted." The woman in Vera's sights, Mabel, Pius's *wife*, merely blushed and no pitchforks were raised. Luckily Pius hadn't noticed, or there might have been at least one pitchfork, socially forward or no. "I look around, and it's lining up to burn my squire to a crisp. I only just got this squire—it's a fun story, she broke into my off—uh, castle, my quarters in the castle to insist that she squire for me—and so I can't let a dragon just burn her. But with its attention fixed on her, she'd inadvertently—"

Charlie broke the wing bone she was eating in half, then more or less stabbed it into a plate of gravy.

"—given me the opening I needed. Now, a dragon's weak point is its eyes. No scales. One good blow there…and you've got a very angry dragon, thrashing and wailing and wanting to fry your innards. But two good blows, and, well, you saw. Roberta saw."

"Robin," Charlie murmured.

"Blow with what?" said Pius, adding, "Just—I want the whole picture," lest anyone think he was backsliding into faithlessness. "And you don't have a sword, so…"

"Well, my armor is my sword. It's…very special armor."

"Enchanted," said Geoffrey, nodding seriously. "You can tell because it's weird-looking. Improves strength and stamina and she can probably do a spell one time a fight."

"Exactly," said Vera, seizing on this belief in magic to solve a story problem she'd evidently been having. "Enchanted. I can go several times a fight, though, no recovery period." She winked again.

"Who enchanted it?" Pius asked. "There used to be a witch in these parts, but there's been no word from her tower in some time."

"Her tower," Vera said, sounding a touch less glib. "Which is… that way." She pointed, unerringly, in the direction she and Charlie had been headed when they'd gotten intercepted by what was now

Vera's entourage. It was kind of a pity a sense of direction was the only sense Vera had.

The guess made sense, though. A witch's tower did seem a likely spot for a tear if that was the context they were working in, and Robin confirmed Vera's guess.

"Well," Vera said. "I did, actually. Enchanted it myself. I do witching as well as knighting. Tomorrow, you know, I might go up, nose around and see what the story is with your missing witch. Tomorrow morning. Well," she smirked at Mabel, looking up from under her lashes as she rested a marshmallowian hand on Mabel's forearm, "maybe lunchtime. We'll see how it goes."

They didn't get a chance to see how it went, however, which was fortunate because Charlie wanted to keep everything she'd eaten on the inside. The unfortunate part was that the interruption was a rags-covered figure throwing the door open and yelling, "The dragon yet lives!"

Charred rags, she realized, as he approached, the remains of a smock and a now mostly brimless straw hat atop a face black with smoke and ash. He was holding a bag, which he upended in front of Vera. It was full of bones.

"Oh, they're just—" she started, releasing the table which she'd gripped in a fit of initial horror before she identified what she was looking at.

"MY GOATS! ALL OF MY GOATS!"

"SHE'S NO KNIGHT AT ALL!" shouted Pius, backsliding like a champion.

"Would you believe that I'm not a knight but I am definitely a witch?" said Vera.

"BURN THE PAIR OF THEM!"

"Would you believe that I am also not a witch?" said Vera.

"BURN THE PAIR OF THEM FOR NOT BEING WITCHES!"

What the fuck?

"Well," said Vera, "that is just completely backward."

Chapter Eight

— THE WITCH OF THE TOWER —

You're burning us at the stake for *not* being witches? This is— I really think you've mixed up your whole superstitious fear thing, here," Vera said, speaking loud and fast to be heard over the tumult of their being grabbed and held—and also the crowd apparently working out the logistics of burning them at the stake. Charlie, meanwhile, had attempted to work out the logistics of fighting an entire town that wanted to burn them at the fucking stake and had come away with the unfortunate answer that they were, well, toast. Burned toast.

How the fuck did Vera get us into this?

"Why would we burn witches?" Pius said. "We've got nothing against witches. It's fine with us if someone's a witch. Good for the crops. Finding lost goats."

"All lost now! All my goats lost forever down a dragon's gullet," wailed Farmer Ash.

"Well, not lost exactly, we know where—" Vera began. Charlie kicked her, the crowd of angry villagers now having manhandled them close enough together that this was possible. It was a small comfort. Very small, since it was probably for the convenience of tying them to the same stake for burning because Vera's big fucking mouth was going to get them rotisseried.

"What's not fine is saying you're a witch when you're not a witch," Pius said sensibly. "That's fraud, that is! Fraud!"

"Awful, awful crime," Mabel agreed. "Disgusting. You must be heartless."

Vera's certainly something, Charlie thought uncharitably. But it was easy to be uncharitable when you were about to get immolated. Her mind kept circling back to the absurdity of their situation. The fire itself wouldn't kill her, not in the Velo—not if she could get the cowl on before her face burned off—but Vera was only fire-resistant at best, and fuck, how were they going to get out of this without anyone dying?

"No," a clear, familiar voice cut through the angry murmuring of the crowd, "heartless are townsfolk who would kill those who saved them from the dragon."

A hush fell over the tavern. The cloaked figure was now standing. A path cleared before her, and she seemed to glide toward where Charlie and Vera were standing together.

"Do you not recognize the Witch of the Tower?" asked the figure. The question welcomed a confused mutter from the crowd as the townsfolk turned to their neighbor to ask each other the same.

Jim raised his hand as he stepped forward. "Er, is that a trick question?" he said. "Only, er, seems to me Sir Vera just said she wasn't a witch, strictly speaking."

"Witches do speak in riddles," Geoffrey allowed.

"They're real big on disguises, too," said Robin. "They're always showing up in disguise to see if they get a proper welcome and then cursing you when they don't."

"That's gods," said Jim. "Er, isn't it?"

"Gods and witches," Robin said with a shrug. "It's pretty much a channeler of the cosmic forces mainstay, dressing up like some haggard old crone. Or, like, a duck."

Everyone turned and looked at Vera, who couldn't muster up "haggard" even having fought a dragon, even mid-lynching. Her hair was mussed, but it mostly just ended up looking rakishly adventurous. Crone was never going to work. She was making a hopeful set of duck lips instead.

"Don't look very crone-y to me," said Pius.

"That's for sure," said Mabel. Vera did not wink, allowing Charlie to consider believing in magic.

"Let's see her do some magic, then," said Pius, crossing his arms. Jim and Geoffrey sidled away from where he was standing. "Not from the armor," he added, as Vera's gaze flickered to her arm. Charlie had just been thinking a solid laser-based light show would probably pass. "We already know that's enchanted. She has to do the spell."

Charlie tried to think if they had anything else they could pass off as magic—the Browning probably would just count as an enchanted artifact, and it was hard to pin down the technological era of this place, anyway; if they'd heard of gunpowder it wouldn't work. The tablet, maybe? Or would that just fall into the same problem, an enchanted mirror? Then she realized the hooded figure was staring right at her and had done a significant head tilt. A significant head tilt to say what? Something about Vera?

"Play along," Charlie muttered, to Vera, and hoped that she'd read that right.

"Oh, you wanna see some magic?" said Vera. Charlie honestly couldn't tell if Vera had heard her or was just being Vera. "You wanna see some magic. You wanna see *me* do some magic."

"Er, yeah," said Jim.

"That's what we're all saying, yeah," said Robin.

"Coming right up," Vera said, clapping her hands together once and then rubbing them before shaking her fingers out. "Promethium! Americium! Berkelium! Californium! Traaaaansuranium!" She threw her hands out on the last, an expansive fling, head tilted back with the conviction that the universe would do whatever it was she demanded of it.

Charlie only just caught it, a slight flick of the cloaked figure's wrist—hardly the show Vera was putting on—but that was all it took. For a moment the air seemed to ripple outward like a stone dropped in a pond, and Charlie's hair stood on end. The townsfolk were, as though by an invisible hand, effortlessly plucked off their feet and returned to their abandoned seats. The overall effect was somewhat disconcerting; it wasn't quite like time being rewound so much as it was like a giant ghost playing with dolls. The townsfolk wore identical expressions of befuddled terror, some crying out with surprise while others simply swore. A trio of musicians was compelled to strike up a jaunty tune. Charlie unclenched her jaw and took a step away from Vera now that she had room to do so.

"So she's a witch, then," Pius grumbled from his seat at the high table. He was very pale. "So what?"

"My goats!" wailed Farmer Ash. He had been placed in Charlie's old seat, and someone handed him a handkerchief, with which he blew his nose. It honked.

"Consider it a sacrifice," Vera said, fittingly unfazed by the magical display. She might've had a big mouth, but at least she could act in a pinch. To Charlie, she added, "That's a witch thing, right? Sacrifices?"

"Absolutely," Charlie confirmed. "Sacrifices. For the dragon we slayed."

"But the dragon's w-what ate my goats!" Farmer Ash cried. Jim patted his shoulder with the awkward care of a stranger.

"I think," the cloaked figure said, at a volume intended for Charlie and Vera only, "it is time we made our exit."

"Yeah, that was a mood killer," Vera agreed, turning to face the crowd. "Official Witch of the Tower pronouncement: burning people alive for fraud is weird and extreme and you should stop doing that. Also, you only barely passed my test. One more week of winter."

They made their exit, to the sound of the villagers murmuring about whether that meant right now or when winter actually arrived in several months, and would it be at the beginning or the end?

Once they were clear of the village, the cloaked figure lowered her hood. Her voice had been familiar for good reason: Dr. Josephine Watson—Sorceress Josephine Watson?—had saved their asses from being roasted. Her dark hair was long in this universe and worn in a thick braid that circled her head like a crown. Her ears dripped with precious stones, and she possessed what Charlie could only describe as an inner luminescence—an otherworldliness that gave Charlie goosebumps if she stared too long. Charlie had had no reason to believe in magic before that day, but the self-styled Lady Josephine, enchantress of a neighboring realm, certainly made a compelling argument in its favor.

"So, hang on," Vera said. "I *am* the Witch of the Tower?"

"You are the counterpart of the Witch of the Tower from across the borders of reality, a reflection in the mirror of worlds."

"Alternate universe version of your witch, got it," Vera said. "Honestly I feel like we should flip that? The crazy witch version is the reflection, obviously. What is that, anyway, is it telekinesis? I would've guessed secret tech to fool the rubes, but I fought a dragon, so, bees."

"...bees?" said Josephine, squinting.

"Don't ask," said Charlie.

"It is magic," Josephine continued, proving she was either good at taking advice or familiar enough with Verity that she didn't need it. "Through careful study and the trained application of will, I access the deeper forces and convince them to affect the natural order."

"You pick people up with your mind."

"The secret language of the world is very convincing."

"It's magic," Charlie told Vera since it was an irrelevant argument. Privately, she kind of figured telekinesis. "So Verity is the Witch of the Tower. Are we going to meet her?"

Maybe this one will actually be useful. Which said something about Vera, really, that the witch was the one Charlie thought might be a reasonable shot at a stable individual who could help her get home.

"She is...not there. She left. There is a plague upon these lands, a curse." Josephine paused with the ease of a practiced storyteller. The raised eyebrow she directed at Charlie was painful in its familiarity. "One that you might be familiar with."

"Big holes in reality," Charlie guessed, with a sigh. "Optical illusions with tentacles eating everything."

"Tears in the fabric of the world," Josephine agreed. "We sought a solution, but Verity concluded it wouldn't be found here, and her only course was to journey beyond the borders of the world to find the source of the fault and set it to rights. She thought someone like you might come along to follow the same trail."

"She predicted that we'd show up?" said Charlie. That was new.

"Well," Josephine said, looking slightly awkward as she gestured toward Vera. "Her. She thought maybe her and...a mirror of me, was her assumption if there was a companion."

Great. Now she was getting burned by a witch she'd never even met. *Haha, burned by a witch, funny joke.*

Past that, though, was an interesting assumption, or conclusion, or soothsaying or however Witch Verity had come up with it; that out there somewhere was a specific cause for the tears, that they weren't just a thing that happened but a thing that had been caused. In the early days of the tears, the initial assumption had been terrorist attack. The first ones were so pointedly located: Times Square, the Eiffel Tower, the Great Pyramid of Giza, Buckingham Palace, the Taj Mahal. Name a landmark, and the tears were there, eating away at reality until there was nothing left but grim and the absence of familiar. It took months to realize no one was going to claim responsibility, that they weren't human acts. Nations were more willing to cooperate once it was clear the tears weren't acts of war but acts of nature, but Charlie had never been able to shake the idea that something was behind the phenomena. They never seemed to show up where they couldn't be observed. There were no reports of tears in a farmer's field, or in the middle of nowhere. They were always in the middle of somewhere. Landmarks. Historical buildings. The busiest and brightest of cities. It was too coincidental to be coincidence.

And Witch Verity thought so too.

"She knew there'd be..." Charlie searched for the word Josephine used. "Mirrors of people. How?"

"I asked her once, and she went and put a potted fern on a table in the study. 'Consider the fern,' she said."

There was a pause as Charlie and Vera waited for Josephine to conclude the anecdote. It extended.

"...she was at times somewhat cryptic. I think she wanted me to work it out for myself, as a lesson," Josephine finally admitted, which Charlie took to mean the anecdote didn't have an end, and Josephine didn't actually know. Which meant the person—witch— who knew wasn't here, which was a pity because there was a chance that would be deeply helpful in figuring out how parts of this worked.

"Or she just liked being dramatic," Charlie said. That could be consistent, although Vera had been slightly quiet. When she turned to look, Vera was intently staring at random rocks on the side of the path, sometimes extending her hand toward them in a claw-shape. "A dramatic weirdo. Okay. She thought we'd be along because...ferns. How was she going to get where she was going?"

"Wrong question," Vera said, dropping her hand, having apparently taken in more of that than Charlie had thought she was listening to. "We know that one. We've done that one. Where was she going, and how was she going to know how to get there?"

"That's what I—never mind," Charlie said. "That."

"When you threw your fire at the dragon, you knew from whence it came. You bent and you turned it, but in knowing the turns it would take, you could aim it," Josephine explained. "Verity thought to follow the thread in much the same way."

"We missed," Charlie pointed out.

"Yes," said Josephine, looking upwards as they rounded a bend and the tower came into view. It was immense, towering as the name implied, and at the top of the mountain they'd been slowly climbing since they'd arrived. Above the tower crackled an absence of space, a tear that pulsed without growing, but Charlie couldn't see anything surrounding it. It was disorienting to see an old, significant-looking structure like the tower so close to a tear without having been consumed, riven, and destroyed. Josephine stared at the tear and continued, "I very much hope she did not miss."

"You don't have a problem with non-Euclidean cockroach squid?" Vera asked once they reached the tower. To Vera's disappointment, there had been no riding lizards. They'd walked, leaving the existence or non-existence of horses up in the air.

Josephine led them past the great wooden doors to the tower in favor of a far smaller door around the side, presumably for servants in times past.

Or now. Charlie didn't know what the staffing requirements were for a witch's tower. There didn't seem to be anyone else around, though, and although the kitchen they passed looked lived in, the rest of the rooms around it seemed fairly dusty.

"There are wards about the tear, as you might have guessed," Josephine said, starting up a long spiral staircase that lay at the center of the tower and appeared to extend all the way to the top. Charlie was reminded of St. Joseph's Oratory before they'd installed escalators (and before it had been destroyed by tears). *How is there still more to climb?*

"Yeah, the building not coming down around our ears was a giveaway," Charlie said. She guessed wards were the witch version of the equipment they'd had back at Veritech.

"So, not just they can't be bothered with the stairs. It'd kill you to put a magic elevator in this thing?" said Vera.

Josephine frowned at her for a moment. If she was trying to square Vera with the woman she'd known, Charlie sympathized.

"There are better uses for magic," she said.

"Yeah, so, what's the job here, anyway? The Witch of the Tower gig. Which is...not you, but you. You're the substitute Witch?"

"I'm standing in in Verity's absence. The Witch of the Tower is an important position. Lower Canatia sits on a critical nexus of magics, and without a witch, its borders go undefended. Not to mention all the usual needs for a witch. Crop maintenance, diplomacy with the under-dwellers..."

"Dragons," Vera pointed out. "You kind of left that one to us."

Josephine looked a little embarrassed. "Dragons are hard," she said.

By the time they got to the top of the tower, even with her enhancements, Charlie sort of wondered if it would have killed them to put a magic elevator in this thing.

Then again, maybe it would have. She didn't know magic, and once they were standing at the top of the tower—a large open platform with a set of stairs, smaller and separate from the ones they'd been climbing, more temporary looking, spiraling up into the center of the tear—she figured she certainly didn't want anything interfering with whatever was keeping it in check.

Which appeared to be a series of symbols inscribed around the edge of the tower. That, more than anything, had her sold on the whole magic business. She'd been wondering if it was telekinesis or something of that order, but this was a set of geometric fucking shapes successfully holding back a tear. She'd never seen anything like it. She'd never have conceived of anything like that.

"Do you have a pen and paper? I wanna just..." she started to say. Josephine interrupted.

"It wouldn't work. To someone trained, that is a language through which we may exert our will on the world. To you, they are simply geometric shapes."

"So if you wrote them down maybe on a big scroll we could unroll around..."

"They must be placed by someone with the knowledge and power to place them. To you, it would just be—"

"A scroll of geometric shapes," Charlie said. "Got it. Just a thought. You've done a lot, anyway. Thanks for helping us out, back there."

"It is not entirely selfless. I would hope that you can find Verity, assist in her task, and then send her back. I don't know that I am doing the best job of pretending to be her."

"Well, don't," Vera said. "Do the rules say the Witch of the Tower has to be me? You're magic, you're in a tower-slash-*the*-tower. Be your own witch. Be the witch you want to see in the world."

Charlie cast a sideways glance at Vera and mouthed "what the hell?"

Josephine, to her credit, only coughed politely. "I have my own realm to attend to," she said, "but it can handle my absence more readily than the Tower can handle Verity's." She gestured to the tear with a shrug. Message delivered.

"Right," said Charlie, before Vera could sneak in another inspirational bon mot. "Massive tear in the fabric of the universe." She cleared her throat. "Look, Josephine, we're not looking to overstay our welcome or anything, but I actually can't remember the last time I slept, so if you wouldn't—"

"Say no more," Josephine said, holding up a hand. With another quick twist of her wrist, a door Charlie hadn't noticed—if it had even been visible a moment before—opened. "You are welcome to rest as long as you need. I am certain you will find the accommodations to your standards."

The last was directed to Vera, but something like relief settled over Charlie's shoulders. Between the climb up the tower and the laundry list of shit she'd put up with since jumping through that first tear, a decent night's sleep and a bath felt well-deserved. She opened her mouth to thank Josephine again, but Vera was already halfway to the stairs.

"Shotgun shower!"

There was no shower. There was, however, a bath the size of a small swimming pool, and a bed that Charlie estimated could comfortably sleep six people. It didn't take much imagination to picture what the Witch of the Tower had probably gotten up to in a room that all but demanded an orgy, but Charlie was too tired to give a damn. She was more focused on getting out of the Velo than anything else, and her time in the army had cured her of any modesty. There'd been no privacy outside the wire, and this was no different.

With the distractions of non-Euclidean cockroach squid and the Wasteland and the Hound and the dragon, it had been easy to forget Vera was fresh out of the hospital. But free from immediate threat, Vera was low on adrenaline, and just getting her out of the Marshmallow exoskeleton proved a challenge. Charlie volunteered her assistance after a long minute of watching Vera struggle with her gauntlets. Stripped down to her under armor and no longer able to rely on mechanical power just to stay standing, Vera was green around the gills and in clear need of a good sit, which she did. On the floor. Charlie was barely certain how the woman was alive, and maybe it was the blatant reminder of her own mortality that kept Vera quiet while Charlie neatly stacked the exoskeleton's various components on the large bureau in the corner of the room. For a moment Charlie wondered if she hadn't just fallen asleep, but then Vera's eyes snapped up and focused on Charlie with their usual keenness.

"Who are you?"

"We went over this," Charlie mumbled, helping her stand and ushering her to the nearest chair. "I exposed all over your office, remember?"

"Not what I'm asking."

"Then you have a funny way of asking it."

"I mean, who are *you*?"

They met each other's gaze. Vera had dark circles blooming around her eyes and was pale and rumpled, but in a way that still somehow managed to suggest a magazine cover and not a deathbed. She was larger than life in the same way Verity was, but youth made her edges rougher, lent her an air of the iconoclast. She didn't seem quite real.

"I repeat. Watts repeats. What are—what are even the odds of that?" Vera said, voice dropping to an excited stage whisper, and there it was again. Vera was theatrical, all grand gestures and endless trains of thought and an expressive face that could be seen from the nosebleeds. "Where are you?"

Charlie didn't want to admit she'd been wondering the same question, but the intensity of Vera's stare compelled her to say, "I don't know. Maybe I'm just not friends with you in these worlds. Maybe I'm just...normal and stay away from fucking dragons and physics and tears. Like a normal person."

Vera didn't seem satisfied with the answer. Charlie wasn't either, but it was easier to think of her doppelgängers as being uninvolved than simply not existing.

"It's a small sample size anyway," Charlie added, changing tactics. Science was sounder. "I've been to three different worlds, and even you've only repeated in two of them. It's not enough data."

Vera half-nodded, temporarily appeased, and then her mind (and mouth) flitted to another topic. This time Charlie tuned her out.

They bathed together, albeit at separate ends of the pool. The sheer amount of space reduced the potential for awkwardness (and opportunities for conversation). Vera stayed by the shallows to keep from drowning by exhaustion, which left Charlie to the deceptively deep end. The water was warm, and the collection of soaps lining the ledge rivaled a commercial inventory. Charlie opted for something that smelled vaguely of lavender and washed what felt like a month's worth of grease and grime from her hair.

She stayed in the water until her toes and fingers were well past pruning and wrapped herself in one of the luxurious golden towels that was kept in a woven basket by the bath. She felt lighter than she had in weeks; idly, she wondered if the water itself didn't have some kind of magical healing properties. Vera, seeming less pale than before, was already sprawled on the bed and dressed in a scarlet robe she'd found in the wardrobe. She was staring intently at the fern Witch Verity kept on her bedside table.

Consider the fern.

Charlie sat at the edge of the bed. "You got anything?"

"It's a plant. It's a potted plant. We're...like plants, in some way. Do you think the potting's important? She didn't say 'consider the potted fern,' but maybe she thought it was implicit in 'the fern.' It'd make it too obvious if she said 'potted.' You take cuttings and then you pot them and they grow into basically the same plant, it's the same plant but growing somewhere else. Is she saying we're clones? Someone went around dropping us off in different universes? I guess it'd explain the recurrence. The many-worlds quantum mechanics explanation went out the window when we hit fantasyland, because there's no way for this to have diverged from one of our worlds. And even if it had, it wouldn't have then produced me. Too many butterflies, too many storms. It'd also explain why Dad was the way Dad was. 'Here's this clone, raise her.' Okay, someone would have had to swap me in; he would not have raised a cuckoo if he'd known. He was big on legacy."

"You don't got anything," Charlie said, which seemed a fair summation in one respect. Vera didn't have anything on the fern front. She had plenty on the issues front, apparently.

"I'll get it. If we're reflections or whatever, I'm as smart as her; I'll get it. Do you think she has a heart thing? Some magical version of a heart thing, some curse. Sliver of ice or whatever."

"I think you put yourself in the exact same circumstances as Verity did and ended up with a similar problem," Charlie said. "If only someone had warned you."

"Right? I'll ask Magic Watts, anyway."

"Josephine," corrected Charlie. "Is her last name really Watts in your universe?"

"What? No, it's Watson. I call her Watts because she's a good source of ideas. Makes light bulbs light up. Watts."

"Oh, right. Obvious, really," said Charlie, rolling her eyes and digging in the closet for a robe that was sized closer to her than Verity. There were a few. She didn't want to think about the circumstances for those.

"It's probably all misdirection, anyway," Vera said. Charlie realized she'd switched tracks back to ferns. You had to get used to a mind that was thinking about several things at once and expected you to be able to work out which one was in active play at any given time. "She probably jumped through a tear or two, did some scouting, and that's how she knew. Magic's all about misdirection."

"That's a different kind of magic," Charlie pointed out.

"Or someone from a different universe swung through. She didn't specify us, specifically."

"She didn't specify me at all," Charlie said.

"Well, it's a big multiverse. You'll probably turn up if you're so desperate to know what your hair looks like from the back."

"It's a big multiverse, so the chances are slim. You haven't seen what your hair looks like from the back. You've just heard about you from other people."

"It looks fabulous. I've seen pictures. It does a little," she said through a yawn, "sweep thing."

"Well, Josephine's hair game is pretty good, so maybe Witch Verity's going to outdo you," Charlie said, but Vera had already fallen asleep. You could tell because she didn't immediately leap to defend her status as the superior…reflection or fern or whatever, and also the general lack of too many words filling up any available silence. There was just the silence, the sound of nothing much. None of the ambient noise of a city, even one rendered quiet by the impact of the tears as Montreal had been. Vera's Montreal had been louder, of course, but that had been the least of Charlie's concerns when it came to sleeping. Here, there was just ambient sound, like a white noise track someone might sell. *Animal and Bird Sounds from the Top of a Tower in Vaguely Medieval Times, So Mostly It's a Lot of Wind.* She'd slept rougher in war zones, and had to wonder if the absurdly soft bed and the quiet would prove counterproductive. Maybe it'd keep her awake.

She woke up to the track called *One Really Persistent Bird that Must Have a Nest Outside the Window or Something; This Bird is Really Going at It.* Charlie groaned, pressing a hand over her eyes. Her body ached in the unpleasant way it did sometimes when she slept in the same position for too long. She couldn't even hazard an estimate for how long she'd been out, but this was mostly because she refused to open her eyes and accept she'd spent the night in the penthouse suite of a magical tower. Her hand slipped from her eyes and flopped on the bed like dead weight. The back of her index finger stung with the particular pain of a fresh papercut.

"The hell—?"

She chanced opening an eye. Vera's side of the (substantial) bed was occupied by several scrolls and piles of parchment. Charlie rolled over and picked up the nearest page. It bore a hand-drawn fern. The whole damn mess comprised of drawing upon drawing of ferns, with the notable exception of a single-page, neatly drawn plan of indoor plumbing for the tower that was simply labeled "You're Welcome."

Charlie snorted. "Christ."

She swung her legs off the clear side of the bed, slowly stretched her hands above her head, and took in the surroundings. Vera was eating breakfast at an impressive wooden table Charlie couldn't be fully certain had been there the night before. That was the thing about this universe, wasn't it? It lacked certainty—defined boundaries and hard fast rules. If Josephine were to tell them today pigs here could fly, Charlie would take the information at face value and say she'd take her bacon to go, then. Nothing seemed impossible. It should've been liberating. It wasn't. Case in point: Vera looked miles better than she had the night before, and Charlie had no explanation for the miraculous recovery beyond "magic bathtub"—and possibly enchanted sleep.

"If you didn't wake up in the next hour, I thought I was going to have to Prince Charming you," Vera said without looking up from her latest drawing. She was getting better at it. The leaves looked lifelike.

"Mm. How romantic of you." Charlie slid into the opposite chair and eyeballed the spread. There were at least three different kinds of breakfast meat that demanded immediate sampling. Charlie made herself a plate.

"Chuck Chaste no more."

Charlie snorted. Vera's easy smile focused into something more thoughtful as her scientific curiosity broke through her jokingly flirtatious veneer.

"You're like a furnace, you know that? Is that a—" Vera wiggled her fingers. "You know, a side effect?"

Charlie speared a piece of possibly-flying-bacon with her fork. "Say you're making a *Canadian* supersoldier—"

"—so there's no side about it. It was just an effect."

"An increased metabolism makes me less susceptible to volatile environmental factors and toxins, so it seemed practical. Unlike whatever the hell you're doing."

"Eating a lot? Extremely practical. We don't know where our next meal is coming from unless we're taking a picnic basket. Are we—it wouldn't survive the trip. Or, do you mean the drawing? Well, I'm getting pretty good. I always liked drawing. This one's the Witch Fern."

Vera held up the pad of paper. There was a drawing of a fern wearing the kind of pointy, large-brimmed witch's hat they had seen exactly zero of in their experience of actual witches. In a border around it, Charlie noticed, were the symbols from the wards at the top of the tower. At some point in the morning, Vera must have gone out there and copied them down despite Josephine's telling them it wouldn't be of any use. Vera probably hadn't been listening. At any rate, it saved Charlie doing it, because you never knew. Maybe they could learn something from them somehow.

"Oh, good, we can show that to people. Have you seen this fern?" Charlie said, sitting down, having piled her plate high.

"Well, we already have the wanted picture," Vera said, indicating her own face. "Should've done a self-portrait. Added the big nose and the warts. So we're chasing Verity Thaum wherever it is she's going?"

Verity Thaum. Jesus. I don't know what's worse: if she's been working on that all night or if she came up with it on the spot.

"It beats jumping randomly from universe to universe hoping we hit the right one, and not another parasite infested wasteland," Charlie agreed. "And it seems like—she has some idea about how things work. She had a lead of some kind. If we can't find her, maybe we can find that."

"Assuming the next world over isn't just another parasite fun park and she wasn't eaten immediately by non-Euclidean cockroach squid."

"Assuming that, because I'm eating," Charlie said, eating.

"Did you ever—I mean, you had them in your world, did you ever see—"

Charlie continued eating for a moment before she picked up the question. "Did I ever see the parasites get someone? Not close up, but… Yeah. It was hard to look at. Not hard-to-look-at *gross*, although, yeah, but just—well, you saw them. It wasn't even like they were eating the person, it was just like…they were present where the parasite was eating. If you can call it eating. I don't even know if they have mouths. It was—"

"Hard to look at," Vera concluded. "Okay. Gross. Why'd you even bring it up? We're eating. That's enough of that."

It was easy to ignore her. There was food.

After breakfast, they went in search of Josephine and found her one level down, in a library that encompassed the entire floor, surrounding the stairs. She was set-up at an inclined table looking through a magnifying glass on an adjustable stand, working with a delicate engraving tool on what Charlie would have ordinarily called a necklace but in the context found herself instinctively thinking *amulet*.

"Cool necklace," Vera said. "Gift for a lovely lady in your life?"

"It's for you, actually," Josephine said, making another, very fine mark.

"Yes, then," Vera said, tipping herself into a well-padded reading chair nearby.

"Oh, that's a mistake I'm not making again," Josephine said, without looking up. Charlie couldn't help but make a satisfied little snort.

"Oh, no," said Vera. "Am I going on a trip where everyone interesting already dated a me? I've changed my mind, I quit. I want off the ride."

"What's it for?" Charlie asked Josephine.

"Emergencies," said Josephine, turning on the stool to hold it out. Charlie took it, a little gingerly, half expecting a spark or something. It mostly just felt like a heavy locket. It had a very finely inscribed series of symbols in a lattice over the entire face and back. Some of the designs seemed as if they were halves that weren't quite lined up. She automatically went to twist it to put them in alignment.

"Don't do that," Josephine said. Charlie stopped short, putting down the amulet in case she'd been about to trigger a magic explosion. It wouldn't have lined them up anyway, she saw, or not all of them. Lining one up would leave the others still in the wrong place. "When you need it, twist, then open."

"How will we know when we need it? What's it do?"

"When you need it, it'll occur to you, and it'll help. I can't say more. It's the nature of the spell. It's meant to be a saving grace. If I told you what it does, it'd just be a tool."

"I thought that stuff wouldn't work for us. Just geometric shapes." *So Vera was listening after all.*

"These geometric shapes were placed on this specific object for a specific purpose by me, and to me—"

"Secret language, got it," Vera finished for her.

"Assuming you had the right shapes," Charlie said, "is there anything magic specifically can't do?"

Josephine cast a suspicious glance her way. "No," she said, "but there's plenty it shouldn't."

The threat was unspoken but clear, yet Charlie pressed on. "I'm just wondering if you can't do something for Vera's heart. Or magic us some sustainable food. We're limited for rations, and—"

"You're injured?" Josephine asked Vera.

"I'm fine. Wonders of modern medicine. I stood a little close to one of those things," Vera said. Charlie held back a comment about the fact that she hadn't simply stood too close, she'd opened the damned thing right on top of herself.

"That's funny, because—" Josephine began, but they didn't get to find out what exactly was funny about it, because at that moment there was a resounding knock that echoed from the tower. It was, presumably, from the larger doors at the base. There were great acoustics, or—

"Someone has a very big fist," Vera said.

"Just a cantrip, so I can hear it. When there were other people in the tower there was at least usually someone on the ground floor to hear and answer," Josephine said, crossing to the window and leaning out to peer down before sighing. "I do wish they'd stand back after they knock. You can't see properly if they're right by the door from up here. Probably just another apprentice candidate, but in case it's not... Nothing for it, I suppose." She crossed to the stairs and started down.

"Elevator," Vera said.

"Well, you should've designed her an elevator," Charlie said. Vera withdrew a piece of paper from her stack and dropped it in front of her on her way to the stairs. It was, indeed, plans for a counterweight-based elevator, although she'd noted at several points "or I guess you could do a magic thing." Inside the diagram of the actual enclosure, she'd drawn several people in business suits holding briefcases, all of whom were wearing witches' hats. Caught up in studying it, it took her a moment to realize that Vera had followed Josephine down the stairs. Vera turning up as she answered the door seemed like it could get awkward, depending on who it was.

Hell, it was Vera, there was no depending. Charlie hurried after her.

"I think she can get a door on her own," she said, once she caught up. "You were just complaining about these stairs. You're gonna go all the way down just because you're curious?"

"Yup," Vera said, firmly. "Also—I am temporarily sort of the Witch of the Tower; maybe I should be there. But mostly—curious. I want to see who comes to see the witch. Maybe it's you! Apprentice candidate, that could be you."

Charlie couldn't help but feel that would be kind of nice. Deeply strange, and it wasn't as if it meant anything that she'd run into Veritys and Josephines and a Salt but not herself, but nonetheless, once Vera raised the idea, she couldn't help but wonder a little if this *was* the moment at which she met herself.

So, of course, it wasn't her. It was a teenager in a smock clutching a very large book—tome, really, seemed the operative word—accompanied by a small shaggy pony, which answered Vera's question about horses. Her name was Fran—

("Francisca?" Josephine had asked. "No." "Francine?" "No." "Faronall'andein?" "No, just Fran.")

—and she had left her parents and five older sisters—

("Five? You are absolutely certain you don't have an extra sister, maybe out of wedlock, maybe a young aunt that looks suspiciously like your mother, and your mother always seemed a little wistful when she looked at her?" "No. Five sisters.")

—to come and seek out an apprenticeship because she'd found this old book of magic—

("Ah, in the attic, hidden away, an old relic of the family. Or perhaps a strange traveler met upon a path of a moonlit night—" "I got it down the local peddler. He said, 'I've got three of these and they're not moving so I'll give you a discount.'")

—and had found she was capable of the magic found within.

"Something deeply prosaic, I suppose. You made some cheese into a little extra cheese. Moved some objects about."

"I turned my friend Ellenda'hara into this strange shaggy hooved thing that isn't a goat," finished Fran, turning to point at the pony. Vera threw up her hands and turned away, shaking her head.

"I had wondered about that," admitted Josephine. She turned to Vera and Charlie. "I am sorry. I had thought to speak more, but I should deal with her friend and then see her on her way. I have, perhaps, delayed you long enough, in any case."

"I wanna see her turn the pony into a girl," Vera said, looking at Charlie. It was Josephine who answered, though. Charlie had been struggling with the fact that she kind of wanted to see it, too, but also kind of didn't. That untethered sense the lack of fundamental rules gave her would only get worse if she witnessed something like that.

Luckily, that didn't seem to be on the cards.

Well, not luckily for Ellenda'hara.

"Unravelling…whatever it was she did will take time," Josephine said, giving the pony a disconcerted look from where she, Vera, and Charlie were talking apart from Fran, who was brushing the pony's mane.

"So…she did some big-time magic that you're not sure how to undo, and you're saying she can't be an apprentice? C'mon, sign her up. She aced the audition. You're down a witch; you need someone to answer the door and help build your new elevator."

"El…e…" Josephine said, mouthing the shape of the words before apparently giving up with the facility gained after spending a few minutes listening to Vera. "Perhaps," she allowed. "Do you think…it's not…"

"It's not disloyal," Charlie said. "Verity would tell you the same. Verity did tell you the same. Sort of. She's not going to come back and get mad because you took on an apprentice. She'd probably—I never met her, but it sounds to me like she'd slap a plant in front of her and wait for her to learn things from it."

"Yes, well," Josephine said. "I hope we find out. I hope you find her. Good luck."

We'll need it.

Two care packages were waiting at the top of the tower, though only one had an amulet, which Charlie carefully slipped around her neck before suiting up. Both the Velo and the Marshmallow had been cleaned overnight, and Charlie had to admit to feeling just a bit the knight.

"A leather satchel and a highly sophisticated, experimental exoskeleton is a lot of look, even for me," Vera said, struggling to get the care package to sit comfortably on her hip. "And how come you get the necklace? That's— That's not fair. She made it for me."

"Safe-keeping," Charlie said, which was the polite way of saying, "You punched a goddamn dragon, and I don't trust you not to blow yourself up with whatever the hell this is." She cut off another complaint with a curt, "Ready?"

Vera made one last adjustment to the satchel's strap, then nodded. It really was a lot of look, but there was no telling where their next meal was coming from. Practicality outweighed fashion.

Together they approached the tear. It was the first time since Charlie's initial jump that she had the time to consider her actions, and it was somehow almost easier to throw yourself into a new world when you were chased out of the old one by a non-Euclidean cockroach squid that was intent on eating you. Without the immediate pressure to jump, there was the impulse to linger—to stare at the half-stabilized tear and force your mind to make sense of the senseless, the absence of familiar. It hurt to look at it, just as it always had. Vera, apparently having less tolerance for self-torture than Charlie, stepped through first.

Charlie huffed and followed.

Chapter Nine

— SUBVERSIVES —

We can't just close it!" Vera repeated for what felt like the twentieth time.

They had been arguing for so long, the new world's sun had fallen entirely out of view. Compared to the lush fantasy setting they'd just abandoned, the city streets felt sterile, lifeless, and chillingly deserted. It was also simply chilly, in the way of Montreal on a November evening, when the leaves had already fallen but the snow wasn't yet sticking. Charlie didn't recognize the alley, but she was sure that it was Montreal. The tear, small and nestled in the back of an alley of some doubtlessly important building, crackled with threatening promise. Vera, while looking less worn than she had after her first two jumps, was still a bit peaky.

"You saw the Wasteland," Charlie said.

"What if this tear is the only way back? What if us closing the tear dooms Verity Thaum to roam the multiverse alone forever? It's stable on their side; what if—"

"I'd sooner doom one person than an entire world. Josephine might be able to handle the tear on her end, but there's nothing to suggest the people of this world are capable of—"

A gleaming white robot with a big blue "B" emblazoned across its humanoid torso appeared at the alley's entrance and effectively killed Charlie's argument.

"You were saying something about being capable?" Vera's dismay over horses didn't extend to not beating dead ones. But Charlie's annoyed retort was cut off by the appearance of a second robot, more or less identical to the first.

They were friendly looking despite their imposing, fiberglass frames. Both stood a few inches taller than Charlie, and they had wide shoulders that tapered into inhumanly narrow waists. Their hands were fully articulated, and they had blank, black screens for faces. Twin expressions of alarm lit up their displays: a red, flashing exclamation mark.

"Curfew is in effect," the closer one said. Played, really, was more apt. It didn't sound as if it was synthesizing the words on the fly so much as repeating a pre-recorded clip. Whoever had done the recording had spoken with the bland pleasantness of an airport announcement. "You are out past curfew, the action of dangerous subversives. Are you dangerous subversives?"

Charlie and Vera looked at each other. "No," said Charlie, before Vera could say "yes." She could see it forming. Frankly, Charlie was a little curious to see what happened if you did say yes, but it seemed too early to pick a fight with the robots.

"I am pleased to hear it," the robot said, with all the affect of someone stamping their thousandth passport of the day. "Please submit index cards for examination."

"Um," said Charlie, wondering if one of the hallmarks of being a dangerous subversive was not having whatever the robot meant by an index card.

"We...lost them," Vera said, making a show of peering into her satchel and patting down a plastic casing that did not have pockets as if she might suddenly discover pockets.

The robots stared—or at least stood still with their faceplates pointed at the pair of them—before the red exclamation marks abruptly changed to yellow question marks.

"In the absence of index cards, please prepare for indexing. A short series of questions will now follow. Please answer as quickly as possible. You are walking in the desert when you come across a turtle on its back. Haha. Little robot humor for you," said the robot, with the same blandly consistent pacing and lack of emphasis. The second robot had stepped closer to Vera, playing a similar set of recordings at the same time. "Are you a turtle or a seal?"

There was silence. After a moment, the robot said, "Please answer as quickly as possible," with the complete same intonation as before. Definitely pre-recordings. Charlie had to wonder if the person had been specifically instructed to do the joke—quote-un-quote—without any feeling. What was the point of that? Be a little extra creepy?

"Seal," she said, at about the same time Vera said it.

"You are walking in the desert when you come across a seal on its back," said the robot. Charlie waited for the recording about this being a joke.

"Please answer as quickly as possible," the robot said.

"Why is there a seal in the desert?" Charlie said, catching a little of Vera saying, "—did it get there? How did I get there? Give me some backstory," to her robot.

"You are driving a trolley which is about to run over a group of people. If you change tracks, it will run over a single child."

"Cut power to the trolley," Charlie said. She understood what that one was about and technically she was cheating, but it hadn't added any provisos that those were her only options, and it had said answer fast.

"You may rescue one item from a fire at your domicile. What is it?"

"My pet seal," she heard Vera say.

"Her pet seal," Charlie said, unable to help herself.

"Sufficient data," said both robots, near simultaneously. "Completing inventory."

"Okay, that cannot be—those things are usually way longer, you cannot be doing whatever you're doing on that elementary—" Vera said. The robot cut her off.

"Sufficient data. Category Opulenti assigned."

"Okay, your system is definitely wrong, because that doesn't sound like me at—" Vera said, over Charlie's own protest.

"There is no way we're in the same category," she said, although even as she said it, it occurred to her that would mean the robots might split them up. Maybe she shouldn't have said anything.

"Category protests noted. You are out of the registered category zone. Category reassessment: Subversives."

"Now that sounds like me," said Vera, as both robots raised their arms, the fiberglass housings widening as barrels extended over their hands. Charlie, not waiting to find if they just looked like guns, took a running jump and hit the robot nearest Vera with both feet. It stumbled back, not going down as she'd hoped but off-balance enough that as she twisted and landed, she pulled the Browning and fired instead at the second.

It pinged off the shell, which she'd kind of figured.

"I hope whoever designed you was dumb enough to put the central processor behind your face," she said, spinning again and driving her fist through the faceplate of the off-balance robot.

"My designer was not dumb enough to put my central processor behind my face," the robot said with bland cheerfulness. The speakers were in its neck, apparently, so she still had to listen to it, too.

She had a follow-up hope, though. She got a grip on the inside of the robot's head, solidly wrapping her hand around circuits and wires and a solid mass that felt like it extended down into the rest of the robot. She used that as leverage to swing the pair of them around to shield herself from the other robot as it fired.

There were further pings. Her hope that the robots weren't armored against each other's weapons—if one went rogue you had to be able to stop it, surely—hit the ground in a series of small taps. Darts, she saw. Not bullets. Tranqs, presumably.

She caught the arm of the robot she was holding as it tried to put its own tranq-gun in a position to hit her, took her hand out of its face to grab the other arm, at which point its head ejected from its body, and the second robot shot a tranq dart through the space where it had been into her neck.

Her third, final hope, was that whatever they were using wasn't calibrated for her and that she'd be able to fight through it.

Her hope plummeted as she did. She had enough consciousness left to wince when the robot's head bounced off hers as it fell back to the ground, and then she didn't have any at all.

"Quit fidgeting."

Charlie didn't recognize the gruff male voice, but she was just cognizant enough to realize the directive wasn't aimed at her. She was still caught in the fuzzy space between sleep and wakefulness, her system fighting through the effects of the robot drugs. Her hands were bound together behind her back, which was bare and pressed against a cold, metallic wall. The Velo had been removed, which left her in a set of plain microfiber under-garments. Her bag and anything else that might have helped was gone, too. Self-preservation ordered her eyes to stay shut and her breaths to stay steady and even. To her right, she was aware of something—someone—rocking back and forth.

"Easier said than done, Zeph," whispered a younger voice, also male. "They've upgraded the cuffs. Gimme a sec."

"'Gimme a sec,' he says," Zeph grumbled. "I'm not getting any younger, kid."

There was a *hiss-click* as the lock on the cuffs gave, and Charlie felt him get up and cross over to Zeph. Each step he took made the floor shake. They were in transport—a truck of some sort, most likely. If she focused, she could hear the hum of a motor over the pounding in her head.

"What, no thank you?" the kid asked, resettling beside Charlie.

"Shut up, I'm thinking of a way to get us out of this mess you made."

The kid made an unintelligible sound of protest. "It was the right call."

"You say that every time B-Tech reels you in?" Charlie could hear Zeph's eyes roll. "No wonder she likes you. Goddamn Vagoses. You're all the same kind of stupid."

"You're a Vagos."

"I'm stuck here with you, aren't I?"

The kid snorted, and there was a lull in the conversation. Vagos. Opulenti. Charlie guessed it was Latin, but she couldn't translate it with any certainty. She never took Latin. Arts majors took Latin. She'd suffered through too many French classes in high school to want to study its older, deader parent in university. B-Tech was more obvious. In Charlie's world, before Verity had taken over the company from dear old dad, it had been called Baum Technologies. If this was another Verity universe—and the signs were pointing to "yes"—B-Tech was a step in the right direction.

But why the hell was this world's Verity—Berity?—having poorly branded robots round up old guys and teenagers for being out after curfew? What was the angle there?

"This your second or third infraction?" Zeph asked.

The kid hesitated. "Third."

"Damn."

"Myriam will make the rendezvous with the TeeVees," the kid said, words tripping over each other in his hurry to spit them out. "Even if we're wiped, it won't matter."

Charlie understood the words, but not the meaning. Why would you meet with a television? What was this—

"It's rude to eavesdrop without introducing yourself."

Charlie stiffened and weighed the option of pretending to still be asleep. Not seeing a point to it, she opened her eyes. The truck box was better lit than she was anticipating, and she winced at the glare. Vera, stripped of the exoskeleton but left with more of her clothes than Charlie, was passed out next to Zeph, whose shoulder-length black hair was streaked with silver. He had brown skin, a stocky build, and an expression that spoke to the lack of fucks he gave about her sizing him up. The kid was no older than fifteen or sixteen, of Asian—if it was even still called Asia here—descent, and too tall to comfortably sit on the truck's low benches. Both he and Zeph had the same markings on their left hand: a dark red swirl that stretched from their wrist to the junction of their index finger and thumb.

"Sergeant Charlotte Chase." She braced herself for skepticism but was met with none.

"Zepherin Benoit. The kid's Wolfgang Do Lee. Where'd the bots pick you up, Sergeant?"

Charlie scoured her memory for a street sign. "An alley," she said, hating that she couldn't be more specific. "I'm...kind of new around here."

Zeph and Wolfgang—*Who named these guys?*—exchanged a look Charlie couldn't interpret. After a long moment, Zeph leveled his gaze on her instead.

"That's fine," he said, "so long as you're on board with the plan."

There was really one thing to say to that.

"What's the plan?"

"That's the dumbest thing I've ever heard," Vera said. "No, I didn't hear it right. I'm woozy. A robot shot me up full of drugs, and now someone's talking nonsense philosophy at me—this is 90 percent of the parties I go to in California." Charlie could believe it; although Vera was slumped in the corner of their cell, there was only the slightest slur in her voice as she jumped from topic to topic with as little consideration for people trying to keep up as ever. "There's categories, and those determine what job you get and what you can watch and where you can live. Sure. Communism plus some psychology from the 19th century, before people started treating it like a science and it was just people making junk up. Well, or modern-day HR." Her face lit up. "Oh, I solved it, this whole thing is just the people who make up the tests making sure they keep their jobs during every company re-org!"

"Good job, congratulations," Charlie bit out. "I'm sure now they'll let us out and not—did you miss the part where there's something called wiping and they're going to do it to us?"

"...yes," said Vera. "They shot me full of drugs. I'm not certain that went well with, you know. Heart condition. I feel weird. Is it just me, or if you have to wipe people, is that not a sign your system is broken?"

"I think we knew that after they put us in the same category. 'Opulenti.'" Charlie could see Vera as an Opulenti. Whatever that was, it sounded very ruling class, fancy and uncaring and whimsical, but it didn't match up with Charlie at all.

"It should be opulenta, anyway," Vera said. "Vocative neuter plural. Honestly, you'd think they just put it in an online translator and called it a day. It means complacent, by the by. That's what we got."

Charlie could still see it. Vera was generally convinced that she knew everything, absolutely secure in her own world.

"So...stay in your complacent little lane, get wiped if you don't. What is the point of that?" Vera finished, throwing up her hands, or making a gesture that would have been that if she'd had complete control of her limbs. Instead she just sort of thrashed them into the wall she was propped halfway up against as Charlie paced the edge of their cell, considering the beams of light that formed the bars. Close up, they hissed very slightly.

"You tell me. They're your robots. B for Baum. Baum Technologies, the architect of...whatever this is."

"Exactly. That is exactly what's—it's all very stupid, but I'm not stupid, so this Verity isn't stupid, so what the hell is she doing?"

Vera was madder about this than she had been the fern thing, although Charlie wondered if it wasn't *because* of the fern thing. Vera was now oh-for-two on working out the ideas of other Veritys.

"We can figure it out later," Charlie said before Vera could begin another rant about her counterparts. "It's time to get the fuck out of here."

"Am I imagining the bars? Is that just the drugs? I could have sworn they locked us in. If they didn't lock us in, they are bad at their jobs," Vera said, sitting up, sloughing to the side slightly as she did and almost toppling off the bed.

"We're escaping. The two guys we were brought in with had a plan, which you didn't listen to."

"I was unconscious," Vera said, standing up, and then immediately sitting back down.

"When I explained it to you. You got hung up on the whole... system."

"'s dumb. Is the plan, 'escape'? I'm caught up," Vera said, bracing herself on the wall and standing up again, sliding along it until she was at the bars. "Okay, you act sick, and I'll overpower the guards."

"That...was their plan," Charlie admitted. Of course, in their plan, it had been Zepherin faking dead and Wolfgang taking out the guards, but it had still been kind of a cliché. That part of it hadn't been great. She'd told them to reconsider. It had become sort of moot since they'd ended up in separate cells.

"Weird plan. They only just met us. I say we just turn off the bars."

"Yeah, I'm sure they put the switch on the inside, that's a real great prison you designed—" Charlie broke off, considering the possibility a Verity Baum had designed this prison.

"Never build a prison you can't break out of," Vera said confidently, pressing her hand flat to a panel that looked just like the others all around it.

Nothing happened.

"...well, that's where I would have put it," Vera said, trying higher and sighing as this, too, proved not to be a secret biometric scanner designed to release Verity Baum should she find herself imprisoned in one of her own cells. "Fine. Put your hand through and turn it off from the outside."

"Excuse you?" said Charlie. "Those bars are—"

"Non-lethal, designed to stun, calibrated for normal people. It's cycling, too. Like an electric fence. There's a couple of seconds where it's just a mild shock before the whole thing will lay you on your back. Stick your hand through and turn it off."

This did not sound like a promising option. Vera had just been completely wrong about there being a secret release mechanism within the cell. She was in the dark about the whole categorization system. Her guess for the fern thing had been potted plants and multiversal storks delivering clones. Her ability to predict other Veritys did not inspire confidence.

On the other hand—Charlie tried not to consider the possibility she'd end up with just the one if this went wrong—it was tech. Vera was good at tech. It was in the company name.

Charlie stepped to the corner, where the cell control panel lay on the other side. Made a fist. Held it close to the bars experimentally. They crackled more, little charges extending toward her hand, a faint sensation of static electricity.

Well, that wasn't so bad. She thrust her hand forward.

Her entire arm seized up. If this was the mild part of the cycle—*how long is a couple of seconds, when does the full impact hit, how long do I have?*—this was going to go very badly in a moment or two because her muscles were locked. She had to shove her arm forward and around from the shoulder, basically a flail, barely feeling it thump against the control panel. There'd been a code. She'd clocked the code when the guards had entered it, but now she had to enter it without seeing what she was doing, with a hand that wouldn't unclench.

Sweat beading, she forced one knuckle further out, whole hand shaking. She knew where the panel was. Where the numbers were. Just basic spatial reasoning, that was all. Just some basic spatial reasoning in one or two seconds with a spasming arm. 4-8-1-5-1-6-2-3-4. The pitch of the bars started to change. With a final jerk, she drove her knuckle into the last number: 2. Just as the sensation in her arm threatened to swell and knock her backward and out, the bars snapped out of the world, just an after-image in her vision.

"Fuck," she said, falling back against the wall, massaging her arm, still unable to unclench her fist. Even without any active effect on it, it was still hundreds of little stabs all over her arm, the worst pins and needles she'd ever felt. Partially because she had no idea when she could expect it to fade. She'd hoped immediately.

It was not immediately.

"I can't believe that worked," Vera said, in the sort of absently impressed way that implied she hadn't believed it would work when she suggested it. Charlie fought down the impulse to put her hand through another piece of Veritech. Namely the company's owner.

"Let's see if we can build some momentum," she said instead, because she was a professional. "Where would you put the control center?"

The control center was in a heavily fortified tower surrounded by armed guards. Vera was two-for-five, which was small comfort when Charlie had to get them past a small army with nothing more than wits and experience.

Good thing she had good old fashioned bioengineered resilience to fall back on.

"Stay here and don't punch any dragons," she said, ushering Vera into a corner that had a reasonable amount of cover. The drugs were wearing off, but not fast enough for either of their likings. Without the Marshmallow to counteract her more reckless tendencies, Vera was more liability than help in a fistfight.

"There aren't even any dragons to punch."

"Then you shouldn't have any problems."

Vera looked like she was about to argue some more, but there was no time. A projectile too slow to be an actual bullet sunk deep into the wall about three inches from Vera's head. Several seconds later, Vera jerked her head to avoid it, although she did it in a direction that put her head in front of the impact point, so the delay had worked out for her. Still, it wasn't a good sign.

"Go, go," Vera said. "Punch the dragoons."

It was an injustice, Charlie considered, that the drugs would put Vera out of it without impeding her tendency to weird wordplay. Still, Charlie did have to go punch some people. She tugged Vera around another corner and parked her farther out of the way. Then she sidled up to the corner, crouched low, and waited.

The thing about being out of the way was, the thing was—

A security guard followed his gun around the corner.

—they had to come to you. She tackled him, grabbing and controlling his wrist as she shoulder-checked him into the far wall, bringing it around and squeezing the trigger to put a dart in his backup.

The dart pinged off his backup's armor instead. The same thing the robots were made out of. Great. At least they weren't actually robots. It meant, too, that she could spin him around and use him as a shield without worrying if his head was going to fly off.

"Surrender! We have yooou…" said the backup.

"Gap in the armor at the neck," Charlie said, with satisfaction, yanking her shield's head to the side and shooting him in the neck, too. Knocking people out by bopping them on the head didn't work like it did in movies. In real life, when someone was knocked out by a punch for more than a few seconds, it was because they were suffering brain damage, and she wasn't here to inflict brain damage.

Admittedly, real life was a strange and nebulous idea these days. Maybe here physiology meant you could just bop people on the head and they went to sleep.

"Put this on," she said to Vera, who woozily regarded the armor Charlie was stripping off the unconscious guard with distaste.

"That…is a downgrade. That is bad for my brand."

"It has your brand on it," Charlie said, tapping the logo.

"It's minion armor with my brand on it. That is bad for my brand. It's ugly and it's a downgrade. I'll just wait for my armor."

"Yours is—it's a spacesuit! It's no—look, we're doing the thing. We're doing the disguise thing. They probably know I knocked out their friends so it'll give us all of ten seconds, but I can use that."

Vera's responding look was withering, and it would have been more effective if Charlie wasn't right. With a forceful, cranky sigh, Vera took the armor. Charlie ignored her steady stream of complaints as she went to strip the other guard. His boots were too small, but Charlie jammed her sock feet into them anyway. Anything was better than nothing, and it was a relief to be wearing something other than her fucking underwear. By the time they were both dressed, Vera was still relying on the wall to stay vertical; the helmet threatened to topple her over. Charlie slipped an arm under Vera's to keep her on her feet.

They ran—or, at least, if Charlie was being generous, she could call it running. It was more like a three-legged race, with Vera tripping every other step, but Charlie adapted to their odd rhythm, kept them at a decent pace. Their disguises bought them a few extra seconds once they arrived at the next checkpoint. The guard's suspicion was a moment too slow to dawn, his look of angry surprise fading as the drugs took effect.

"It's a retinal scan," Vera remarked from where she was slumped on the floor. She thrust a shoulder in the vague direction of the secure door, and sure enough, there was a slim panel with a pictograph of an eye flashing red on the wall beside it.

Charlie frowned at the unconscious guard. "Do you think our pal is authorized?"

"Could be."

The movies made prison breakouts seem so glamorous. In reality, it involved picking up a man twice your size and prying an eyelid open long enough for the scan to take. The panel flashed green, and the door slid open with a hiss. Five pairs of eyes turned in their direction. The closest goon was reaching for his comms, probably to call for backup. Charlie fired her new friend's tranq gun. The dart stuck in the man's neck, and he was down before he could utter a word.

The other four weren't as easy. Charlie felt the prick of a needle, the burn of the drugs working through her bloodstream to lull her to sleep. She pushed through, digging deep. Her system had been exposed to it already, had built up a tolerance. That was how the enhancements worked: they were adaptive, could help her survive in environments and situations no human body should. The drugs were like a weight she had to carry, slowing her down, yes, but no longer stopping her. She shouldered a blow to a head, a sharp pain at the back of her knee that made her leg buckle. She rallied, growling with equal parts frustration and determination, and weaved through the other guards with as much speed as she could muster. Tranq gun in hand, she dropped them with tastes of their own medicine.

"Get in here," Charlie said to Vera, who was leaning on the other side of the door with just her head poking around, helmet askew. Vera more or less rolled herself around the doorframe until she was on the correct side, fumbling behind her for the button to close it, before lurching across the room. Charlie hooked a roller chair with her foot and kicked it across the room, where it hit Vera in the leg, and she fell into it. Almost over it. Charlie winced. She'd kind of thought she had more motor function back than that.

But she did have enough to wheel herself over to a computer while Charlie tore out the door panel, sealing it.

"Right," Vera said. "Hacking, hacking. Stuff about mainframes and trojans."

"Type?" suggested Charlie, glancing at where Vera's hands remained at her sides. *You'd think she was the one who just got another dose of the tranqs.* Charlie considered sitting down but decided she didn't want her body thinking it could relax. Then the drugs probably would hit her.

"Good start," Vera said, typing and then immediately pausing. Charlie began to sigh but realized Vera was just peering at the screen, and then down at the keyboard. "Huh. DVORAK."

"Is that going to slow you down? Because we're not exactly stealth, here," Charlie said, glancing at the screens that lined the walls, trying to work out where in relation to the control room the flood of security personnel was.

"Yes," Vera said, which had to be the drugs, an admission of weakness like that. "But not so much you'd notice. I'm still, you know, me." She started typing again, pausing periodically to study the screen and then type some more. "Also, this is pretty easy. They kind of figure if you're in here, you have the right to, say..."

She held her hand over the enter key, then brought it down dramatically. Stared at the screen a moment, then looked at the keyboard, sighed, and lifted her finger off the shift key to hit enter.

"Open all the cell doors," she said, a little deflated.

Charlie confirmed this on the screens. A lot of bars winking out, and Zepherin and Wolfgang immediately barreling out of theirs, stopping to exhort the somewhat slower crowds in the other cells to likewise follow.

"Have you found our stuff?" she said, leaning down to tap at the keyboard on the terminal next to Vera's. "Or any sign of Verity Thaum?"

"Nope," Vera said, shaking her head. The Witch of the Tower was still in the wind, then. "Nothing. I tried the keywords 'KICK-ASS SPACESUIT' and it didn't come up, so it's gonna be tough. They don't categorize properly."

"Well, we established that," Charlie said. "'Opulenti.' Honestly." She looked for a map, somewhere she could find contraband storage or something, then glanced up and stopped looking. Instead, she grabbed the back of Vera's chair and wheeled her to the side of the room furthest from the door, trying to stash her in cover as much as possible. Herself, too. She didn't know that she'd be able to fight through another tranq dart this soon. Two or more, definitely not.

And the screen that showed just outside the door contained decidedly more than a couple of security guards. In her favor was the fact that not all of them appeared to have the tranq guns.

Against was the fact that instead some of them appeared to have something closer to actual guns. Another pair of guards had brought forward a contraption like the jaws of life, evidently for prying the door open, given that they were currently prying the door open. Charlie tried to get a bead on them through the gap, but they'd evidently seen some of their buddies on the way and were staying in cover.

They had to come in sometime, though, and when they did, she dropped two of them right off, and then the gun clicked. She was woozy. She should have picked spares off the unconscious guards in the room. She threw herself into a roll toward where the guns lay, snatching one up even as she carried the motion through to slam into the legs of the nearest conscious guard, coming up to level the gun—

Stopping when she realized all the guards had stopped, because someone was shouting, "Wait, wait, hang on!"

Not Vera. Familiar, though.

"Professor Baum?" said Nathaniel Salt, which Charlie thought just figured.

Chapter Ten

— CUTE METAPHORS —

A fire crackled merrily in Professor Baum's office, which had the lived-in quality a room acquires when its owner is a reclusive academic. Unlike the monochromatic sterility of the rest of this world, the office almost exploded with color: rich reds and browns and golds that invited the eye to rest easy for a while. Charlie was seated in a perfectly stuffed leather armchair that molded to her body. Vera, Wolfgang, and Zepherin flanked her sides in similarly comfortable seating arrangements. All save Vera were fighting off sleep, and the drugs were only partially to blame; the office was downright cozy. Charlie sipped at her tea, thoughtfully prepared by Nathaniel, who was fussier and more nervous than the man she knew from home.

"Professor Baum disappeared about a year ago," he was saying in hushed tones, though there was little risk of them being overheard. The office was deep underground, and Charlie had counted no fewer than eight biometric security checkpoints on their way in, the last three of which were keyed only to accept Nathaniel's and Professor Baum's authorization.

"How did you know I wasn't her?" Vera asked. "I could be back from my trip...wherever." She was more alert than she had been in hours and was sitting at the edge of her chair, her posture straight. Her eyes were narrowed in deductive thought. Charlie recognized the look enough to be wary of it.

Nathaniel's expression pinched. He cleared his throat. In a delicate tone, he replied, "Baum Technologies is capable of many wonderful, terrible things, my dear, but cellular regeneration is not among them."

Charlie snorted. "That means you're a baby."

Vera glared. "So what? I went crazy and escaped from the old folks' home?"

"Ah, not quite."

"It'd explain a few things," Wolfgang muttered.

"See?" Vera said, waving in his direction. "Crazy old woman comes up with an insane sorting system to—what, exactly, what purpose does bad Latin ever have except to show off how pretentious grandma is?"

"There is a logic to the system, Doctor."

"I'm not seeing it." Vera sat back, throwing up her hands with palpable dismissiveness. This was Vera the Businesswoman, used to holding court with intellectual inferiors. For the first time, Charlie was able to appreciate Vera's unique conversational style. Even Nathaniel seemed torn between defending his old friend and cowering in front of her younger model.

"Perhaps we should start from the beginning," Nathaniel hedged, standing up from his chair. He pulled off his glasses and took half a minute to clean them—a nervous twitch Nate had never exhibited. Maybe it was just the drugs talking, but it was strange to Charlie how different the same face—the same body—could be depending on who was piloting. He had as much in common with

Nate as Vera did with Verity: a name, a face, a voice. It was disquieting. "Our world was stricken by bleeds. Imagine, if you would, a tank of—"

"Holes in reality destroying the place. Spare me the colorful, easy to understand, oversimplified to the point of inaccuracy metaphor. Assume we know," said Vera, cocking her head to the side and leaning it on two fingers next to her temple.

"I don't know," Wolfgang said, sitting so far up in his chair he nearly came out of it. "What? *What?*"

"You're caught up. Let the adults talk," Vera said, waving him down with the hand she wasn't leaning on.

"...right," said Nathaniel, pausing for a moment. "Professor Baum devised the system as a methodology for minimizing our susceptibility to bleeds. Historical homogenization, she called it. Things that left a mark on history had to be removed—"

"Because historic buildings get hit first," Vera said. Charlie was briefly startled that she knew that, before recalling that she had mentioned it, on their first meeting. She'd just assumed Vera's dismissive attitude at the time meant that she either wouldn't have heard or retained that much. "Someone's aiming at you, you take the bullseye off your chest?" She looked around, at the walls. "You lose the bright colors?"

"Thank you for the colorful, easy to understand, oversimplified to the point of inaccuracy metaphor," Nathaniel said. To his credit, he flinched only very slightly at the look Vera gave him in response. Charlie cut in.

"That explains the boring architecture, but where do the robots administering avant-garde Scientology-grade personality tests come in?"

"It was part of the homogenization. Individuals couldn't be allowed to stand out, either. Categories were a means to that end. 'People are like cats,' she said. 'Give them a box, and they'll go sit in it.'"

"Bullcrap," scoffed Wolfgang. "We rebel all the time. We're constantly—"

"Yes. Constantly," said Nathaniel. "In little, predictable ways, and then the classes with more devise ways to put you down, convinced that they deserve what they have, because why else would they have it? It all ticks along. Or at least...it did. Curfew used to just be a thing we gave Vagos so they'd occupy themselves breaking it, but then we had to *actually* enforce curfews because the tears got worse. We've used holograms to disguise the damage, but there's only so much we can do, and Professor Baum isn't here to work out what went wrong."

"Don't tell me. She teamed up with a witch to go find the source of the problem."

"...what?" Nathaniel said, his genial air of confidence slipping in the face of this apparent non-sequitur. "No. She said it was part of the homogenization. She had to disappear. No one stands out, no one makes history."

"Her office stands out plenty. Looks to me like she left herself something fancy to come back to," said Zepherin.

"Yes, well," Nathaniel said. "Professor Baum was not without her flaws. But lack of foresight was not among them. She mentioned someone with her face might come along."

"Did she say how she knew that? If you mention ferns, I'm going to throw...something at you," Vera said, looking around for something to throw.

Nathaniel's befuddlement returned. "Er, perhaps an easier to follow metaphor?"

Charlie waved him off. "It's a long story. Answer the question."

"She didn't say."

Vera flashed a smile with too many teeth. "Convenient."

"It is, actually," Nathaniel said, brightening slightly. Off everyone's confused glances, he added, "She instructed me to help you however we can."

It was a lonely piece of good news, but it was good news never-theless. Charlie, trying to get a read on Vera's reaction, tilted her head and eyed her sidelong. Vera's expression was muted, but their new friends' faces reflected suspicion. If they'd been fighting against a rigged system for this long, Charlie couldn't blame them.

"Your system's shit," Charlie said. "What's the guarantee your help won't be?"

"That's a *strong* wo—"

"I can think of stronger. In both official languages."

Nathaniel sat back in his ostentatiously decorated chair and visibly deflated. "What would you accept as a sign of our goodwill?"

"Let them have their prison break," Vera suggested. "A real one. Flip the table over and start a new...whatever this is. System. Game."

"You're talking about people's lives," Wolfgang butted in, in a tone Charlie couldn't help but dub Universal Teen.

"Hey! I'm not the bad guy here."

"No, you just look like her."

Vera sniffed. "Newer model. *Better* model."

"She's at zero systemic models of oppression designed," Charlie had to admit. *Although...* "As far as I know. Look, *we* can help *you* with the tears, at least a little. We have a way of closing them."

"It tends to strand people in the wrong place, forcing them to throw themselves on the mercy of brilliant, charismatic indus-trialists," said Vera, "but depending how smart you can get your robots, there may be a way around that."

"If robots worked, do you seriously think *I'd* be here?"

Charlie had the sudden thought of one of those robots wandering around Josephine's land of dragons and magic, trying to sort people into made-up classes. When the time came to program them, maybe she'd suggest getting them to bury themselves in a cave afterward or something. The ones they'd unknowingly sent to Vera's universe had been mistaken as litter. Who knew what they'd've been mistaken for in Ye Old Land of Magic.

"And in exchange...?" Nathaniel asked. Charlie thought about noting that a moment ago this help had been freely offered by mandate of his boss, but maybe it made him feel better to think of it as a deal. Then again, maybe she didn't care how he felt. She was still deciding when Vera started naming things.

"I'm raiding your stores, obviously. We have upgrades to make. Chuck, I'm gonna need to take apart one of your lures to see how it works, so I can make more."

"I *know* how it works and how to make—"

"Then we fix up the tear gear. Think of a better name for it than the tear gear. What else?"

"It has a name," Charlie muttered, but given that "the Coupler" wasn't a very good name, the defense was self-conscious at best. With more confidence, she added, "Holograms. If they can hide tears, they can make you look less like a marshmallow."

Vera looked all the world like she wanted to refute the idea that she resembled a marshmallow, but even her ego couldn't deny so plain a reality. Her mouth snapped shut before she pointed at Charlie. "Holograms. You heard the lady."

It took three days to put everything into place, which was three days longer than Charlie had wanted to spend in this particular universe. Josephine's place might have had the occasional dragon in need of punching, but magical folks, it turned out, had a much more developed sense of hospitality. Of course, it had helped that the Tower wasn't smack in the middle of a revolution led by the improbably named folk hero, Myriam Webster, and her followers, the TeeVees, of which Zepherin and Wolfgang counted themselves members.

The extra time had allowed them to search for Verity Thaum, but neither B-Tech's impressively dystopian security apparatus, nor the Velo's sensors, after some fine-tuning, turned up any leads. With Thaum herself a dead end, they changed tack, looked for a semi-stabilized tear the likes of which they'd seen at the Tower, but that hadn't yielded anything either. If Verity Thaum had passed through this universe, she was better at stealth than Vera, no doubt about it.

There wasn't much in the way of goodbyes, though Nathaniel, Zeph, and Wolfgang were there to see them off. Against her better judgment, Charlie instructed them to keep the tear to Josephine's land open as long as possible—just in case it was the only way Verity Thaum could get home again. God only knew Charlie would've appreciated the same were circumstances reversed.

They'd chosen another tear to make their departure. It was on the smaller end of the spectrum, about the size of an apple, and in the middle of an abandoned robot warehouse near the Fleuve. Unlike previous jumps, Charlie and Vera both appeared to be wearing the local fashion of slate gray, long-sleeved tunics with standing collars and fitted black trousers. Vera's shoes were a violent violet to compensate for the drab sartorial choices of their hosts, but Charlie's shoes were a boring white. The holograms were undeniably impressive, hiding not only the Velo and the Marshmallow but their accessories as well.

"Hopefully you have better luck with the robots than we did," Charlie said to Wolfgang, shaking his hand. "Try not to get stranded in the multiverse, all right?"

"I think we have enough on our plate right here at home," Zepherin assured her.

Nathaniel smiled a thin smile. He looked distinctly more ruffled than when they'd first met. His eyes had picked up a few bags. "Quite."

"Right. Enough jibber-jabbering," Vera said. She lowered her visor, though with the hologram on, it merely looked like she was adjusting her hair. "Let's roll."

The process of stabilizing a tear was almost old hat by now. Charlie's movements were sure and steady, as though she was squirting water into a clown's mouth at La Ronde, not trying to steady an instability in the fabric of reality that could tear them all apart, using about a fist's worth of metals and plastics.

It didn't help when she thought about it like that. Shoot the clown, win a prize. That was better. In short order, the tear had been smoothed out, and they were jumping through.

That part was a little less old hat, for all they'd done it the same number of times. It was just far harder to get used to, although the landings were getting better. This time, for instance, she didn't feel like throwing up.

That came just *after* landing. She had to fall down and nearly get stabbed first.

Chapter Eleven

_ THE SHIP IS ALSO _
NAMED VERITY

What the fuck?"

There was a lot to take in, which was unfortunate, seeing as they'd landed in the hold of some kind of old-fashioned ship, and most of that *lot* was water. The tear had eaten a hole through the ship's side and the ocean was rushing in, leaving them ankle-deep in water already. If that and closing an interdimensional threat weren't enough immediate problems to have, there was also a dirty looking asshole waving a sword in her face.

The categorization dystopia universe was looking better by the second.

Vera fell to her knees and retched into the water. No help there. The tear was more help. Literally, because Dirty Asshole's confused distress about the sudden appearance of the two of them and the hole in the side of the ship was probably why neither Charlie nor Vera had been more efficiently stabbed so far.

Which gave her a few seconds to adjust her outfit.

"BACK," Charlie barked, leveling a flintlock pistol at him. It was the Coupler in a holographic costume, hastily applied, and she wasn't entirely sure what the rest of her looked like because she'd just found the template that seemed closest to whatever the hell age of sail business this universe had going on and activated it. The hologram flickered, but a swift knock of her wrist against the side of the ship not currently being consumed by a hole in space-time righted the disguise.

Luckily, he recognized the gun and froze, backing up. A relief, since he could have decided that, at close quarters, a sword could beat a gun, and since her gun was not actually a gun and would do precisely nothing to him, he would've turned out to be right.

"I can fix that," she said, pointing across herself at the tear. Another set of boards snapped. The ship groaned alarmingly. The tear groaned alarmingly, a high-pitched drone of white noise because they were stuck in a ship's hold with the thing, absolutely too close.

"Then fix it!" he said, so at least he was a dirty looking asshole with correct priorities. She wasn't about to stop holding him at fake-gunpoint, though, using her free hand to pass her backpack, disguised as a leather satchel, to Vera, who had recovered enough to stumble to the side of the hold farthest from the tear, if not the guy with the sword. She looked a little like she'd been preparing to tackle him, actually. Again, Charlie wondered if the Marshmallow was sword-proof and had to conclude there was a fair chance whatever plastic it was made of actually was.

"I don't know about you," Vera said, taking the bag and fishing out an undisguised Einstein-Rosen Coupling, setting it and lobbing it into the tear. She barely had to move her arm to do it, and if she had she might have stuck her arm in the damn thing, so close were they stuck. "But I'm suddenly having a lot of thoughts about how much of the world is covered in water and the apparent lack of geographic consistency between universes. We should have asked for floaties. We should be jumping in some kind of boat."

"Tears like architecture," Charlie said, hesitating with her fake-gun still on Dirty but Reasonable Asshole. She was going to have to point her flint-not away from him to close up the tear, and that was probably going to give away that it wasn't actually the kind of gun it looked like. But the tear had to be closed. She swung the Coupler away and fired. The tear knit itself out of existence with an unsettling suction sound.

The situation did not improve. Where previously there'd been a hole in reality to suck up at least some of the water (and contaminate the rest in such a way that it wasn't water anymore, and therefore no longer traditionally filling space), the hole in reality was now just a hole in the boat. There was a lot more water rushing in. The whole ship listed, the timbers groaning more, water immediately rising past their ankles.

"You said you could fix it!" shouted Dirty Panicking Asshole, pulling his sword back to thrust. Charlie kicked him in the chest and then overbalanced, splashing backward. She'd trained for a lot of things and fought in a lot of places, but ankle—no, shit, shin—deep in water on a sinking ship wasn't one of them. She was having to adjust.

Still, the other guy had more experience and he'd fallen completely, so she was doing okay. "I don't want to fight you!" she said, wading over to him to try and stomp the sword out of his hand, only to miss with her view of the floor obscured by the flooding water, and the surface moving under her.

"I know, I know, you're just legally obligated! You could at least try less!" said Dirty Confusing Asshole.

"As my first act as president of the multiverse, I'm getting rid of all the weird confusing laws," Vera said, pinning the sword to the deck with her knee as she fell into a crouch. Charlie couldn't tell if it was a deliberate move or not. "Legally obligated?"

"Well, yeah," said Dirty Expounding Asshole. "I'm a pirate currently engaged in an attempt to gain illegal possession of goods contained upon a ship on which you are passengers. Not fighting me is a failure to uphold your duties as lawful persons in maritime transit. It's basic sea law. I'm just saying, you could just make the token effort."

"So we're clear," said Charlie, the absurdity of the situation demanding repetition instead of action, "you're saying we have to fight you."

"Or risk failing to uphold your duties, aye!" said Dirty Clarifying Asshole.

Charlie exchanged a bemused shrug with Vera. "Guess we gotta."

Vera shot her such a terrifyingly gleeful smile that Charlie couldn't help but return it. Between the dragon, the robots, and the pirate, it was almost like being a kid again—but with considerable more awareness of one's mortality.

The ship listed again to the side, and with it went their temporary advantage over their legally sworn enemy, DA. Using a large wooden crate for leverage, he sloshed to his feet and brandished his sword. He looked a little green.

"We should really invest in some swords!" Vera shouted, slowly getting back to her feet.

"I've got a better idea."

No matter her backpack's disguise, Charlie would be a piss-poor soldier if she didn't know where she kept her actual-facts gun. The weight of it was familiar in her hand, and while holographic leather wasn't waterproof, space-age polymer was, meaning they were officially in business. As Vera flopped out of the way of DA's wobbly thrust, Charlie took aim and fired at his knee. He yelped and dropped face-first into the water. He surfaced seconds later, mouth gaping like a fish as he sputtered.

"What in Moran's name is going on there?" yelled a suspiciously familiar voice from above deck. There was no time to entertain hiding. The keen gaze of Nathaniel Salt, Pirate, trapped them all where they stood. They made for a strange tableau: Dirty Asshole was still on his knees, surrounded by a pool of pinkening water; Charlie, dressed as a naval officer of unknown origin, was still aiming her gun; Vera, who had the presence of mind to flick her holosetting to a headless lobster mascot—*why the fuck was that even one of the presets?*—at the last possible second, stood with a wide stance to keep from toppling over.

Salt stared at Vera the longest. "Captain?"

They stood now on the deck of the *Verity Baum*, a ship belonging to the pirates that had been looting the merchant vessel in whose hold they'd landed. They were not on the merchant vessel partly because the vessel had sunk…well, mostly-to-entirely because the vessel had sunk. The pirate crew's reasons for taking them aboard ran secondary to that; they might have ended up on the pirate ship even if their arrival hadn't torn open the side of the merchant vessel. Possibly. It was hard to tell. Had the tear been there before they'd come through? Smaller, maybe? Charlie didn't know what the mechanics had been, and no one had been making scientific readings on account of being boarded by pirates—and also by being a merchant vessel not working on solving the collapse of universes.

Whatever the reason, they were certainly on the *Verity Baum* now, along with some of the merchant crew, although they were systematically bundled into rowboats at the angry behest of the pirate captain, who was still ranting about it.

"If we go around *sinking* ships, we can only rob them once. We let them go, we can rob them every time. Also, the Royal Navy doesn't decide we're a priority and send all of their ships to come fucking kill us and all of our friends."

She's swearing, Charlie thought vaguely, as she watched the captain stomp up and down the deck, following the length of one of the many ropes strung across it for support, pegleg making a solid thwack every time wood met wood. Pirates, like soldiers, swore more than industrialists, Charlie guessed. Maybe it was an optics thing. In spite of the tongue lashing, the pirate crew had lugged aboard an impressive amount of spoils, including an impossibly ornate chest that called to mind cursed treasure. It had certainly cursed the merchant vessel, at any rate.

Charlie turned to look at Vera, beside her, who appeared to be experiencing her own optics thing. One eye was twitching. It didn't look entirely involuntary. More as if she was experiencing complete physical indecision about whether to squeeze one eye closed. Eventually, she did, tilting her head to the side. She'd also lifted one foot just barely off the deck, although they weren't close enough for her to hold on to any of the ropes, so she kept putting it down again every time the ship listed. She'd abandoned the lobster getup, at least, though the hologram kept her in red, the type of outfit that might earn her a nickname like the Scarlet Siren if she stuck around this universe awhile. Charlie doubted they'd be welcome that long.

When she'd seen the name of the ship, she'd thought maybe she'd misheard Salt. Part of her had even wondered if, this time, maybe he'd meant *her*. That maybe this time it would be Captain Charlotte Chase of the *Verity Baum*.

It was not. It was Captain Verity Baum of the *Verity Baum*, now stomping over to get a better look at her younger self. She wasn't as old as the Verity from Charlie's world. Charlie figured her for maybe early forties, although the salt-weathered skin made it a trickier guess. She had an eye patch. Charlie was wondering if this was because she'd lost the eye, or if it was that thing about preserving low-light vision for going below decks.

"You're me," the captain announced, reaching them and striking up a position, legs wooden and real apart and one hand thrown up on the guideline.

"I'm Vera Baum," said Vera. "You're...Captain Verity Baum."

"*Queen* Verity Baum."

"But," Charlie butted in, because this had been bothering her, "your *ship* is named—"

"Yes."

"You named your ship after—"

"*Yes.*" The pirate sneered at Charlie. "You're not me. I don't need to know your story. You. What is—I don't have a sister. Do I have a secret sister? No. Does this have something to do with the whirlpools and cursed beasts following us around?"

"...probably," Vera said, now holding one hand up to her eye.

Captain-slash-Queen Verity reached up and flipped her eyepatch up.

It was not, it turned out, to preserve low light vision for going below decks.

"I don't recommend it," she said. "Salt, tell the cook I have guests for dinner. I'm dining with myself."

They were joined for dinner by First Mate Jack Watson, who still had both her legs and both her eyes, though the state of her teeth was best left undescribed. Like Queen Verity, her exact age was difficult to pin down, but Charlie guessed she couldn't have been much older than Josie back home. Judging by the deference afforded her, she was definitely older than the Queen. Neither of them seemed to recognize Charlie. Hell, they were barely paying her mind at all. Vera was, once again, the center of attention.

Which meant Charlie had first dibs on the food. It tasted like boiled shit warmed over, but there was protein and that was all that mattered. She'd eaten worse things.

"...and that's how we ended up here," Vera said, with a flourish of her fork, concluding the somewhat embellished saga of how they'd ended up on the merchant vessel in the first place. She stabbed what Charlie identified as some kind of pork product and got as far as putting it in her mouth before promptly spitting it clear across the table. It landed in a fishbowl containing a single goldfish and sunk to the bottom.

Queen Verity and Jack exchanged a glance.

"Landlubbers," Jack said.

"Aye."

"Pirates," Vera said in much the same tone and downed a glass of sour wine that left her lips puckering. "Bleh, seriously?" she asked the glass as though it were to blame, then set it down on the table. Some wine sloshed onto the incongruously clean tablecloth.

"Tell me more of the beast you encountered in the dead land," the Queen said more than asked. Charlie got the sense she didn't do a lot of asking.

"The parasites?"

Queen Verity waved a hand. "No, the other one."

"So when you said beasts..." Vera started.

"It's the first and only time I've seen anything like it," Charlie said, filling in the silence once it was clear Vera wasn't about to continue, lost in some unspoken thought. Finally, Charlie had the Queen's full attention. The intensity of her gaze wasn't in the least diminished by her missing eye. Charlie found herself sitting a little straighter in her chair, though she didn't think pirates cared all that much about posture. Then again, she didn't think anyone could be legally bound to swordfight, either. It was to her advantage to play it safe.

"The parasites are organic."

This was met by a slight narrowing of Queen Verity's eye. "Those'd be the squid, aye?"

"Aye. Not that we've ever caught one to make sure, but they act like an animal. We know what they eat."

"Reality itself, mostly," Vera said.

"Pretty much. But the Hound—it was different. Mechanical." Techno-organic, if she had to get fancy, but Charlie was aware of her audience. "We didn't get too close a look, honestly, but if I had to guess, I'd say someone made it."

"Made it?"

"Maybe to hunt the parasites? I'm not sure. Fuck, there's so much about the tears we don't understand, let alone what lives in them."

"But you've met one of these things," Vera prompted the Queen.

"Aye. The *Verity Baum* has run afoul of this machine creature, though 'twas the whirlpools we encountered first. There's been rumors around these parts since I was a lass, but I thought it a ghost story, the type of shit the Royal Navy sells its babes to keep them on the straight and narrow. Would that I could be so certain now.

"We were sailing to Île du Feu Rouge. I'd promised the crew some rest after a very successful bout of pirating, see, and we knew the locals well." The Queen flashed the table a lascivious grin. "Jack was especially popular, weren't you, Jack?"

Jack looked especially grim, truth be told, but she lifted her glass to take a sip of wine, her lips curling in a pained smile as she bowed her head and listened to her captain's tale.

"We arrived as the sun was setting, only the sky wasn't right. No pinks or oranges, but colorless. Wouldn't be right to call it gray, even. It was as though my eyes didn't wish to see the sky, nor the sea, nor the island itself. It was all simply…gone. We lingered. We were damned fools for it, but we lingered. Thought we might find a survivor or two who could explain what in damnation's name had happened. Instead, we found your hound and its friends."

"Then bye-bye eye, huh?" Vera said. The Queen snorted, and Charlie was suddenly very glad they shared a similar sense of humor.

"Aye," said the Queen. Dry.

"How did you survive?" Charlie asked. They hadn't lost any limbs, but that had been a near thing, and their technology far outpaced anything on the *Verity Baum*.

"A Navy ship happened 'pon us and assumed we were the ones who torched the isle," said Jack. "The beasts got caught in the crossfire."

"I never thought I'd be grateful for the Navy trying to kill me, but the bastards saved me life. The cannonball struck your hound as it was about to make its killing blow, distracted it long enough for the surgeon to slip me away below deck. Once we were some distance from the whirlpool, the...parasites, issit?" The word fit strangely in the Queen's mouth, which was a funny thing given that she shared it with a preeminent genius who could probably have spelled it in the womb. "The parasites were distraction enough, I s'pose." Her expression darkened.

Silence fell over the table, the four of them lost in their own thoughts. Someone had made the Hound to hunt the parasites, but who? It was a stopgap measure at best—the Hound couldn't close the tears, or at least had never been observed closing tears, but that train of thought was heading straight toward the hypothetical, and who would want to stick around to test such a hypothesis?

Well, Charlie, probably. Vera definitely. But maybe in a different universe, one where they had better weapons at hand than the flint-not and Charlie's favorite gun and swords and—

"Good talk," Vera said. She shot to her feet and clapped a hand to the Queen's shoulder.

A whip of thunder cracked through the ship. As one, they were thrown to the far side of the room. Charlie's nose connected with the wall and painted her face bloody. A shout sounded at the door, and Salt rushed in uninvited.

"Captain!"

Charlie felt more than saw Salt lift the Queen to her feet. Jack was already standing, her front stained with wine. Vera groaned from underneath Charlie, impatient hands pushing her away. Charlie rolled off and staggered as she righted herself.

"Fucking Christ."

"A whirlpool's appeared off the bow, Captain."

"Well, steer the bloody ship away, Salt!"

The Queen strode with her distinctive gait toward the upper deck. Salt and Jack followed after, overtaking her in the narrow stairwell. The *Verity Baum* was not the most accessible ship on the seven seas (assuming there were still seven seas in this universe). Charlie collected her backpack-cum-satchel from where it had fallen under the table and slung it over her shoulder. She took out the flint-not to make room for a few handfuls of dried pork. They were on the move already.

"You've got a little—" Vera said, pointing to her own face.

Charlie sniffled and immediately regretted it. She dragged her nose along the back of her forearm, smearing her holographic getup in blood. There wasn't any time to puzzle the physics of that, though she desperately wanted to.

Judging by Vera's curious expression, she wasn't alone.

"Later." Charlie waved a hand and followed the sounds of shouting above decks. As they came outside, she was immediately struck by the lack of smell—a real feat considering the state of her nose. Everything before had reeked of salt and fish and sweat and rum and the underside of a drunk vagrant's shoe, but all of that was gone, replaced by the ozone no-smell of a tear. A headache bloomed between her brows and stopped her in her tracks. Vera turned back to look at her, concern—if that's what it was—cut short when a crewman shoved a length of rope in her hands and told her to pull.

Above their heads was a choreographed dance of pirates swinging from ropes. Queen Verity stood solid at the center of it all, barking orders to her crew. Charlie ducked just in time to avoid a boot to the face, stumbling forward a few paces when the ship listed sharply.

The tear was nowhere in sight. They were in the middle of the ocean, no architecture to speak of. Tears liked architecture. They seemed to feed on history: the older, the better. There were few significant landmarks left on Charlie's Earth. But there was nothing here except the *Verity Baum* and a few rowboats containing the merchant vessel's crew dotting the horizon.

"Bow is the front," Charlie said, to no one in particular, although a crew-woman darted past her and made the universal face for "no duh." *Multiversal*, Charlie reminded herself. Stumbling a little against the violent roll of the ship, she took the stairs to the forecastle two at a time for half their length, and then one at a time when this proved to be a terrible idea under the conditions. At the top, the ship crested a wave and she skidded down to catch herself on the railing beside the figurehead. It was Mermaid Verity Baum. She'd seen it already. It was still weird.

Right now, she was staring more at the whirlpool. She didn't really know much about whirlpools. She knew a bit about waterspouts as they related to atmospheric dynamics because it had been one of the things they'd looked at when they were trying to model tear behavior, but strictly ocean-related phenomena had never come up.

She was practically certain the water around them wasn't meant to boil and steam, though. Tears were usually unnerving because of their hard to categorize appearance. It turned out when you could categorize them, it wasn't any better, because here the category was "horribly Biblical."

"VER-A!" Charlie hollered. Vera crashed into the side of her wooden mermaid doppelgänger a moment later. Charlie wasn't sure if she'd just gotten her sea legs, or if she'd already been on her way.

"Lemuria?" Vera said.

"Lemiwhat," Charlie said, "...ia."

"You know! Mythical underwater city."

"Atlantis?" Charlie said, squinting. She thought maybe she had better things to do than try to understand Vera's weird digressions, but she didn't exactly know how to steer or crew a ship, and that seemed about the only thing that'd do any good with a tear somewhere a tear shouldn't be because there wasn't any— "You think there's underwater architecture," she said.

"Not anymore I don't! That's last minute's theory. It'd be way too deep. The boat would be getting stuck on church steeples if it was high enough for...that," Vera said, gesturing at the whirlpool. They weren't exactly getting farther away, Charlie couldn't help but notice.

"But there is definitely a tear in that whirlpool, and close to the surface," Charlie said. Which completely tracked, because there was a huge disturbance in the water and also above the water where it was steaming. And there was the other thing.

"Because of the non-Euclidean cockroach squid now crawling out of it to eat us," Vera said.

"Because of the non-Euclidean cockroach squid now crawling out of it to eat us," Charlie agreed.

They weren't even swimming. It might have made the multi-faceted tentacles easier to bear if they were applying them to a recognizable form of propulsion. Instead, when they did twitch and beat, it wasn't in any relation to the water they were sometimes in, sometimes not, extradimensional limbs flailing absolutely heedless of the existence of sea and air both.

The water sure as shit wasn't slowing them down.

Charlie checked the load on the flint-not—she couldn't help thinking of it thus, even when she was prepping it for its original use, mostly because it was still holographically camouflaged. She couldn't spare the time to muddle about with the settings to reset it to default and had to hope that the projector was making it look loaded because it was actually loaded.

"And then what?" Vera said, looking at Charlie's hands. "That's, what, a couple of minutes? To sail—" They both looked at where they were in relation to the whirlpool, which was *oh fuck closer.* "—nowhere?"

"I don't know, I'm good with another couple of minutes of not being eaten, sort of in general! That'll buy time for maybe one of the supposed geniuses on board to come up with something!"

"I mean, is she a genius like me, or is she just a genius at being a pirate? Because I feel like—not the time," Vera concluded. Charlie felt this was a point in favor of "supposed," but Vera had gotten there in the end.

"Exactly."

Charlie took tentative aim at the bubbling water below and lowered her arm a moment later. The flint-not's range was good, but not that good. They needed to get even closer to stabilize the tear, but getting closer to the tear meant getting closer to the insurmountable swarm of tentacles licking at reality, and who the hell even knew what they'd be meeting on the other side once they made the jump to close it. More parasites? More water? Plan, plan, they needed a fucking plan.

Instead, they got an inhuman roar: the wounded growl of mechanical gears, the high pitch whine of metal on metal. Charlie's skin erupted into goosebumps, the hairs on the back of her neck and arms standing on end. Vera shuddered and looked to its source.

The Hound could fly. It surfaced from the sea and kept going, upward and onward even as Charlie kept expecting it to reach the apex of its jump and curve down, back toward the water, back at a safer distance. It didn't. It opened what passed for a mouth to unleash another shit-yourself-inspiring scream and whipped its body around with agility that belied its bulk to snag a cluster of tentacles from the air.

"It's missing a leg," Vera observed. Clinical. Like they were in a lab.

"It's missing a lot of legs."

"Not the non-Euclidean cockroach squid."

Charlie narrowed her eyes. It was hard to track its movements, but she could see it. The shape of the Hound suggested a body in need of four legs. There were only three.

"Eye for an eye. Leg for a leg."

"Definitely just a genius at being a pirate, then, right? Good. That's settled."

"Just. Shut up."

"CREW THE CANNONS!" This was not Vera. This was the other one, from the main deck. It was uncanny. It seemed like a sort of weird ventriloquism, except ventriloquists generally went with a completely different voice. Not just the same voice, but angrier and raspier.

"I take it back if she's made a cannon that shoots up...because unless she's built a cannon that shoots up, it's up there, and we're down here. And it's kind of working for us, anyway. It's killing the things we don't like that eat the world. Why would it even go after her in the first place?"

"Maybe it listened to you talk," Charlie mumbled, eyes still fixed on the Hound in the sky. One on one, it could take a parasite, evidently. If she could believe in the "enemy of my enemy" bit, that might have been encouraging. But she found it wasn't reassuring in the slightest.

Not just because there wasn't just one parasite. They were swarming. Some were in the air, going after the Hound, moving with more identifiable purpose than she'd ever seen. Probably because she'd never seen anything that was a legitimate threat to them before—they hadn't exactly stuck around to watch the show in the Wasteland. The Hound would tear one directly in its path to shreds, but then another would dart in, tendrils wrapping around a leg, and it howled.

Her eyes were watering. She wasn't entirely sure the parasite had latched on to any of the legs the Hound still had.

She threw herself backward, snagging Vera by the back of her holoshirt and hauling her away from the railing as the flicker in the air resolved itself into the first tentacles of a parasite swimming up and through the side of the ship. The wood peeled and splintered in random, disjointed places.

Vera put two fingers in her mouth and whistled, as if for a cab. She was backing up with Charlie, though, all the way to the stairs and down. Crazy, but not all-the-way stupid.

Wait, was she trying to get the Hound's attention? Charlie took all of that back. Complete fucking idiot.

A moment later, the Hound crashed into the parasite and straight through the deck into the cabin at the back of the ship where they'd been dining. Charlie refused to revise her sentiment. Big fish ate medium fish. It didn't make them friends with little fish.

"Scylla and Charybdis."

"Gesundheit," Vera said.

"No, no— It's a story. About being stuck between a rock and a hard place."

"Why didn't you just say that?"

"Because—"

BOOM!

The *Verity Baum* had cannons that shot up. Not directly up, because even if this Verity was a pirate and not a physicist, it didn't take degrees to puzzle out why that was a bad idea. But a lot up. The entire ship shuddered with the blast, but only Vera and Charlie lost their footing. The holograms might've dressed them up like sailors, but there was no faking sea legs. Charlie watched the trajectory of the cannonball, but as it approached its intended target, it became impossible to follow, the visual distortions of the parasites suggesting it simply disappeared without doing anything.

"Argue later, run now." Charlie hauled Vera away from the side of the ship, closer to the center, before the boards under their feet could collapse.

"We're on a boat!"

"A sinking boat, yes, I know. I know."

She needed to work the problem, but her thoughts were stuck in a loop. She was dimly aware of her heart racing, of the foreign weight of panic pressing down on her chest. They needed to get closer to the tear to stabilize and close it, but they were on a sinking ship. They needed to make sure a bunch of pirates didn't die in the jaws of a technological monstrosity but had no effective weapons save for a cannon that, yes, shot mostly up. She needed to get home and hug her parents and her Verity and save her world. She needed, she needed, she needed—

"—are you even listening?"

Vera was snapping her fingers in front of Charlie's face. She'd lost time. Queen Verity was standing in front of them now, though her attention was understandably divided between the two of them, her crew, and what her understanding of the situation could only describe as "beasts from hell."

Charlie was in no place to disagree with that description.

"What?"

Vera made a gesture that roughly translated to "can you believe I have to work with this?"

"We're jumping."

"But the—"

"Let us handle the beasts, lass," said the Queen.

"Oh, cool. The parasite-killing swords were stashed below, then, because I didn't—"

"Is this helping?" demanded the Queen. Charlie wondered if constantly being at sea somehow made this Verity more stable. Or, no, her own might have had little patience for that. *Christ, when did* Vera *become the default? If it weren't for literally every other fucking thing currently happening, I'd be scared.*

"If you engage them, they'll just tear you apart," Charlie said. "That Hound is the only thing I've seen hurt them, aside from—"

"There's an aside from?" said Vera, looking up from where she'd removed a lure from Charlie's backpack-turned-satchel.

"We could hurt one or two if we got them when they were solidly phased with our reality. Eating something, usually. But hurting them just attracts more. They eat each other."

Vera and the Queen looked at each other. They shrugged opposite shoulders in unison.

"Hurt a couple, have them eat each other, give you a chance to close the whirlpool threatening to eat my fucking ship."

"Strap these to the cannonballs," Charlie said, hurriedly thrusting lures at the Queen. It was a fair amount of their supply, and who knew if there'd be the resources to make more in the universes ahead, but if they were dead before they got there it wouldn't matter. "They'll think it's food."

"We'll fire it straight down their gullets," said the Queen, passing them off to a crew member, "and you into the eye of that whirlpool. Get in the boat."

Vera and Charlie turned to look at the rowboat. As they did, the ship violently rocked, setting it swinging in its rigging to smash against the side. It didn't break. It didn't look especially whirlpool proof, either. It barely looked waterproof.

"This is the worst fucking plan we've ever had, and you once punched a dragon," Charlie said, starting toward it. The ship rocked again, and she only just caught herself on a rope. One of the ones strung about for Queen Verity, because she only had one leg. Which was an apt summation of Charlie's balance at present.

They reached the rowboat at the same time as the first lure-equipped cannonball went up. Charlie watched as one of the parasites, two, darted, faded into near-complete focus in its path—

Only for more legs than it currently possessed to be shredded from it by a glancing impact. Immediately, the second turned on it, tentacles penetrating the remains, threading right through. Then another was there, and then another, both diverting from their fight with the Hound and coming from seemingly nowhere.

Another cannonball careened through the now teeming mass, sending them further into a frenzy.

"Hey, that's worki—" said Charlie.

The Hound landed directly on the ship, red eyes laser-focused on Vera. Not literally, Charlie hoped. If it had lasers this would go very badly. The crew had swung them out over the ocean but had only lowered them a few feet. They hadn't dropped below the level of the deck yet.

"Down, down, down," Charlie said. She wanted to scramble somewhere. The rowboat did not have any room for scrambling. Maybe if she shot it with a lure, the parasites would descend on it, and they'd go back to fighting?

Only, it would be on the deck of the ship, which would mean the ship would begin coming apart, and everyone aboard would be eaten.

Only, they'd just handed most of their lures over, and she didn't have one loaded. She'd have to get one out of the bag, get it into the gun, fire, hope the parasites reached the Hound before it reached them—

Which wasn't going to happen, because it had charged. Biomechanical jaws wide with a distinctly non-mechanical, biological slathering of mucus. She could see right down its throat. There were lights along it. It was not a pathway she felt needed guiding lighting.

It covered the distance between them in the time that it took for Vera to throw her hands up in absolute futility, and in less time than Charlie had to shove her out of the way.

A cannonball rammed it out of its path and into the ship, boards splintering apart. Charlie had time to look and see a cannon, a rope hurriedly whipped around it, evidently wrenched around to fire straight across and into the ship. And, following the rope, from up where it crossed the mast and back down to the loose end, Queen Verity swinging down into that same hole.

"It's not her you have business with, beast!"

The rowboat hit the water, was immediately thrown up against the hull of the *Verity*, boards scraping and making noises Charlie did not know that rowboats were meant to make. But a moment later the motion spun them away and past, the ship passing beyond them, leaving them only assailed by the pull of the whirlpool. Which was where they wanted to go.

Theoretically.

Charlie prepared the Einstein-Rosen Coupling.

"What do you think the chances are this spits us out on land?" Vera said.

"Why would you bring that up now?" Charlie snapped, starting to stand up in the bow of the rowboat and nearly tumbling out. Instead, she inched forward and took up a position with her stomach resting on the front end of the boat, hand thrust forward, as if assigning herself the duty of figurehead.

This was going to be a complete shithouse of a shot, and she wasn't going to be able to watch their six.

"Watch our six," she said.

"Our six what?"

"Is anything about to eat us?"

"Everything is eating everything but us," Vera said. "Except the whirlpool, which—here comes the fun part."

The rowboat tipped into the maw of the whirlpool. Charlie fired as the boat tilted, spun. Flipped and began to come apart, sending them helplessly into the tear.

It was not the fun part.

Chapter Twelve

— CARS CHASING DOGS —

Charlie narrowly dodged the smoldering remains of the rowboat as the tear spat it out. There wasn't much left of it to dodge. The wooden hull had splintered and twisted, leaving behind only a bleached, gnarled husk that would've still hurt if it had landed on her head instead of a few inches next to it. On her other side, Vera was vomiting, the wet splatter of sick hitting metal a sign she'd managed to open her visor in time. Charlie swallowed her own bile and blinked up at an impossibly blue sky, her view unimpeded by the tear.

It was much smaller on this side, barely visible to the naked eye, a micro tear a few feet above her head according to the confusing string of stats the Velo's HUD flickered across her line of vision, though it wasn't going to stay a micro tear for long, already growing. Groaning, she sat up, a wave of vertigo catching her unaware when she realized they hadn't landed on the ground. They were on a raised platform of some sort, about ten feet off the pavement below, and to one side was a familiar stretch of concrete wall, the kind that dampened the sound of traffic from the highway.

The platform lurched. In rapid succession: a car door opening and slamming shut; feet on the ground; horns honking; a gun cocking.

Not a platform.

"Oh, f—"

"Get down from there!"

"In a minute," Charlie grumbled from atop the armored truck. Vera moaned unintelligibly. Her face was a worrying shade of green. They'd need to look into that, provided they didn't get fucking shot first.

Charlie fished an Einstein-Rosen Coupling from her backpack, still disguised as a leather satchel, but the sudden movement wasn't appreciated by the guard—guards, plural, fuck, she wasn't seeing double—on the ground. A warning shot went wide. She was safe in the Velo so long as her cowl was deployed, but the Marshmallow wasn't as sure a bet. They didn't need this right now. She was shivering with adrenaline, heart still racing from their last near-death experience, the anxiety of what else could come through that tear a heavy weight on her mind, numbing her to the smaller issue of Guards 1 and 2 waving guns around. She got onto her knees, positioned herself between the guards and Vera, holding the Coupling like a grenade.

The tear was widening, another reality spilling into this one, and the guards, though uncomprehending, took note. They backed off a step, guns wavering. Their eyes were comically round. The rows of cars stopped behind the truck tried, in vain, to back away. A few more impatient drivers simply got out of their cars and ran.

"I can fix that," Charlie said, jutting her chin toward the tear. She needn't have bothered. They weren't looking at her anyway, eyes stuck on the hole in space-time. Good. She took out the flint-not. "Give me a minute to fix that, and I'll—"

The next shot landed, punching Charlie in the chest. She flashed Guard 1 an irritated look.

"Hey! What the fuck—" She peered down at Guard 1's uniform to make out her name, printed in white block letters over her front pocket, while blindly *thwhacking* the holosetting dial with the palm of her hand until the image flickered and faded. The flint-not was no more, though the Coupler was still gun-shaped. "—Lafleur?"

Lafleur's partner, a six-foot giant ironically named Little, fired this time. His shot went wide, ricocheting off a lamppost. Charlie fought the instinct to duck.

"I said—"

Charlie's tirade was cut short by roaring engines and a crash in the distance. From her vantage, she watched as cars made futile attempts to peel away from the main road, trying to divert themselves onto non-existent shoulders to get out of the way of an onslaught of slick jewel-toned sports cars driving well past the speed limit and showing no intention of stopping.

"—get back in the fucking truck and drive!"

There was a split-second of hesitation, but a small army of cars was an easier danger to understand than a shapeshifting gun and two assholes dressed up like pirates. The guards lowered their weapons and scrambled back in the cab, the truck shifting into gear moments later. Lafleur gunned the gas and Charlie grabbed hold of Vera, in danger of slipping off the edge.

Though falling off the back of a truck was probably safer at this point. The tear was a foot across now, eating away at the heavy cement wall. A sign designating the route 134 hung from the traffic lights.

"Oh, thawassabaddone," Vera said. "Th'ground still hasn't stopped moving."

"No, we're—hold on," Charlie said. She couldn't spare the attention. The truck was moving now, which meant they were going to start getting farther away from the tear. But if she let go of Vera and she slipped, she was going to get run over by one of the sports cars, which were distinctly not respecting the road rules or even just the basic idea that you didn't drive full speed through congested traffic.

Charlie spared a moment's attention. Vera was holding on, although Charlie wasn't one hundred percent sure about her grip. She tapped one of Vera's boots and engaged the magnet and hoped that'd do it.

She looked back up. The security guard was just motoring now as if this truck was going to outrun the absurd sports cars tearing down the road toward them. The distance between Charlie and the tear had grown alarmingly. She wound back and pitched the Einstein-Rosen Coupling like a baseball, then immediately dropped to lie flat, bracing herself to aim the Coupler.

They'd never tested the distance on it. There'd been no real way to test the distance on it, and also they hadn't really anticipated that she'd be closing the tear in the middle of a car chase. She lined it up. Squeezed the trigger.

The truck veered, yanked to the side by a sudden new force. Charlie seized the back of the truck with one hand and just managed to catch the lip of the roof to the side with one foot. She looked down to see that there was now a metal hook in one of the back doors. A steel cable ran from it to a bright blue sports car.

She looked back. Vera had canted over the edge, prevented from sliding entirely over the side by one boot. She threw up again, which seemed fair.

Well, now Charlie knew what to look out for. A couple of seconds, and while the truck was moving at what seemed like a ridiculous pace for an armored truck, she could make the shot. It would be fi—

The Hound tore through, coalescing into the world in one long bound, landing in front of a bright green sports car that was lining up a shot with another grappling hook mounted on the side. The car veered off, the two running side by side. Charlie could just make out the driver's head—was that Wolfgang, from the categorization dystopia? A sports car joyriding version of him, at least—snapping back between the car-sized biomechanical dog-thing that had just jumped from literally nowhere and the road. Inexplicable robodog, road full of potential crashes, inexplicable robodog, crashes.

Charlie pushed off the roof of the truck with her hands, getting her feet under her, crouching long enough to squeeze the trigger and experience the faintest relief as the tear knit itself out of existence. At least there wouldn't also be parasites to deal with.

Only some criminals in fast cars and a biomechanical death machine bent on killing Vera.

She ran to the front of the truck, grasped the side of the cab, and dropped down to shout at the window. "PLEASE GO FASTER."

It was probably a dumb request. This thing was already somehow traveling at the same pace as the high-performance sports cars surrounding it. The guard in the passenger seat shook his gun at her but thankfully didn't fire, because of the bulletproof glass. She was also bulletproof with the cowl up, but that didn't mean a bullet to the face at point-blank range wasn't going to have some unpleasant side effects.

She hauled herself back on the roof of the truck.

"—bringing a robot dog, you have to tell me."

It was a male voice, and it was in her ear. She had time to process that it was the Velo picking up comms chatter before the Hound landed on the back of the truck. It looked at her, dismissed her, and honed in on Vera, who had just scrambled her way back to what had been the relative security of the center of the truck's roof. Except now it was probably the most dangerous spot in this whole dimension.

"It's not our robot dog!" Charlie said.

"Well, it's stealing our score."

The Hound opened its mouth, muscles tensed and servos shifted to lunge.

A grappling hook smacked into its side, cable snapping taut and dragging it off the roof.

"Like hell it—awww, shit, I think I made it mad!"

Wolfgang was probably understating it. The Hound hit the ground, metal claws striking sparks as momentum carried it forward. It dug in, twisted, turning itself around, then flung itself at the car.

Charlie felt terrible. He hadn't been trying to help, maybe, but he had, and now he was going to get torn apart for it.

"Oh, I definitely made it mad, guys, guys, it is—"

"JUMP!"

Not Charlie yelling, or even thinking, but a stranger's voice cutting through her comms. This alternative plan just meant instead he was going to smear himself over the asphalt trying to avoid being torn apart. That wasn't exactly—

The Hound hit the hood of the car, the whole thing beginning to wrap itself around it. As it did so, Wolfgang popped up through the sunroof, kicked off and, with the transferred momentum, jumped over the Hound, traveling at the full speed of the car. In the grip of gravity. About to meet the road at that speed. Smear.

A flash of yellow caught Charlie's eye. It was, as she shifted her head, the detachable roof of a convertible, skidding onto the road from who knows where, the convertible itself unerringly positioning itself under Wolfgang's fall, fishtailing in such a pronounced fashion that the backseat was parallel with his falling body.

He landed in it. Entirely. In the absolutely tiny back seat that had to be precisely his size or smaller. The yellow car straightened out.

"No fucking way," Charlie said.

"Way," said a female voice in her ear. Charlie half-expected it to be this universe's answer to Verity Baum, reimagined as some hotshot stunt driving bank robber, but the register was all wrong. The yellow car's driver had a mane of impractically long black hair, dark skin, and, even at a distance, the type of brilliant white teeth that could sell a lot of toothpaste.

Not that there was a lot of distance. The driver was almost overtaking the (improbably fast) armored truck. Was she going to jump? Have Wolfgang take the wheel so she could steal whatever the fuck was so valuable from the truck? Charlie almost wanted to see that. This universe treated physics the way an action movie did: some rules may not apply.

But Car Lady didn't perform some physics-defying stunt, unless one counted driving with one hand to dramatically lower her sunglasses with the other, as though Charlie was sitting right next to her instead of crouching on top of a moving vehicle.

They made eye contact. The HUD zoomed in on Car Lady's face; she was no one Charlie recognized. Before she had a chance to assign the woman a charming sobriquet, the HUD, of its own accord, connected to the local 5G network. That was different. The damn thing had been on the fritz since the very first jump, and now here it was, displaying Loa Ram's lengthy police record.

Meanwhile, the holosetting was still stuck on fucking pirate.

"Listen, lady," Loa said, "I don't know who you are, or where you came from, but you're standing on top of our stuff."

"Charlie Chase, you wouldn't believe me if I told you, and I couldn't give a rat's ass about this truck," said Charlie in a rush. The Hound could navigate realities with the same facility as parasites. It wouldn't be put off by a car accident for long. She needed to get Vera off this truck and somewhere safe, but Lafleur was gunning for employee of the month with her evasive driving, and the Car Crew seemed unlikely to slow down.

The blue car still had its hook in the truck. If they kept enough tension in the rope, maybe they could climb from the truck to the car and steal the car—it was probably stolen in the first place, no one drove like that if they had to pay insurance. Then again, if this universe ran on cartoon physics, maybe they could just jump from the truck and they'd be all right and not sitting ducks for the murderous robot.

I'm starting to think like Vera. That was right up there with "punch a dragon in the face."

Then again, punching a dragon had—

"Shit. *Shit shit shit.*"

"I don't like the sound of that!" said the Miraculously Alive Wolfgang, while Charlie's line of vision flashed red, the HUD lighting up with warnings of a rapidly growing tear that came out of fucking nowhere.

Whipping her head toward the source, her stomach dropped when she saw it: the Jacques Cartier bridge. It was daytime, meaning it wasn't lit up like a Christmas tree, and it was early enough in the afternoon to be between rush hours. Traffic was circulating at a decent clip by Montreal standards, but if that tear got any bigger, it would endanger the structural integrity of an already notoriously structurally unsound bridge and likely kill everyone on it.

Not to mention it'd be parasite bait if they couldn't stabilize it.

Not to mention the Hound had recovered from its car accident.

Not to mention a passenger from the blue car, Bernard "Burn" Kim, a Korean guy with a ponytail and a death wish, was totally stealing her terrible climb-the-rope plan to get onto the armored truck.

"GET BACK IN THE FUCKING CAR."

He looked at her with a politely stunned expression, as though he couldn't quite believe someone would take issue with a death-defying stunt when he was minding his own business, and Charlie resisted the urge to bang her head against something.

"YES, YOU. BACK."

"Lady, I got a job to—"

"Did you see the murderous robotic dog? Did you see it? Did you see the fucking robot murderdog?"

"I don't know if I believe it, but I sure as hell saw it."

"Well, it's going to be back any second now, and if you are on a goddamn cable between a car and a truck you will definitely die and probably will die anyway because we're fucked. I don't see any way to—"

This wasn't true. She kind of did. It was right there, in front of them, about to rip the bridge apart. She just didn't want to say it, or even think it, really.

"Car. Tear," Vera groaned, apparently conscious enough to have terrible ideas and less compunction about saying them out loud.

"You mean that freaky looking wavy patch in the air?"

"Shit, that looks like some kind of space-time breach," said the driver of the red car, a Haitian guy named Casim Dupont, which Charlie found a more ludicrous event than the jumping out of the crashing car into another car thing.

"Charlie'll steal your thing if you do our thing," groaned Vera.

"I'll steal your thing if you do our thing. If you…"

"Yeah, I got it," said Loa. "Burn, quit hanging around. Cas, someone's gotta be the stick."

"Aw, hell no, Wolfgang can't be the stick? Wolfgang makes a great stick!"

"Wolfgang already trashed his car. Now line that dog up for me."

The cars were already changing position, swinging into a new formation. It was like they'd practiced it, except they could not possibly have practiced it. Within moments, the yellow car had swung off who-knew-where, and a red car had swung into position behind them. The blue car, driven by Adi Pinto, remained where it was, cable still stretched.

The stolen goods had to go somewhere, Charlie supposed. Which meant she now had to steal them. Which she definitely had not practiced. Last time she'd been down there, she'd gotten shot in the face. She had to hope things would go better this time.

What the hell had she just promised to steal, anyway? It was an armored truck, and they had a five-person team in place to rob it. There was no way in hell she could send bags full of money over the cable while they were racing down a fucking highway toward a bridge that might collapse. How was she even going to open the—

The rear door of the truck swung open with a deafening clang. Off Charlie's shocked expression, Vera gave a slight shrug, made awkward by the fact she was clinging to the roof of a speeding truck and looked as though she was about to pass out at any second.

"Magnets."

"Magnets?!"

"Magnets."

With no more time to spare arguing, Charlie trusted the explanation at face value: Vera picked the lock of an armored car with magnets because apparently, that's just how shit fucking worked in this universe, no matter how absurd. Lowering herself to her knees, Charlie gripped the edge of the roof and swung herself inside the truck. She landed in a crouch in the middle of the surprisingly empty floor, swaying a little as the truck took a curve. The cable between the truck and Adi's car groaned from the strain, but Burn was already clear, having mercifully listened to Loa's order.

"What the fuck am I looking for?" Charlie wondered aloud when large bags of money failed to materialize.

"There should be a briefcase," said Casim.

"You're doing all of this for a briefcase?"

"Nah, we're doing all of this for what's in it."

"You can't even fit that much money in a briefcase," Charlie grumbled.

"We're not after money."

"No shit."

The briefcase was secured to the floor by a single strap and made of an alloy the HUD couldn't immediately place. Charlie tugged the case free and stepped back toward the door.

The Hound was gaining on them.

"You get this, you help us with that, remember?" she said, hefting it to throw. Holding it back until they'd actually gotten rid of the Hound wasn't going to do any good. Charlie couldn't risk them holding out until delivery, which meant she had to risk them just driving off once they had it.

"We got it. Just slide it here."

Charlie shrugged, hung the briefcase off a hook at the end of the grappling hook attached to the truck, and gave it a push. It seemed, for a moment, a little anticlimactic.

Then the Hound finished catching up. It landed with enough force to shear through a layer of asphalt in the spot the blue car had just been. But it wasn't, because it had skidded into a handbrake turn and released the grapple. Charlie saw the briefcase disappear into the open window a moment before it was obscured by the sudden presence of the Hound.

It skidded, but even as it did so, it was positioning itself to leap.

The red car sideswiped it, then peeled off, the Hound now in pursuit. It didn't like Veritys, but apparently, it liked things that tried to hurt it less.

Charlie hauled herself back onto the roof of the truck to watch them go past, heading for the bridge, yellow car swerving into position behind. The Hound leaped from car to car, gaining height, throwing itself into a high arc.

The bridge ahead started to collapse.

Loa changed lanes, pegged the side of the highway sound barrier with the grappling hook, immediately winding it in, putting the car up high enough on one side that it could ramp off the side of a truck, go airborne. It was still turning, so that when it struck the Hound in mid-air it was almost sideways, with Loa pulling herself out the driver's side window and running down the side of the car to throw herself clear—

—through the window of an orange car Charlie hadn't even been tracking, that had come from somewhere to jump on a perpendicular course, putting it right in front of where Loa was jumping. Of course. That seemed reasonable. That was a thing that happened.

The Hound and car disappeared into the tear. The armored car came to a screeching halt before it reached the collapsing bridge, sending Charlie stumbling forward a couple of steps, swaying at the very front as she rummaged for an Einstein-Rosen Coupling. She threw it into the tear, stabilized it.

She looked over and assessed Vera's chances of surviving another trip through a tear right now. It seemed about as likely... as, well, literally anything involving a car that had just happened, but they probably wouldn't be landing in a magic car universe on the other side, so she couldn't risk it.

Which was why they were still there when the cops arrived.

"I refuse to believe all you have is food poisoning."

The doctors had left, leaving Vera and Charlie alone in their hospital room, handcuffed to their respective hospital beds. A pair of cops were posted outside the door, just in case they decided to stage the kind of daring stunt that had landed them in this mess in the first place. The privacy curtain separating the two beds was partially open, just enough that Charlie could get a glimpse of Vera through the gap. They were wearing identical baby blue hospital gowns (which had been a headache—not one of the cops had understood why the hell Vera's inexplicable pirate outfit needed a handful of guys to carry it and Charlie, by being the only one conscious at the time, bore the brunt of their questioning). There was a very good chance they'd be trading the gowns in for orange jumpsuits soon. Assuming they were even orange in this universe.

"Right? Who'd have thought pirates wouldn't meet health and safety codes," Vera replied, looking somewhat better than she had magnetized on top of an armored truck, but nowhere near one hundred percent.

"Vera."

"What?"

Charlie frowned. "You were barely conscious after that last jump."

"It was a bad one. There was a murderous robot dog. You were there."

"Right, I was there, meaning I saw how you—"

"Came up with another plan to save the day? You're welcome."

"I was gonna go with 'had to be stuck onto an armored truck like Junior's macaroni art,' but sure, let's go with your phrasing."

"Really, if you think about it, we should be getting sick more often."

"I have thought it about it. My whole team thought about it. You have no idea the amount of bioengineered crap I got put in me before I was deemed travel safe," said Charlie. "Bioengineered crap you don't have, which is why this whole food poisoning angle is a little tough to—"

"They said more tests were required, didn't they?" Vera snapped. Her gaze was fixed pointedly at the ceiling, the heart monitor beeping a staccato misstep as her pulse spiked, then settled.

"—swallow," Charlie finished, then cleared her throat, awkwardly. "I'm just saying…"

But any further show of concern for Vera's wellbeing was put on hold by the sudden arrival of a fresh set of police officers, moving with the kind of punctuated impatience that signaled they were there to collect, not guard, a couple of would-be thieves. Charlie, ignoring the cuff digging into her wrist, sat a little straighter in the bed.

"...already signed the paperwork," the taller of the two officers was saying. It was Zepherin, from the categorization dystopia, but a version that clearly spent a lot more time drinking protein shakes and hitting the gym. He was built like a brick house and had a shaved head that could put him anywhere between the ages of twenty and forty, unlike the older mentor type they'd run into before.

"We weren't expecting you dee-oh-jay types 'til tomorrow," replied Officer Chronopolous. He was just a rookie and had fumbled through the questioning earlier. Charlie hadn't held it against him, and in return, he'd gotten her some jello.

"The case was expedited," said the shorter officer, glancing up from a very official-looking memo pad to make eye contact with Charlie.

It was Wolfgang.

Maybe there was honor among thieves.

"Honor among thieves, y'know?" said Burn, some time later. They'd been escorted out of the hospital under the false auspices of Zeph and Wolfgang, to a remarkably understated getaway vehicle that nonetheless drove like it was trying to jump twelve school buses. Now they were at the Car Crew's Car Headquarters, where exactly none of the cars were understated. (The getaway van was parked outside. Vera had nodded approvingly and pointed out it would ruin the aesthetic.)

"Yeah, you did us a solid. Got us our score and helped deal with that dog thing that showed up to wreck our score."

Charlie shot Vera a warning look. Vera was already looking in her direction, eyebrows raised, the picture of innocence. Or at least the picture next to innocence, marked "antonyms."

"Where'd you get your toys, anyway?"

They'd also retrieved all of Vera and Charlie's gear. Charlie wasn't sure how they'd accomplished that. She assumed cars, somehow.

"Ah, well—"

"Another dimension," Vera said. They all turned to look at her, Charlie included. Although, in retrospect, what the hell else was she going to run with? They'd all seen the giant mechanical horrordog, and at least two tears. They laid it out for their new friends.

"So when one of these things opens…someone's gotta get on that shit, fast, shut it down."

"By going through it. To somewhere else entirely."

"Hell, we're always saying we could do with a vacation. Any way to pick where we end up? I could go for a beach and ladies dimension, y'know?"

"If I could pick the beach and ladies dimension, I would be in the beach and ladies dimension," Vera said. "I mean, I can't say I wouldn't have stopped here first. Those are some nice cars."

The Car Crew preened a little.

"It's also more complicated than just going through it," Charlie felt compelled to add. She glanced pointedly at Vera. "There can be…*side effects.*"

"Side effects?" asked Loa, a woman Charlie had seen jump out of a speeding car, through the window of *another* speeding car, and land without a scratch in the correct seat, all while dodging an evil robot dog and a fucking tear in the fabric of reality.

Charlie rethought her stance. Caution clearly didn't apply to these people. "Which one of you is the tech person?"

"You sent the package?"

"It'll get where it needs to go," Cas the Tech Person confirmed. The package in question was a full-detailed report on everything Charlie knew about tears, parasites, and the Hound, and included a new tear tech prototype that Vera, during her weeklong convalescence, had cooked up for this world's version of the UN.

The lady was just physically incapable of sitting still and doing nothing. Charlie was almost glad to be getting on the metaphorical road again, if only to stop Vera's bellyaching about needing to take a fucking rest day. But with the Hound on their scent, staying in one universe for this long was already a calculated risk, a fact Vera was keen to point out every time Charlie implored her to "please just take a goddamned nap, Christ, Vera."

"Then until next time," Charlie said, briefly clasping Cas's hand before he headed off, giving Vera a nod in goodbye. It was a bit of interdimensional travel humor, maybe. Maybe they'd end up in the same universe again someday since the Car Crew thought the whole exercise would be a vacation, or maybe she'd just see someone with his face. The evidence so far pointed to the latter.

The tear situation in Carverse was further along than Vera's but not near the catastrophic levels of Charlie's own. They were small enough still to evade detection by the masses, more conspiracy theory than actual threat. Nevertheless, they didn't have to wait long for another microtear to show up in Montreal.

The Baum family were, evidently, bankers instead of celebrity scientists in this world, and Charlie was somehow unsurprised that the next tear had opened inside one of Baum Banks' vaults. If all roads lead to Rome, then all tears lead to Verity. Naturally, the Car Crew wanted to use cars to access the tear, but Charlie vetoed the idea. They needed something a little less high profile, considering the last heist brought down a fucking bridge.

Which meant going with Vera's plan of staging a bank robbery. Charlie already regretted the plan, but, as she was forced to acknowledge, there really were only so many ways to see a high-security vault. Verity existed in this world, they'd learned, but she wasn't an adult. A simple impersonation was a no-go.

They were back in the Velo and Marshmallow, disguises set to something that passed for inconspicuous in this world. Their getaway crew was sitting out front in a different nondescript van, just in case the Hound made a reappearance. If anyone else had offered to help out, Charlie would've declined, but the Car Crew had some kind of improbable immunity to injury.

"Ready?"

Vera nodded. Charlie wasn't sure what part of the Marshmallow was disguised, but whatever the hell Vera was holding in her hands looked like a gun.

They tugged down their balaclavas and strode into the bank.

"Nobody move," Charlie said. "This is a robbery."

Nobody stopped moving. Maybe they should've gone with the cars.

"You need more oomph," Vera suggested out of the corner of her mouth.

Charlie sighed, unholstered the Browning, and shot a round into the wall.

"This is a ROBBERY," she shouted.

Unsuspecting patrons looked up as plaster snowed down on their hair and shoulders. At least a few of them had stopped moving, but most were murmuring to each other. One man was actively trying to look around Vera and Charlie.

"What?" Charlie snapped.

"But where's the cool car?"

"Oh, for fuck's sake."

They couldn't get out of there soon enough.

Chapter Thirteen

— TEAM CHARITY —

The last few jumps had been random, out of necessity. Or, at least, the first had, because there'd been that whole whirlpool situation, and then things had been too chaotic and dangerous to consider taking a trip backward if such a thing were even possible. Which meant they had no idea if Verity Thaum, who they had been theoretically following, had come this way. Their paths had probably diverged from the start. The dystopia universe was littered with tears. Which meant they had no lead, and the Hound was on their trail. They could hope that every jump made it harder for the thing to track them down, but there was no way to tell. Maybe every jump gave it another chance to pick up the trail. Either way, they couldn't stay in one spot for too long, since then it was guaranteed to catch up with them.

Problem was, Vera couldn't take too many jumps in a row. Charlie's best guess was that the Marshmallow was insulating her enough for her to simply not die, but it still did a number on her constitution. They needed to space them out.

So to speak. Space was sort of the operative word. This latest stop on their interdimensional road trip was something straight out of a space opera. Technicolor aliens of all shapes and sizes walked through the halls of the Montreal Spaceport, a towering building that housed, according to the digital placards at the front entrance, one of the world's first and most sophisticated space elevators.

Given Dr. Verity Baum was listed prominently as the port's chief engineer, Charlie was unsure how much of the sophisticated claim was personal ego at play, but the building, stretching up as far as the eye could see, certainly defied simple imagination. Parts of the exterior seemed more beanstalk than building, and Charlie wondered if her own city might have adopted a similar architectural style had the tears not ravaged through the Old Port. Urban farming had been gaining traction for decades, and this was the same concept taken to the extreme: kilometers of green (though still not the right green) bracketed by levels of floor-to-ceiling windows. Swarms of Flying Personalized Vehicles—FPVs, the locals called them, though Charlie overheard a grumpy old man cursing them as "those frogging faps buzzing around"—were docked on every other floor, and Charlie's throttle-thumb itched to take one for a spin. She'd been eying a particularly sleek model for the past hour. Painted candy apple red with chrome accents, the fap's angular, agile frame called to mind a wasp. It was roughly the size of a sports bike and similarly designed with only one (bipedal) passenger in mind. Its security features were well beyond Charlie's capabilities as a hacker, as the state of the art here was even more advanced than her state, but she had half a mind to try hot wiring the thing anyway.

Security, it turned out, was proving something of a problem in this universe. Up until that point, they'd been able to rely on Charlie's sheer technological superiority and hardiness to ease their way. But this universe made the Coupler look like the Apple II. While they'd been lucky to arrive through an unmonitored tear—luckier than they'd initially realized when they arrived two weeks ago—their way out necessitated some subterfuge to access.

Charlie checked her watch, because they'd apparently made a comeback in the far-off future of an alternate Earth and didn't look out of place. The hologram tech was too outdated to pass muster when it seemed everyone and their brother had a cybernetic eye with enhanced sensors, and they had to locally source some new clothes to fit in. ("Locally sourced" was Vera's charming euphemism for falling in with the sprawling metropolis's criminal element and getting their hands on a device that could fabricate everything from currency to clothing. But seeing as how that same criminal element landed them a meeting with a security agent who had Tear Clearance, Charlie could live with a little theft at the end of the day.)

A startlingly lifelike news broadcast was projected on the opposite wall, but, already short on patience, Charlie found it difficult to follow the story about something called the Council Victorious. It sounded a bit like a heavy metal band but was, from what little she could gather, some sort of futuristic foreign empire disappointed with the current status quo. Space politics for the space opera.

Vera insisted on taking point for the meeting, but she sure as hell was taking her sweet time. Charlie craned her neck to get a better look down the impossibly long corridor lined with doors that went *whoosh*. The level they were on was some kind of hotel and prioritized anonymity above much else. Charlie understood why their contact chose the location. She didn't understand what the fuck was taking Vera so long.

The answer arrived some five minutes later (or about two minutes before Charlie was scheduled to go in, guns a-blazing): Vera oozed from the room five doors down from Charlie's lookout at the balcony. Vera's body had the loose-limbed, feline quality of a woman whose brains had just been truly and spectacularly fucked out. She wore a grin from ear to ear, and her futuristic shift dress hung at an artfully mussed angle on her shoulders. She braced herself on the wall and tossed an undoubtedly flirty look over her shoulder. An Amazonian green woman followed after her. (Amazonian in stature, not species, and still the wrong green, Charlie decided, which maybe made no sense because she had no existing frame of reference for Amazonian green women, but she was Annoyed.) She wore the more casual attire of a smile and a bedsheet.

Oh, and a wink. A smile, a bedsheet, and a wink.

Vera giggled.

Charlie's mouth silently worked around several responses to this turn of events. The one her brain ultimately supplied was, "YOU HAVE A HEART CONDITION."

A pair of aliens on the floor below collided due to the outburst. Vera only batted her eyes and reached up to slide a hand over the Amazonian green woman's chest, her fingers tracing the prominent line of her collarbone.

"Are you a Martian?" Vera asked.

The Amazonian green woman laughed. Her voice was surprisingly high. Smile widening, she framed Vera's face in both hands and said, "Don't be silly, darling. Everybody knows those don't exist."

It took five more minutes of flirting and suggestive tones before the two dared to part ways, AGW slipping back into the room with a whoosh. Charlie's jaw hurt from clenching, the space between her brows red from furrowing. She didn't wait to get to a more secure location before snapping, "Did you even get it?"

Vera, who was still riding her hormonal high but wasn't, somewhat irritatingly at this moment, a complete idiot, held out a translucent data drive containing the biometrics needed to break into the tear's facility. She smirked, and Charlie, fuming, snatched the drive away.

"Aw, come on," Vera said, clapping Charlie's shoulder. "Don't get all Chuck Chaste about it. Tell you what, why don't we get you one too? You're all...tense. You deserve a break from me doing all the work."

Charlie's indignation winded her. "Ex*cuse* me?"

"No, seriously, what do you like? Boys? Girls?" Vera squeezed her shoulder. "I'll be your wingwoman. It'll be fun."

Fun. Right. Between being a science major, a soldier, and a science experiment, Charlie's idea of fun was conditioned to include a lot more clothes than Vera's. She never had time to even consider she was maybe missing out. She still didn't have time. She didn't say that. She was still seeing red—the right color of red, because it was metaphorical and therefore familiar.

"Like anyone'd even pay attention to me with you standing right there."

"That's bugging you. It's a big multiverse!" Vera ushered Charlie into the empty elevator and held no apparent suspicion about the fact Charlie desperately wanted to throttle her. "We'll find another Chuck, Chuck. Just you wait."

Most Montrealers never left city limits. They were not unlike New Yorkers in this regard, local pride eclipsing the pitfalls of urban living: the potholes, the pollution, the rush hour press of people. But when Charlie had been a little girl, before her life had been swallowed by the military and physics and the first hint of the tears, her family would take a trip up north every summer. Lanaudière had seemed like an entirely different country at times, with its wide-open spaces that narrowed into twisty mountain roads punctuated by the distinctive Canadian shield. As a child, she'd been fascinated by the farms, the well-worn fields holding cattle and the long silver barns housing chickens. When the wind was right, the air smelled sweet and green. When the wind was wrong, you never thought the stench of chicken and horse shit was ever going to leave your nose.

The old-timey jail smelled a lot like those farms. Charlie was seated opposite Vera in a cell no larger than her U1 dorm. They were dressed like characters out of a bad Western, Vera opting for what she'd decided was a more fashionable black hat while Charlie stuck to the hologram's default white. Vera was on her back, one leg bent at the knee, the other extended out, and was tossing a ball belonging to one of the cell's previous tenants over her head, palming it, and tossing it again.

"I never figured Nate for politics," Vera said.

"No?"

"Nah. Too plebeian."

"Well, I bet this version of him never figured legendary outlaw Vera the Kid would drop out of the sky and ruin his baby girl's wedding day, so I guess you're even."

Vera had vomited in the cake before introductions could be made. You'd've thought stopping the chapel from collapsing via tear would've warranted a thank you, but it had earned them a jail stay instead.

Vera flashed Charlie a shark's grin. It didn't reach her eyes. "She was cute. The bride. His daughter, I guess." A beat. "Weird."

"I didn't get a good look," Charlie said. "I was too busy trying to talk down Papa Salt from pulling out his shotgun."

"*Mayor* Papa Salt."

"*Mayor* Papa Salt of the Wild Wild West Island's daughter was not high on my list of priorities is what I'm saying." Charlie tipped her head back and pressed it against the wall. "I don't think mine's ever been married. My Salt, I mean."

"Mine's married to his work."

"And by work, you mean 'managing you.'"

"Veritech has excellent dental."

Charlie snorted. For a moment, they fell into companionable silence, but the false edge of Vera's smile was caught in Charlie's conscience like a thorn.

"You wanna talk about it?" Charlie asked.

"No."

"All right."

Vera palmed the ball but didn't move to throw it again. A mixture of gratitude and incredulity played across her face as she sat up. "That's it?"

Charlie blinked. "Yes? Yes."

"You're not going to, I don't know..." She waved a hand. "Get all psychoanalytical on me?"

"Do I fucking look like a therapist?"

Vera gave the question considerably more thought than it deserved. "In some universe, maybe."

"We'd have to find another one where I exist first," Charlie pointed out, crossing her arms.

"Aw, see! I *knew* that was bugging you."

"No!" Charlie huffed. "Yes. But. You *definitely* don't look like a therapist, so. Shut up."

Vera hummed, but whatever retort she had sitting on the tip of her tongue evaporated at the sound of footsteps. The deputy was returning from his piss break.

"Saved by the bell."

"Thank God," Charlie addressed to the ceiling. "Time to go find that gateway to hell in the mines they're afraid of and get out of here."

Vera tossed Charlie the ball and stretched. "Do you want to be the sick prisoner, or shall I?"

"You. Obviously you."

Verabucks did not make especially good coffee. It didn't even have especially speedy Wi-Fi, which Charlie considered the bigger sin. (Vera disagreed; she'd argued a Verity putting out a substandard product with her name stamped on it was an affront to all things Baum.) But this particular location, one of four on this street alone, did boast the comfiest chairs. Vera was already sprawled in an overstuffed loveseat when Charlie returned with their drink orders. Vera's name was spelled correctly, while Charlie suffered the quiet indignity of having Chuck scrawled over the Verabucks logo: a mermaid with Vera's face. *You'd think looking friendlier than the* Verity Baum*'s figurehead would make it better, but somehow it's worse.*

Charlie frowned at her cup and sighed. "Why did you have to tell Fran my name was Chuck?"

"Because this universe is boring, and I'm bored?"

"That's not a reason. Regular people are people. They have lives."

"You're just grumpy Fran's got a doppelgänger and you don't," Vera said, stretching to grab a handful of sugar packets from the counter behind her. "You should be grateful. You could have a copy who makes coffee with your face on it."

"You're still rich."

"Not the point!"

"Pretty sure that's the point."

Vera sniffed. "My defining characteristic is that I'm a rich *genius*, not a *rich* genius."

"You literally just said the same thing twice."

"It's all about the emphasis. I can be smart *without* being rich!"

Charlie waved her off. "And you can be rich without being smart, fine, I get it. You're still some fancy CEO, though. Only instead of redefining technology as we know it, you're…supplying coffee to the young and pretty."

This universe really was boring. Charlie scanned the shop. The clientele was predominantly white twentysomethings wearing earth tones, and judging by the number of laptops and books, they were either students or aspiring writers or both. The colors in this world were even more discernibly wrong than any previous one they'd visited, like someone had slapped a golden filter over her eyes that made everything seem overly sharp and muted at the same time. Everything smelled of pumpkin spice, even outdoors. The weather seemed perfectly calibrated to lure you into a coffee shop, too: rainy and gray, with red and orange and yellow leaves plastered to wet sidewalks. They'd been hopping between Verabucks locations to kill time and to warm up. There really wasn't much else to do after they'd stabilized their way out. It was the only tear in town besides the one they'd already closed.

Charlie looked back at Vera, who was doodling a cybernetic eye on a napkin. Earlier, she had insisted on dropping into a pharmacy to grab an eyepatch, "just in case." If they'd sold prosthetic legs, Charlie didn't doubt she'd be lugging one of those around too. She almost felt bad for yelling about her heart condition.

"Is it just me, or does nothing seem to actually happen in this universe?" Charlie ventured, hoping that a rare moment of agreement between the two of them might stir Vera out of her funk. "Everyone's just gorgeous and really likes coffee."

Vera scoffed, gaze flicking up from her drawing. "Excuse you, there is lots of drama." Now she was just disagreeing for the sake of disagreeing. She nodded toward a trio of coffee drinkers no more distinctive to Charlie's eye than any other patron in the shop. "Just look at those lingering glances. Stupid T-shirt Guy is clearly in love with his best friend, Classic Americana Man."

"You really need to get better with names."

"Those are their names. That's what Zee—"

"—Zepherin," Charlie said in a flat tone since the dystopian revolutionary was a barista in this universe.

"—called out. He said 'Stupid T-shirt Guy.' Maybe this universe has weird names; you don't know."

"I do know because we've been sitting in coffee shops for the longest hours of my—"

"I think Classic Americana Man's pining for someone, though. Watches the door every time someone comes in. And Obvious Horse Girl has just been drawing Fran this whole time. Barely touched her coffee."

"Which has her name on it, which is a normal name, which I know because," Charlie said, pointedly holding up both of their cups, side by side.

"Hey, neat! You'd be 'Cherity!' I ship it," said a passer-by, who Charlie involuntarily thought of as "Buttons" because Vera possibly was catching.

They both watched her continue on to the counter in equal bafflement.

"Well, that's ridiculous," Vera said.

"For once, we—"

"It's obviously 'Charity.'"

An argument was happening in the street. It was loud. It was extremely off-putting. Charlie had seen a giant biomechanical predator eating parasitic entities that existed beyond space and ate reality, and she thought this might be the most off-putting thing she'd seen.

Well, heard, technically. The choreography was only a minor part of it. Mostly it was the singing. The in-time counterpoint layered singing. She'd have assumed it was a stunt, that this was just a universe where flash mobs were still a thing, except this was the second argument they'd seen. There'd also been the cab driver singing a vengeful anthem about having been stiffed on a tip. The dirge for fallen ice cream. Everyone just sang. She'd tried to order at the café where they were sitting, watching the fight, and the person at the counter had become extremely solicitous, as if she had a speaking disorder that might be indicative of some other condition, singing very slowly and patiently.

Vera had wanted to see if she could make something that would autotune them, but Charlie thought that would more or less have the same effect, like using a text-to-speech program.

They were dealing with it mostly by keeping quiet.

Well, no, that was completely inaccurate. Charlie was dealing with it that way. Vera was apparently doing her utmost to become a freestyle lyricist in the space of a day.

"Hey, this world has rhymes, this world keeps time, I think I know how they do the—I was just going to say rhymes again. This is tougher than it looks. It must be like—you know how some languages don't have left and right, just compass directions? So everyone who speaks it is just always calculating that in their head, they don't even think about it. Song as language. Everyone's probably singing in their heads, too."

"Please only sing in your head," Charlie said.

"Hey, Chuck, don't see red—"

"Oranges oranges oranges."

"Oh, hardy har." Vera took a sip of her coffee and grimaced, either because she'd been foiled or because the coffee wasn't a patch on Verabucks. Faced with a world of inferior products, Charlie was forced to reevaluate her opinion of Verabucks. Maybe that Verity *had* been a genius at coffee. "What are they even arguing about?"

"Fender bender. Probably a gimme. She is really steaming about it, though. Practically operatic."

One part of the argument was, indeed, reaching a crescendo, scaling up in pitch and holding the note. Charlie and Vera watched a glass on the table vibrate.

"Oh, wow, she's gonna do it," Vera said. "Check it—"

The glass on the table exploded. They both looked at the jagged bottom that remained. Then immediately at each other.

"Resonance," they said simultaneously.

(Vera might have hummed it a little.)

Resonance was a cutesy metaphor, and they were beyond cutesy metaphors, but Charlie's thoughts were racing with implications. Vera pulled a napkin from the dispenser and was spreading it out on the table to doodle, though Charlie couldn't make sense of what she was doodling. It was more nervous tic than art, a part of her process, and Charlie could only find herself grateful for the fact that at least it meant no more singing.

"So everything vibrates at its own frequency—"

"—and when something vibrates at the same frequency as something else—"

"—and is strong enough—"

"And is strong enough—"

"—and close enough, that's when things—" Charlie gestured to the shattered remains of the glass.

"Go 'splodey."

"For lack of a better term."

"Naturally."

"The whirlpool tear—"

"—appeared right after I touched Yarrity. So it's more than just looking alike. It wasn't just some hairline fracture in reality, we tore apart the ocean with that thing. Doppelgängers must have the same frequency," Vera said, leaning forward and slamming a hand on the table, "and that's why we keep running into Verity Baums.

Why we keep ending up in versions of Montreal. The tears are a result of like calling to like, adjacent Earths drawn together and causing fractures in reality."

"But it's more than that," Charlie said. Her body thrummed with the adrenaline of realization, and she was on her feet, struck by the wild idea she might start dancing. At least then they'd blend in with the locals. Space had been cleared around them, the shop's other patrons clearly put off by their lack of meter and rhyme. "Tears like history. They like places of significance, places that come to resonate louder and louder because they're the same setting for countless events, that's why New York was the first to go, and it's not just adjacent Earths and people and places, it's adjacent ideas. Think of the places we've been, it's all shit that's straight out of—"

"Stories," they finished together.

"So it's like—another kind of building block," Vera continued, eyes narrowed. "Stories as DNA, stories as a chemical reaction. With certain elements as proteins, molecules, what-have-you. Or, I don't know, as likely consequence. Oh, goddammit."

"...what?" Charlie said. She'd been with her up until then. It was interesting. Invigorating. It was, if not a lead precisely, then progress. It made the pieces fit together. You had to be wary of a good story, she knew, because you then had to go and try to prove yourself wrong and not be so taken with your grand explanation you assumed it, but this was a good hypothesis. She didn't know what Vera was annoyed about.

Although she didn't seem that annoyed.

"Logarithmic spirals," Vera said. "Patterns arising naturally, not because of engineering but just as a product of the math. Galaxies, shells..."

"Ferns," said Charlie.

"'Consider the,'" Vera quoted. "I cannot believe the woo-woo magic me had this first. So it's not...clones, or universes diverging on choice quantum mechanics-style. I'm a fern. I'm a shell. Except if you put two shells together, they don't explode."

"Put two galaxies together and things get pretty hairy, though."

"Aw, you think I'm a star. Or, well. Stars."

Whereas I'm whatever you found around those things that aren't a fern, or a shell, or a galaxy. Dirt. Sand. Space dust.

"Still big question marks over parasites, and the Hound, and what started putting holes in things," Charlie said, blinking past the thought. "Put two of you together, tear. In theory. But we had plenty of tears forming back home, and there was only one Verity. Somehow other universes were vibrating close enough that the architecture was setting it off."

Vera drew a very angry looking fern at the edge of her napkin. "A question that would be easier to figure out if it was strictly science. But it's not, is it?" The fern grew eyes and jagged eyebrows. It scowled. "Don't get me wrong, I *will* throw math at this problem until we figure out a way to get you home, but I'd bet Magic Me's been laughing at us for a reason."

Charlie frowned. "Because it's not just science, it's...art. Possibly *magical*...arts." That didn't sit right. It was like the colors being wrong all over again, a subtle, disquieting shift in worldview. She blinked hard and stuck out a hand. "Quick, give me a napkin."

"All right...?"

"Let's crunch some numbers."

Vera grinned.

Chapter Fourteen

— SAVAGE WOOD —

The numbers didn't help.

That was disingenuous. The numbers alone didn't help. The math supported the Resonance Hypothesis, sure, but they needed to replicate what had happened on the *Verity Baum* to proceed, and the musical universe's Verity Baum had died some years prior in an unfortunate opera house fire.

So they needed to find a universe with another—still living—Verity Baum, and they needed to be prepared to deal with a tear the moment they did, along with the ever-looming threat of the Hound finally catching up with them, which they agreed was a matter of when, not if. Until they could figure out a way to put the pooch down, though, the best thing they could do was figure out why the tears were happening in the first place. Maybe that would lead them to whoever made the Hound so they could tell them to keep their fucking dog on a leash.

It was winter in the first universe that met their criteria, and the snow covering the streets and sidewalks was fresh enough to still be white and fluffy: postcard perfect. It would be only a matter of hours before the illusion would be shattered, the streets thick with brown slush that stained your boots and pant cuffs with salt, but the view was nice while it lasted. Strings of white lights festooned the fake trees the city put up around the holidays as wards against winter's too-short days, and these only added to the postcard feel, the sense that they were walking through a moment that couldn't last, a veneer that covered something unpleasant.

Money could open more doors than any key. Of all the technological odds and ends they'd picked up on the road so far, the Fabricator was, once they'd accounted for a universe's unique quirks, worth its weight in gold—though in this particular universe, at least, that wasn't a literal sentiment. Vera had a large, discretion-inspiring stack of the colorful local currency tucked inside a brown envelope. The bills were all forged, but there was nothing about this Earth's technology to suggest their crime would ever be discovered.

Christ, zeppelins were hanging above the Montreal skyline, subtle as beached whales. Vera said something about the locals' "post-war sartorial choices," and Charlie nodded along as though she knew what that meant. While her enhancements reduced her need for sleep, she hadn't managed so much as a wink in two jumps, and exhaustion was fraying the edges of her vision. When Vera had suggested they book a stay at the Ritz-Carlton, Charlie hadn't fought her on it. The promise of rest had been too tempting an incentive, and she was only (a slightly modified) human.

The hotel lobby was empty of clientele save Vera and Charlie, but service was at a standstill. The concierge had been called away from the front desk the moment they'd walked in, leaving reception unattended. Charlie threw herself into a wingback leather chair and daydreamed about what a life would be like where such quality furniture was the norm and not the exception. She slouched a little to palm her cheek, elbow propped on the generous armrest, and kept a watch on Vera, who seemed oddly entranced with their latest host Earth. There was a romantic quality about this Montreal, the world painted in broad strokes as though it were designed for a film set rather than real life. Everything was clean and stylized. Even the graffiti in the alley they'd passed on their way here suggested an artist's intent instead of some dumb kid tagging his existence. Maybe Vera could picture herself here—*like calling to like, we came up with that theory weeks ago and still haven't figured out how to make it work for us and*—

A man entered the lobby. Normally such an event wouldn't capture Charlie's attention so completely, but he triggered some kind of hindbrain response that demanded her focus. He walked much like how Vera walked, the swaggery strut of someone unused to hearing no. But where on Vera it was a novelty, on him it was tired. The kindest adjective Charlie could ascribe his face was "symmetrical." He had dark hair and dark eyes, and he wore a dark bespoke suit. He was the dictionary definition of attractive, and the smirk marring his expression said he wrote the dictionary in question.

Charlie had a very bad feeling about this. It grew worse when he approached the front desk; he slid into Vera's space like he belonged there. It was like watching a nature documentary, and they'd arrived at the moment where the innocent woodland creature was about to be devoured by a snake.

Vera, of course, was the snake. And the bad feeling was less a matter of sympathy for Monsieur Dick as it was the sinking realization that getting a room was going to take even longer if the bastard was trying to cut the line.

"Oh, fuck no." Charlie got up.

She'd taken five quick, purposeful steps in the direction of the desk when the concierge reappeared. His brow was shiny with sweat. He did not pay any attention to Monsieur Dick, who slunk back a respectable three feet at the intrusion. Vera, in a rare lack of loquaciousness, raised a cool eyebrow that dismissed Monsieur Dick's flirtations before they'd even arrived for class. Charlie, for good measure, occupied the newly opened space and plopped her elbows on the counter.

"Dr. Baum," the concierge greeted because of course he did. They hadn't passed any skyscrapers with her name on them yet, but it was only a matter of time before the Vera of it all introduced itself. "Mr. Potter will escort you to your rooms."

A disconcertingly *young* Pius Potter, dressed as a bellhop, materialized at the desk.

"Rooms," mouthed Charlie.

Vera simply shrugged. Charlie supposed she was the type of woman who expected *rooms*.

Charlie was face-first on a bed-shaped cloud when Vera floated the idea of room service. Food was the only thing that could distract Charlie from sleep, and she lifted her head enough to ask, "Do they have hot dogs?"

"Seriously?"

Charlie pushed herself up until she was kneeling on the bed. She hadn't even bothered to take off the Velo, which was hologrammed to resemble a full, high-waisted skirt, a sleeveless polkadot blouse, and an ankle-length wool coat. The mattress molded to her legs, and she longingly looked back at her pillow.

"What's wrong with hot dogs?"

"'What's wrong with—' Are you even listening to yourself?"

"What kind of Quebecer *are* you?"

"The English kind."

Charlie rolled her eyes. "So am I!"

"We're in a five-star hotel, and you're asking for hot dogs."

"And poutine."

"And pou—" Vera bit back a frustrated noise and threw up her hands in defeat. "Fine." She picked up the rotary phone and began the laborious process of dialing the front desk. "It's a good thing I'm the one with the heart condition. Five-star hotel and you're making me order hot dogs. This is embarrassing."

"But delicious."

Vera mumbled something insulting under her breath, but it was drowned out by the impatient rumble of Charlie's stomach. The last time she'd had hot dogs, Montreal had still been mostly intact. They were comfort food, the nutritional equivalent of her cloud-like mattress, and if Vera could indulge in her rich people digs for a night or two, Charlie could damn well indulge in a trip down starving student lane.

"Hot dogs are en route," Vera said. "They will either be really quick because they're friggin' hot dogs, or they'll take forever because some schmuck is right now running around the streets trying to find a high enough standard of hot dog. You're lucky this is going on the reputation of an entirely different Baum. I mean, there's a solid chance it just becomes a charming peccadillo, but my charming peccadillos will be my own. I don't need your charming peccadillos."

"Aw," said Charlie, intending to follow with a joke about being thought charming and getting to about the "you think" before it became an indistinct murmur. She did not find out how fast the food delivery was, it turned out, because the time passed at the blurred hop of dozing. She was vaguely aware of a knocking, and she thought maybe she should try and pull herself awake, but she only got as far as turning her face so it wasn't nestled quite so deep in the pillow.

The bed shifted slightly as it was bumped. "'m waking up," she mumbled, flapping her hand in the direction of the bump.

Vera body-slammed her. This seemed unnecessary, to Charlie's groggy mind. She'd said she was waking up. A moment later the weight was gone. Charlie considered that maybe she wouldn't call it the Marshmallow after all. That had been plenty heavy. That had been like…

Two people?

She raised herself up on her elbows, spitting hair out of her mouth and twisted to look with bleary eyes until she found Vera in the room. She hadn't rolled far, it turned out. Just to the floor next to Charlie's bed.

Monsieur Dick from the front desk was on top of her, strangling her. Bemusedly, Charlie pulled her leg back, shifted it into the space beside the bed, and kicked him in the face. Then she rubbed some sleep out of one eye.

"What—" she began. It was as far as she got before the man, having rolled with the kick and come smoothly to his feet, seized an icepick out of the bucket and threw it at her. Charlie grabbed the pillow and rolled, staring a moment later at an inch or so of ice-smashing metal that had penetrated the pillow. She threw the pillow and pick aside as her roll brought her to the edge of the bed and her feet.

"—is—" She caught the bucket, which he'd pelted at her face. A moment later, she deflected the heavy rotary phone with it; he'd torn it out of the wall and was handling it like a ball and chain, spinning back and forth on one side, then the other, then sending it stabbing at her face. She scooped it out of the air with the bucket and slammed it to the floor, trapping it underneath.

"—happen-ehhhhh-ng." With her head lower, bent as she was, he leaped into a spinning kick aimed at her face. She caught his foot and shoved, toppling him. He landed, immediately flipped back to his feet, and went over again as Charlie beaned him in the face with the bucket on the way up.

He learned from his mistake and rolled backward, coming to his feet out of her immediate range. His eyes flicked across the room, from Charlie to Vera, then the objects in it, stopping on the backpack.

"Bodyguard," he said. "Where's your gun, bodyguard?"

"Safe," croaked Vera.

"Bag," he said, and threw himself in that direction, elbow coming up to block the bucket Charlie threw at him.

"Did you not tip?" Charlie squawked, more awake but not anywhere near all the way. She was half on autopilot, but the half that wasn't was trying to catch up to why this fucking guy was in their room trying to kill them.

Well, her as collateral, it seemed. Trying to kill Vera, then. Even autopilot could come up with some reasons for that. He reached the bag a step ahead of her, stooped to grab it. She didn't bother trying to stop him, simply launched and came down elbow first on his back. She grabbed an arm and twisted it, forcing him further into the floor, giving him no leverage to do anything with the bag he was stuck on top of, pinned down.

With their assailant secured, she looked across the bed at Vera, who had pulled herself up, just her head visible, chin resting on the mattress as she stared over at Charlie.

"Well, I'm definitely not tipping *now*," Vera said.

The hot dogs were cold but edible. (The poutine had been unsalvageable. Melted cheese curds didn't taste particularly good with carpet, no matter the skill of the chef.) Vera was humming around a bite of filet mignon (which was actually rabbit, Charlie realized, but filet mignon was the only fancy rich person food name she knew offhand).

Monsieur Dick was beginning to stir. He groaned. This was a reasonable reaction to getting hit in the head by a genetically enhanced soldier and tied to a chair, yet still managed to annoy

Charlie, who wanted to enjoy her cold hot dog in peace. She shoved the rest of her food in her mouth and stood up. She thudded a heavy foot onto the sliver of seat showing between his spread legs. This expedited his waking considerably. He jerked back.

"Bodyguard."

"Sergeant Chase," Charlie corrected.

He stared at her in sullen silence. She inched her foot forward.

"...Sergeant."

"And you are...?"

"Savage. Holt Savage."

Vera snickered.

"I really don't give a fuck what your name is," Charlie said. "*Who* are you?"

"A concerned citizen."

There were no inches left, but Charlie pushed her foot forward anyway. When Savage spoke next, his voice was notably strained.

"A surveillant."

He had an accent. It wasn't local.

"All right, so you're Holt Savage, International Dick of Mystery. Great."

Fucking spies.

"Why is there a hit out on Verity Baum?"

It was Savage's turn to laugh, though unlike Vera's, his bore more incredulity.

"I know Baum pays her stooges to be loyal, but I didn't realize she also paid them to be stupid."

Charlie kicked Savage in the chest. This was a reasonable reaction to having insult added to attempted injury. The chair tipped backward onto the floor. Charlie knelt beside a wheezing Savage and raised her index finger. Her middle finger felt a bit left out.

"Okay, first of all," she said, "I do not get paid. So your whole premise there is shitty right off the bat. Second of all—" She hitched a thumb toward Vera, who was only just visible from this particular vantage point. "—that is not Verity Baum." She cleared her throat. "Well, not the one you were trying to kill, at least."

"What?"

"That is not the Verity Baum you were hired to kill."

"It's true," said Vera. "Or I'm reasonably sure it's—quick sidebar: you weren't hired to kill someone from an alternate universe, were you?"

Savage looked wary. Probably he thought they were crazy.

"We're not crazy," Charlie said. She was uncomfortable including Vera in that statement, but it was important to show a united front.

"No," he replied.

"No, you think we are crazy, or no, you weren't hired to kill someone from an alternate universe?" asked Vera.

Savage squirmed in the restraints as Vera knelt opposite Charlie. "*Both!*"

"Look, pal, we need to be on the same page here," Charlie said. "Because it just so happens, we're also in the market for finding Verity Baum."

Vera raised an eyebrow at her, but Savage was too preoccupied to notice the silent exchange that followed. Where there was Verity, there was, undoubtedly, a tear. Vera nodded a tacit agreement for the plan if a pointed look could constitute a plan.

"Finding, not killing," said Savage.

"Killing would be in poor taste," said Vera, dryly.

Savage tried the restraints again, teeth gritted together, a vein popping out in his forehead threatening his face's unnerving symmetry. When neither his arms nor feet budged, he eyed the two of them. Charlie met his gaze.

"There was no hit on Baum," he said slowly.

"Really? 'Cause you sure looked pretty murdery," said Charlie.

"My orders had...wiggle room."

"Elaborate," said Vera. Despite the fact she was dressed in a marshmallow space suit disguised as a dress and had a spectacular looking bruise forming around her neck, Vera reminded Charlie of her own Verity at that moment. Her tone announced Business and intolerance for fools who might waste her time. It was a comforting tone when it was directed toward someone else.

"You're really not her, are you," said Savage, his tone not quite a question, as though he were attempting to convince himself. "Only, I suppose if you were, I'd be dead by now. Rumor has it Dr. Baum is much more...elaborate with her interrogations."

"Yeah, I don't do torture," said Vera. "Kind of a standard policy at Veritech."

"Veritech?"

"Don't worry about it."

Interesting. No Veritech, but definitely a Verity. If she wasn't in charge of a tech conglomerate, why would a foreign intelligence service maybe want her dead?

"Why do you want to find Verity Baum?" he asked.

"You first," said Vera.

The last of Savage's skepticism was either satisfied, or he figured he didn't have anything to lose by answering their question.

"I want to gain access to her airship to retrieve some government property she stole."

"Define stole," Charlie said. "Governments can get weirdly proprietary over scientific inventions they didn't, you know, invent."

"Dr. Baum is a genius and a monster, but this creature is beyond even her intellect."

Charlie glanced at Vera for another silent exchange but was disappointed to find that Vera's brain had clearly tripped up over the wrong word: "monster" instead of "creature." While most of the Veritys they'd learned about could, at best, be said to occupy a kind of moral gray area, none of them could be neatly categorized as "evil," per se—not even the architect of the categorization dystopian universe.

Charlie straightened herself out and tugged Vera aside so that they were out of Savage's line of sight, though he remained in theirs.

"Don't move," Charlie said to Savage, who scoffed at the suggestion. To Vera, she lowered her voice and said, "I appreciate you're maybe having an existential crisis here, and we can get back to that in a second, but do we think your Evil Twin managed to get her mitts on a parasite or a hound?"

Vera returned to the driver's seat at the same speed she'd vacated. "Definitely parasite."

Charlie frowned. "Really? My forged money was on hound. My Earth's tech is eons ahead of this place, and we never managed to get a parasite in captivity. It'd just eat whatever was holding it and call a bunch of its friends in the process."

"Weren't you listening? He said it wasn't manmade."

"No, he said that it was beyond her—"

Vera waved her off. "Same thing."

"So much for that existential crisis, huh?"

"It's resolved. I remembered how he tried to choke me to death just now and that I don't trust his moral judgments at all."

Charlie had to wonder at that. Callous murderers didn't generally go around calling the pure-hearted monsters. Suckers or fools or cowards or some diminutive that let them categorize them as "less than," generally. You didn't throw out "monster" unless their behavior gave you pause and concern, and as Vera herself said, he'd been trying to choke her to death just now.

"Well, do we trust his intel? We never managed to hold one, and we weren't calling people on phones you can use to bludgeon people. Or, you know—" Charlie shot Savage a humorless smile. "—try."

"Because they ate the cage and their friends turned up," Vera said. "Your digs. Sort of historic? You had a tear, they had a little history."

"We tried new. They still turned up pretty quickly. Anywhere we kept them long—" Charlie paused. She and Vera looked at each other.

"Random spots in the sky don't have history. She's floating it around up there in an airship—"

"—so there's nothing for them to latch their eye-watering little paws on."

"For now," Vera said. "Yarrity had a boat, and that had enough resonance for us to land on the next boat over. Eventually, her airship's gonna get enough hype the extradimensional nasties are gonna find it."

"All the more reason you should help me retrieve it," said Savage. Charlie didn't know if he'd followed all of that—he was hard to read—but he'd gotten enough to work it into his point.

"Gosh, I want to say yes, but for some reason, my throat just won't say the word..." Vera said, lightly rubbing the bruise and wincing.

"You need my help. I have the interior schematics. I have resources. I can get us on an airship headed in the same direction. We fake an engine problem that puts us on a parallel course, shoot a cable across, zipline over, cut a hole—"

"That sounds—" *fun, actually, but not with so many parts and with Savage in charge of all of them* "—like something people without a hologram generator do. We can do disguises."

"Which also need information you don't have. Details on the people you'd be impersonating. If you're from another dimension, you don't know the things you'd need to know."

"I know I don't need a disguise," Vera said, lacing her fingers together and putting her hands behind her head. "Concealer, maybe, for the attempted murder bruises—I don't know if someone's tried to strangle her to death recently. But as far as anyone knows, it's my airship. They've gotta let me on."

"You still need me along," Savage said.

"You definitely need me along," Charlie said. She thought her case was stronger, given she was the reason Savage hadn't murdered Vera.

"I can see bringing her along," Vera said. "Why would I bring along my..."

"Arch-nemesis?" Savage suggested.

"Ugh, I'll be so disappointed in me if that's true. You, anyway."

"Fake prisoner routine," Savage said. "Me and the sergeant as prisoners."

Charlie frowned. "Okay, that gets us in, but only if Vera can pass for a different her. You'd have to act like a different you, the mannerisms, the behavior. You'd have to be, you know...subtle."

"You think I can't be subtle?"

"I think I have not once seen you be subtle."

Vera planted her hands on her hips.

"Oh, please," she said. "I run a multimillion-dollar business. That didn't want me running it, by the by, so I went out and started my own, undercut them, and then when they were just about to start selling the furniture..." She punched the flat of her palm. "*There* I was with the hostile takeover. I've been convincing everyone on my vision of the future for *years*. I present an image. I'm an icon. I do an interview and I say outrageous things and people talk about the things, and then the things happen. I can't pretend to be me?" Vera scoffed, tossing her head back. "I change the world pretending to be me. I can *do subtle*."

Chapter Fifteen
— SHE CAN'T —

The zeppelin was on fire.

They were still too far away to smell much smoke, but the flashing red lights and ear-piercing siren were big enough clues that something had gone horribly awry between the moment Vera-as-Dr.-Baum ordered her minions to escort Charlie and Savage to the prisoner hold and now. Charlie winced, slotting the pad of her thumb near the corner of her eye as though that might relieve the pressure of her building migraine. It wouldn't, but there was a power in remaining optimistic when your dumbass travel partner decided to set a worryingly flammable vehicle on fucking fire. It wasn't going to explode—it wasn't hydrogen—but that didn't mean fire on the big floating balloon thousands of feet in the air was a-okay.

"I suppose the opposite of brilliant and evil is good and incompetent," Savage remarked, pitching his voice to be heard over the din.

Charlie's temples throbbed. "She'll be here," she said, willing her words to reflect earnest belief rather than sarcasm. Charlie should have played the part of Baum. They could have fixed the hologram tech to do faces. She could not be stuck in a brig, separated from their escape gear, on a goddamned flaming zeppelin.

But Vera had said she could do subtle, and despite all evidence to the contrary, Charlie had believed her. Because that was the thing, wasn't it? When she turned on the charm, you wanted to believe Vera. That was probably why they kept running into versions of her, and not different iterations of Charlotte Chase.

No, apparently Charlotte Chase is a dispensable foot soldier who's going to fall thousands of feet toward the ground while having to listen to Double-Oh-Asshole think he's being clever. Yay me. (The Velo meant she wouldn't burn, but falling was falling. Maybe she'd pass out first. That would be swell.)

"Yes, well, forgive my impatience, Sergeant," Savage said drolly. When Charlie opened her eyes, she found him on the other side of his cell door, the *better* side of his cell door. He was holding an unfamiliar gadget whose purpose was nevertheless clear. Namely: breaking out of cells.

He was also walking away without popping the lock on her door.

"Hey!" Charlie called out to his retreating back. "Hey! What the *fuck*, asshole? We had a deal!"

She managed conviction on that one, even if no part of her was actually surprised the guy who'd tried to kill Vera double-crossed them. He was a spy. Double-crossing was what spies *did*.

"Oh, I'm sure you'll figure something out, darling." And then, just as he disappeared from view, "Ta!"

Charlie's knuckles turned white from her grip around the cell's bars.

"'I can do subtle,'" she said, shoving herself back and away from the bars, scanning the room and the mechanism. "'I can do subtle,'" she mimicked, again, this time in a higher, lilting register that sounded nothing like Vera. "'C'n do subtle,'" she muttered, kicking at the frame that held the small bed up until she had one of the metal rods free. It tapered enough that she could just use it as a screwdriver, so long as all she wanted to do was lean through the bars and mess with the hydraulic pressure running to the door. She jacked it up so the door was practically hissing.

She took a deep breath and kicked the cell door clear off its hinges.

"*Subtlety!*" she shouted, at an empty corridor.

She ran after Savage but soon lost his trail when the corridor split. Left or right? Vera had the schematics. Faced with the choice between running after Savage or trying to find Vera, she opted for the latter. Finding Vera would be easier. All Charlie had to do was follow the chaos.

Only there was a lot to choose from.

While she could only guess at how much damage the ship had sustained, it was clear the zeppelin was struggling to stay in the sky. The groans of metal under strain played counterpoint to the wail of the siren. The floor shook, giving the disquieting feeling it might give away at any moment. Charlie deployed her cowl once the smoke started to tickle her throat. The hologram, which still had her dressed in the same skirt and blouse, registered the cowl as a scarf, and she couldn't help but think a silent thank you to the fact her kitten heels were likewise an illusion. Running in heels belonged solely to the silver screen.

She took a right down a hallway marked AUTHORIZED PERSONNEL ONLY and ducked into an alcove to avoid a rush of presumably authorized personnel. Who were either rushing to deal with the fire or with whatever Vera was doing, which was no doubt related to the fire. The direction to go, probably.

The stampede had been fast enough that there'd been no time to try and capture the look of the uniforms, and reconfiguring the hologram would take time that she couldn't help but think, to coin a phrase, they were burning through. Instead, she just banked on them not looking back and staying about one turn behind, which went well for about two turns before it turned out they were holed up at a door that was stuck closed, working on getting it open.

Being the presumably authorized personnel, Charlie had to figure they were also presumably authorized to be opening that door, and if it wasn't opening, it was because someone had been fucking around with it. Which placed Vera either on the opposite side of it or hurrying away from a door she'd locked. It was hard to say which was preferable. If she wasn't there, that meant Charlie had to keep looking for her. If she was there, there was a whole squad of guards about to force their way through.

Also, Charlie finding her might itself not be in Vera's best interest. The zeppelin was on fire. She'd been locked up in a burning zeppelin.

She considered her Browning. She considered the fact they were on a zeppelin, which was on fire, and that these were henchmen drawing a paycheck. She didn't know exactly how villainous any of them were, and being on the opposite side of matters to Holt fucking Savage didn't selling her on anyone's irredeemable villainy, frankly. Injuring them to the point where they'd need the kind of medical attention you just didn't get on burning zeppelins seemed uncalled for. Knocking them out meant leaving them unconscious on a burning zeppelin.

The burning zeppelin was really complicating matters. *Who'd've thunk?*

She sidled up close, then looped an arm around the closest henchperson, putting the Browning to his head. It was a universally understood move. One of the universes was, fortunately, this one. He froze. She cleared her throat, and two more of the guards looked over and also froze.

"Freeze," she said, just to reinforce that this was the correct decision.

"You freeze!" said the one she concluded was the most hench of the people.

Or, wait. Did that imply that they were the most subservient and dutiful, and thus had the smallest amount of initiative? Least hench?

"I think your friend would really prefer it if you did," she said.

"I would," said her hostage.

"It doesn't matter what he thinks," said Least Hench, leveling his gun at her.

"Karl!" said her hostage.

"If you shoot him, then what? Your leverage disappears!"

"*KARL!*" said her hostage.

"Then I have a body to take shots while I one hundred percent shoot you first," Charlie said.

"...I don't know your name," said the hostage.

"You and the universe," muttered Charlie. "Look, you guys want to get to the fire, right?"

"There's an imposter on board who set the fire—"

"Yeah, okay, but is that *really* the most pressing part of this? We're on a zeppelin. Where are we going to go, except, you know, down in flames if you don't get this under control? So I would suggest: My friend's going to open that door."

It occurred to her that she wasn't one hundred percent sure Vera was on the other side of the door. This was going to get considerably more awkward if she wasn't. "Then you're going to trade places. We shut the door. You go fight the fire and stop us all from dying, hooray."

"Seems solid to me, Karl," said her hostage, who was kind of making a case for himself as Most Hench.

"I think we can take her," said Karl, at which point the zeppelin listed sideways. Charlie managed to prevent herself from skewing too far by kicking a foot up and catching the wall, the gun never wavering. Karl tripped over a panel that had been removed from the door to get at the workings and tipped headfirst into the same wall. There was a moment of silence as they all watched Karl lay there, unmoving.

"Sounds good to me," said Second Least Hench, regarding the unconscious Karl.

"VERA!" Charlie yelled. "OPEN THE DOOR!"

Vera popped into view in the porthole, like a meerkat with a really good stylist.

"That seems like a really bad idea," she said, muffled by the barrier.

Charlie lifted her gun-free hand from Most Hench long enough to indicate the whole hostage situation she had going on.

"Okay, but then they're all on the same side as me. What if they take me hostage?"

Second Least Hench's eyes lit up.

Fucking hell. Now she had one of those logic problems with the sheep and the wolf and the farmer to deal with, only it was set on a zeppelin which was on fire.

Those were always ridiculous, too. If you were a farmer, why did you even want to transport the wolf? It seemed like you'd be in the wolf-shooting business.

Then again, she'd decided against shooting or knocking these guys out. (Karl's situation was his own damn fault.) She couldn't criticize overly moral theoretical farmers.

"If you don't open the fucking door, Vera, I swear to God I might just let them!"

"Wait, I thought she was an impostor!" said Most Hench, trying to twist in Charlie's grip, not to evade, but to get a better look at Vera.

"Of course she is!" argued Second Least Hench. "You know how...sensitive Dr. Baum gets about people calling her—" He looked around, making sure there was no one to hear him over the fucking siren—God someone needed to turn that shit off already. "You know. That name."

"What's wrong with Vera?" asked Vera, through the door, because it was still fucking shut.

"Nothing's wrong with it," Most Hench said, deference bleeding into his tone. "Dr. Baum just prefers formalities!"

Again, Charlie saw a familiar shade of red. "We. Are. On. A. Ship. That's. On. Fire. *VERA.*"

There was a click and a hiss. The door inched open. Charlie knew little about dancing, yet the next moments played out like choreography. She caught Most Hench around the shoulders and swung him bodily into the room as Vera slipped out. Second Least Hench struck forward, but not before Charlie had twisted back around, hands-free, and caught him by the wrist. She pulled, hard, and he tripped over his feet, arms splayed to regain his balance. He didn't. Instead, Charlie helped him along to the floor, shoving him into the room along with Most Hench. She spun again, taking crisscrossing steps to a non-existent beat. Swooping down, she grabbed the unconscious Karl by the ankles and yanked him through her spread legs. He slid through the doorway, and Vera shut the door the moment his head cleared the threshold.

Charlie dusted her hands. The henchmen blinked owlishly at her through the porthole. Charlie stared back, expression expectant in the face of their dumb inaction.

After a long moment, she screamed, "PUT OUT THE FIRE!"

The conscious Henches sprang to life at the order. It occurred to neither of them that the door locked on their side, not Charlie's, but she supposed critical thinking wasn't the desired skill set when hiring henchmen. The only correct answer to "put out the fire" was a prompt "yes, ma'am."

Charlie turned to Vera, who was a shining example of the problem with critical thinking. Because Critical Thinkers were prone to Ideas—Ideas that deviated from the Plan and set the damn fire in the first place.

Charlie threw her hands in the air. "What the fuck, man?"

Vera was leaning against the wall. The Marshmallow was disguised in Period Villain Chic: a black, high-necked sleeveless blouse tucked into black, high-waisted wide-leg trousers. A skull pendant was tucked between the two pointed ends of her collar. Between the smoke, the flashing lights, and the vaguely industrial quality of the parts of the zeppelin not currently on fire, she looked like she was posing for a photoshoot for *Fashionable Villain Monthly*. She wasn't jumping to attention at a direct question. If anything, her posture suggested defensiveness.

"Look, there was too much security for me to make a move without being discovered," Vera said. "So I had to contrive a distraction, and I thought—well, what's more distracting than a fire on a zeppelin?"

Charlie couldn't actually disagree with that. She'd been thinking of little else thanks to that fucking siren. How infuriating.

"Fine," she bit out reluctantly. "Except the point of a distraction isn't to have everyone come running to where you are!"

"I wasn't trying to distract them from me."

"Jesus—" Charlie threaded an arm through Vera's and pulled her from the wall. "Come on."

Vera followed without withdrawing her arm, despite Charlie clearly outpacing her. "Wait, aren't we supposed to be a threesome?"

"Please rephrase that."

"Chuck Chaste, just because I don't care for that kind of thing doesn't mean I can't be supportive—well, actually, you never did answer me about what you liked. Should I check off—"

"Murderous scumbags who don't break out their, for lack of a better word, teammates?"

Vera hummed. "So that's a no on bondage, then."

"Ugh."

"Look, I'm just trying to be helpful."

"Then at least tell me you know where the lab is."

"Sure thing. Hang a left."

Charlie turned left at the next possible opportunity, just as the zeppelin listed again and propelled her and Vera into the wall, and then, soon after, the floor. Vera, having fallen on top of Charlie, was first to her feet, and extended a hand to help Charlie up. Her face lit up with self-satisfaction when Charlie took the hand.

"See? Helpful."

"And modest as ever."

"Modesty is for people without convictions."

Charlie snorted. "Jesus."

"What?"

"You say shit like that, and I can definitely buy you as a bad guy."

"Hey!"

Charlie didn't answer. She focused on running, which in turn prompted Vera to focus on giving her directions. By the time they reached the lab, it was abandoned by staff. To Charlie's relief, Vera's handprint was enough to fool the biometrics in this universe, and they were able to waltz inside as though at least one of them owned the place. They spread out. Charlie tried the light switch, but the lights had blown, casting the room in the eerie half-light of the emergency system.

The lab boasted the same retro-future tech as the rest of the ship. Much of the nearest wall was occupied by a single computer, and Charlie nabbed the latest printout and hastily folded it to cram inside her backpack, which was disguised as a purse. Vera was gathering notes from one of the tables into a battered folder. There was no time to read over the data, so it was a simple matter of taking everything and hoping some of it—any of it—was useful.

The large sign declaring CAUTION: DO NOT OPEN above a reinforced door sure as hell seemed useful. She darted toward the door, but when she peered through the porthole, she took an instinctive step back.

There was a parasite on the other side. It hovered in the air, unmoving, as though in repose, its countless tentacles hanging limply below, the tips brushing against the floor. While terrifying in motion, something was unsettling about its utter stillness. Her mind couldn't quite process what she was seeing. She felt vaguely nauseated, though that could easily be the turbulence. If possible, it was getting worse.

Where's Savage? Charlie tore her gaze from the porthole and realized the door wasn't just a door. It was some kind of module. Her eyes landed on a large red button that was behind glass. The connection was clear: press the button, eject the module, save the zeppelin from the parasitic threat in case of emergency. Savage's complicated-I'm-a-spy plan had necessitated a separate team in an airplane and a curious amount of wires to steal back the parasite, but he'd been annoyingly vague about the specifics. Charlie could guess at least some of them involved pressing the big red button. She resisted the urge to press it.

"We should get—" Vera had materialized at Charlie's shoulder, but the parasite stole her train of thought. They both stood and stared at it, the only sound the continued scream of the siren. Frustration burned in the pit of Charlie's stomach. They had to settle for another woman's research when there was a parasite right there, if only they had the time to study it. But between Savage's unreliability and the zeppelin that was on fucking fire, a fact that was getting no less ridiculous, time was the one thing they didn't have.

"I've never seen one so still."

"Yeah, they're usually more—" Vera wiggled her fingers. "You know. With the tentacles and everything."

"Non-Euclidean cockroach squid. You've said it a couple times. I know."

"Good. That's…good. Good listening skills. So like I said—"

"We should get going. Right."

"About that," said Savage, from behind them, because of course he did. Charlie turned to find he was in the doorway to the lab with a gun trained on her. She wished any part of this was surprising. "I'm afraid this is where we part ways."

"…I haven't seen you this whole plan," Vera said.

"I mean in terms of our temporary alliance," said Savage, shooting Vera a look. "I can't let you have that research. These tears? One of you Baums is responsible. Maybe it's you, maybe it's not, but I certainly can't trust you with it." Charlie took a step forward, mostly so he wouldn't get any ideas about changing where he was pointing the gun after dropping the new—but honestly unsurprising—information that one of the various Verity Baums in the multiverse was behind this whole mess.

"What, leaving me locked up on the burning zeppelin wasn't enough?" she said.

"Well, no," Savage said and shot Charlie in the head.

She was getting real sick of people doing that. The cowl had long been extended for the smoke, but the impact was doing nothing for her migraine.

"Ow," she said. "Round two, I guess."

Savage paused with the gun already halfway to Vera and wavered for a second between targets, reaching with his other hand to grab a handrail set by the door. More of his improvised weapon business. Except then he fired, pointing at neither of them. A loud klaxon of a different timbre to the persistent "This zeppelin is on fire, what are you still doing here alarm" sounded, localized to the room. A glance confirmed that he had, in fact, shot the big red button.

"Aw, man, I wanted to press that," Vera said.

So he was actually holding hard to the handrail to hold on to something. Which meant that loud hissing and mechanical snapping—

The cage containing the parasite ejected from the room, the air inside rushing out to follow into empty sky.

Along with Charlie and Vera.

The cage was falling but already beginning to swing on an arc, secured by cables to a plane that had been shadowing the zeppelin. Very soon the cage would cease falling, and they wouldn't, and that would be extremely bad. Charlie spread her hands and legs, a mental note about adding wingsuit functionality into the Velo burning itself into her brain upon a single look past the cage toward the ground.

Just intercept it before it swung away, that was all she could do. Then Vera, then she could, fuck, *fuck*, how could she possibly—

She was going to miss the cage, anyway, she wasn't going to get close enough fast enough, she was going to be beneath it when she reached—

A hand thrust itself out. She seized it.

The cage had turned as it fell, concealing the fact that Vera had managed to turn on the magnets in her boots fast enough to be stuck to it, dangling upside down.

Charlie opened her mouth to say something, or maybe just scream a little, but Vera cut her off.

"Dolt Ravage, your south!"

"What does that—" Charlie began to say, at which point Holt Savage rammed into her back and knocked her loose. She twisted, grabbing for whatever she could, managed to get hold of whatever she could, which proved to be the strap on his jetpack. Because he had a jetpack. Because of-fucking-course he did.

She felt the distinct focused and repeated moment of sharp pressure that indicated he was trying to stab her. She supposed that was reasonable. Bullets didn't work, try stabbing. Stabbing didn't work, well dislodge her from the cage, and then gravity would do his job for him. She scrambled for a better hold, trying to get her arm around his head as he tried to throw it off entirely, neither succeeding entirely. They corkscrewed dizzyingly through open-air, which did not help. He was only using one hand to try and throw her off, which did. Why one hand?

Jetpack controls. She twisted her head enough to spot the thumbstick his other hand was using. She hooked her arm through the strap on the jetpack so that she could leave off trying to choke him and swing that hand loose to grab at it, try to take control of their flightpath.

I'm one thousand feet up in a fucking thumb war for my life, she thought, slightly hysterically.

And winning, or at least not losing, managing to twist their path enough that they were angled back toward the cage swinging along beneath the plane. If she fell, momentum would put her on top of it. Probably. Possibly.

She clicked the snap on the jetpack harness and both of them fell. She had a heart-stopping moment to regret every part of this idea, as well as every decision in her life that had led to this moment, and then she hit the roof of the cage. She bounced. She bounced clear of the cage but got her arm out, catching one of the cables securing it to the plane in the crook of her elbow, spun around it, feet scrabbling for purchase. Her eyes were watering.

Or, no. No, that was a weft in space forming below them.

Faintly, she heard Vera's voice from somewhere on the side of the cage. "Scientific inquiry pause, I'd like to note that Colt Scavenge had to have a really dramatic exit and jetpack fight, so now we have—"

"Resonance," Charlie said, with her, albeit not at a pitch that anyone else could hear, considering the circumstances. She clocked Savage's current whereabouts: he'd caught himself on the cable kitty-corner to her, likewise trying to get his feet.

"You want us to fix that, or you want to be a murderous asshole some more?!" Charlie shouted at him across the swaying cage, pulling out the Browning and leveling it at him. She really didn't feel good about the positioning here. No handrails, nothing to hold on to except the cables at each corner. Also, a fucking parasite some inches below them and no way of knowing if the principles that had kept it quiescent so far were going to hold up. She kind of doubted it. "Because I'm going to have to jump into that fucking thing from here! And that's insane! And it's going to be doing you a favor and it's the right fucking thing to do, but I don't feel good about it because you are such! A! Dick!"

"Eh, I say we go in style," said Vera, taking a clanking step into view, then laboriously trying to make the change from standing on the side of the cage, secured by the magnets in her boots, to standing on top of it. She couldn't use her arms to do it, because she'd caught the jetpack. Which, a moment later, she threw to Charlie.

Who had to do a nerve-wracking bit of juggling as she caught it without dropping the Browning or letting go of the cable. She managed it by just putting her arm out and through one strap, letting its momentum carry it around onto her back. Then she strapped it into place, stepping away from the cable since that was less of a concern now.

"You can do that?" said Savage. "You'll do that?"

"Yeah, because we're not supervillains," said Charlie. Although apparently, somewhere out there, one of the Veritys was.

"Or murderous assholes," Vera said.

Savage considered this, along with his own precarious position, faced with his only exit being slowly climbing up the cable or very rapidly descending to the ground, sans jetpack.

"I don't suppose—"

"Nah," said Vera and Charlie together, as they worked out the carrying-a-person-wearing-marshmallow-power-armor situation.

"It's just I'm kind of...stuck, here—"

"You'll figure something out," Charlie said, beaming at him, and stepped backward off the cage.

Maybe she should have checked she knew how to turn the jetpack back on before she did that. But it just wouldn't have been as satisfying.

"Oh," she said, a moment later, examining the controls instead of the wildly spinning horizon and city spread out quite far below them. "Obviously. Big red button."

She hit the big red button. The jetpack ignited, momentarily increasing the rate with which they were wildly skewing about, until she got the hang of the controls and steadied, pulling out of the falling spin and into a rising arc. With the arm not looped around Charlie, Vera pulled the Coupler out of the backpack squished between Charlie and the jetpack, cocked, and readied it.

Charlie realized she was cackling. Then she realized that Vera was cackling too. She aimed the pair of them square at the tear and didn't stop.

Chapter Sixteen

— LITTLE GREEN MEN —

The newspaper clippings from Dr. Baum's lab painted a compelling alternate history of the tears in the world they'd just left. The first portal had opened during D-Day, disrupting—though not quite ending—the battle while the world's armies contemplated the existential threat and concluded it could wait until the war was won. Important dates were shifted around from those Charlie knew, some occurring earlier, some later. The atomic bomb was first used in an attempt to close a tear over Paris; it was unsuccessful but itself caused no casualties. (The tear, on the other hand, was a different matter.) The post-war landscape was where the differences really started to show. The space race wasn't just a bipolar affair between the Americans and the Soviets. Other countries, notably England and the Commonwealth, had thrown their hats in as well. There were repeated entries about Baum Technologies and punny, sexist headlines about its eccentric new CEO, Miss Verity Baum. Curiously, no efforts were being made to put a man on the moon.

There were a lot of efforts being made to put a man on Mars.

The headlines boasted variations on a theme: LITTLE GREEN MEN? PARASITIC ORIGINS MAY BE MARS EXPERTS SAY. There was no mention of Verity by name in any of those articles, though there was a nod to Baum Technologies' founder, Dr. Victor Baum, having died at Juno Beach.

Dr. Verity Baum's notes were preoccupied with his death. She blamed the parasites and therein was born an obsession. Vera had taken on the task of decrypting her notes—"You can tell she was a genius because everything's in fucking code," Charlie had remarked before dumping the lot on Vera to figure out—and the notes were supporting even the more hyperbolic headlines.

"More coffee?" asked their waiter, a suspiciously lifelike robot named K.A.R.L.

"Hit me," Vera said, sliding her mug to the edge of the table without looking up from her decryption. In spite of their current host universe's impressive technology, she was working with pen and paper, an adorably analog approach she claimed helped her think better. Charlie, meanwhile, had scanned everything they'd stolen from the zeppelin's lab upon arrival and was reading off a VeriPAD, a thin digital reader she bought courtesy of more forged funds.

K.A.R.L. filled Vera's mug with automated precision and rolled away. The diner was between rushes and mostly empty save for the robotic staff. A lone human employee was at the front of the house, fiddling with her smartphone. Charlie almost missed the luxury of boredom.

Vera finished scribbling something and slammed the pen down on the table. Her grin stretched from ear to ear, and she grabbed her coffee to down the rest of it. She was vibrating, and Charlie figured the caffeine was only partly to blame.

"So what's the verdict?" Charlie asked because she could tell Vera wanted to show off. Charlie supposed it was a survival instinct. Being the most significant mind since Einstein wouldn't have been worth a damn to shareholders if she couldn't sell an idea.

The grin was back in full force, shaky at the corners from barely restrained giddiness. "We have to go to Mars."

Charlie blinked. "Come again?"

"Don't you have—" Vera made an irritated gesture at her own ears. "I don't know, enhanced hearing? You heard me."

"We have to go to Mars," Charlie said, because yes, of course, she had heard her.

"We have to go to Mars," Vera tried again, pumping her arms in an aborted cheering motion. Charlie's mouth twitched briefly into a smile in spite of herself. "Turns out VeeVee—"

"Vee...Vee?"

"Villain Verity," Vera clarified. "No, wait, I changed my mind. Villainy Baum is better. Has the same rhythm. I think it's questionable whether she *is* a villain, but I don't have anything catchy involving zeppelins, so. She was at the CSA while we were busy slumming it with Revolting Cabbage. She was conducting trials for some kind of Martian ATV. She had a lot of data on possible origins for her tentacled friend, which I'm...still decoding. Doesn't matter. Point is, she was going to go, we have to go. All of this—" She swept an arm over the table. "—says we have to go to Mars if we're going to get any answers."

"Right, but didn't your...friend," Charlie's tone curled peculiarly around the word, "from the space opera universe say there was no life on Mars?"

"Well, maybe in her universe."

"There's no life on mine, either."

"That's a faulty premise, though. There's no magic in either of our universes, but that hasn't stopped us from finding worlds where magic trumps physics. And—look, right there in the headline. Little green men. Martians are little green men. That's the joke where I'm from. That's—resonance. You—You can't deny there's something there. Maybe not on this universe's Mars, or the space opera's, maybe even not on Villainy's—which would make all of her, y'know, *villainy* for nothing, poor thing—but on one of them. But we're not going to find out which from down here."

Charlie had to concede the point, though she still wasn't entirely convinced what the point meant.

"All right, so we have to go to Mars."

"You're missing the—do the arms."

Charlie raised her arms in a V—for Vera. "We have to go to Mars."

Vera mouthed a little "yay." "Right, so I was thinking—maybe we steal a ship from the spaceport we passed on the way here."

"First we steal a jetpack, now you want to steal a spaceship." Charlie ruefully shook her head. Where was the Car Crew when you needed them? "I feel like I'm leading you down a life of crime."

"You did break into my office that one time."

"*One* time!"

"Just—I mean, morally, I'm still a lighter gray than you are."

"It was in the name of saving the multiverse. I figure a little B and E balances out at the end of the day."

Vera grinned again. "So some grand theft spaceship should be nothing."

Charlie rolled her eyes. It could pass as fond. "You're *really* jazzed about going to Mars."

"And you're not?"

Charlie shrugged and tapped in a few keywords on the VeriPAD.

Vera reached across the table to shake her, nearly sending the coffee over the edge. "Come on. I've been wearing a spacesuit for how many months? Who doesn't want to go to Mars?" She held up a warning finger. "Don't answer that. So what's the plan? I distract the guard while you use some of your natural-born criminal talents to hotwire a ship from one of the parking levels? Or—no, maybe you pose as a valet at a fancy restaurant. That's—That's a classic. Or—"

"Actually, I have a better idea."

Vera had likely never looked so miserable flying first class. Booking a flight to Mars on Ares Astrolines had proven as simple as a few keystrokes on the VeriPAD and a creative money transfer. The flight itself was similarly easy, if predictably long. In that way, jumping between universes had spoiled them. Interplanetary travel took days, whereas inter-dimensional travel only took as long as finding and stabilizing a tear.

That said, there were advantages: a lack of motion sickness. In-flight entertainment. Meal service. Hot towels. (Charlie really liked the hot towels. Vera, searching for anything to complain about, said they were too hot.)

They didn't even have to wear their suits. Vera had had to check the Marshmallow since the hologram couldn't fool the x-ray, and the astroline had surprisingly strict protocols about powered spacesuits. She'd been tetchy ever since, picking at the sleeves of the souvenir MONTREAL SPACEPORT hoodie they'd had to buy since her under armor had seen better days. Out of solidarity, Charlie wore civvies too, though the Velo had passed the security scans no problem. She thought it would help curb some of the complaining.

She was mistaken.

After the first twelve hours, she had enabled her seat's privacy settings and requested a perfectly-hot hot towel before passing out for the night. Because they were in space, night mostly just meant they dimmed the cabin lights, but the effect was more or less the same.

When she came to, in that vague liminal plane-state of wakefulness without any tangible sense it was morning or any specific time at all, Vera had the Velo draped over her tray table and was taking notes and sketching in an overpriced notebook. Charlie supposed that's what she got for a gesture of solidarity.

"If you've touched a single wire—"

"My fingers go only where asked, Cee Cee," Vera muttered, still notetaking. "I'm looking at your threads because I think they frown on tossing blood in a centrifuge on spaceflights. I'm guessing. I don't have a centrifuge, anyway. Just, okay, how much is you and how much is the Velo?"

"I don't know," Charlie admitted. "It was all…insurance. Make me as survivable as possible, put me in something as survivable as possible. And then it turned out we didn't know nearly as much about tear mechanics as we thought. Not real eager to test levels."

"Yeah," said Vera, almost absently. "Yeah. No going through tears without my armor on."

Charlie began to suspect Vera had taken the other approach to travel, where because it was never night, you just treated it as one extended day. Considering the flight was going to be days with an "S", she hoped that changed. Normally Vera was a lot. Completely loopy Vera was a scenario she wanted to deal with almost as little as she wanted to test how she did in a tear without the Velo. Already Vera was a bit off. Her conversational stream of consciousness was usually a little less unconsciously telling.

"If tears are rare in empty air, in the vacuum of space they've gotta be…it's space! It's nothing but infinite nothing!"

Vera looked up at the ceiling, then over at Charlie. "Yes. That makes me much happier about how I'm not wearing my spacesuit right now," she said. "How long did your whole…makeover take, anyway? How invasive are we talking?"

"Months of being weak and sick and probably putting a lot of stress on my heart," Charlie said, emphasizing the last word slightly.

"Right," Vera said, looking annoyed, but not in Charlie's direction. "Look to discover something, get a heart condition. Look to stand up to something, lose a leg, lose an eye. Here is the lesson, Verity Baum, observe your futures. Better learn to be cautious and behave or the universe will punish you for being uppity. Be a good little genius and disappear yourself from the narrative, there's a good girl. The world will run smoother if you pretend like you are not."

Charlie frowned. "Not...?"

"Not special, not you, not in the narrative, not *anything*. The world won't be colorful, and it will suppress everyone into indifferent conformity, but hey, you'll have all your parts! You know what, I reject the lesson. I reject the arc. I will not learn caution. I will learn to make better tools with which to be reckless and alarming."

Charlie resisted the urge to go with one of her first instincts, which was to just say an "okay" that was five minutes long or to turn the privacy settings back on and go back to sleep.

"I think that counts as caution," she pointed out, at last.

"I'm going to sleep," Vera said, enabling her seat's privacy setting.

"You know what I mean, anyway," Vera said, a moment later, having turned it back off. Then she turned it back on.

Then back off. "I just mean—I am going to punch another dragon. You watch me, I will punch a dragon. Upgrading my outfit before I do it doesn't negate the, the Just Vera of punching the dragon."

"You're very reckless and I am alarmed by your behavior," Charlie said, with autocue formality.

"Thank you!" Vera said and turned her privacy settings back on.

It turned out there was plenty of life on Mars, only none of it was Martian. The Mars colonies were the crown jewel of an international coalition of space agencies and had only been open to civilian travelers for the past ten years, though humans, mostly military personnel and professional lab rats, had been living there in some capacity for decades. The planet was still only partially terraformed, with the majority of the population living under the central biodome, Athena, which was large enough to be viewed from orbit and a frankly spectacular feat of human ingenuity. Charlie couldn't tear her eyes away from the window as they landed, keen on taking in every technicolor detail. If the red was different, well. It was *Mars*. She didn't have anything to compare it to, beyond pictures. But she was *here*.

The spaceport was newer than its counterpart in Montreal, and a female voice that was just on the creepy side of pleasant thanked them for flying Ares Astrolines as they disembarked the ship. It felt good to stretch her legs, and even better to take a piss in a stall big enough to turn around in without banging her elbows against the sides. The showers were likewise built for someone of Charlie's height in mind. The extra room made it easier to get changed back into the Velo, and while Charlie hadn't felt naked without her suit, she couldn't deny her relief at having it back on, and her Browning within reach. She tugged the MONTREAL SPACEPORT sweater back on over the top. From a polite distance, she could pass for a young woman on her way to the gym instead of a soldier-turned-interdimensional-traveler wearing a multimillion-dollar suit her travel buddy had better not have fucked with.

Vera took longer in the bathroom. Charlie figured the Marshmallow was only partly to blame, and her suspicions were confirmed when Vera emerged in a hologrammed outfit and a clean head of artfully tousled hair. Charlie's own hair was still damp and pulled back in her usual regulation French braid. Some habits never died.

"Feeling better?" Charlie asked.

"Much." Vera could never be described as relaxed, but she was certainly less tense, the set of her shoulders loose and head held high. She was back to strutting around like she owned the place. Charlie wouldn't have been surprised if some version of her did.

They fell into step. It was a slightly jauntier step than normal due to the difference in gravity. They'd taken long enough in the washroom that the rush from their arrival had cleared, leaving them to walk through the empty halls of the port. A kiosk selling MARS SPACEPORT sweaters caught Charlie's eye. They were identical to the ones she and Vera had purchased in Montreal, save for the one important difference in wording. She resisted the impulse to buy another, but even if she didn't strictly need it, she couldn't quite refute the voice in the back of her head that asked, "How often do you get to go to *Mars*?"

"So where are we starting?"

"Where else do you go when you want to learn some facts about shit?" said Charlie. "And, you know, you've already exhausted your search engine."

"Museum?"

"Museum."

There'd probably be better souvenirs there. Did Mars do gift shops? Maybe she could get a magnet for Mum. That'd fit in her backpack. When she'd been on duty overseas, Charlie had always gotten her parents a little something from the airport gift shop, just enough to mark her time in a foreign land. Being on an alternate reality Mars certainly counted as foreign. It was probably optimistic she was considering souvenirs at all, but Charlie had found it hurt less to think of home if she believed she'd see it again, intact.

"I saw an advertisement for the Martian Natural History Museum while we were on board," she told Vera. The commercial had aired during a twelve-hour marathon of action flicks, and it seemed like the best place to start looking for more information about the local theories about the tears and parasites.

"All right, so we hit the museum, check out the—"

Charlie stepped out in front of Vera. She whipped out the Browning and trained it on the Hound that had rounded the corner. Its eyes flashed red, and Charlie had only a second to realize that drawing a fucking gun in a futuristic airport was not her wisest idea. But security did not descend in droves. It was just the two of them and the...

"What the fuck is that?"

It wasn't the Hound—or even a hound. She could tell because it wasn't murdering the two of them or possibly just Vera. (Charlie wasn't clear on where the Hound would draw the line, and she wasn't exactly raring to find out.) It looked like one, but now that it was standing still and continuing to not launch itself murderously at the two-or-maybe-just-one of them, she could see the differences. It was smaller, and while still biomechanical, the mechanics were simpler. Bulkier, in a similar way the tech in Vera's universe compared to that in Charlie's own, the design of someone approaching the same goal but without the same level of advancement, of miniaturization.

It seemed simultaneously like a cousin to the Hound, a mountain lion to a cheetah, and an earlier hardware generation. Probably several.

Considering they were standing on Mars, that made her a little alarmed about whoever might have made this thing's cousin.

But it didn't appear to be airport security, given that she'd pulled a gun and, again, it wasn't murdering the two-or-maybe-just-one of them.

"A question for the museum, or anywhere it's not staring at us," Vera said, reaching over and waving her hand in the air just beside where Charlie had the gun up. Charlie put the gun down, if only so that Vera wouldn't paw at it.

The protohound continued to stare. Apparently, it wasn't the gun that it was staring at. When they reached a set of escalators down to the next floor and the exit, it didn't follow.

Maybe it didn't have to. When they reached the museum, there were two more protohounds standing on plinths outside, flanking the entrance for all the world as if someone had animated a pair of statues.

This pair watched them, too. Not any of the other people walking the steps to the museum, Charlie noted, just them.

"So if the one we've encountered before was designed to hunt parasites—"

"And me," Vera noted.

"—then these are probably in the same line of work."

"Well, I don't think they're staring because they're admiring my snazzy hair," Vera said. "If they were programmed to eat me, they'd be eating me. I think we just smell."

"Like parasites, or like tears?"

Vera just shrugged. "Maybe just foreign. We're not from around here, but they don't know if we're the kind of not from around here they should be attacking. So they're not, making them a possible improvement on every human who guarded a border."

"Still staring, though."

"Well, built by people. Partly built by people."

"And partly grown." Charlie suppressed a shudder. Here she was, a walking, talking lab experiment herself, but the unbidden image of a scientist surveying a vat full of half-formed body parts flashed in her mind.

"Creepy."

They stared a moment longer, and then, as one, started inside through the automatic doors. Charlie immediately felt underdressed. The interior of the museum was immaculate, the borderline sterility that belonged exclusively to the massively wealthy: white marble floors, gleaming walls that doubled as information screens, a distinctly minimalist decor. There was no line at the front counter, and they purchased two adult fares with forged funds from a woman in a tasteful all-black uniform. In lieu of tickets, they were given stickers to attach to their clothing and a wireless earbud that would act as an audio guide.

"If you have any questions, one of our attendants will be happy to help you."

"Thanks," said Charlie, and Vera echoed, though hers had a considerably more flirtatious bent to it.

They attached their stickers and put in the earbuds. An unobtrusive song was already playing—futuristic Martian Muzak. It continued to play until they entered the first exhibit, THE ROAD TO MARS, which was guarded by a heavyset man in a similar uniform to the woman operating the front desk. A posh male voice replaced the music and launched into an explanation of the early days of the space program. The exhibit's staging resembled that of a fine art gallery more than a history museum, each artifact carefully curated rather than an explosion of curiosities. There was a replica of Buzz Aldrin's flight suit. A lunar rock given a prominent place on a pedestal. A life-size model of *Sputnik* suspended from the ceiling. Photographs of *Sputnik*'s launch in 1957, and the *Explorer 1*'s launch in 1958. The smiling faces of Yuri Gagarin, Valentina Tereshkova, Alan Shepard, Neil Armstrong, Sally Ride, John Glenn, Chris Hadfield, Mae Jemison, and others, a *Who's Who* of famous astronauts.

"I always wanted to be an astronaut," said Vera, reaching up to touch the portrait of Sally Ride. "The CSA never wanted to take me on, though. Something about not being a team player."

"I can't imagine where they got that idea."

"Hey! I mean, *we're* a team. Baum and Chase. Charity, like the coffee cups said."

Charlie looked over to gauge Vera's sincerity. "Remember that the next time you want to punch a dragon."

"Why, because you want to punch one too?" Off Charlie's arched brow, Vera continued, "Oh, don't give me that look."

"And what look is that?"

"The look that says, 'Who me? I'd never laugh like a loon while skydiving from a burning zeppelin.' I saw you, Sarge." She squeezed Charlie's shoulder and pulled her closer. It wasn't quite an embrace, but it was fast approaching one with its familiarity. "You might act like you're the responsible one—"

"Because I am—"

"—but that's only because I—"

"Ruin the curve. Like...just obliterate the curve. See: punching dragons."

Vera guided Charlie away from the photographs. "Okay, point taken, but my point is, we're a team."

"Fine," said Charlie. "We're a team. Let's do a trust fall and sing a song by the burning zeppelin."

"You set fire to *one* zeppelin..."

Charlie laughed so loudly one of the guards flashed her a warning glare. She resisted giving him the finger.

LIFE ON MARS? asked the sign above the entrance for the final exhibit. They passed through the double doors into a large hall. A solar-powered space exploration vehicle roughly the size of a large SUV was slowly rotating on a turntable. Its information placard read "Belonging to the first confirmed life on Mars." The audio guide explained the Rover belonged to the first crew who landed on Mars in 2036. Despite the Rover's disappointingly slow top speed of 16 kilometers per hour, it was built to last for thousands of kilometers—though it was famously a very bumpy ride. Mars—at the time, at least, Charlie couldn't speak about the present yet—didn't exactly have a highway, and the astronauts spent as much time peering through the large-windowed dome that made up the front half of the vehicle as they did trying to stay some approximation of seated.

There were other odds and ends from the first Martian settlers: video diaries, uneaten meals still vacuum sealed, spacesuits. A multimedia station pulled Charlie's attention away from an old computer module, and as she made her approach, the audio guide changed from a diary entry by Martian settler Loa Ram to the familiar voice of this universe's Verity Baum, who was speaking animatedly on the screen.

She was about the same age as Vera, maybe a little older, and the chyron beneath her face named her as DR. VERITY BAUM, NOTED ASTROPHYSICIST.

"...evidence strongly suggests there was once a full-blown civilization," said on-screen Verity. Vera ambled over once she noticed Charlie waving at her and came to a stop beside her. The station had the feel of a sideshow, one of those less serious exhibits intended as something of a lark, a fringe theory to smile indulgently over. You could tell because there was an interrobang on the sign. Underneath the video of Verity Baum expounding on her beliefs was a touchscreen option to play SPOT THE UFO or EXPLORE THE MARTIAN ARCHITECTURE. Either it was a response to what Verity was saying, or she'd anticipated it because she was talking about how there weren't any artifacts or signs of building or any of the archaeological finds traditionally associated with a society having existed. Her theory apparently had to do with the wrong kind of dirt, some of which contained elements not usually found on Mars. As she put it, you either had to figure on a lot of asteroid impacts, or people moving things from one place or one planet to another or performing manufacturing processes on the dirt. Without ever leaving any products of manufacturing behind.

(The on-screen Verity did not say that last part. A passive-aggressive on-screen chyron did.)

The video ended. Vera played SPOT THE UFO for a while. Every time you spotted a UFO, the screen explained how it was a shooting star, or a weather satellite, or a media-informed hallucination forming part of a sleep paralysis episode. Then Vera played EXPLORE THE MARTIAN ARCHITECTURE, a game in which life on Mars turned out to consist of a race of passive-aggressive chyrons popping up to tell you that actually, this was just natural erosion, or wind, or human pattern recognition playing tricks.

Then Vera started hacking the station to install a game she called "Oregon Odyssey," and before Vera could program it to give anyone dysentery, Charlie figured they were done there.

"Well, it's a start," said Charlie, dropping off her earbud in the designated bin outside of the exhibit.

"Sure, now we know I'm maybe crazy in this universe."

"The chyron *did* say 'noted.'"

"Fine, yes, then I'm the *noted* maybe crazy Verity Baum. Stellar."

They started down a long hallway lined with digital posters advertising upcoming museum events. Most were geared toward children, but one looked promising. Charlie stopped walking, and it took Vera a few seconds to realize no one was pretending to listen to her grousing before she turned back around.

"Hey—"

The advertisement was for a black-tie charity gala taking place at the museum tomorrow night. A number of speakers, most of whom Charlie recognized from the exhibit, were listed at the bottom, with Maybe Crazy Verity Baum occupying the last slot.

"Look at that," Vera said. "I'm invited. Let's go to a party."

"A party *you'll*," Charlie said, nodding significantly at the list, "be at."

"I'll probably be late," Vera said. "We need the info they don't put out in the fun interactive experiences, right? The actual research. We attend, we ditch. If nothing else, we can pick some people's brains. The best brains in their fields, presumably."

"And also alternative you," Charlie said. Vera looked playfully faux-insulted. But Charlie had to admit she didn't have an alternative plan to "party on Mars," and also, *party on Mars.*

"Okay," she said. "Let's go to a party."

Chapter Seventeen

— TYPICAL BAUM BULLSHIT —

The hologram, somewhat unsurprisingly, did not have a ready-to-go futuristic space party option programmed, and they spent the hours leading up to the gala tinkering with settings. With another Verity Baum likely in attendance—even if she would probably be late, as Vera predicted—the possibility of a tear opening was too great to risk going unprepared, though their research had shown there were no previous tear sightings on Mars. On one hand, Charlie was averse to needlessly risking lives, but on the other hand, if Crackpot Verity showed, it could be their first real opportunity to test the Resonance Hypothesis, see if they couldn't get Crackpot Verity on board to recreate what had happened on the *Verity Baum*. Either way, leaving all of their gear at the hotel while they played dress-up simply wasn't an option.

Vera did insist on at least having their hair and makeup done. Charlie had no strong opinions on makeup, mostly because she couldn't remember the last time she'd even worn any that wasn't for tactical purposes. Maybe her high school graduation, which felt like another lifetime ago. While she wondered why Vera even needed a professional to do her hair when she seemed to do a plenty professional job herself, Vera wasn't budging on the issue—a creature comfort, she called it. The concierge of their hotel recommended a salon within walking distance, and before Charlie could muster up a token protest, she was seated in a hoverchair while Artemis the Martian Hairstylist, a tall boulder of a woman with platinum hair that stood on end, cut and styled her hair.

It said so, right on her name tag: Artemis on the first line, and then, beneath it on its own line, MARTIAN HAIRSTYLIST. The distinction wasn't, strictly speaking, necessary, but Charlie figured that if she worked on fucking Mars, she'd want "Martian" affixed to her job title too. It was remarkable to see how the colonists had made a home here, on another planet. The human species was resilient, much like Artemis's gravity-defying hair.

"It's mostly just a lot of hairspray," she confessed as she put Charlie's hair in some kind of curler. "We're only supposed to have thirty-eight percent of Earth's gravity, but to be honest, my hair can't really tell the difference. I've got no volume in the morning, mark my words."

By the time they were ready to leave an hour later, Vera looked the same to Charlie's eye—improbably polished as ever. Charlie's hair, meanwhile, had enough pins in it that she was concerned about metal detectors, and the subtlety of the makeup belied how many products she'd had slapped on her face. She didn't look especially different, except maybe more rested. They paid a small ransom in forged currency for the service and donned their new holograms before returning to the museum. Their gowns inversely mirrored each other's, Vera in form-fitting black and Charlie in Grecian-inspired silver. Minimalism, by all accounts, was in, so they'd programmed no jewelry.

The charity gala was ostensibly open to the public, which meant getting in was a simple matter of buying tickets. Of course, the tickets were exorbitantly expensive, but then money was as effective a gatekeeper for undesirable guests as any security force. Fortunately, they had the Fabricator. It did a better job in this universe than in some, apparently more in line with the rules of the universe from which they'd acquired it, although it was still a little fractious. Charlie suspected the fact they had to keep messing around with it was having its own inevitable degrading effect. You could only do patch-up futz work to something so much before the patch-up futz work became part of the problem. They bypassed the press line—*do they have little badges designating themselves as MARTIAN PAPARAZZI?*—using an apparently well-honed tactic of Vera's called "using the back entrance" and arrived at the event fashionably early. As he scanned her ticket, the usher gave Vera a weird look and informed her that as a guest speaker she hadn't needed to buy a ticket.

"Any excuse to donate to a cause I care deeply about," Vera replied, which was a convincing enough impression of Crackpot Verity for the usher not to press the issue. Charlie followed after with no problems.

The gala was held in a cavernous banquet hall. The room's impressive architecture was deemed sufficient decoration, as the black marble pillars stood bare. About twenty large tables occupied most of the floor, and there was a small stage at the front of the room. Illuminated glass display cases dotted the lengths of the walls. Charlie clocked seventeen guests, six waitstaff, four stage techs, and zero Crackpot Veritys, which meant the first part of their plan was a success. Their tickets placed them at Table #6, but given that they probably wouldn't be able to stay for dinner anyway, they didn't bother settling in. Charlie grabbed an hors d'oeuvre from a passing waiter and popped it into her mouth.

"Space chicken," she mumbled thoughtfully.

"Watts," Vera said.

Charlie swallowed. "I said 'space chicken.'"

"No, I got that. *Watts*. Look."

Josephine Watson's latest counterpart stood at the entrance of the hall. She had close-cropped hair and wore a deep purple halter gown. Vera's expression suggested more than intellectual interest, and Charlie was briefly tempted to ask if she'd ever dated Watts, if that was another resonant thread between the universes, though Verity and Josie had already been ancient history by the time Charlie made their acquaintance.

"We should go talk to her," Vera said.

"Uh-huh," Charlie said.

"No, not for—Wattses tend to have some association with Baums, right? She probably knows the deal. We'll ask her."

"About a thing we—*you* are supposed to be the resident proponent of."

"We'll ask her subtly," said Vera.

"Oh no," Charlie said, but Vera was already moving, and Charlie could either abandon her to the disaster or try to steer into the skid. She hurried along in the eddy that formed as Vera created a lane between her and her target just by deciding there would be one.

Admittedly, there were only twenty-six people to not be in the way of that, but nonetheless, the beeline existed. Charlie just had to hope Vera wasn't going to waste their one sting on the wrong play.

"Josie!" Vera said effusively, sliding it into a "—phine!" when Josephine of Mars looked momentarily confused. "I like the hair."

"I've had this haircut for two years," said Josephine of Mars.

"And I like it," said Vera, with a heedless cheerfulness that actually did belay the look of confusion on J of M's face. "Ready to spread the good word?"

"*Your* good word, you mean," J of M said. Charlie couldn't tell if this meant she didn't believe in the theory, or just accredited it entirely to Verity.

"That's why it's so good. Since, as we know, it's a pretty compelling theory once it's all laid out."

"Well, you would say that," J of M said. Calibrating her position was still pretty hard.

"I would, wouldn't I?" Vera said, downing half a glass of something Charlie wasn't even sure when she'd picked up. She suspected Vera might have willed it into existence. "Well, what would you say? Lemme hear it. Fresh take."

"You've *heard* my take," J of M said, looking confused again. But a nettled kind of confused. "We both know your pet theory—you *just* said, 'as we know.' Why would I lay out your own theory to you? I'm not here to massage your ego."

"Well, see, it's—Chuck!" Vera said, seizing Charlie by the arm and attempting to yank her into closer proximity of the conversation, instead just tilting herself about thirty degrees off vertical before she tipped back and pretended she was just patting Charlie's arm. "She was wondering about it. I thought you could hit her with the talking points."

"*Your* talking points," J of M said. "What is this? Is this some kind of test? Are you checking if I'm up on my scientific literature? In front of—I don't know if she's a new hire or what. Is that it, a pissing contest to show off to the newest intern at your think tank? That's ridiculous. That's the kind of competitive B.S. we should be above, even when we don't agree. We don't prove assholes like La Roche wrong by being assholes like La Roche! Honestly."

Josephine of Mars swept off.

"That went well," said Vera, in a tone that meant she was mostly convincing herself.

Charlie popped another space chicken ball into her mouth. "You see anyone who looks like a La Roche?"

Vera wrinkled her nose and looked away. "Can you—has no one ever taught you to chew with your mouth shut?"

"Increased metabolism," replied Charlie, like that made sense, as a boisterous group of men entered the hall. One man, in particular, drew attention to himself. His bespoke suit signified wealth over taste, the fabric's jewel tones flattering against his bronzed skin but clearly faddish. His tan begged the question of whether or not there were Martian tanning beds. Most of the locals had ashy complexions regardless of race, but he stood out like a sun-soaked beacon. He probably spent more time on Earth than on Mars, Charlie decided, and more time outside than in a lab. An actor, maybe, who played an astronaut in a movie once upon a time and was now trotted out to charity events to raise awareness of the space program. His fawning entourage—and that's what it was, she realized, an *entourage*, not a group of colleagues, but a pack of sycophants—suggested a celebrity, not a scientist. Even Vera at her peak Just Vera hadn't needed an entourage to simply walk into a room.

Then again, J of M said asshole, right?

Charlie narrowed her eyes and started walking. The growing crowd parted, not with the effortless ease Vera might have commanded, but with glared looks and the occasional swallowed curse at Charlie's back as she passed. Vera was on her heels.

"Where are you—? Oh. Really? Him?"

"Do you spot a bigger looking asshole?"

A pause as Vera looked over the room. "Point."

"Exactly. Go introduce us."

Vera squared her shoulders, which was wholly unnecessary as she had enviously good posture, and donned her best boardroom smile, the one that warned the wise she was a shark and fooled pricks into a false sense of superiority.

"Dr. La Roche!" she exclaimed, extending a hand, which he ignored. His answering smile was paternalistically wolfish, and he cupped her elbows to draw her in for a quick kiss to each cheek.

"Verity," he said, pronouncing it *"vérité."* It was hard to tell if they were old friends, or if he was simply *French.* (*Not Québecois, though,* Charlie noted. *His vowels are all wrong. Parisian bastard.*) He did not immediately let go of her arms, instead taking a fractional step back to allow for a better view of her dress. His gaze swept up and down and up again, with a notable detour spent at the level of her chest. Vera's smile remained static and practiced, though the set of her brows was at once both knowing and disgusted. "It's been too long. But please, call me Roman. I insist."

So they knew each other. Or they'd met before, at least.

"Well, you know how it is, Roman," Vera said, gently disengaging from his grasp under the pretense of giving her empty glass to a passing waiter. "Work, work, work."

His face split into another wide grin. Charlie showed remarkable restraint by not punching him. He had a very punchable face.

"Of course, your *théorie* about life on Mars is fascinating," said La Roche. Jackpot. Yet Charlie's interest was like blood in the water because La Roche inclined his head. "But who is this?"

Goddamn it. La Roche's appraising body scan was no less subtle for Charlie, but she wasn't as practiced as Vera at ignoring it, and her expression plainly spoke her irritation.

Fortunately, La Roche was as handsome as his name was apt, as he didn't seem to notice.

"This is Chuck. She's my new intern," Vera said, a hint of alarm around her eyes as La Roche reached for Charlie's hand and kissed her knuckles. Charlie mentally counted backward from ten. Her saving grace was that she couldn't feel his perfectly moisturized lips, that he was actually kissing the Velo's gloves, though the hard light of the hologram meant he couldn't tell the difference. "Very fascinated by my research."

The word choice was deliberate, Charlie could tell, mirroring his phrasing to get him back on track. He gave her hand a squeeze and let go. She resisted the impulse to go burn the suit. It was fireproof.

It would take more time than they had. It would probably be worth it.

"*Enchanté, mademoiselle,*" he said.

"Sure," Charlie said, trying to look simpering or interested or anything appropriate. She didn't know what to play it as, or really how to play things. Not punching him or looking horrified was about the limit of her skill.

"And you are captivated by the romantic thought that we walk in the steps of a great Martian civilization?"

"For which there is plenty of evidence," Vera said, having shifted half a step, placing herself such that she was just slightly to the side and behind La Roche. If he looked for her to supply further details, she wasn't immediately in his field of view.

He didn't look.

"*Mais oui,*" he said. "As you know—" Behind him, Vera winked. "—none have ever found artifacts or architecture on Mars. But nonetheless, the pieces are there, the signs that a civilization existed. Perhaps they even traveled the stars, as we do! For there are elements here found only on other worlds, or not at all. The usual explanation is asteroid strike. Pah! So prosaic. Indeed, from whence did the asteroids spring?"

"They haven't always been there?" said Vera, squinting into her glass as she swirled it around.

La Roche, paying no attention to the fact that Verity Baum, renowned astrocrackpot and progenitor of the theory he was explaining at length was asking this obvious question, barreled on. "*Mais non!* In all likelihood, a planet once lay between Mars and the God-King, Jupiter. There is a tremendous cataclysm, a strike worthy of the gods, and the planet is destroyed. Its remains spin on to become the asteroid belt. At the same time, the magnetosphere of Mars collapses. What are the chances, *chérie*, that such cataclysms would occur about the same time? On the scale of universes, it is rather like—"

"Roman, I know all this, it's my theory," Vera said. Charlie had seen her head snap up on "magnetosphere" and knew why. That was what linked all this in, because they'd seen a place where the magnetosphere was wearing out, and could even pin it on a cause.

Too many tears. There was important data missing, because many of the worlds they'd been to hadn't been in a position to study Mars, and she and Vera hadn't been looking for that information. But each of the spacefaring versions of Earth they'd hit, Mars had always been a dead planet or in the process of terraforming. They'd never seen a Mars that had been a green, living world since before humanity got a look at it.

She'd seen Vera hit the same mental conclusion she had: it was possible that what was happening to their Earths was what had happened to Mars. With that in mind, they didn't need to talk to this pompous ass anymore.

"Kind of surface level, really. How about we leave, and you explain the actual science?" Charlie said.

"Or how about I do it," said a stomach-sinkingly familiar voice.

Crackpot Verity was not late. Crackpot Verity was there. *Crackpot Verity was there* and already rubbing elbows. Worse, she was grabbing elbows—Vera's elbow, specifically.

The sound of a pebble being dropped in water reverberated throughout the room as a tear the size of a tennis ball opened in a nearby display of astronaut helmets. The tear did not stay the size of a tennis ball for long, swelling as people stared in mute shock.

"Shit *fuck*!" said Charlie, which was evidently the correct sequence of words to inspire swift and sudden action.

Vera tore away from CV's grip. CV's expression was twisted in understandable—but no less frustrating, fury—as she locked eyes with her impostor. They didn't have time for the Doppelgänger Paso Doble. They were about to jump realities while on another planet. Charlie's head was spinning with logistics. While resonance was a strong idea, a compelling idea, like the best stories all were, the data they had was still anecdotal. They'd considered asking CV for her help, maybe, with the intent to avoid physical contact until they had their ducks in a row. They didn't always land in convenient places. Resonance alone was no guarantee they'd have access to food and water and, more basic still, air.

The Velo was capable of producing oxygen indefinitely. The Marshmallow was not.

They needed a plan. Plans had not exactly proven their forte, but they would need some form of transportation, a mobile base of operations to work from in the event they arrived in a universe where humans hadn't yet started colonization. They needed—

"The Rover," said Charlie, at the same time as CV was saying "Who the hell are you?" to Vera, as though Vera, and not the tear in reality, was the most pressing thing in the room. Typical Baum bullshit.

Charlie swung her arm back and dropped CV cold. It was a punch several realities in the making, and she could hardly help the slight thrill of satisfaction as CV swayed on her feet before falling onto the floor in all her finery. Hopefully this was a universe where blunt force trauma just meant a nice nap.

"Get that woman out of here immediately," Charlie barked at a Martian usher.

"Also...everybody," Vera said, putting her hands on her hips and surveying the forming tear. She looked almost as if she would glare it out of existence. Almost, because the effect was ruined somewhat by the fact that she was edging backward. Her holographic dress was clipping through the other Verity's everything. Nobody appeared to notice, not even the usher who was seizing CV under the arms and pulling her away.

Nor La Roche, who looked from the Verity on the ground to the Vera sidling away from the very dangerous hole in the world and declared, "Fear not, *chéries*. It is, obviously, a side effect of this dangerous phenomenon. An echoing. A visual hallucination."

The usher paused, looked down at the weight in his arms, immediately became a better scientist than La Roche by concluding the woman in his arms existed and continued hauling her to safety. Vera began to strategize. "You're a fancy museum on Mars, you keep your Rover in pristine condition, right? You look after it, it's history. Because if it's an empty shell—"

"We're fucked," Charlie concluded. "It might just be sawdust under the controls, though. Nothing for—I don't know, Martian mice to chew on."

"Well, if there's Mars mice—Marce? Those don't combine well, let's hope for different rodents—at least we'll have something to eat. Otherwise, Fabricator. Can also get us patches for anything they took out of the Rover. You know what I'm wondering?"

"How infinitesimal our chances of surviving are, even in comparison with where they usually are, which is fucking tiny? What the hell is La Roche doing?"

He hadn't backed away from the tear. Vera and Charlie at this point were half the room away and honestly should have been further. Charlie was just kind of hypnotized by his complete refusal to recognize the danger. He had produced what appeared to be a large rod, because of course it was a large rod. It had dials. He was turning them.

"We have, of course, been researching the phenomenon, and have devised a way of bringing the instability into phase, thus rendering it inert."

Vera and Charlie both paused. This universe had protohounds. Maybe they had tear tech that was further along than Charlie's was? They'd tried sticking stabilizing equipment on a pole or on a tether, of course, but maybe there was a trick to getting that to work, or possibly there was something you could do from the inside?

He finished playing with his rod and thrust it inside the hole without ceremony. A jagged line spread from it, expanding like reality was a layer of cracking glass.

"And now I simply—" he said, and then the tear surged wider, further, and La Roche was gone.

Most of him. All of the solid parts.

"Maybe if I throw up now, I'll be fine going through," Vera said, covering her mouth and bending a little forward.

"Jesus fuck," Charlie said, and then, "Rover."

They ran for the display, vaulting the red rope blocking access to the rest of the museum. The stands dragged behind the rope tangled around Vera's ankle for a few steps before she shook it loose. Only to skid to a halt a few steps later to nearly collide into Charlie, who had already stopped. Two of this world's protohounds were coming down the corridor. Their eyes were set red. This did not seem promising. They hadn't seemed especially focused on Vera, not like the evolved, advanced version that had been hunting them across worlds, but now things were going sideways. Now they'd met her.

One crouched. Lept. Charlie tackled Vera sideways—

Out of the way of an arc that had been going above them both, and into the parasite behind them.

"Oh," Vera said. "Well, at least that's—"

The protohound came apart in a shower of sparks and viscera.

"Fuck," Charlie said, hauling Vera to her feet as the second protohound went past them. Had the parasite seemed hurt? Less tentacles? Impossible to tell, impossible to count. "Fuck, *fuck*."

"Rover," said Vera.

"Come over," said Charlie, which Vera wouldn't even get, because of the whole alternate universe thing, and now they were either going to die in this fucking universe from parasites or a tear in reality, or they were going to die on an alternate Mars from not having what they needed to survive because they had to put it together in five fucking seconds or a lot of people were going to die.

They rushed into the room containing the Rover, which was several rooms over from what had been the gala and was now a disaster. There was a logistical problem there, but they didn't have to consider it for several more steps, because they had to get this thing working first.

"Well, they left the parts in it, at least," Charlie said, hopping up on the front as Vera checked the back. "They took the power out, though, almost like they didn't want someone just driving off with it."

"How frustratingly forward-thinking of them."

"Tell me about it."

"I did, those were the words coming out of—hang on."

Charlie huffed but said nothing. The Rover was solar-powered, but the panels hadn't been properly charged in god knows how long. The exhibit had windows, sure, but how much sun really penetrated the glass and the biodome? If she could reconnect the engine, there was a chance it would go, but there wasn't exactly a handy user manual.

She looked up. Vera had disappeared. This seemed alarming.

Vera reappeared, awkwardly dragging one of the dead proto-hounds behind her. A trail of fluids led back where she'd been. Charlie couldn't tell if it was mechanical or organic and wasn't about to go sniff.

"Let's see, what looks like...power," Vera said, rummaging through innards before producing a core, with a bunch of wires hanging off. "Also, bunch of wires. And it's probably compatible, because—"

"Same world, same tech. It's probably not plug and play, but—"

"We're smart ladies," Vera said, hopping up on the front beside her, hurriedly examining the set-up and wiring things into place. It looked like it would start.

"Okay, what else do we need," Charlie said, heading for the driver's side door and arriving there at the same time as Vera. They stood there, at an unstated impasse, as she ran through the list. "It drives. It recycles air, and my suit and your confection do air, so we can work out air solutions. Fabricator for food and drink. I'm driving."

"I'm driving; you're making sure we don't get eaten or shot or, I don't know, hounded on our way there," Vera said.

"...fuck," Charlie said, opening the airlock, getting in, and shuffling over to the passenger side. Vera got in after her, holographic dress jutting through random parts of the Rover, and they sat there and looked at the logistical problem they'd wordlessly put to the side earlier.

The Rover was a large vehicle. It didn't fit through the doors they'd come in. It could go elsewhere in the building, the museum had had to get it in, but it did not have a route specifically to where the tear was shredding this dimension one passive-aggressive interactive display at a time.

"Tell me you're not going to just gun and ram it," Charlie said, already knowing the answer. If they damaged the Rover, they died on the other side of the tear. Maybe in the tear. The La Roche parts still on the floor were fresh in her mind. She could almost smell it.

...actually, that might be the protohound innards on Vera's hands, as she said, inexplicably, "I'm not going to gun and ram it. You've still got the lures, right? At least one left? Shoot the wall."

Charlie, already rummaging for it, looked up, trying to follow this to a conclusion. She reached one. It was terrible.

"That's terrible," she said.

"I could just gun it..."

Charlie swore, took out the lure gun, leaned out the airlock and shot the wall in front of them.

Tentacles clipped through it a moment later. It was so much worse than what was happening with Vera's holographic dress.

"Sure, great, now it eats maybe a little of the wall, we drive at it, and it eats us. Good solve," Charlie said.

"Wait for—" Vera started, but waiting wasn't required. The parasite burst through the wall, or rather the wall burst around it as a protohound slammed into it, two of them, both curling around the parasite, biting, tearing. Not as effective as the actual Hound, but enough of them could serve. How many did they have here? Probably not enough if the tear kept growing. Well, it wasn't going to get the chance.

Vera gunned the engine. The Rover leaped forward, enough clearance to go over the awful pile of protohounds and parasite. A single-double tentacle whipped upwards, dead center through the rear of the Rover. Charlie and Vera both plastered themselves as far to the sides as they could and then they were clear, they were past. Something sparked in the back.

They crashed through the hole in the wall, weakened from, well, the hole. Something snapped off the Rover. Charlie had to hope nothing vital.

She leaned out the airlock again, got off the stabilizing charge just before scrambling back within the confines of the Rover and shutting the door. They passed through. They hit La Roche on the other side. He was all vitals, now spread out over the window.

She joined Vera in throwing up.

Chapter Eighteen
— MARTIANS —

"**F**UCK."

Charlie slammed a hand against the Rover's dash, the impact hard enough for pain to shoot up the length of her arm. The dash escaped unscathed. That was the good news. She tried to focus on the good news because she was sure as shit bracing herself for the bad news. There was no way in hell a fucking museum antique made a universal jump without sustaining some kind of damage.

The pink-sprayed remains of Roman La Roche on their windshield didn't count.

The technology behind the Hound far outstripped what was available on Charlie's Earth, but Veritech's thinking had followed the same lines: that surviving a trip through reality required a biomechanical approach. That's why the jumps were so much harder on Vera, even with all the tinkering she'd done to the Marshmallow to make it more specialized to exploring reality instead of just space. A little trip through Lady Josephine's magic bathtub might've undone some of the damage of the initial jumps, sure, but it was nothing compared to the months of therapies Charlie had suffered through in the name of science.

La Roche's trinket never really stood a chance. Now he was mist on a dead planet, and they were alive… For now.

They needed to close the tear.

"I'm not—I'm not saying I *disagree* with the… very concise assessment, but maybe we don't hit the life-sustaining vehicle," said Vera, holding up her hands in an approximation of a placating gesture. Vera was not built for placating, though, so she mostly just looked awkward, like she was preparing herself for arrest. She went to wipe her mouth with the back of her hand and met with the resistance of her still-deployed visor, hidden by the hologram.

Charlie took in a deep breath and aborted her attempt at meditation before even starting because *fuck, we need to check the life support systems.* She turned from Vera, who was enough of a genius to get the hell out of her way and sat down at the console to pull up their oxygen levels. The parasite's phasing hadn't left a hole in the back of the Rover. They weren't going to asphyxiate if their suits gave out, at least, though the climate control was a bit concerning. They'd gained a few degrees since the museum. Probably a wiring issue. Not a priority (yet).

"How's the Marshmallow for temperature control?"

"There's a cooling system." Her "why" was unspoken.

"Good," said Charlie.

"Are we making s'mores?"

"Hopefully not."

"Well, I wish I had a better segue than a veiled reference to cannibalism to mention this, but." Vera shrugged, holding up the Fabricator. It had seen better days, sure, but Charlie couldn't spot the cause for Vera's frown. She wasn't left in suspense for long. "The power source got damaged. Once the charge goes…"

Right. That would be it, then. Charlie resisted the impulse to hit the dash again. Instead, she huffed out a breath and slapped on a toothy smile.

"Guess who's glad *her* suit isn't food-themed?" She hitched a thumb at her chest. "This gal."

"You wouldn't eat me."

They stopped their damage assessment and met each other's gazes, both willing the other to crack first. Charlie lost, letting out a loud snort, shaking her head. "I can't believe you just said that."

Vera shrugged one shoulder and went back to work.

While they were in better shape than they had any right to be, they were nowhere near out of the woods and needed to prioritize. The first order of business was the tear. Once they established the Rover's integrity was stable enough to risk opening the airlock, Charlie ventured out to close the tear, a disquietingly *quiet* process in Mars's thin atmosphere. As the tear blinked out of existence, she surveyed the barren landscape that remained; her sensors didn't pick up any other tears on the planet, which meant they wouldn't have to worry about parasites or hounds showing up, but it also meant they didn't have a convenient way off fucking Mars. They could open a tear themselves—a Hail Mary move Charlie had been reluctant to put into practice again, seeing as the first time they'd tried that, she got Vera stuck on this interdimensional road trip, too—but repairing the tech to do so would take time since it had taken a beating on the trip over.

When Charlie returned inside the Rover, Vera greeted her with the good news that they probably wouldn't die of starvation or asphyxiation before fixing the tech. The bad news was there were a lot of other fucking things they could die from because they were *stuck on fucking Mars*. The potentially worse news was that Charlie's sensors were unreliable. Maybe there were other tears. Maybe there were plenty of parasites that could kill them. Mars's magnetosphere had collapsed, the same as the Wasteland's.

Shouldn't there be other tears? Or was resonance impossible once a planet was dead? The thrill of being on another planet, in another universe, was superseded by the fact that space was a scary fucking place to be without a plan and three backup plans.

They decided to explore anyway. They came to the decision mutually, or as mutually as one could get when crammed into a relatively small space with two large personalities.

"We need to start traveling between Marses, not Earths," Vera said.

"Hell of a fucking detour to get back home," Charlie muttered, finally scrubbing the vomit from her cowl before the smell was permanently etched into her nostrils. It might already be too late.

"Right, but the more we understand what we're dealing with, the better our chances of figuring out a way to navigate."

Charlie kept scrubbing.

"Anyway," Vera continued, "it's the best lead we've had since 'consider the fern.' And if Verity Thaum thought she could travel between realms, or…whatever the magical nomenclature demands alternate realities be called, then there has to be a rhyme or reason to which tears go where."

"So what, we try to find a Mars that isn't already a dead husk? Ask the little green guys hey, what's up with the magnetosphere? Would they even understand English?" Charlie stopped her scrubbing to ponder, "Ever notice how weird it is that everyone we've met does speak English?"

"Resonance, probably," Vera said, waving a hand. "Like calls to like. If we were French, we'd be hitting up all the French universes—you could sound more excited, you know."

"Sorry," said Charlie, who wasn't very sorry at all. "I'm just caught up in the logistics."

"We're out of good options," Vera pointed out. "So why not try one of the iffy-but-not-terrible ones?"

Maybe there weren't any tears or lifeforms, but that didn't mean there weren't any answers.

The Rover wasn't going to win any races. It was a rough, bumpy, *slow* ride across the bleak Martian landscape, and while the view was nothing to sniff at, it was also the same view for a very long time. Charlie was reminded of Afghanistan, of being stationed in Kandahar, of the peculiarly acute boredom that came with soldiering where every day was a case of hurry up and wait for shit to go wrong. Once she'd been stuck outside the wire for three weeks, in an LAV III that had been equipped for a mission meant to last only three days. If life as they knew it operated on the law of stories, then maybe she had to consider that experience as *foreshadowing*.

"You really wouldn't eat me," said Vera, jarring Charlie from her light doze. She'd been dreaming of lip-syncing to ridiculous pop songs on a sandy army base.

The Rover was stopped in the midday sun to recharge its battery. Vera was tinkering with the Fabricator's settings and had one tiny screwdriver hanging precariously from the corner of her mouth.

Charlie yawned, rubbing sleep from her eyes. "This again?"

"I'm bored. Humor me."

"I'm not your dancing monkey, Vera."

Vera implemented her frustrating tactic of selective hearing. "But you wouldn't. So what is it?"

"What is *what*?"

"Your, you know, your deal."

Charlie blinked. "Are we seriously having this conversation? Seriously."

"Yes."

"Why?"

"Because I'm curious?"

That was more honesty than Charlie was expecting, even if she didn't see how it was any of Vera's business. She smoothed her hands over her head, mussing her hair, and tugged at a handful of Martian bobby pins to undo her updo and do her usual braid.

"I'm...I don't know."

The angle of Vera's brows was skeptical. "You don't know."

"I'm not sure if you've noticed, but I've kind of had a lot going on!"

"Right, sure, but—"

"But *what*?"

Charlie longed for the rumble of the Rover's engines to fill the awkward silence, but there was no reprieve. Vera plucked the screwdriver from her mouth and pursed her lips in thought.

"You know what I think? I think you don't have a deal."

"I have a— Of course I have a deal." Charlie abandoned her hair and crossed her arms. "Everyone has a deal."

"No," said Vera, eyes narrowing, "I don't think you do."

"Maybe I just don't think about my deal because of— Because of fucking priorities!"

"Excellent word choice, Chuck."

Charlie spun around to look back outside. "Ugh. *Shut up*. Just... *shut up*."

For a brief, beautiful moment she thought Vera was going to abide the request. She was mistaken. "Okay, but now I kind of feel like an asshole for the Chuck *Chaste* thing."

"Don't." The word was clipped, a reflexive instinct to end the conversation as soon as possible, but the sincerity of Vera's tone compelled Charlie to look over her shoulder and make eye contact. This wasn't a conversation she'd ever had with anyone, not even her parents, though a part of her suspected they knew something was up. Even before the tears, she'd never brought anyone home. It was easy enough to dismiss it as a lack of *time*, not *interest*, but the reality was that it was a lack of *both*.

"Right, but...I do. So."

Charlie waited.

"Sorry."

"Vera..."

The apology, rare as it was, served to make the Rover feel even smaller. They didn't *do* heart-to-hearts, and not just because Vera's had a condition. Heart-to-hearts meant emotional vulnerability, meant considering just how far they were from home, and how much they stood to lose. She swallowed, her throat a little tight, and nodded. Apology heard and accepted. Time to pivot.

"Vera, that is the most Canadian thing you've ever said to me."

She scoffed.

"What kind of road trip doesn't have music?" Vera asked much later.

"The kind without roads?" Charlie replied. "Trip implies we have a destination. That we're going somewhere. We're just driving around hoping we're going to roll over something note-worthy enough that it's got a tear around it. And that that tear will take us somewhere other than *another* dead Mars where we'll repeat the process."

"Okay, well, that's what the sensors are for. I've spent the last day jury-rigging sensors for everything I can think of that can be sensed and now I am very bored. I solved like three career-defining equations in my head already, the proofs of which, alas, are too long for the condensation on the window of the Rover to contain. Also, there's condensation on the window, so we've got some internal climate problems."

"Then fix *those*."

"I'm just saying, we're cruising on the open…" Vera said with a pause to peer out the front, "dusty plains and canyons of Mars. There should be music. I feel like music would solve our problems. Stories, right? If we provide some music, maybe we get a montage and we get out of this."

The problem with that, Charlie considered, was that even if it were in any way accurate, *she'd* still have to live all the in-between bits. If it were a training montage she wouldn't have minded. Working at something, improving at something, having a goal and getting to it, that was fine.

Finding ways to aimlessly waste time while their only source of food ran down, stuck in the cabin of a not-small-but-feeling-increasingly-small all-terrain exploratory vehicle with someone who was, now, drawing designs for a more stylish all-terrain exploratory vehicle in the condensation in the window and managing to be bored doing it, that was less so.

"If you start singing, I am turning this Rover around."

The Rover broke before they ran out of food. The good news was it turned out to be a problem they could fix.

The bad news was it was a problem they could fix by cannibalizing parts out of the gear they'd brought with them. In particular by hooking part of the Fabricator system into the engine, meaning they could produce food or move forward, but not both at the same time. After they'd depleted their existing rations, whenever they ran out of the nutritious mush Charlie had worked out as the most efficient way of getting what they needed to survive out of the least amount of power and resources, they had to stop the Rover, rework the parts back in and sit around while it generated more.

Christ, "cannibalizing" really is a bad choice of word vis-à-vis our food set-up.

She was pretty sure the Fabricator was getting less efficient every time they did it, too, and that was on top of the fact it was burning out. It had always taken a bit of fucking around on every world but its own, presumably because they were trying to make it work in places that had slightly different fundamental rules and under-pinnings, or maybe because taking it through the tears damaged it in some way. They'd never had time to completely understand how it did what it did, so they'd been running on hasty guesses and experimentation. Now it was under a lot more pressure than it ever had been, and also they were regularly yanking it apart and putting it back together. Eventually, it was just going to stop working.

The Fabricator had stopped working. The engine was still going, running on the now permanently cannibalized parts. It had developed a kind of whine that set Charlie's teeth on edge. She would have blamed it on her enhanced senses, but Vera's boredom had gotten proportionally more extravagant as time dragged on, so tempers were clearly short all around.

It was becoming increasingly apparent they needed to focus their energies on repairing the tear tech, threat of the Hound and parasites be damned. Whatever answers they'd hoped to find here could be found on another Mars, preferably one with amenities and a way back to Earth—*any* Earth. The thought briefly occurred to her that she could be in her home universe and have no way of knowing it—briefly because she refused to consider it any longer than that when she could be yelling at Vera instead.

"How does that make *any* fucking sense?" Charlie said, with a wild gesture.

Beep.

"Right, because a magical locket that gives you a makeover and superpowers makes *so* much more sense than Greek deities disguised as rad teens!"

Admittedly, she was yelling at her about a children's cartoon, but in their current state of hunger, it felt important to educate Vera about the shittiness of her childhood entertainment.

"There is nothing rad about an abacus!"

"An *enchanted* abacus! That helps them beats bad guys!"

Beep.

"All a fucking abacus does is *count*! There is nothing *rad* about counting!"

"Tell that to the legions of *Eureka Magical God Girls* fans!"

Beep.

"Eureka. Magical. God. Girls."

"It's a global phenomenon!"

"It's fucking word salad!"

"Ex*cuse* me—?"

BEEP.

One of the sensors Vera had rigged up was impatiently flashing red. The end of Vera's rebuke went unheard—possibly unsaid, though she was no longer paying attention to Vera at all—as Charlie rushed to the dash to pull up the appropriate screen. The resulting image forced her to the back of her chair.

It was a Martian base.

Chapter Nineteen

— DIRT —

Y ou're seeing what I'm seeing, right? That's—"

"A base, yup. That's...definitely a base," said Vera.

"All right. As long as we're on the same page, then."

"Definitely same page. Maybe not the same page as whoever made that. If they used pages."

Which wasn't just a question of whether the civilization that had built this had still used paper. It was a question of whether they had, for example, eyes. Hands. It was the question of whether this was a Martian base in the sense that it was a base on Mars, or whether it was a Martian base in that it was a base that belonged to Martians.

Right now, it was hard to tell, mostly because all they could see of it was the tunnel in, and if it weren't for the signs on the scanner that indicated somewhere down there was power, and some things weren't rocks and dirt, they might have just dismissed it entirely as just a cavern.

A very straight cavern. Fortunate, because the Rover only just fit and if they had to execute any kind of turn they would probably be shit out of luck. Backing up if they ran into any sort of cave-in or blockage would be problem enough. But then, there wouldn't be much point to that, because it wasn't as if they were going to find another mysterious cavern leading to an apparent base on Mars.

Except we just found one, so maybe I can't rule that out. But they probably wouldn't find one before they ran out of supplies and were dead. It would be better to just try to find a way through any cave-ins.

The thing was, there weren't any. The edges of the tunnel were rough, whatever geometry they might have once had obscured by the passage of time. They drove the Rover carefully, oh so carefully, down. There was a bump or two of rock or pothole, but the way was clear. The way was, the deeper down they got, ever more clearly a way, a built passage. It had a shape. The proportions of it were odd, the angles set jarringly, but there were angles and there were proportions. The farther they got, the more it looked like architecture.

Even Vera was quiet. It wasn't every day you drove down an alien hole.

Hands tense on the controls, Charlie watched the beam of headlights illuminate each new yard of passage. She didn't know what she was expecting. It was impossible to know what to expect. She'd seen a dragon. She'd seen aliens. She'd seen Vera apologize. There were apparently no limits to the possible, which meant anything could get upset and come tearing out of the dark to eat them.

Or there could just be automated turrets or something. Getting shot by an automated turret seemed like it would be a terrible anticlimax, even if it was a laser.

The close walls suddenly opened ahead as the tunnel led into a larger space, and at the same time, Charlie sawed on the breaks. The Rover gently skidded and whined to a halt.

"So," she said, "that is—"

"A door," Vera said. It was set slightly into the far wall of the cavern, an opening with a clearly crafted shape protruding partway into the open space, rising out of the floor. A way beyond it was a repeat of the same. "Two doors, a short distance apart. You know what that looks like to me?"

"I dunno about you, but it sure looks like an airlock to me."

"Or a…whatever-they-breathed-here-lock. What are the chances it does air?"

Charlie opened her mouth, then considered again, then simply gave a huge shrug. Probability would argue against it. But at this point, probability would argue against her whole fucking life, so. The only way to find out would be to poke at it and find out.

"I'm gonna go poke at it and find out," Vera said.

"Of course you are."

Charlie, eyes locked on Vera's vitals, was perched inside the Rover. While it was more responsible to send only one of them outside, it was simultaneously less exciting and more stressful. She had no doubts the Marshmallow was up for the job—Vera did build it, after all, and she'd been paranoid about keeping it in working order ever since their encounter with Yarrity—but she also had no doubts that Vera was often pointedly, gleefully reckless, and who knew what kind of trouble she'd get herself into?

A small part of Charlie thought she should have gone instead. Her fucking job description was professional guinea pig, and she had more than willful enthusiasm with which to defend herself. But Vera hadn't wanted to hear it, so here Charlie was, ground control to Major Vera.

"I think I've got it," said Vera. Her voice through the intercom sounded canned, like she was an old-time radio star.

There probably was a universe where she was an old-time radio star.

"Yeah?"

"Uh-huh. These components are ancient, and I clearly don't speak Martian, but— Yeah. Hello, genius? Of course I've got it. Running her now."

From Charlie's vantage point, nothing seemed to be happening. Space wasn't like the movies. Mars wasn't quite a vacuum, but the Martian atmosphere was too thin for sound to travel at a speed audible to human ears. Vera's dramatic moment wasn't even a whimper, let alone a bang, but Charlie couldn't bring herself to feel too disappointed about a lack of things exploding. If anything, it was a nice change of pace.

"Update on the readings?" asked Vera.

Charlie tore her eyes away from the Marshmallow's stats. "Sensors are detecting a marked increase in oxygen."

"Looks like Martians do air. *Did* air?"

"We'll figure out the grammar once we get a better look inside."

"'We?'"

"We."

Inside suggested more bunker than base, though that might have something to do with the lighting. Absent a convenient light switch, they were relying on flashlights and headlamps scavenged from the Rover. Despite the air circulation, they kept their respective suits sealed. You couldn't be too careful in space, and they were already throwing sufficient caution to the wind getting out of the Rover in the first place. They walked through a long empty corridor for some time before confronting another door.

"What are the odds this is the universe full of space horror tropes?" Charlie wondered aloud.

"Increasingly higher the longer we walk down a dark creepy corridor. Did Martians not do lights?"

"If they were cave-dwelling people, it's possible they didn't."

The decor was certainly spartan enough. They hadn't encountered so much as a pictogram since the airlock. Even this latest door was nondescript. It was circular in shape and recessed into the wall, with no obvious markings. There wasn't so much as a handle. But maybe there was some kind of keypad. Charlie and Vera each took one side of the door and ran their hands over the wall. Poking around was becoming a habit.

"Got something," said Charlie. Buried under a layer of dust was what deduction revealed to be a motion sensor. Slowly, lights flickered to life, and the door haltingly slid open just enough for them to squeeze through. It could probably do with a good greasing. Nothing about the Martian(?) bunker screamed frequently visited in the past decade. Or century, for that matter.

"Physical bodies, vision somewhere close to our visible spectrum, not significantly taller," Vera concluded, waving a hand through the dust their progress through the door had disturbed. "If they're just an ahistorical Earth society that made it to Mars generations ago, I'm going to be mad. I want aliens."

Charlie smirked. "Yeah, I noticed, the last time we met aliens."

"Alien aliens. Not people with antennae and body paint. I mean, it wasn't body paint, I can be absolutely certain of that, but you get what I mean. Real weird aliens."

"Aaand we're back to space horror," Charlie said, approaching a dust-covered mound. "I've had enough of tentacles, you know?"

"It's not the tentacles I mind. It's the whole— I could do properly Euclidean tentacles, you know?"

"Wait, 'do' like...handle the sight of, or do like—shit!" Charlie exclaimed, reflexively darting back from the mound after she'd brushed the dirt off and found, not rocks or structure, but robotic-looking remains. Hard to say if it was plastic or metal at first glance, especially given how dirty it was, but it definitely had joints, was meant to move.

It did not move. She tried to get a sense of what shape it was meant to be, under normal circumstances, but it was hard to say. Fortunately, it wasn't because it was in defiance of conventional perspective or geometry. It just didn't conform to any shape she was used to. It had parts sticking out that could be wings or paddles or feet. Very carefully, she tried to move one. It was crusted in places, but very lightly; she could shift it.

"It's missing parts," Vera said. Charlie looked over at her, then back at the thing. Now that Vera had said it, she could see it, but in another kind of perspective, that part of what had been challenging her to make sense of it was that it was built around gaps.

"Stolen?" Charlie ventured. Vera just shrugged. Hard to say without more information, Charlie had to agree.

A little farther in were two more mystery paddles, both in similar states of decay. "Gaps in the same places," Vera said. "Either those were the valuable parts, or whatever was there was made of something more prone to decay."

"...biomechanical," Charlie said, turning back to look where they'd come. She went back to the door, wedging herself in the gap and forcing it a bit further open by putting both her feet on the moveable portion and shoving. Then she used the extra space to turn and look into the door frame.

With the lights on and more space, she could see what they'd missed on the way through the first time. The internals had a similar look and build to those on the airship where the parasite had been held. She left the door frame and ran her hand along the wall until she found a panel that time had rendered loose enough for her to tear off.

The design was entirely foreign, of course, built on fundamentals completely different from what she was used to. Any assumptions about function were utter guesswork. But in the same way that a door was a door was a door, even though she couldn't identify individual components or something recognizable as a circuit, if you assumed that was a circuit and that was a power source and that was a conduit, then the whole thing could have been a take on a design they'd tried once, an inversion of the Reality Jig she'd been carrying this whole time. A system for deterring parasites, or at least convincing them nothing was interesting to eat.

"Hey, check it out!" Vera called, from farther on in. Charlie jogged inward to join her, passing several columns and more of what she was now guessing were Martian hounds. She paused to consider the patterns in the dust around the columns, the way the light passed through the dust not quite right.

"Chandelle," Charlie told the column. "You are a Chandelle. I helped design a version of you!"

An underground bunker full of what she now suspected was the equipment used to deter and discourage parasites. Martian Veritech, maybe.

If it was just the work of a green Verity, Vera was going to be so disappointed.

She found Vera a short distance on, looking at more technology she couldn't identify. Even trying to relate it to the tech they'd been working on at Veritech didn't come up with any linkages here. It was just unfathomable device after unfathomable device sitting in half-spherical depressions in the floor. Intricate scratches in the stonework surrounded each depression.

"I bet you could spend a year here and not have any idea what even one of these gizmos was," Vera said. She sounded delighted. "Look at the carvings. Are they circuit designs? Writing? Magic spells? I dunno! It's too alien! Look—"

Vera waved her hand by one of the carved circles, at a similar spot to where the door motion sensor had been, and a glow suffused it. The space above it bent and Charlie was tensed to dive sideways and take Vera with her before she realized it was flickering in and out. Dust was gently drifting through the glow. It wasn't a tear; it was a hologram of a tear. As she watched, the hologram resolved into the activated depression; the "tear" closed.

"They're displays," Charlie said. "This is some kind of..."

"Museum, maybe," Vera said. "Maybe the specific sort. The Martian Museum of Martians Knew About Tears A Long Time Ago, Holy Crap. Kind of an unwieldy name, but those Martians, right?"

"Those Martians," Charlie agreed faintly, crossing to the next depression. Not all of the holograms worked, or maybe not all of the displays had them, but there was enough to get a sense of what the room was exhibiting. This device closed a tear. The next hologram along seemed to imply that the device did something to maintain a tear without closing it, which would have been nice for Charlie to have, oh, say, at the beginning of this trip. This one directed a tear to a particular point, or perhaps just ensured that whoever passed through went there. It was hard to say which precisely it was. Either way, the hologram showed their best look at a Martian yet, assuming the creature it showed was the same as had made all of this. Vera was happy; it had antennae, yes, but there was no mistaking them for a model made up in body paint. The simplest way to describe it was alien. It was insectoid in appearance, but stood upright, not entirely unlike a quadrupedal, rust-colored praying mantis. It passed through two tears and went to different places; then it activated the featured device and went to the same place twice in a row.

That was about it for that room, or at least that was all they could get to work and puzzle out. The next room more heavily featured the holograms, seemingly less focused on displaying individual pieces of technology so much as telling a story about their use. It started with a civilization on Mars, the kind that no evidence had ever been found for. Buildings, vehicles, spreading across the world, a Mars teeming with life.

Then different versions of the same. All populated by the same Martians, but many different. Maybe all different, in ways that it was impossible for her and Vera to recognize because they were dealing with a wholly different culture. There were Marses with more water, with different levels of technology. There was a Mars where all the Martians paused and then started moving in sync; there was a Mars where a Martian moved things with a wave of a proboscis. There was a Mars with dangerous-looking fire-breathing reptilian giants.

As the holograms progressed, the Mars of the first images seemed to spread. Martians that looked similar to the ones from that interacted with those of the later ones. The lower-tech Martians suddenly had lasers with which to shoot at the giants. The giants suddenly had lasers with which to shoot at people the Martians riding the giants didn't like.

"Never mind punching," Vera said. "That. Next time. That."

"Yeah, this definitely all worked out for them," Charlie said, looking around at the dust in which they stood. She activated the next one and again, had to resist leaping back.

This hologram was parasites. Swarming each of the worlds they'd seen. The Martians of each fighting back. Attempting to divert and contain and kill with various kinds and levels of technology. Failing, and failing. Marses that resembled the blasted

Wasteland, on the way to becoming the Mars outside this bunker. Tear after tear closing, some of the linked Marses trying to close themselves off.

Trying not to feel like she already knew how this all ended— they'd just spent days driving over a dead world, identical to the dead world Mars was in every universe they'd visited bar the ones where humans were trying to terraform it—Charlie moved to the next display.

It turned out she didn't know how this all ended because this display was of the solar system. Except there was an extra planet, and not in the sense that they'd included Pluto. (They hadn't.) They'd included Theia, the theoretical planet once at a Lagrange point, a consistent orbital position with respect to the sun and Earth. The hologram zoomed in, showed it teeming with more parasites than Charlie had ever seen.

"Does your universe have any of those horror movies where someone knocks a hole in the wall and cockroaches just swarm out?" Vera said, in the dreamy, distracted way she sounded when she was disturbed or scared.

"That's definitely a nest, right? That's what this is saying. That whole planet was a nest," Charlie said.

"Please tell me the next one is the Martians developing the universe's largest and greatest bug bomb," Vera said.

The next hologram was Theia being forcibly crashed into Earth. Charlie had always learned that theory as the probable influence of Venus, but she supposed no one had had the data on extra-dimensional parasites and the Martian civilization trying to eliminate them. By destroying the parasites' planet. By crashing it into what would become their planet, causing the formation of the moon in the process.

"Go them," Vera said, but she didn't sound comforted. Charlie didn't feel comforted, either, and the next hologram bore it out: a view of many, many Marses, most of them dead. And then world after world after world changing to match the majority. Each world fading from its original, individual state into a dead husk, until the hologram seemed to just be an unending picture of the same Mars.

"All of the stories about Mars are about Earth," Vera said, staring into space.

"Well, I mean, I've read ones where there's civilization there, so that's—" Charlie began, struggling to connect this line of thought. Struggling more with the simple fact of what they'd just watched spelled out, the end of a whole civilization, across all the worlds that civilization could exist on.

"But it's always—someone from Earth goes to Mars, has adventures. There's no stories about Mars that aren't vehicles for stories about people. It's always us because their story is just...dirt. Parasites ate all their stories and now every Mars is just a story about dirt."

They'd been wrong. This wasn't a base, or a bunker, or a museum.

It was a tomb.

Charlie circled back to the hologram featuring the parasites. This was not to say she wanted to circle back, but at some point, without her noticing, her feet carried her in front of the appropriate depression. There was something there, she could feel it, her brain at the edge of a precipice of understanding if only her train of thought could make the jump. She was mixing metaphors. She didn't care. There were no parasites before the tears, but that made sense. That fit with their current working model. Parasites and tears went hand in hand. There *wouldn't* be parasites before there were tears. The parasites came *from* the tears.

Only that wasn't quite right. Maybe. The parasites came from this mysterious planet, if it was even a planet at all and not simply a planet-sized non-Euclidean *nest*. The parasites had a base of operations, and judging by the holograms, they'd been happy to stay there until the Martians went exploring. Had the tears disturbed them, in some way, or had they just been an easy ticket to the multiverse? Parasites appeared where there were tears, but they didn't *travel* by tears, necessarily. Did tears make things more permeable, so they could do it easier, spread farther, or did they provide a new food source?

She went back again, to the beginning of the holograms. The Martians had demonstrated an unprecedented control over the tears from the outset. There was little evidence of a learning curve. No record of any scientist suddenly developing, say, a *heart condition* from standing too close. (Though maybe there was. She didn't read Martian. She shouldn't be so quick to rule it out.) The holograms went from one set of Martians right to the same set of Martians exploring.

Which meant they didn't just *find* a tear.

They *made* a tear.

Why the fuck would they *make* a tear?

Because that's what sentient species did, isn't it? Go exploring, to make sure they aren't the only ones out there. *Or is that just me making it a story about Earth again, because that's what* people *do? We're so desperate to not be alone.*

But no, that wasn't the point. Who cared about the *why*, when what mattered was the *what*?

"They made the tears."

Vera glanced up from where she was seated on the floor near the last of the holograms. In her hands were two Martian components. Even from a short distance, Charlie could see Vera silently work the hypothesis. She looked from Charlie back to the components.

"It's not a natural phenomenon."

"It's *not* a natural fucking phenomenon. They *started* it."

Vera stared harder at the components. "And we're in a base full of their tech," she said absently, thoughts lightyears ahead of her mouth, and Charlie couldn't help the laugh that bubbled from the dark, twisted recesses of her gut. She was bent double, arms wrapped around her middle.

"Fuck *yes*, we are!"

They scoured the base. Charlie labeled anything that looked familiar to her technology with duct tape and a sharpie from her backpack, because no matter what universe one was in, duct tape would always be useful. Everything that was labeled was then knolled across a swath of the cleared floor. The organizational process was almost soothing. Maybe it was the clean, orderly Euclidean geometry, everything along 90-degree angles. More familiarity might help them crack the mystery of exactly what they had on their hands.

Vera's process was somewhat messier. She was hunched over the data they'd stolen from Villainy Baum, a lone figure in a sea of papers. The VeriPAD with the digitized documents served as a very expensive paperweight.

They knew the Martians could not only start tears, not only create stable, two-way portals but also control where those tears went. It was a hell of a step up from the bastardized Veritech they were working from now, and it was just a matter of figuring out how the hell any of it worked. (If it still worked, a doubt neither of them had dared to voice aloud.)

"Do you think Martians counted on their legs, or proboscises, or antennae? I'm trying to guess at what base their math would be. I mean, at some level the tech is probably binary, because everyone has on and off, yes and no. Well, on and off. Maybe they had liminal agreement states, who knows. Maybe tech based on circuit on/circuit off is too much of an assumption. I think we use Veritech for the navigation system. At least the bit where we tell it where to go. Which still leaves...making an interface between their tear-guidance system and our controller. Without any common base. I am starving. They have air, do you think they have vending machines?"

"Sure, maybe," Charlie said. Vera started to perk up, hunger apparently outweighing logic enough she didn't see the next part coming. "If you eat proboscis food."

"I'm going to set the coordinates to a Mars that's made of food. Candy Mars, that's where we're going."

"Oh, c'mon. Mars bar is right there. It's right there!"

Vera looked beside herself as if Charlie were pointing out an actual physical place. "For...drinks? I'm after food, not drinks. Oh, great, now I'm thirsty, too. Only we can't go to a Candy Mars or your...Mars bar, you lush, because...all Marses are dirt. Except, hopefully, the one in the universe our blimp-living tentacled friend was originally from. Which I think I can point us at. Once we've worked out the math for focused dimensional traversal through spaces with non-uniform physical laws. Not really through, more...resonate a certain way to have the non-reality unspace curve over additional axes to deposit us at the desired— have you been stashing any protein bars against a situation like this? Please say yes."

They'd eaten them all already. Which left only getting back to work figuring out how to jury-rig a control system they could speak to in a math they could rely on as having foundational principles they understood that would achieve the desired effect when wired into alien technology that definitely didn't.

Which was, put simply, really fucking hard.

Luckily, they were really fucking motivated. Also, smart.

For instance: the base was running on something. So Charlie spent a solid while chasing that down, which gave them a sense for at least the fundamentals of how the Martians had powered things at the stage of development they'd been at when they made the base. How lights functioned, basic mechanisms like the doors. Which were fire and sticks with stones tied to them compared to tear tech, but it was useful context.

A lot of it was still going to be trusting that the tech did what it said on the tin, once they could get it running. And more math. Always, always, more math.

Charlie's hunger was about to gnaw a tear through her stomach. No matter what, they had a way out. The bastardized Veritech would open a tear. They could load up the entire contents of the base and head out whenever they needed to. The problem was, if they missed something critical here, there would be no guaranteed way back. There was a lot of incentive to get things right the first time around, since it turned out finding a specific universe was about as straightforward as finding a needle in a haystack, assuming the needle was also made of hay, and maybe you had no hands.

There was also a lot of incentive not to starve. They didn't have a lot of time to waste on tests. The human body could go for weeks without food, but they needed their wits about them. The math was tricky enough without factoring in delirium. At some point, they simply had to decide that what they had was as good as it was going to get. That point coincided with Vera passing out after standing up too quickly. They loaded the Rover with everything that wasn't bolted down—and a few things that *were* bolted down—took pictures of every hologram with the VeriPAD, and punched in the fruits of their mathematical labor into their brand new navigational system cobbled together with Martian and Veritech parts. The coordinates: Villainy Baum's fabled Mars. Not the one from *her* universe, but the home of her pet parasite, the Mars where all of this began. They were going to trace it right back to the source.

"Better buckle up," said Charlie, doing one final pre-jump check. They were already both strapped in, but nerves compelled her to talk.

"It can't be any rougher than the landing we had on the way here."

"We can hope. On my mark."

Vera shifted to grab hold of the Rover's steering. Charlie was manning the tear tech.

"Three, two, one. Mark."

For a second Charlie thought it didn't work. There was no discernible change in the viewfinder, just the same red rock as ever, but then the red seemed to disappear. It vanished in slivers, replaced by a growing spiderweb of data the mind couldn't process and therefore registered as non-color. A tear. Only it seemed hyperbolic to call *this* a tear. It was the difference between a gash and a surgical incision, the scalpel so sharp the skin took a while to realize it was cut. The universe didn't even know it was bleeding, a steady expansion of energy that engulfed the Rover's field of vision. And that was the word for it: *steady*. Tears in Charlie's mind were inherently violent. This was a ripple in a pond on a Sunday afternoon. Pleasant, as far as holes in reality went.

"*Huh*," said Charlie.

There were no side effects. Interdimensional travel was no walk in the park, but Charlie had gotten a bigger headache puzzling out the math with Vera than she did casually driving through the tear. *Portal*, she mentally corrected. Not that the wording mattered. As the holograms had proven, the parasites would come regardless if it stayed open, and they closed it shortly after passing through.

The base in this universe was distressingly similar to the one they'd just left. On the one hand, that was a good thing: it meant Villainy Baum had actually been on the right track with her research. On the other hand, that meant there was still no fucking *food*.

There was also a distinct lack of Martian tech.

"Picked clean, like the rest of the rooms," Charlie reported when she returned to the foyer where Vera was waiting. She was drinking a bottle of recycled water under Charlie's orders.

"All right, so we've got two options. Either *this* Mars isn't as dead as the last one—"

"Or we've got ourselves some astronauts with sticky fingers. There's just one room left. You staying or coming?"

"Coming," Vera said, getting to her feet. If she smirked a little around the word, Charlie pretended not to notice.

The final room had a different door than the others, namely, in the sense there was actual security. Or there had been actual security, as, by the time Charlie and Vera found it, the system had clearly already been disabled. This was evident by the fact a panel had been torn off the wall, its circuitry gutted and strewn all over the floor.

"Well, that's promising," said Charlie.

She shouldered open the door, a heavy-duty beast made of some kind of metallic alloy. Whatever was behind this door wasn't your garden variety museum exhibit, that much was for certain.

"Oh, hello beautiful," Vera said, pushing past her the moment there was enough space for her to do so. Actually, from the way Charlie was pressed into the metal by the plastic of the Marshmallow, maybe a moment or two earlier than that.

Once the Marshmallow was done compressing her lungs, Charlie could follow through and see what had so caught Vera's attention.

It was, indeed, not garden variety. Although probably there would be museums that exhibited it. Aeronautics museums, for instance. Aeronautics and space museums, in particular.

It was a rocket ship. Not the mass-produced, space travel as standardized commercial venture kind they'd taken on their trip out to Mars a couple of universes ago, either. For one thing, it looked more exploratory, more multipurpose. For another, there was the styling, in that it had some. Someone had taken time to make it look good, rather than building it to the barest necessities to function. Admittedly, Charlie didn't entirely agree with their idea of good. It had fins. It looked sort of like it belonged on a sign next to an old diner. But whether that was period or contemporary to the maker, they'd been working with an aesthetic.

Which made sense, given the logo on the side. Not one they'd seen before, but nonetheless, it didn't take multiversal mathematics to figure out who the stylized letters were going to belong to.

"VB," Charlie read. "I mean, *obviously*."

Chapter Twenty

— TAKE ME TO YOUR LEADER —

Try open sesame," Charlie suggested.

Vera had already ordered the spaceship to open with a variety of commands, to no avail. Frankly, Charlie had her doubts about whether it was voice-operated at all, given that there wasn't so much as a tell-tale ding when Vera said *anything*, so she was doing a tour around the craft while Vera shouted gibberish at it.

"I don't know why you think any old nonsense is going to work," Vera snapped. "And, actually, it's very rude to be suggesting random food words to a starving woman. Spaceship, list commands!"

The spaceship did not list commands. The spaceship continued to sit idle. Charlie had found the door, though, and set about accessing the control panel. After the time they'd spent muddling around with the Martian tech, the hardest part was honestly just looking at circuits as ordinary circuits and not as the unfathomable products of an alien consciousness to be guessed at and worked with by a series of guesses and impulses that felt right but couldn't be consciously explained. She could just work out what triggered the door and then trigger it.

It hissed open.

"Open sesame," she said, purely for her own satisfaction.

"Spaceship, this isn't over," Vera said, strolling over and joining Charlie on the other side of the airlock. The inside was...*homier* than she'd expected. She'd expected a private plane sort of vibe, plush seats, maybe an absurd bed of some kind. Instead, she was reminded of a motorhome. There *was* a bed, but it was a bunk. It was there to be slept on, rather than to entertain. There were chairs, but they weren't expansive luxury chairs. Whoever had designed this place hadn't wanted to spend that much space on a comfy chair. This was a rocket ship with other priorities. Workbench priorities. Kitchenette and little dining area priorities.

Charlie kind of approved, which put the Verity Baum responsible for this closer to the one from her own universe than to the one who'd just pulled her arm out of her own spacesuit just so she could waggle her fingers inside a too-large glove she'd found in a drawer.

Charlie's own priorities lived in the kitchenette. Food over fashion. She nearly wept when she spotted a stash of space food securely Velcroed to the inside of one of the cabinets.

"Praise be Vee-*Bee*," she crowed, victoriously thrusting a vacuum-sealed pouch of beef stroganoff in the air.

They ate in silence, though they didn't eat silently. Both were too hungry to bother with any semblance of table manners, and they shoved food down their pie holes until their stomachs ached. Some part of Charlie knew you were supposed to reintroduce food slowly when starvation had settled in, but that part was her brain, which had to get in fucking line behind her stomach.

A food coma followed. Several hours later, Charlie woke to find Vera tinkering with the engines.

"Do you ever sleep?" Charlie asked around a yawn. She was sore from passing out on the dining room table, and she slowly tilted her head from side to side to get rid of the crick in her neck.

Vera popped out from under the dash like a Jack-in-the-Box, her red-lined eyes comically large behind the lenses of a set of a magnifying headgear that didn't fit quite right.

Charlie jumped back. "Fuck!"

"Is that a rhetorical question?"

"It's a—"

"—no, see, *that* was a rhetorical question," Vera interrupted, whipping off the headgear and tossing it onto the ground. "I figured it out. The spaceship. How to turn it on."

"How do I turn you *off*?" Charlie muttered.

"Doesn't run on fuel in the traditional sense, but based on my calculations, it should get us to where we're going."

"Where *are* we going?" A pause. "That *wasn't* rhetorical."

"Glad you asked." Vera climbed into the pilot's seat and toggled several switches. The ship began to hum with electricity. Lights flickered on in the cabin, and several holographic projections materialized in the viewscreen. One was labeled "flight plan." Vera mimed pinching the corners of the screen and magnified it with a quick flick of her wrists. "We are going to...huh."

"That says the moon. Our moon. Well. Earth's moon."

And it did. The ship's last (and only, from the looks of things) point of origin was the moon.

"Can't really get proprietary in someone else's universe. Lunar base, probably."

"Well, a lunar base screams supervillain, so we're on the right track so far," said Charlie, folding her arms.

"Now hang on a second," Vera said. "Just because someone has a lunar base—"

"—and a monogrammed spaceship—"

"Just because someone has a lunar base and a monogrammed spaceship doesn't mean they're a supervillain. Maybe she just happens to own property on the moon!"

"Yeah, her evil lunar base."

"Look, no self-respecting supervillain would have a kitchenette. Supervillains have style."

"Maybe she's still early in her villainy days. Maybe that comes later. Maybe— No, you're right, no self-respecting supervillain would have a kitchenette."

Vera looked smug.

"But she clearly hasn't been *here* in a long ass time," Charlie pointed out. "So I'm reserving the right to say I told you so just in case she was a late bloomer in villainy."

"*Anyway*," Vera said, "we're going to the moon."

"Yes," Charlie agreed. "Because we're looking for an evil you, and a lunar base is a *great* fucking lead."

"What! Says who?"

Holt Savage was the only person to outright say it, and he wasn't the most reliable source of information. Still, Charlie had come to agree with him—reluctantly, *begrudgingly* agree with him—along the way.

"Isn't it obvious?" she said. "We keep running into yous for a reason."

"Yeah! Resonance! Resonance is the reason!"

"Vera. Come on."

Vera scowled and Charlie pretended not to notice. While they now had an idea of how the tears started—not to mention an idea of how to *navigate* between worlds—they still had no idea how to stop the parasites for good. Without that piece of the puzzle, the multiverse of Earths would be as doomed as Mars before it, even if they managed the impossible task of closing every tear.

"Let's pack up our shit from the Rover and go."

The spacehome could fucking *motor*. The decor might've looked like a family of four's RV, but the engine was all Ferrari. At these speeds, it was going to take them a hell of a lot less time to get to the moon than it had to get them to Mars. After some cajoling, Charlie had managed to wrestle the controls from Vera for a bit, but now Vera was back at the wheel while Charlie rehydrated an individual-sized cheese pizza.

She sat down in the passenger seat, folded the pizza in half, and took a bite. Objectively speaking, it wasn't great; the rehydrated cheese scalded the roof of her mouth, and there was a distinct shortage of tomato sauce. But subjectively speaking, it was fucking space pizza, and that made it the best pizza she'd ever eaten by default.

"I'm making one of these when I get back," said Vera, absently handing Charlie a rag from the dash to clean up her pizza fingers. "Maybe with a nicer kitchenette. Some kind of lounge."

"You could just retrofit this one."

"You don't steal a woman's monogrammed spaceship, Chuck."

"You have the same initials! And what do you call this, anyhow?"

Vera sniffed. "Creative borrowing."

"If we run into a version of you that's a lawyer, remind me not to hire you."

"You couldn't afford me anyhow."

"You couldn't, either. We'll need to figure out a way to fix the Fabricator if it turns out we need to pay for shit on this definitely on-the-level lunar base." The moment she said it, Charlie realized the pressing nature of that point and immediately went to fetch the cannibalized remnants of Fabricator from the back. The road so far couldn't be characterized as easy, but without money, they would've been considerably more screwed. She returned with a box of parts and a handful of tools. She was about to station herself at the little dining table when a flashing tab on one of the viewfinders caught her attention.

"What's that?"

"What's what?"

"Second viewfinder from the right. There's a thing."

Charlie decided Vera was probably one of those people who let their inbox balloon with email. With a wave of her hand, the flashing viewfinder expanded: INCOMING FREQUENCY.

"Someone's calling us?" said Vera.

"Looks like."

"Well, pick up."

"They're probably looking for Vee-Bee," Charlie pointed out. "Or expecting Vee-Bee, what with your...*creative borrowing* of her spaceship."

"*Our* creative borrowing of her spaceship."

"We should—"

A piercingly loud alarm filled the cabin. Charlie doubled over, hands covering her ears. The lighting switched from mellow yellow to hellish red. The end result was so disorienting it took Charlie a while to source the sound: all of the holographic viewfinders were flashing with a skull and crossbones, WARNING: PARASITE PROXIMITY written in block letters underneath, along with an impossibly large number of lifeforms detected. The advisory was so over the top Charlie's instinctive fear was on a ten-second delay.

"TURN IT OFF," she bellowed.

Vera blindly swatted at the dash until the noise stopped, but in doing so, she also answered the call. For a moment, Charlie thought a parasite might fill the viewfinder, but the face that greeted them was almost worse.

None other than Roman La Roche's maddeningly rugged features glared stonily from just above the dash. It was the expression a particularly constipated male model might make in one of the fashion magazines that often featured Vera. Charlie wanted to punch him, but her ears were still ringing from the alarm. At least he wasn't mist this time.

Also, she reminded herself, he was just an impressively lifelike hologram. She could practically count the stitching on his slate gray uniform. Her gaze caught on his badge reading HEAD OF SECURITY. Shit.

Were they holograms on his end? She couldn't see a camera, but that didn't mean there wasn't one.

"You are entering Baum space without authorization," he said. His accent was no less annoying than it was during their first encounter, slithering in her ringing ears. "Identify yourself."

"La Roche, did you forget your reading glasses again?" Vera said, all J.V. bluster. They'd been traveling together long enough for Charlie to pick apart the pieces of her transformation from scientific weirdo to unflappable CEO of a multimillion-dollar tech company. She held herself to fill as much of the screen as she could. "It's me."

There was a pause. La Roche's gaze flicked away from the camera, and his hands fell into frame as he typed something quickly onto an unseen keyboard.

"I hope I'm not home," Vera said without moving her lips.

"The *Rocket* has been decommissioned for years," La Roche said. As if on cue, the lighting in whatever security post he was manning turned a menacing red. "Identify yourself immediately or be destroyed."

"Well, that seems a little overkill," muttered Charlie, bracing herself on the dash. Her focus shifted back to the viewfinders warning about the endless fucking horde of parasites about to breathe down their necks. La Roche and his itchy trigger finger were the least of their fucking concerns. Where the fuck was he to not be worried?

"*Roman*," Vera entreated, rolling her R like a pro. "We've got a wonderfully worrying amount of parasites on our tail, so maybe we can save the roleplaying games for later."

She winked.

Charlie suppressed a shudder.

The hologram blinked off. Another alarm—a different alarm— sounded, accompanied by another round of bold text, this time reading: INCOMING PROJECTILE. Fucking shit.

"Well, guess I'm home!"

"Evasive maneuvers!" Charlie shouted because it seemed like the thing to shout. They were being fired at by a skeevy Frenchman, and they were still in danger of being fucking eaten by a bunch of reality destroying non-Euclidean cockroach squid. They needed to fucking evade.

But they were flying a goddamn motorhome. And while it could motor, that proved to be an entirely straight-line kind of deal. Charlie slammed the stick to the side and the ship wallowed, began to slowly skew to the left. Emphasis on slowly. If the incoming projectiles were purely kinetic, maybe they'd be fine, but no one with a moon base was going to be shooting at spaceships with purely kinetic projectiles.

"*Fuck fuck fuck*," she said, punching at the controls. She had to be able to get something out of the maneuvering thrusters. You had to be able to park the thing, which meant you had to be able to make very specific movements, which meant control.

It was just that the design assumed you were going very slowly when this was happening, thus the exceptionally slow impact it had on their path. If they'd been going faster, maybe it would have been enough to blow past the projectiles, but they'd slowed down to approach the moon. Now, with the turning rate, if they sped up in a straight line, they'd just hit the fucking moon.

She looked for the weapons systems. She did not find the weapons systems. There were no fucking weapons systems.

"I gotta retrofit the engine," Vera blurted, vaulting her chair and dashing for the back, Marshmallow making a low clunk as she bounced off the kitchenette on her way down. "Introduce a variable fuel right to the sides of the main thruster, no time to wire it to the controls but if I can manually adjust, we can turn faster, no side to side unless I can get more juice to maneuvering but I'd have to open up the side and be outside and—"

This was all solid thinking. It might have worked, too, had they thought of it yesterday. Ten minutes ago. Anytime before—

The ship finally threw itself violently to the side.

Not all of the side came with it, because it had disintegrated on missile impact.

The good news was the violent forward corkscrew they were in now made them very hard to hit.

The bad news was she could barely control the violent forward corkscrew, and the atmosphere was rushing out of the ship. The cowl wasn't deploying. The impact had thrown her into the dash, had jostled something that shouldn't have been jostled, and the fucking cowl was not deploying. She could hold her breath and hope, she supposed.

A dome fell over her face. The whistling of their oxygen disappearing became a strange rippling sound that she realized was duct tape. The dome was one of the spare spacesuit helmets from the back. Vera had dumped it over her head and was now duct-taping the loose neck portion to the upper part of the Velo.

"Seal the breach," she yelled, hoping there was enough air left for that to travel.

"In progress," Vera yelled back. "I ripped the workbench loose and any moment now—"

The wail of air leaving the ship capped out. Charlie couldn't look back, both because she had an unwieldy helmet duct-taped to her now, and because she had to watch the controls to not die in several other ways. She could figure it out, though: the suction of the vacuum would have pulled the bench to the breach and would hold it in place until such time as it broke.

She didn't know how long that would be, but probably it was longer than they had until another missile hit them and finished the job.

The good news was that they were going to hit the fucking moon before that happened.

She'd developed a real shitty idea of what "good news" was.

"Hold on to something," she said. "Not me."

Vera threw herself back in her seat and assumed the airplane crash position. Charlie figured it was as good as any, in that if she fucked this up, they were probably going to be minute particles and it didn't really matter.

They were careening wildly, tumbling about the axis. She could use that. Only one decent thruster, the ship mostly did forward, but forward was now a direction that changed split second to split second, so if she cut power and then jerked it back on now and now and now, she could turn the spin into something she could control enough to get thrusters facing the surface and burn and burn and maybe slow them down enough that they wouldn't disintegrate entirely when—

They hit.

Charlie was not aware of when she first woke. Consciousness came in shades of gray, a gradual shift from sleep to waking. Her ears were stuffed with cotton. Her head pulsed with each beat of her heart. She could taste copper. There was pain. There was a *lot* of pain. A dislocation, maybe, if she was lucky. Given that she'd apparently survived a crash landing on the fucking moon, luck seemed like an interesting concept to think about.

She didn't have time to think about it.

Rough hands hoisted her up to her feet. She was tall, but the men speaking gruff words she couldn't make sense of were taller. Threats, she realized, when a hand struck her face. Well, that made sense, she supposed. They *did* crash a spaceship on their lunar base. She spat at their feet and dimly registered the red spattering the floor. Her vision was clearing up, fuzzy images coming into focus.

They were on the ship still, or what remained of it, but the men weren't wearing spacesuits. Probably they'd recovered the wreckage and brought it—and, consequently, *them*—inside.

Vera.

She jerked out of her captors' grasp, scanned for any sign of the Marshmallow among the debris. A group of men struggled to get Vera standing, the weight of her suit posing a challenge, though they managed it just as more hands grabbed at Charlie. She let them, her attention divided between her own survival and making sure Vera was still alive.

Fuck, she *had* to still be alive. *C'mon, c'mon, c'mon. Sign of life, Vera.*

The men removed Vera's shattered helmet, and her eyes fluttered at the change in lighting. She made a small, displeased sound, a frown flitting between her eyebrows. It was too early for relief to hit, adrenaline from the crash making a welcome return though Charlie knew there would be no fighting out of this one. Not yet. There were too many moving parts to consider: the guards, the fucking *swarm* of parasites, another Verity, a way *off the fucking moon*. Maybe she could fight them off. Maybe she could get them to a secure spot. But she didn't like the odds. The story had brought them this far: a parasite stronghold, echoes of the nest in the Martian worlds. This didn't have to be the end if she played it right.

Charlie let out the breath she'd been holding and went slack in the captors' arms. She tongued at her split lip and lifted her head to look at the nearest guard. It was thankfully not Roman La Roche.

"All right, boys," she said. "Take me to your leader."

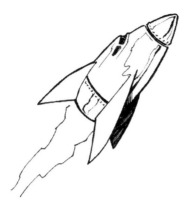

Chapter Twenty-One

— DILETTANTES —

They did not get taken to the leader.

That line always worked in movies. Charlie was almost annoyed by the twist real life had dumped on her narrative, but her nascent disappointment was quickly eclipsed by extreme concern regarding their surroundings. The long, utilitarian corridor wasn't noteworthy at first, the type of setting one expected of a lunar base: all cold hues and metal and concrete and rivets. But as they walked—well, walked was a bit generous of a word, the henchmen were half-dragging, half-escorting her—the hair on Charlie's neck began to stand on end. Her arms tingled with goosebumps underneath the sleeves of the Velo. The air shivered, like a heat mirage on a sunny day, only they couldn't be further from a fucking beach, and Charlie knew, knew the implausible number of parasites that had called this part of space home, and her stomach sank with dread.

There was a heavy-looking door when they reached the end of the corridor. A candy cane stripe painted across its width served as a warning, though the small plaque near the door frame was verbosely vague: DEMARCATED INDIVIDUALS EGRESS CHAMBER. Charlie's stomach sunk deeper. Anything with "chamber" in its name wasn't going to be good news. A DIE chamber less so.

"Hey, fellas, how about we try door number two?" said Charlie.

"There really does seem to be some kind of misunderstanding," Vera added. Her speech was still somewhat slowed from having her bell rung in the crash, which meant normal-speed for anyone not named Verity Baum. It was probably a miracle she was even walking, though Charlie had to wonder how much of that was the Marshmallow.

Not that she was going to have much time to worry. Either Roman La Roche was a terrifying boss, or this world's Verity had dished out for a much higher caliber of henchman than Villainy Baum.

"You know, when we got her helmet off, I was worried for a moment," said one of them. It was hard to assign him a descriptor. Charlie wasn't sure if that was wooziness from the crash, or just a more uniform set of goons. Less quirk. "What if she threw some of that creepy juju around, like that one a few times back? But she's just normal."

Creepy juju? They'd lost the thread on Verity Thaum so many jumps ago, they'd more or less given up on picking it up again. Was she here too? Maybe this story only had one ending, a Choose Your Own Adventure that finished the same way no matter which path you took.

"Excuse you," Vera said, glaring first at a point to the left of his face and then to the right, and then finally approximating somewhere in the middle.

"It's not even nano," said another. "I mean, check how bulky this thing is, it's like she's lumbering around in a loaf of bread."

Charlie felt a perverse sort of possessiveness toward food-based joke analogies. It was a marshmallow, obviously, and this asshole didn't get to make comments about it.

"Charlie, beat this guy up first," Vera said.

"That's the plan," Charlie said. Only, she didn't have a plan. They had her solidly at multiple gun points, and not the kind of guns that shot darts. They looked to be working on a contingency system. Some of them looked like, well, guns, which would shoot bullets that at this distance would probably go through the Marshmallow. Maybe not the Velo, but definitely through the empty space where the cowl wasn't. But interspersed through those were what looked to be energy weapons, which meant all bets there were off.

Energy weapons. Something about that tugged at her mind, but she couldn't quite get it to settle.

"Yeah, real tough, in your bread and your leotard. Hey, hey, get this: maybe the critters'll fill up on bread. Get it? Fill up on bread!"

Chuckling at his own joke, he punched a code into the pad by the door. It hissed open, and they ushered Charlie and Vera through.

Beyond the door was a catwalk, terminating halfway into the circular chamber that was the room. The shaft, Charlie amended, glancing to the side and down, because on either side of the railing was a drop. She couldn't tell how far down it went.

She couldn't tell because below them was a swarm of parasites so dense she couldn't make out individual shapes, just a heaving mass of innumerable tentacles with carapaces floating amongst them. She couldn't tell, because staring down it seemed as if the shaft might bifurcate, or trifurcate, or be any number of shafts, except at the same time there was a clear straight line. Her vision was doubling and tripling and quadrupling and resetting. It was like staring into a kaleidoscope filled with bugs. There was a smell wafting up. No, all smells were wafting up, including ones she had never smelled but her brain somehow knew, the precise opposite of what it was like near a tear.

She thought she might be sick.

"Oh," said Vera, sounding as distant as she ever had, like she was sleepwalking.

"Welcome to the Demarcated Individuals Egress chamber," said the first henchman. "You are the Demarcated Individuals, and that is your Egress."

Now would be when she needed some kind of plan. If she'd had the Reality Jig she could have...attracted the biggest swarm of parasites she'd ever seen, a fucking nest. Not an option, there. With the Browning...one or two of the guards, probably, maybe she got a human shield, but Vera almost definitely got capped in the head, and maybe one of them shot her through the shield with a fancy energy gun. She wondered what kind they were. Plasma, laser, some tech completely new to her? She supposed it didn't matter. Dead was dead. It didn't matter if it was superheated gas or an intense beam of—

"Hey, Vera," she said. "Remember that dragon? I'm sorry you won't get your rematch." She patted Vera's arm as she said it.

"Yeah," Vera said, slowly, glancing down at her hand, and at Charlie's hand patting her hand. "I don't care what anyone says, we won that fight."

"We sure did," Charlie said, angling the half of a mirror she'd pulled free of its position on the Velcro on Vera's arm until by angling it back and forth she could shift the image reflected between several of the guards. "Hey, which of you guys is the bread guy? You're all really...generic."

"That's me," said that henchman. "You're one to talk. Who are you, anyw—"

"Chuck Chase," she said, putting him in the frame. Vera fired the suit laser into the mirror. Because the thing was, she'd never dialed that back down. It was still supercharged for blinding dragons.

Or these guys. With a twist of her fingers, Charlie rapidly swiveled it across at head height directly behind them, to sudden screams, then dropped into a turning crouch, coming up under the guard of the nearest henchman. He'd just started to scream and clutch his eyes. The guy behind him was just starting to say, "What's—" when Charlie threw the guard into him.

But not the guard's energy gun.

"Ah," she said, a moment later. "Plasma."

A small hole sizzled dead center in the henchman's chest, and he staggered, toppling over the edge of the catwalk. There was a brief, sickening whine as the parasites devoured their latest snack. Hopefully, it'd spoil their appetite for bread.

Charlie leveled the plasma gun at the remaining guards. "We can do this the easy—"

A blast of energy singed her hair and any thoughts of mercy. They were fast. She was faster. Maybe it was adrenaline, maybe it was determination, maybe it was just that she was not going to die by getting eaten by fucking parasites. She pressed the trigger in rapid succession, and soon it was just her and Vera still breathing.

Vera, eyes wide, asked, "That…that was the hard way, right?"

The lunar base was not especially well-staffed. Or maybe they didn't see a need to have additional security personnel on a level that housed a giant shaft full of reality-eating parasites. The parasites were about all the security one needed.

They made it all the way to the guard station—now devoid of guards, thanks to their misadventure in the DIE chamber—without running into anyone else. Charlie immediately set to barricade the door, while Vera threw herself into one of the henchmen's chairs.

They took a moment to breathe. The room didn't smell like much, but in the normal way, and not a tear imminent way. Sweat, leather, some sort of cheap aftershave, the kind favored by teenage boys trying to impress someone. It was a welcome change from the overwhelming olfactory fucking *bouquet* in the shaft.

Charlie fell back against her barricade and sank to the floor.

"Jesus *fucking* Christ."

Vera swallowed audibly. "Agreed."

"I told you so. I fucking *told* you so."

"Evil lunar base."

"Evil fucking lunar base."

"But the kitchenette—"

"See, that's how they get you. Put a kitchenette on your spaceship, and you almost forget about the monogram. Makes you seem like an astronaut of the fucking *people*."

"I need to go yell at someone," Vera said, eyes unfocused. "I need to go yell at myself."

"Yeah," said Charlie. "And tell her where she can go put her lying fucking kitchenette." Under her breath, she added, "Fucking *DIE* chamber, Jesus Christ. Jesus *fucking* Christ."

Vera stood up. She hovered over Charlie.

"Where are you going?"

"To yell at myself," said Vera, as though this were a perfectly reasonable plan. Her voice sounded more present than it had a second ago, her gaze turned outward.

Charlie sprung to her feet. "Woah, hey, maybe—"

"Yeah, no, this isn't a debate. My other half just tried to kill us!"

"I'm aware! But I'm not sure ripping open another tear in reality is our best—"

"You *saw them*," Vera said. "The parasites. How bad is a tear going to be when we're already in the belly of the beast?"

"*Less* bad than you going off to get yourself kill..." Charlie trailed off, frowning. "Actually, that's a confusing sentence given the context."

"It'll buy you time to find a way out," said Vera. "La Roche will be expecting those guards to check-in, and when they don't, he'll send others. And you heard them. They won't be looking for you."

It stung. It probably shouldn't have. It was a tactical advantage, and one they were lucky to have. Charlie looked away, hands balling at her sides, frustrated that she couldn't offer up an alternate plan that wasn't even stupider.

"We're getting out of here together," she finally said.

"Well, *yeah*," Vera scoffed, though it lacked a certain punch. "*I'm* not dying today."

"I'm holding you to that."

"I'm counting on it."

The guard station seemed too empty once Vera left. Charlie watched her progress across a row of screens that showed this level's corridors at different angles, but once Vera reached the elevator, there was no telling where she went.

God, this was a stupid plan. Right up there with punching a fucking dragon. Hell, it was the *same* fucking plan, wasn't it? Only Vee-Bee was the dragon, and she had an evil lunar base built over parasite-central at her disposal. Punching it hadn't even been the thing, in the end. They'd needed an advantage. Now they needed an advantage again. Were there security systems? Automated turrets she could hack, modify the friend or foe detection. There were *missiles*, could she get at the missile targeting and launch controls from here?

She cycled through the menus, getting a sense for what she had access to on default guard permissions, no hacking required. She didn't have a lot of luck. Missiles were done from the main control room. Apparently, *someone* was paranoid about being shot at from their own base, because there wasn't even a way to do it if she managed to hack herself better clearance.

Which she had yet to do. This wasn't Vera's world. The tech was ahead, and she didn't have that advantage.

She tried other places. She could get at the reactor systems, and that seemed promising—for a hot minute. Turn out all the lights. Genius. Except it turned out it was the kind of doomsday reactor that you didn't just turn *off*. You could turn off the regulators, at which point a lot of alarms went off and someone turned them all back on. It might even be her because she could only see doing that as a giant bluff. It wouldn't just be the base. The only reason to actually do it would be if you genuinely wanted to—

Well, suffice to say she did *not*. She wasn't the supervillain here. She needed an option with less collateral damage. She needed to find their way out of here. They'd need functioning spacesuits, in case the next moon didn't have a lunar base. The tear tech. Some kind of vehicle, ideally. Rations. It was a short list, but each item was a big ask on an impossibly short timeline, and could they have come *up* with a stupider plan?

Her answer came in the form of another deafening alarm, and the by now familiar flashing red lights.

"Fuck. *Fuck*!"

WARNING: TEAR IMMINENT appeared in bold type on every screen.

The only comforting word was "imminent." *Imminent* meant that Vera was close, but not *too* close. But that didn't matter. Splitting up had been a terrible idea, and maybe going after Vera wasn't much wiser, but they got *this* far working together, and like hell was she going to let Vera get herself killed. Kill herself? It didn't matter.

With the hologram busted, Charlie went old school and dug around the small row of lockers for an extra uniform, which she slipped on over the Velo. A duty roster stuck to the inside of one of the doors gave her an idea of how many hired guns to expect and where, while bad gun ownership practice supplied her with another gun to call her own. She cast one last glance at the screens to make sure "imminent" was still the warning in play and then left to go do something incredibly stupid.

The upper levels were organized chaos, though not so organized that Charlie couldn't blend in with a rush of guards sight unseen. It was all hands on deck, and no one had counted the hands. The guards she was trailing seemed more concerned about what might be ahead of them and glad of the numbers. Not because of the tears or the parasites, which they called "critters" in what she had to assume was a coping mechanism to deal with the fact they were living above a critical mass of reality eating horrors.

No, they were again worried that they might be running into more "weird juju." Which, again, Charlie thought was an odd concern considering what they were living above, which was the weirdest creepiest shit she'd ever seen. But then it wasn't actively trying to kill them. Just her goddamned universe.

Verity Thaum *had* made it this far, it seemed. And no further. Which was alarming, because while she'd obviously left an *impression*, she also hadn't done any damage that couldn't be fixed, since everything here seemed to be running fine. If Verity Thaum had been able to do the kinds of things the Josephine from that universe had, and hadn't pulled it off…

Maybe magic didn't work when you rolled out of the universe it was from. Or, no, she'd been able to do something, because "weird juju," but maybe it was like the Fabricator. Maybe she'd been futzing it.

It was all a lot of maybes that weren't going to do her a lot of good because she couldn't do magic, could she? All she had was what she had on her, and her own self.

And hopefully whatever Vera brought to the table if she wasn't dead already. This was a very deep and very real concern, considering the utterly matter-of-fact way they'd tried to toss the both of them down a villainous death shaft in a room with a deeply on the nose name.

A concern immediately alleviated by the sound of voices raised in disbelief, a kind of angry incredulity. Only Vera made people incredulously mad like that.

Only, when Charlie followed the rush of guards into what was evidently the control room, the raised voice *was* Vera's. "...you *kidding* me?" she was finishing up, yelling at—

Not another Vera. It was a man. One that could have been Vera's twin brother, had fraternal twins the same level of genetic similarity as identical twins. It was uncanny, give or take a beard (him) and shorter hair (her).

"It's perfectly sound! Yes, I saw what happened on Mars. You know what I have that they don't?"

"Bad facial hair choic—"

"I know what happened on Mars, that's what! They had time to build an empire, it was perfectly reasonable to expect more time."

"Okay, *Victor*, how's that working out for you?"

Victor Baum. Vee-Bee. Well, that explained why La Roche had been so quick with the missiles. There was no Verity Baum to be in charge here because this universe had a Victor Baum instead. If she'd been picturing a culprit behind all of this, she'd kind of figured on someone taller. The goatee seemed dead fucking on, though.

"I'm handling it! I'm not just scrambling around without a plan. Here we are, living quite happily—well, living in, okay, not harmony, but there's a certain symbiotic relationship developing—"

"Is feeding them people you don't like *part* of that or is that just an added bonus for you? When you decided to build a murder shaft, did you sit around trying to think of a catchy acronym *yourself*, or did you give the job to someone else?"

"Shouting isn't really helping your case, you know. This really calls for a reasoned discussion of our relative points without just throwing insults and accusations about. But I suppose you would be more emotional."

"Right, because 'DIE chamber' really screams 'emotionally stability.'"

"Well, what would *you* have called it?" he snapped, peevish.

"I wouldn't have built it in the first place, you ludicrous goatee-stroking psycho."

Victor took a very visible moment to compose himself. The guards made no sudden movements, or even attempts to get closer—a curious strategy for *guarding* that again spoke volumes of their wariness of whatever Verity Thaum *had* managed to do.

"Are *ad hominem* attacks *strictly* necessary?" said Victor. "You don't *understand.*"

Vera took a small step back and raised her arms in a challenging shrug. The room, save Charlie, collectively held its breath. "Try me."

And exhaled.

Victor laced his hands together and stepped down from what Charlie couldn't help but think of as a dais. "Well, where to start," he said.

"The beginning," said Vera. She rethought that almost immediately, holding up a finger. Tension shivered through the guards.

"Not the very beginning. When it gets interesting. I'll be the judge of what's interesting. Obviously."

Victor bristled. His knuckles turned white.

"Victor Baum Senior—"

"Oh, *brother.*"

"*Victor Baum Senior,*" Victor began again, in a louder voice, "was the greatest explorer in a generation of great explorers. Naturally, I wanted to live up to my father's legacy, but how could I hope to do so, when there was nothing new I could possibly achieve? My father made his name through discovery. But what's another star or planet? There was nothing left to discover—not in this reality. I wanted to explore a *different* kind of new world—one that wouldn't just carry on the Baum legacy but *redefine* it, forever.

"When I found the portal technology, how could I do anything *but* leap upon it? Instead of traveling from dead rock to dead rock with the hopes of *maybe* finding a microorganism or two, here was a multitude of worlds, brimming with life and variety! With one jump, I had changed our understanding of life as we know it!"

He lapsed into an expectant silence. Was he waiting for applause? As far as evil villain monologues went, this one had the practiced feeling of a keynote speech. He'd given this before, probably in front of shareholders.

Vera yawned loudly. A tic of annoyance crossed Victor's features. His face was easier to read than Vera's had been. Charlie considered the fact it was easier because she knew Vera and then dismissed it out of hand.

"I'm sorry," Vera said, not sounding very sorry at all. "You were saying? You know, about the part where you apparently *knew going in* about the parasites?"

"So I gave the Martians undue credit!" he said. "How magnanimous of me, thinking they might have actually killed them all!" A sharp inhale, his next words more measured. "I figured even if they hadn't, I could simply stop using the technology the moment a parasite appeared. *One* would be manageable, surely."

"You played the odds," Vera said flatly.

"Yes, I suppose I di—"

"—you played the odds with— With everything. Literally, *everything* hanging in the balance."

"Well, when you put it *that*—"

"How would *you* put it?"

"I would tell you if you would stop interrupting me!"

"Really? I should get credit letting you yap that long *without* interrupting you. Blah, blah, blah, *daddy issues*."

Victor glowered. It should have been menacing. Charlie had no doubt he thought it *was* menacing. "The odds were in our *favor*," he said, stubbornly pressing forward with his story. *History.* "We assumed, and the data supported, that the parasites would be easily managed in small numbers! Baum Technologies even developed a bioengineered predator—"

"—yeah, we've *met*," Vera groused.

"—as a precautionary measure before opening the first portal," said Victor. "But when the parasites showed up, they didn't *stop* showing up. Portals started to open on their own, which we hadn't known was possible. The BioPred proved at best a delaying measure. We were at risk of going the way of Mars before us, but as I've said, we knew their mistakes. We knew where they went wrong."

"If you can't beat 'em, join 'em."

"In essence, yes. The parasites, I came to understand, are a natural part of the multiverse. But as man did with the wolf, I did with the parasites."

"Except you ended up with cats, not dogs. Assuming the cats were soulless, non-Euclidean cockroach squid who left bits and pieces of other realities on your doorstep, which— Actually, yeah, that metaphor works out nicely. Cats."

Vera evidently wasn't a cat person.

"It's a symbiotic relationship," insisted Victor, who apparently *was*. "We devised a means to cultivate them, to tunnel through the multiverse to give them other worlds to eat, worlds where foreign realities were leaking into each other. They would have no need to damage m— Our world. The Prime reality's existence would be preserved." A twitch of amusement along the line of his mouth. "You look confused."

"'Prime' reality," Vera said, complete with scare quotes that had every henchman's trigger finger extra itchy.

"Well, all the other ones are just full of other people from my world, aren't they? Spinoffs. Distaff versions of *me*, everywhere." He looked pointedly at Vera, who scoffed. "Please. As if the female version of me that's a *witch* is going to be the original? When she invaded my world with the intent of destroying my work—my *reality*, I might remind you—I did what was only reasonable."

"You threw her in a fucking kill chamber," said Charlie. She meant to think it, but the words spilled from her mouth before she could stop them, a rising tide of anger crashing against her sense of self-preservation. "You're crazy. You're fucking crazy, and you're killing my universe so you can feel like a *hero*." The word tore from her throat, more scream than voice.

"Who is that?" Victor demanded, peering into the crowd. "Who— Karla, is this one of your jokes?"

A murmur passed through the crowd. The guards, quickly realizing Charlie wasn't one of their own, gave her a wide berth. She stepped forward to fill the vacuum and stopped beside Vera.

Victor scrutinized her from the tips of her toes to the top of her head. Charlie wanted to take a fucking shower, but she stood her ground. Her jaw clenched, and she raised her chin.

"You're not Karla," said Victor, seeming genuinely perturbed. "Who even are *you*?"

"Nobody," she said, because that was what the multiverse had told her all along. She was a nobody, and that didn't fucking matter. "I'm a *nobody*. But there are lot more of those than somebodies, so that's gotta count for something, right?"

He stared at her a moment later, then, seemingly unable to put this in context, turned back to the known quantity. "Did you pick up some random bit of background information and drag her along on your attempt to undermine my reality? That's almost… inhumane."

Charlie wasn't done with him. In fact, after that, she was additionally not done with him. "*That's* inhumane?! That's where you draw the line? My entire reality is dying, you fuck! Not just mine! Just because—what, you don't think they're as *real*? Because naturally, you're King Shit Central, from whom all King and Queen Shits descend."

"Uh," said Vera, but then stopped and put up her hands, apparently allowing Charlie room to say whatever she was going to say without interruption.

"Well, obviou—"

"IT IS NOT YOUR TURN TO TALK. Consider the fern, you motherfucker. Consider the fucking fern! There's no Fern Prime! There's just—the fucking infinite multiplicity of life, abiding by mathematical principles! They're shaped like galaxies, but that doesn't mean galaxies need to bow down to a goddamned fern and accept it as the one true fucking spiral! And vice versa! Ferns are as goddamned important as goddamned galaxies!"

"A fern would say that," Victor said, cold with fury. "You are nobody! You said it yourself! You are a nobody, and *she* is a reflection of the kind all heroes eventually face, unable to stomach the tough choices all heroes eventually must make, and I will *not* be lectured by a pair of…a pair of dilettante *ladyhoppers*. The Martians crashed a single Theia into a single Earth! *This* Earth, because here the parasites turned out to be, in the moon that event formed! This is the nexus point that I am *preserving*!"

"But you're not," said a new voice. "Victor, it didn't work. It isn't working." Charlie turned her head just enough to see, keeping Victor in view in the corner of her vision. A muscle in his forehead was twitching. He didn't seem far off deciding he was justified in just ordering them shot. Frankly, she was pretty sure the only reason he hadn't already was that he'd been caught up in selling them on his bullshit reasoning. She'd have liked to believe he was having to sell himself on it, too, but it was tough to say. Maybe he just really did not see anyone else as real people. Other realities didn't factor in unless they were somewhere to expand to, to take over or to use as fuel or discard, as he saw fit.

But the woman who'd spoken seemed considerably less sold. Mournful. The guards had turned slightly when Charlie had but had then turned back once they recognized her. Charlie tried to put her in context. A little younger than Victor, buttoned-up, hair in a very tight bun. Quite...wound.

"Miss Salt, this isn't—"

"It didn't *work*, Victor," she said. She looked at Charlie. "The world down there is stripped clean. Mars-state. The plan was—we evacuated everyone we could, and then Victor said he could use the reality the parasites have in the nest to...rebuild it, and then we'd bring everyone back, but...for god's sake, Victor, can't you see this has to stop?"

"Just because it's hard? I thought you understood the work we're doing here, Miss Salt, but I suppose in the end you're just as irrational as they are. I am *done* explaining myself to people who refuse to engage in reasoned discussion. No more talking."

"Yeah," Vera said. "Yeah, you know what, let's get *irrational*."

Charlie saw it coming, and not just because Vera didn't know how not to telegraph the move. Because it was what Vera did. She was impulsive. She was reckless. She was, on occasion, righteous. As for irrational…

Vera backhanded Victor across the face with machine-assisted strength. Backhanding Victor Baum Junior with an arm backed up by a motorized designer exoskeleton seemed a perfectly rational course of action, with only one minor flaw.

The smell of nothing tore through the chamber as a tear shredded into existence where Vera and Victor were standing.

Chapter Twenty-Two

— LADYHOPPERS —

Vera was out cold.

Victor was not. He fucking *lived* over a tear. He rolled from his back onto his knees. An angry welt marred his cheek. He spat. His teeth were stained with blood.

The tear raged, but Victor would not be outdone. He pushed himself up and barked at the guards, "What are you *waiting* for?"

He had to yell it again before anyone moved. He'd been flung quite a distance.

The circle of guards became smaller. Charlie and Vera were surrounded. But Charlie's attention was divided, aware of the increasing outside threat while preoccupied with ensuring Vera would live. Kneeling, Charlie pulled Vera's mirror from her pocket and held it close to Vera's face. It fogged up. She was breathing. She would live.

Or rather, the tear wouldn't kill her. The guards still might.

Fuck.

"Guess she wasn't no witch after all," a broad set henchman remarked to his friend. He was tapping on some kind of scanner that looked tiny in his hands. "Kinda anticlimactic, really."

"What about her?" said Henchman's equally large friend. He was armed with something more lethal-looking than a scanner. Charlie ran through a list of moves she could use to gain the advantage, all of which would've been fine if Henchfriend didn't have several dozen buddies with similar weapons pointed at her head.

"Didn't know I was supposed to be scanning *her!*"

"Gentlemen," said Miss Salt. She was working her way through the crowd, her shoes click-clacking against the concrete floor. On her heels was a man Charlie thought looked familiar but couldn't immediately place. He hovered at Miss Salt's side, expression worried, his own weapon holstered, though his hand stayed close by. Between the pair of them, Charlie and Vera were somewhat shielded from half of the circle, at least. "This madness must stop. Victor sold you a lie."

"Victor *gave* us the multiverse, and this safe haven," said, oh great, there was Roman La fucking Roche, here to be the loyal lieutenant. "If you wish to leave, Natalia, you are free to...*egress.* Really. Faced with this *weakness*, your choice is to side with it? So be it. The scans show they have no magic? Then *fire.*"

"Uh," said Henchman, whose scanner had just chimed once, as if to provide the foley for the realization that Charlie had just had.

She did, in fact, have magic.

Not in any "the power was in you all along" sense. In the sense that she'd been carrying a witch-certified hand-crafted magic amulet across quite a few universes now, that had been specifically given to her with the instruction, *"When you need it, it'll occur to you, and it'll help."*

What occurred to Charlie, in fact, was that Josephine, Witch of the Tower, had spoken in a lot of symbolic terms, had believed in the power and significance of concepts. That Verity Thaum had known a lot about how this all worked. That maybe witches knew a lot about stories. And when one had shown up to help Victor and his people with their story problem, they'd thrown her down a kill shaft.

Well, Charlie might not be an expert, but she knew what you did with the magical item you'd just remembered at a moment when you were about to be killed a dozen different ways by the minions of the guy responsible for the death of your universe. She plucked it out and twisted the face. She'd been right when she first considered it. Twisting wouldn't put all of the various designs into alignment, just one at a time. But when the first lined up, it flared up with light, that portion of the design staying lit even as she twisted—

"*Merde*," said Roman. "I SAID FIRE, *CONNARDS*."

—and then the next, and then the next, until the amulet was all overlapping lines of fire, making a series of symbols that lay in the same space somehow without interrupting each other. It looked pretty, but somehow Charlie had the sense that something a little more was called for. This might have seemed a failure of instruction, but actually, she knew exactly what she wanted to do with it to finish up.

"Abracadabra," she said and spiked it into the ground, where it shattered, even as a dozen fingers squeezed a dozen triggers and a dozen superheated balls of plasma erupted through the air toward them—

Only to hit the expanding bubble of swirling light that had exploded from the amulet and slowed as if they were marbles thrown into jelly. The plasma coasted to a stop in midair. Expressions of slow consternation threatened to bloom across the faces of the guards who'd fired them before they, too, slowed to the point where any movement was nigh undetectable.

Roman was poised in mid-air, mid-dive, hand outstretched to try and catch the amulet. Charlie crouched beside him. She considered poking him, just to see what it would do, but smashing instincts aside, she really didn't know how the spell functioned. It could snap him out of it.

"Wait, so you're—" Miss Salt said.

"Good at on the job procurement," Charlie said, crossing hastily back to where Vera was lying and heaving her over her shoulder. "I have no idea how long this is going to last, we need to get gone."

"'This' being...frozen time?" said Miss Salt.

"Why aren't we frozen?" asked Miss Salt's friend.

"I don't fucking know! Magic! We need to *move*, people!"

"I can take you to the escape pods," said Miss Salt's friend.

"Great," said Charlie, because she wasn't about to look a gift horse in the mouth, especially a gift horse that *couldn't* resist poking La Roche in his stupid face. (His cheek jiggled like gelatin as the friend retracted his finger, but as mesmerizing as that visual was, nothing else happened.) "I'm gonna need to make a pitstop at the reactor first. Lead the way, uh— I didn't catch your name."

"Joe Watson," said Joe.

Joe, who was *very* not-Black. He did have an objectively nice head of hair, she supposed.

"Of course it is," said Charlie, because this was apparently the topsy fucking turvy universe. "Anyway, let's just—"

Joe hesitated, like he wanted to ask something, but then simply nodded. "Right."

As a trio, they bobbed and weaved through the discharged plasma shots. Joe, unencumbered by impractical footwear or a CEO in a heavy fucking spacesuit slung over his shoulder, had the easiest time of it, with Miss Salt taking up the rear behind Charlie. The spell wasn't localized to the control room. A half dozen guards, weapons drawn, were frozen in the hallway. She had to give it to Lady J; the woman knew her magic.

"How far do you think it extends?" asked Miss Salt.

"No fucking idea, but I've got my fingers crossed for *far*," said Charlie.

It was magic. It was last-ditch-save magic. That had to mean *far*, right?

They turned a corner and Charlie got her answer when she got a face full of tentacle. Her heart stuttered. Her grip on Vera tightened. A scream died in her throat. She was frozen, not from magic, but from good old-fashioned fear, fear that overwhelmed her fight or flight response so that she could do nothing but stand still and wait to die via non-Euclidean cockroach squid.

That didn't happen. The parasite was frozen in motion, a living still from a nature documentary. That she'd thought the hologram lifelike seemed laughable in retrospect. She could fucking *smell* it—it smelled like the DIE chamber, of too much distinct reality for the brain to possibly process. Even frozen, it hurt to look at. The glimpse of *teeth* she caught before glancing away would haunt her nightmares for the rest of her life, presuming they got out of there alive.

It seemed like an awfully optimistic presumption.

She blinked hard, shaking her head. When she opened her eyes, she swore the parasite moved. Was it an optical illusion? The spell wearing off? How in the flying fuck were they going to *beat* these things? Turning tail and running was a great short-term solution, but a stopgap wasn't going to cut it forever.

"We need to evacuate the base." Her voice came out shaky, the plan in her head not quite formed but taking shape.

The parasite was definitely closer. Joe and Miss Salt didn't look quite as perturbed, like it was just another day with the critters and their homicidal fucking boss. It probably was. Verity Thaum hadn't been the only Verity to make it here. Charlie stepped back and around the parasite, willed her pulse to steady. They weren't even that far from the amulet yet, and they were only headed farther at a quick clip.

The reactor was two levels down. At that distance, time was flowing fast enough for the straggler guards' expressions to pass from "confused" right to "oh shit," but not quite have time to draw *and* fire their weapons before Joe programmed a bulkhead door to fall shut with a resounding *CLANG*.

"We need to evacuate the base," Charlie said again, stronger. She peered through the bulkhead's reinforced window, at the plasma beam still moving toward them in slow motion.

"You won't have much luck convincing the others to leave," Miss Salt said. "You saw them up there."

"True believers, all of them," Joe chimed in, tapping in another code on the control panel to unlock the hangar bay. "They're so far up Vic's ass, they can almost see La Roche."

The doors opened with a hydraulic hiss to reveal the base's reactor room, which lived up to her expectations: It was an imposingly large room with high vaulted ceilings that strained the neck to look at and thick walls of concrete and metal, as prototypically masculine as the rest of the base. The reactor itself was a tall column encased in unbreakable glass, painting the room in eerie blue-white light.

"Good thing I'm leaving the convincing to you two," said Charlie, rolling her shoulders back. She might have to rethink Marshmallow as a name. That thing weighed a ton. "There another way out of here?"

"West entrance," Joe said, jutting his chin in what Charlie could only assume was a westward direction. She took a second to orient herself in the room. If right was west, that meant they'd just come in through the southern entrance.

"Great. Go out that way and drag anyone you can to the escape pods. Things are about to get a little messy. They'll want to leave."

Joe and Miss Salt, wearing twin expressions of concern, exchanged a glance.

"What are you going to do?"

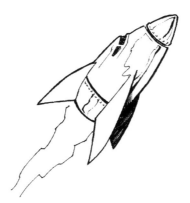

Chapter Twenty-Three
— #BLOWUPTHEMOON —

Wakey wakey, Sleeping Beauty, I could really use some help here!"

Yelling at Vera seemed like a questionable strategy at best, seeing as the blaring alarm systems hadn't yet woken her, but when it came to questionable strategies, Charlie was on a run. They were barricaded in the reactor room, the lights flashing red, red, *red*. Charlie's fingers were flying over the reactor's primary console, flicking buttons and inputting code to manually disable the reactor's many fail safes, but she wouldn't be able to complete the sequence without another set of hands. On either side of the reactor were two levers that needed to be switched off simultaneously. Once flipped, Charlie judged they'd have about five minutes to get their asses on an escape pod before the whole thing blew.

It was a lot to be handling all on her own, hence the yelling at the unconscious woman. Also, even if she *could* flip both switches on her own, she didn't want Vera unconscious while making their mad dash to the pod; she was a lot to carry in the Marshmallow.

Also *also*, she'd been out for a while and that was generally kind of a worrying sign. Maybe in other dimensions, people really did stay unconscious that long without brain damage? She hoped so.

"Whuzziz," Vera said, not exactly helping these concerns before she added a slightly more coherent if no less blurry, "What is—are we escaping?" She rubbed her eyes and then forehead with one hand, leaning forward to peer up at the console.

"Getting there," Charlie said, voice straining as she leaned over to the far right to hit one of the last switches.

"Chuck," said Vera. "Why are we not escaping?"

"We have to blow up the moon first," Charlie said.

"Right, right," Vera said, sitting back and squeezing her eyes shut and then opening them again, working her jaw. She paused. "Wait. *What.*"

"That's where they live. I'm blowing it up. If we blow it up, it's just...space. Big empty insignificant space. No tears. They'll be stuck here. So while everyone was frozen—"

"Froz—"

"—I told Salt and Joe to evacuate everyone through the tears, close 'em as they go, and I found the reactor and I—well, *we*, you need to stand over there—are going to set it to overload. Because of course there's a reactor you can overload. That asshole is *such* an overloading reactor kind of asshole."

"And the moon is going to blow up..."

"In about five minutes, once we disable the fail safes. A little more to your right. Yeah, that switch there," Charlie said, watching as Vera woozily lumbered over to the far side of the panel. "Good. We have to switch it off at the same time, or else they'll be able to reinstate the fail-safes remotely."

"Which we don't want."

"Correct."

Vera pawed at the switch, using the rest of the console to keep herself balanced. Still woozy, then. Charlie might end up having to carry her to the escape pod after all, but that was a problem for thirty seconds from now.

"LADIES," boomed a loudspeaker in Victor's voice.

The spell had worn off. Great. Charlie kept inputting code.

"Not now, asshole!"

"YOU DON'T INTEND TO LEAve me a later," Victor said. Vera paused in the process of turning the speaker down and looked at Charlie. Widening her fingers a little so that they weren't touching the dial, she gave them a little rotating wiggle and raised her eyebrows in a question. It was a good question. Did they really want to listen to this guy?

"And you're ripping my world apart like a fucking *afterthought*. A whole reality! I'm just blowing up a fucking moon!"

"You're the one resorting to an act of *astounding* destruction, and you still think I'm the bad guy? There'll be no coming back for this Earth! How can you even be sure this will work?"

"I already explained this to someone I trust more than you, and she's pressing buttons here with me, *so*, not doing it again, asshole!"

Vera made an exaggerated hand on heart and head-tilt. Charlie considered taking it back or maybe leaving her behind.

"Okay. Okay! You are obviously...very upset about what's happening to your world. I understand. I understand! I'd do anything to save mine! There is, surely, there has to be a compromise. I could preserve your world. Off-limits to parasites. You can close tears, now, and I have a map of the multiverse, all worlds currently affected by...parasitic sub-infestation. You could go home. You could *save* it. Or, you could just...destroy to satiate your own anger."

Charlie thought about it.

"Yeah, that sounds good, actually."

"Have fun exploding!" Vera said and turned the speaker off.

The escape pod handled better than the spaceship that had gotten them off Mars. It was smaller. It was designed to avoid obstacles. There was an expectation of "imminent threat" to the design that indicated Victor had anticipated someone shooting at them.

No one was shooting at them. They were all busy. Charlie had seen to that. It would have made escaping easy if that was the plan. Where would they go? There was a moon full of parasites and an Earth that was just dust.

Some of those parasites were trying to eat the pod. Charlie corkscrewed through the stutter-jerk as they lashed out at her, trying not to remember what their teeth had looked like up close. She didn't know if they knew what she was up to or if they were just reacting to the presence of something out of universe that smelled good. Maybe the magic. She didn't know. They were trying to eat them, she was trying to avoid being eaten.

"Could you watch that panel and tell me when it goes red?" said Charlie. "I connected it to the reactor core temp. I'd like some warning before spacetime gets completely fucked up. I feel like this is really going to fuck up local spacetime, you know?"

"Charlie," said Vera, sitting back in her chair and eyeing the panel Charlie had indicated. "You're very reckless, and I am alarmed by your behavior."

"Thank you," Charlie said.

"Also, the reactor just went critical, so I guess the moon—"

The moon exploded.

Without a sound, it was as if a huge chunk, a third or more, simply leaped apart from the rest, shattering out as it did. Charlie couldn't quite process it. She'd come up with the idea, she'd executed the idea, and now that the moon was *fucking exploding* in front of her, it was hard to believe that the moon actually was *fucking exploding* because she'd decided it was a good idea to *blow up the fucking moon*.

She didn't have much time to process or freak out about her choices re: blowing up the fucking moon, because then, as if the flat black emptiness of space was just a cloth that could be bunched and crumpled and twisted, everything in front of them folded in and fractured, flared. The spacetime distortions began disintegrating the rest of the moon, cracks shearing through it.

"Holy shit," Vera said. "So our exit is…"

"Tear in the middle of it," Charlie confirmed.

"So we're flying—"

"Into the exploding moon," Charlie confirmed.

"You've officially lost the right to complain about me punching a dragon that one time."

"Noted."

"Assuming we survive."

"Assuming we survive," Charlie agreed. "Fingers crossed."

"What? No! That's bad luck!"

"Seriously?"

Vera lifted her arms in an emphatic gesture. "Yes!"

"Not where I'm from!"

"Well, let's hope it's not bad luck in *this* universe," said Vera, not sounding convinced. "Who knows how superstitions operate here?"

Charlie set a course for the eye of the explosion, or at least she tried to. The navigational system was going haywire, the heads-up display streaming nonsense data before giving up the ghost and turning an unpromising blue. Terrified that she was going to have to eyeball flying into a fucking spacetime *minefield*, Charlie *thwacked* the casing. The system flickered from blue to black, and then the HUD was back online.

Just in time for the next crisis. Though maybe that was thinking too linearly, ascribing an order to events. Space was folding in on itself and duplicating like a fucking kaleidoscope on acid. There was no *next* crisis: there were infinite crises, existing simultaneously. The parasites, the tears, debris. Not that there would be tears for much longer, that was the whole point of her plan: remove the resonant moon, cut the parasites off from the rest of the multiverse. Already they were closing or merging, she wasn't sure yet. There were fewer. There was no weapons system. She had no idea what kind of shielding, if any, the pod had. Wouldn't even take that big of a rock to blow a hole through the hull and kill them dead, not at those speeds.

She hit the acceleration anyway. They were really givin'er now, maxing out the digital odometer on the console. A proximity alarm went off, and Charlie punched the reverse thrusters to turn the ship out of the path of a parasite. The sudden tug-and-shove of the seatbelt winded her, leaving Charlie gasping until there was enough slack to breathe.

The closer they got to the moon, the more disjointed their path became: stops and starts that made Charlie's chest ache and Vera slip worryingly in and out of consciousness. The proximity alarm was white noise, a constant background wail that barely registered over the adrenaline-drunk pounding of her pulse in her ears. The parasites warred against the moon's gravity warred against the tears. She threaded the pod through the parasite's nest as it collapsed around them, the route a series of desperate gambles wherein each new detour was picked in a fraction of a second.

She miscalculated. Zigged when she should've zagged, and a parasite was too close, and they were done for.

Only they weren't. The parasite bounced off a second pod and through a tear like a non-Euclidean bumper car.

Charlie gaped. "Who the fuck—?"

The pod fired.

Victor. Of course it was Victor. Of course his pod had guns and could repel parasites. It was even a different color from the rest of the fleet, an ostentatious gold that gleamed like a miniature sun.

"Oh, come *on*!"

The pod rattled from the force of the direct hit, but that they were still flying suggested they were equipped with some kind of shielding.

"That is far too much gold," Vera agreed. She shifted in her seat and reached for her console.

"We don't have any weapons," Charlie said, redirecting her attention to flying. She knew better than to question Vera when she had an idea, but Vera also had a probable head injury. "I checked already."

"Not looking for weapons."

"Well, unless you're suggesting one of us jump out, go over there and punch him in the face, I don't think—"

"Not that, either."

Charlie hadn't been serious, but she had to admit she was a little bit disappointed. Vera had gotten to hit the guy, and Charlie had the far more personal beef. The opportunity to punch that fussy little goatee right off Victor's smug fucking face wouldn't have gone amiss. But the moon was exploding, the tears were closing off, and all of Victor's works were crumbling down. It'd have to do.

Vera punched a button. A new tear appeared on the scanner. Charlie juked them out of the way of another parasite. This didn't seem to *help* them any. Tears were nothing to Victor. Tears were his *business*.

"You're gonna want to dodge in a sec because I figure it's coming through right…about…"

Vera paused. The space where "now" should have been failed to be punctuated by whatever she'd been planning on.

"Ah. Damn," Vera said. "I really thought—"

The Hound—*clearly* the same one they'd met before by the array of battle scars it had accumulated, metal parts torn loose or missing, two or three or maybe one tentacle still embedded in a sparking wound in its side and flapping loose—tore through the tear, shredding through a pair of parasites that had been darting for the tear. Charlie didn't know if they'd been trying to block access or, if in whatever parasites used for a brain, they could tell what was happening was intended to rein them in. If they had enough intelligence to be escaping.

Not those, though. Or the next parasite along, at which point the Hound landed on a tumbling lump of moon, head turning and searching before it locked on.

"Yeah, now. Now would be the time for—"

"I got it," Charlie said, not dodging or turning but steering directly on at the Hound. Victor fired on them again. *Then* she hit the stick, spiraling them out of the way and around the fragment, even as the bolts of energy blew it apart, grazing the side of the Hound. Its eyes locked down red, chose a target, identified the greatest current threat.

"A boy really shouldn't be separated from his dog," Vera said, as the Hound launched itself through the space between it and Victor's pod, the ostentatious gold hull crumpling and beginning to split with the force of the impact. The pair tumbled in a wild spin back into the maelstrom of debris and destruction that was the remains of the moon, the Hound clawing at a gap in the hull, beginning to tear it apart before the two were lost from view, blocked by dust and rocks and more dust and more rocks.

There'd been the possibility it *wouldn't* go for Victor. It might have only gone for his distaff—no, fuck that. It might have only gone for *Verity* Baums, excluding the masculine side. What would you call it, if you were engaging in his kind of fuckery and calling one the spin-off? She supposed it didn't matter. If she survived the next five minutes, she might look it up. She'd tried to weigh the die by getting Victor to shoot it. She'd seen it going for whoever had last attacked it before. It made sense, on the basis that if you were a rabid cybernetic predator, you probably ate whatever was shooting you first. She wished them well of each other. As satisfying as seeing the result of that would be, they wouldn't be seeing it. Bearing straight for the Hound meant that she'd born straight for what was *behind* it, as well, and the dodge hadn't cleared them of it: the scintillating weft in space, the last extant tear in the crumbling moon.

Vera urgently tapped on the console, furiously pulling up and dismissing menus to find and activate the pod's tear-stabilization, slamming a button just as the pod hit the edge of the tear and the world dissolved.

It wasn't exactly the calm portal journey of the last time. The trip was uncomfortable. They came through hard, the pod plunging on a one-way trip toward the remains of the Wasteland Earth's atmosphere. Charlie's second alternate universe, Vera's first, and possibly their last if this crash went badly.

And it was absolutely going to be a crash. The good news about the low atmosphere was that it meant they weren't going to get as hot on re-entry. The bad news was that they weren't going to slow down a lot. The tear fucked with the pod's power, the console blinking in and out. There was enough juice left to shut the tear behind them, but the hits they'd taken from Victor and from debris had limited the amount the thrusters could control and slow the descent as they engaged in a full-on reentry. What other choice did they have? It was Earth and possible death, or space and certain death. Charlie picked the option where living was at least on the table. Flames licked at the viewscreen—"not as hot" wasn't "not hot." An impossible inferno engulfed the pod, the heat becoming unbearable. Sweat crowded Charlie's vision, but the G-force was too strong to wipe at her eyes. Vera was out cold, front drenched in fresh vomit.

When the hellfire gave way to the expansive gray of the Wasteland's barren landscape, it was all Charlie could do to steer into a slope, fighting gravity to grasp at the controls, using each tooth-rattling bounce to bleed off speed so that when they finally did hit and slide and skid and careen, they would bruise but not break.

The pod at last slowed and rolled and stopped. Charlie looked at the scanner. Not a single parasite signal lit up. Not a single sign of anything adjacent to life, aside from her and Vera.

She supposed that was a win.

Chapter Twenty-Four

— EPILOGUE —

Ow," said Vera. "Wait. What's stronger than 'ow'?"

"Jesus fuck I'm sore," Charlie said, falling back in the seat of the pod to take a couple of breaths. She'd been busy trying to kick the escape pod's door open. The crash had dug them into the dust that coated the surface of this Earth. Every kick was against the weight of both door and piled up dust, an exercise in digging a little more space every time.

"That," agreed Vera. "Hey, Chuck?"

"Yeah," Charlie said, looking sightlessly at the ceiling. She kind of wanted to take a nap. That was fair, right? After what had just happened, she could take a nap if she wanted. Not even necessarily if she *needed*, she could just briefly take some sort of fucking *break*.

"Did we just save the multiverse?"

Charlie considered this. Eventually, she concluded, "I have no fucking idea." She thought about it a little more. "I think at least we helped."

With a groan, Vera leaned forward and seized a panel, sliding it loose into a free tablet so she could collapse back into the seat next to Charlie. The pod had rolled such that the seats faced up, toward the sky. A little like a space shuttle on the launch pad. The fact this meant she was effectively lying on her back when in the seat wasn't helping her on the nap-front.

Vera tapped the screen. The tablet made a little siren wail, the "fuckload of tears" alert, prompting Vera to hastily tap it again and silence it. They already knew about those, after all. They'd been here before. It did indicate that the damage hadn't just immediately healed up because they'd blown up the source, which was the moon.

Well, *a* moon. But blowing up *a* moon didn't have the same ring to it.

Charlie reviewed this thought, then decided she'd been around Vera far too long.

Her eyelids drooped, and she blinked them open, once, twice, and then it was a lost cause. She drifted into a dreamless sleep.

Charlie woke all at once, the rude awakening of someone whose unconscious mind realized they'd pressed the snooze button one too many times. Disoriented, she fell ass over teakettle from her seat and landed in an unceremonious heap at the back of the pod.

"Morning," chirped Vera. "Or— Whatever the local time is. Can't really see the sun, so it's hard to tell. Do you think the parasites bought into time zones?"

Charlie lifted a bleary gaze upward and began the laborious process of righting herself.

"Time zones, yes," she decided, thumbing her temples. "Daylight Savings Time, no."

"You think?"

"Vera."

Vera looked up from whatever she was doing. It was hard to tell from this angle, but Charlie thought she was still tinkering with the makeshift tablet. "Mm?"

"How long was I out?"

"Uhhh... About ten minutes."

Charlie frowned. "Seriously? That's all."

"Yeah, I didn't even know you were asleep until you woke up. Woke...down?" She cast a glance at the hatch. "We should really get out of this thing. I'm losing my sense of direction, and I'm working on some very complex navigational equations. I can't work in these conditions."

Charlie snorted. "'Can't work in these conditions'."

"I'm a delicate flower."

They locked gazes and fought to keep neutral expressions. Vera cracked first, Charlie following at her heels, and they laughed until they cried.

They sat with their backs against the escape pod's dusty exterior, legs extended, and took turns drinking from a bottle of water scavenged from the pod's emergency rations. The Wasteland's sky was darkening, a grim watercolor of brown and orange, the horizon dotted with unstabilized tears. Even absent of reality eating, non-Euclidean cockroach squid, it was not a beautiful landscape, though it was awesome in the historical sense of the word. A world with a failing magnetosphere but enough air to breathe. Doors to other realities as far as the eye could see—and some distance beyond even that.

She didn't know for sure if they had actually *killed* all the parasites, but she'd figured blowing up the moon would be enough of a resonant event that they'd all go over there. Lured by the significance of it. Trapped, now, by the sudden lack of any link to Earths That Have Stories. Crashing the parasites into Earth, destroying their nest, that had worked for the Martians. It had just been too late.

Somewhere along the way, the meaning of the last hologram had become clear for her. It hadn't just been Marses so identical they blended. It had simply been one Mars. So many of them, telling the same story, pushing past a tipping point to change all the others to match, too. Identical realities collapsed in on each other. In the end, there'd only been the one story. Maybe that's what parasites were *for,* when someone wasn't messing around with them. Preventing realities from becoming so similar that they collapsed in on each other. And before stories, there'd only *been* one Earth, really, in that space after the end of Martians and before humans. Victor had been one hundred percent wrong about that. He'd been looking at it from the wrong angle. His reality hadn't caused the others. He'd just been the first to start feeding the parasites.

"I lost count along the way," Charlie murmured against the lip of the bottle. She lowered it, held it out for Vera to take.

"Of?"

"How many jumps we made."

"Over a dozen," said Vera. "Plus one for you."

"Plus one for me." Charlie scratched under her chin. "Huh."

She had no concept of how much time had passed since the initial jump, or if it would even correspond directly to how much time had passed at home. Would home still be there? How long had it been since she last hugged her parents? Had seen *her* Josie? *Her* Salt? *Her* Verity?

The last gave her pause. She'd known Verity Baum most of her adult life, but the woman beside her, ridiculous marshmallow power suit and all, was as much hers, really. Charlie slumped a little, let her body relax until her head rested on Vera's shoulder. Vera shifted, lifted her arm so Charlie could fit more comfortably, though the Marshmallow was not particularly comfortable.

There were a lot of worlds on the other sides of those tears. They had a lot of work to do. But Charlie knew where she wanted to start.

"Vera?"

Vera hummed. She was tracing an absent pattern on Charlie's shoulder. *Consider the fern.*

Charlie hesitated. It felt childish to say aloud. Certainly selfish. She almost reconsidered saying anything at all, but Vera gave her shoulder a reassuring squeeze, and the words rushed out: "I want to go home."

"No problem."

Charlie twisted just enough to meet Vera's gaze.

"I know the way," said Vera.

"You— What?"

"Yeah, I jacked all of Victor's navigational data." Vera shrugged the shoulder Charlie wasn't leaning against. "Seemed like it might be useful."

Useful. Fuck. Charlie huffed a disbelieving laugh. Forget about a map to the stars. They had a map of *reality.*

"I mean, it's unlabeled, but it's a map," Vera continued. "A map's still a map even if it's unlabeled."

"We figured out Martian tech. We can figure out a map."

"Exactly! Hey, I said I'd get you home, right?" She gave Charlie another squeeze. "I'm getting you home."

Charlie's throat grew tight. Tears pricked at the back of her eyes. It was too big a possibility than she had the energy to consider, and she pushed the emotion a safe distance away.

"Well," she said, "hopefully it goes better than the last time you promised."

Vera scoffed. "Let's reframe it this way: it can't possibly go any worse."

"Okay, now *that's* bad luck."

"*How* is that bad luck? I swear, your universe has the strangest superstitions."

"Just. Take it back."

Charlie was first and foremost a scientist, but she'd stopped time with a magical amulet not that long ago and had a renewed appreciation for rules she could not possibly understand. Superstition fell neatly under that category. It was a necessary precaution.

Vera pursed her lips. "Fine," she said. "It will *definitely* go worse. Happy?"

Charlie considered the question and then smiled. "I will be."

— ACKNOWLEDGMENTS —

As best I can tell from digging around my inbox, the idea that became *Ladyhoppers* started as a one-line email I sent to Scott in 2016. We'd had some thoughts about a #blowupthemoon story about a year prior, but the characters that morphed into Charlie and Vera were born in that very long 2016 email chain. We've been working on the idea ever since.

And now you're reading the fruit of that idea! How wild is that?

First and foremost, I want to thank Scott, without whom this book would not exist. (Also, a shoutout to Livejournal, where we first met!) If you laughed at a joke while reading *Ladyhoppers*, it's probably one of his. Hilarious, insightful, and sharp as a tack, Scott has made me a better writer through our collaborations over the years.

But Scott and I didn't do this alone. A huge thank you to our editor, Alana Abbott, and the whole team at Outland Entertainment who helped make this strange book a reality: Gwendolyn Nix, Ariel Kromoff, Jeremy Mohler, Chris Yarbrough, Mikael Brodu, Shannon Potratz, and Em Palladino. Lastly, thank you, Mum and Papa, who told me my first stories.

Sarah Thérèse Pelletier
December 14th, 2022

As much as it would be very funny to follow that with "I also would like to acknowledge myself" and nothing else—think about it, sitting down here as a single line, signed—I cannot do it; it's too important. It's more important than the joke, that's how important it is.

Ladyhoppers is a story about stories, and so the genesis is in all the stories I've been given before. It starts with Mum and Dad and my sisters letting me read everything I could get my hands on, with Dad handing me a grown-up fantasy novel and henceforth letting me treat all his books as my books; continues through the family members who, upon being told ten-year-old me was plugging away at a *Jurassic Park* sequel, did not dissuade me. The school friends who would ask for more stories about particular characters; the Livejournal friends at various communities that I've written with over the years.

No book is written alone, and that's especially true when you fully wrote it with someone. Don't let Sarah convince you all the good jokes are mine. Let me convince you that there are great swathes of this thing that only make sense because of her; any place that feels particularly real is probably one of hers.

Then there's the team at Outland, who Sarah already mentioned, but I'm going to fully do it again; they get to be in here twice. Alana Joli Abbott believed in a very weird and specific multiverse mélange, and now you get to read it. Thanks to her and Jeremy Mohler, Gwendolyn Nix, Chris Yarbrough, Ariel Kromoff, Mikael Brodu, Shannon Potratz, and Em Palladino, *Ladyhoppers* exists. Thank you for reading it.

Scott James Taylor
December 15th, 2022

— ABOUT THE AUTHORS —

Sarah Thérèse Pelletier is a Canadian writer living in Quebec. Under the pseudonym J.T. Rogers, she co-authored her first novel, *In from the Cold,* while pursuing her teaching certification. A perpetual student, Sarah has degrees in anthropology and education from the University of Calgary and McGill University. She is an ESL educator and editor, a budding seamstress, a novice gardener, an enthusiastic artist, and, when she finds time, a voracious reader.

Scott James Taylor lives in Auckland, where he watches television for money, a career option surpassed only by making up stories for money. *Ladyhoppers* is his first novel, the conclusion of a journey that began when he first read a Terry Pratchett novel at age eleven and learned that fantasy could have jokes in it. He has joint psychology and computer science degrees, a combination probably only useful in writing weird science fiction novels. This is handy in retrospect as it makes it look like there was some kind of plan.